ISLAND
OF
SPIES

ISLAND OF SPIES

BY SHEILA TURNAGE

DIAL BOOKS FOR YOUNG READERS

Dial Books for Young Readers
An imprint of Penguin Random House LLC, New York

First published in the United States of America by Dial Books for Young Readers,
an imprint of Penguin Random House LLC, 2022

Copyright © 2022 by Sheila Turnage

Visit us online at penguinrandomhouse.com.

Library of Congress Cataloging-in-Publication Data is available.

Printed in the United States of America

ISBN 9780735231252

1st Printing

LSCH

Design by Cerise Steel
Text set in Macklin Text

For my mother, Vivian Taylor Turnage,
a 1940s science kid,
and my sister, Allison Turnage,
who left us much too soon,
and for Rodney, as always.

A NOTE TO THE FUTURE
IF YOU FIND THIS

There's three graves hidden in the heart of Buxton Woods, all three held down with ballast stones painted white. We aren't saying who's resting in those graves and who's not. We aren't saying who dug those graves, or who wanted the bodies to never float up and give their secrets away.

All we're saying is there's three graves if you know how to find them.

If you want to know more, everything's here in this book, which we wrote for Ada Lawson's library. You can read it as soon as Rain finishes drawing the cover. We'll add another book to that library bookshelf too—*A Thin Book Written by a Spy*—as soon as Neb finishes decoding it.

Fact: If you'd asked us Dime Novel Kids eight months ago if even *one* mystery strolled our white-sand roads or swam our crystal-blue sea, we'd have said no. "Life on our island moves steady as the breath of the tides," we'd have told you.

We would have been wrong.

We live on an island of mystery and change, double cross, and spies.

Alphabetically yours,
Neb, Rain & Stick—the Dime Novel Kids
Hatteras Island, North Carolina, August 30, 1942

CHAPTER 1

A TIME FOR DANGER

January 12, 1942

Fact: Change rarely shows up the same way twice.

It might stroll up comfortable as old boots, and take a seat on the porch. Or smile at you from across the room, shiny as a new friend. It might attack from the deep of the sea or the dark of the heart and slam your world hard enough to wobble your stars.

No matter how it shows, you can count on this: It never leaves until it's done.

It first slipped up on us Dime Novel Kids one lazy Saturday afternoon as, downstairs, the door to the abandoned Hatteras Lighthouse scraped open.

My best friends, Neb and Rain, looked up from their work, and I closed my weather journal. Footsteps scuffed across the stone floor below and stopped at the foot of the spiral iron staircase leading to our headquarters in the very top of the lighthouse.

Neb snapped his ragged Boy Scout Handbook shut and straightened his neckerchief. He's pale as a ghost crab—odd for an island kid. At twelve and a half, he wants to be a man so bad, he can taste it. Rain pushed her crayons aside and closed her latest artwork—*Portraits of Island Cats, Volume 2.*

She's only ten, but her shipwreck of a life has matured her beyond her years.

They pointed to me—twelve-year-old Sarah Stickley Lawson, apprentice scientist and pre-FBI agent if the FBI ever writes us back. Everybody calls me Stick.

"You talk," Rain said. "You're a scientist. You're good with the unknown."

Fact: The unknown calls to me like a long-lost friend. "The Dime Novel Kids are in," I shouted. "Who's down there?"

Silence.

I glanced out the window at our homemade flag fluttering from our rusty balcony rail. Beyond it stretched sand dunes, Neb's house, and the sparkling blue Atlantic Ocean. The flag means we're in, and everybody knows it.

"Could be a lost tourist," Rain said, pushing her wild halo of sun-bleached curls from her light-brown face. She's sturdy, Rain, and graceful as the live oaks along the edge of Buxton Woods. Last year this time, she might have been right about the tourist. But my grandfather, aka Grand, says with a war coming, tourists are rarer than fish lips here on Hatteras Island.

War changes everything. That's what Grand says.

It's not changing us. That's what us Dimes say.

As it turned out, of course, we were dead wrong.

Downstairs, something clunked. "Hello below," Neb called.

He turned to me, his dark eyes glistening. "Maybe it's a *rich* client," he whispered, and straightened our poster:

```
DIME NOVEL KIDS FOR HIRE
Surveillance (after school preferred)
Solving mysteries of all kinds (pre-FBI certified)
Fishnet Mending
Yard Work
Housework
Babysitting (no diapers)
```

We went into business last year. So far we have two cases. First, we're closing in on a thief—Tommy Wilkins. Second, we're trailing Postmistress Agnes Wainwright, a possible spy. We self-assigned both cases to get the attention of the FBI, and hope to go famous nationwide. While waiting for fame we do chores for cash. For fun, we stake out my snotty sister, Faye, and her good-looking boyfriend, Reed Connor. They kiss.

Something rattled downstairs. "They're touching our fishing gear," Neb whispered.

"Let me," said Rain, who's practicing using good manners while being assertive. They don't always go together. "Back away from our supplies," she called, stamping her foot. "State your name. Now! Please!"

A voice floated up to us. "It's Otto Wilkins the Second. Invite me up, Seaweed Brains."

The hair on my arms rose. *Otto Wilkins II.*

Otto's the meanest boy in sixth grade and also the best looking. I used to think time would make Otto as shiny inside as he is outside, but that hypothesis has proven false.

Fact: Otto's a bully. He hates anything odd, and here on Hatteras Island we Dime Novel Kids are stand-out weird. Neb's a fake Boy Scout with a faint polio limp and black hair that spikes up like he bit lightning. Rain draws like the angels kissed her fingertips, and lives in the island's oddest house. Her skin's darker than most islanders'—a point of interest for Otto and his mother. Me, I'm a fire-haired, freckle-faced scientist in a world of ghost ships and hurricanes.

In short, we're walking targets.

"Hey Mollusk Brains, I'm waiting," Otto shouted, and someone snickered. *Otto's goons!*

"Jersey and Scrape, wait outside. Now!" Rain bellowed. "Thank you. Otto, stand by."

Otto's goons, who've flunked sixth grade twice, hover around him like flies around stink. Downstairs, the door opened and they shuffled out.

"Don't let Otto up here," Neb said, his voice low.

"I wanna discuss a paying case," Otto shouted.

Neb's dreamed of a real case since we started reading dime novels, three years ago. He says once we start landing paying cases, we'll *be* somebody. He looked at Rain. "Otto may have changed. Let him in."

"He hasn't changed," she said. "Otto was a rat yesterday and he'll be a rat tomorrow. I don't want his business. Stick?"

I hesitated. On one hand, I trusted Otto as far as I could spit him. On the other hand, science supplies cost money. "I vote yes. We can pump Otto for information on his thieving brother, Tommy."

Rain sighed. "Otto! Relax in the lobby until I buzz you up!"

"You got no lobby, Seaweed."

"Sit on the bottom step now please," she shouted, stomping again.

Technically, Otto had a point. We don't actually have a buzzer or a lobby. Here on the island, this year looks like every year. But thanks to the brightly colored dime novels lining our shelf, we know modern even if we've never seen it. My stuck-up sister, Faye, says dime novels are trashy and pointless. We say they're full of clues to life beyond the island.

Rain strolled to our Coca-Cola calendar and circled today's date with her red crayon: Monday, January 12, 1942. She glanced at my sundial and wrote: *Meeting—Otto, 4 PM*.

"Hide the valuables," she said, slipping the gold ring she wears on a leather necklace inside her dress. It's a man's ring, engraved with the letter *M*. So far, the *M* stands for *Mystery*. She scooped her crayons into a cigar box with *Titus & Son General Store* written across the top. *Titus*, aka Grand, runs the store. *Son* means Papa, who sails up and down the coast, buying and selling.

Faye says Papa stays gone so much, she almost forgets what he looks like. I never do.

Neb shot to our bookshelf and slipped his Boy Scout Handbook behind the dime novels. I stashed our cash box behind my Curious Plant Collection. Current balance, $7.15—enough to buy each of us a suit of clothes and a new hat, if we want them—which we don't. There's no dress-up to the island, unless you count church.

Top Secret: Thanks to our hard work, we're the second-richest kids on the island. We'd be *the* richest if we stopped sending off for things: art supplies (Rain), pony supplies (Neb), and science supplies (me). No Secret: Otto is *the* richest kid on the island. His preacher daddy married money from the mainland, and Otto makes sure we know it.

As Neb and Rain arranged our chairs and dragged up a Pepsi crate for Otto, I reviewed our second poster:

```
LIFE RULES LEARNED FROM DIME NOVELS
#1. If you must lie, use true details to avoid slip-ups.
        #2. Never give your heart to a suspect.
            #3. When undercover, blend.
        #4. In times of danger, bet on each other.
            #5. Make up new rules as needed.
```

"We're in unknown territory. Use Rule Number Five," I said.

I shrugged into my lab jacket—technically one of Papa's white shirts, but it looks scientific when I roll up the sleeves. Neb straightened the yellow Boy Scout neckerchief the surf tumbled ashore at his feet a couple years ago, making him the island's only Boy Scout. Rain adjusted her trim pink-and-white-flowered dress and pulled up her white socks, one of which still had lace.

"We won't ever look more normal than this," Neb said.

We put our fists together and whispered our motto: "*Non tatum sursum*"—Latin for *Don't mess up*.

Everything sounds better in Latin.

"*Bzzzzzzz*. You may enter," Rain sang, and Otto began the long trek up our iron stairs.

Neb counted Otto's steps under his breath—a nervous habit. "Two hundred fifty-five, two hundred fifty-six, two hundred fifty-seven."

Otto stepped in wearing shiny, store-bought clothes and a smirk.

If the sun swallowed a boy and spit him out golden, that boy would be Otto. Yellow hair, sky-blue eyes, rosy pink cheeks. He'd have what Faye calls Leading Man Good Looks, except for his ears, which stick out like dinner plates, and his soul, which is dark as the inside of a widow's chimney.

Otto stuffed his hands in the pockets of his new red jacket—$1.29 from the Sears catalog—and checked out our headquarters: Neb's neat posters; Rain's bright cat-and-Jesus art; my weather vane, thermometer, bottles, and barometer. He eyed my photos of First Lady Eleanor Roosevelt and scientist Dr. Madame Curie, autographed by me on their behalf.

I followed his gaze to our desk. *No! I left my weather journal out!*

Otto swaggered over, licked his finger, and ran it down the page. *"January 12, 1942. Unseasonably warm. 67 degrees F, SSE Wind 10 mph."*

"Step away from my data," I said.

"Data. Okey-dokey," Otto said, turning to the windows. "Nice view."

Actually, it's a very nice view when Otto isn't in it. From our headquarters, you look down on our long, thin island as it stretches north and south—our white-sand dunes edged in sea oats, our fishing village on the sound-side of the island. To the east, the Atlantic Ocean glittered like sapphires, sea and sky melting into a hazy, blue-gray horizon. To the west, a few boats dotted the dark blue Pamlico Sound.

"Otto, please sit," Rain said. "What can we do for you?"

We quickly took the chairs, leaving Otto to crouch on our Pepsi crate like a frog in a prince's jacket. Behind him, on the ocean's horizon, something flashed. Sunlight off a northbound ship, bringing oil or sugar, I thought. Or a southbound ship laden with passengers, machinery, or goods. Fact: All East Coast ships pass along the North Carolina shore. The trade winds and strong north-south currents see to it.

"Tick tock," Rain said—a line from *Dime Novel #5: A Time for Danger.*

Otto licked his lips. "So, America's at war. Pearl Harbor, attacked by Japan," he said, swooping his hand in like a bomber. "Hitler spreading death and destruction across Europe." He rose and tugged his red jacket neat. "I hate to think of war coming ashore *here*, but ..."

"Daddy says it won't," Neb said, very quick.

"When it does, I figure my brother Tommy will join the navy," Otto said, like Neb hadn't said a word. "He's hero material."

Tommy Wilkins? *A hero?* Tommy filches anything unguarded, and sells it on the mainland. Nets, fishing gear, boots. He even stole Mr. Olsen's tie pin. I smiled. "I hear your hero-material of a brother has a camp in Buxton Woods. Have you seen it yet?"

He ignored me. "Point is," Otto continued, "I want to buy Tommy a going-away gift. Something nice."

Rain frowned. "If you came to borrow money, the answer's no."

Fact: Trusting Otto's like lip-kissing a snake.

Otto smiled a little too long. "I worry about you kids," he finally said. "Neb, you're too thin. You should eat more."

Neb flushed. Lately, somebody'd been robbing Neb's dinner pail at school. We knew it was Otto, but we couldn't prove it. Yet.

"And Rain," Otto continued, "it hurts me the way people talk about you and your batty mother. And this stuff you call art," he said, glancing at her latest masterpiece on our wall. Rain's colors shriek and leap across her oceans and skies. Her people and cats walk with their bodies front-ways and faces sideways, like ancient Egyptians from our history books. Her portrait of her father she keeps at home. It's a work in progress.

"If you ask me, this isn't *art*," Otto said, squinting at her masterpiece. "It doesn't look like anything I've ever seen."

"Yet it's true," I said. "Which is why it's art."

"And Stick, my pale, gangly, carrot-top friend," he continued. "I worry about your good-looking sister, Faye. She walks four miles to high school—alone, some days. With your papa always gone, who'll keep her safe when the Germans come?"

My stomach dropped. If Faye was a chemistry experiment, I'd dump her down the drain and start over. She's a self-worshipper, pushy and annoying. Still, she's blood. "We have that in hand," I lied. "If you have a case to discuss . . ."

"The Germans came in the last war," Otto continued. "U-boats sat right out there." A shiver whispered across my shoulders. "They'll be back. In fact, I say they *are* back, and waiting to rush us. Rain, they'll get you first. Or you, Neb, and your folks. Your daddy was a big man when he was keeper of this lighthouse, but now he's sick and you're, well . . . you. Your folks need protection. Yours too, Rain *Lawson*. Or whoever you are."

Rain's claimed the name *Lawson* since first grade.

Mama had walked Rain, Neb, and me to school that day. "Miss Pope," Mama had said, herding us into the schoolhouse, "I've come to enroll these children in school."

"We're a three-fer," I'd added. "Where do we sit?"

Miss Pope had stared into Rain's face. It's a pretty face—square-jawed, and a Caribbean shade of brown. Not a fisherman's crusty surface tan, but a warm, always-tan. Rain's zigzag hair's a tumble of dark-and-light blond curls streaked in brown.

Rain smiled at Miss Pope, her dark eyes dancing. She'd

wanted to go to school since she was three. Miss Pope cleared her throat. "Ada, the law says . . ."

"Rain *needs* to be in school," Mama said. "There's nobody to say she can't be."

Except Miss Pope, I thought.

Fact: The law is, white children go to the white school. One drop of Black blood, and you go to a Black school off the island or you don't go to a school at all. Rain's mother is white and freckled, and has curly blond hair. Her father's a lost page in their personal history. His blood's an unknown.

"Rain reads like she could drink the ink off of the page," Mama continued. "Rain, please spell something for Miss Pope."

Rain nodded, setting her curls rocking. "*S-o-m-e-t-h-i-n-g*."

Neb shifted to stand like his daddy, Mr. Mac. "Rain and Stick found each other in the sea," he said. "What the sea gives is yours to keep. Stick and Rain together are a given."

Miss Pope tapped her pen against her role book and gave Mama the look women share when they've hatched a rebels' plan. She picked up her pen. "Welcome, Rain. Your full name?"

I went still inside. Rain didn't have a last name, only the ring with the letter *M*. Rain looked at Mama. "May I? Mama Jonah said I could ask." My mother nodded and put her hand on Rain's shoulder. "My name is Rain Jonah Mystery Lawson," she announced. Her parents plus the second family she'd found at the edge of the sea—mine.

"Good enough," Miss Pope had said, and that's how Rain and me became sister-enough.

Fact: There's two ways to break a rule. Bust it wide open,

like I do, or ask an insider to help bend it. People underestimate Miss Jonah's smarts: She had asked for Mama's help.

Now Rain rose. "Otto, you know who I am and you know my name."

"Rain, Rain, go away," Otto sang. He swiped at her hair, and she slapped his hand away.

Otto picked up the unmarked bottle of distilled water I keep for my experiments, and tossed it hand to hand like a baseball. "Put that down," I said.

Otto glared. "Say please."

"It's nitroglycerin," Rain said, her voice even. "You could blow us all up."

Nitroglycerin. A reference to *Dime Novel #12: Boom Times.* Rain might look waifish and naïve in her homemade, pink-flowered dress and hand-me-down Mary Janes, but she's a thunder-clap thinker.

Otto gingerly lowered the bottle to the desk. "Listen, Seaweeds. Our men will go to war, and you'll need me to keep your families safe. I'll let you in *now*—at a reduced rate."

So that's it. He wants us to pay protection money.

"A paying case—*us* paying *you*. No thank you. *Bzzzzt,* meeting over," Rain said.

"Two bucks a month buys your safety. You can afford that. I hear you fixed up that shack for Postmistress Agnes Wainwright," Otto said. "She pays good, right?"

Fact: Miss Agnes pays great. She also swore us to secrecy, maybe because cleaning up a guest shack without tourists is flat-out stupid. "What shack?" I asked.

He sneered, trotted down the stairs, and slammed the door behind him.

"Two dollars a month?" Neb said. "Who has that kind of throwaway money?"

Faye does, I thought. In her secret box under her bed, with her diary. So far she'd saved forty dollars in get-away money—a fortune. She plans to leave for Hollywood the day she finishes high school. In fact, lately she wanted us to call her that—Hollywood Faye Lawson.

Faye would never tell Otto about her cash, but she tells Neb's sisters everything. Gossip flies around the island at the speed of a gale-force wind.

I jumped up. "Let's go. Otto will shake Faye down too. We need to warn her."

"She's with the sisters," Neb said. He never says *my* sisters. Only *the* sisters. "At least Otto won't be hitting *my* folks for money," he added, like that would be a good thing.

Fact: Neb's family is dead broke, from Neb's daddy being sick for so long. Faye says the sisters have elevated Making Do to an art.

I grabbed my spyglass and swept Neb's whitewashed brick house fifty yards up the beach. No Otto. I turned to Rain's house.

Rain and her mother, Miss Jonah, live in a giant wine cask that rolled off a ship in a storm. It's just bigger than a pickup truck—small for a house, huge for a barrel. It lies on its side with a door cut into one flat end and a window cut in the other. It's tall enough to walk around in and nice if you don't crave corners, but Miss Jonah prefers to sleep outside beneath the stars.

"No Otto at your place," I said as Rain stepped up beside me.

As I searched for Otto's red jacket, two men darted from the dunes—one man blond and slender, one bulky and dark-headed. The Island Bus, which chugs up the island once a day, stopped and they hopped on board. "Strangers," I said, frowning.

Rain took the spyglass. "Worse than strangers. Kinnakeet's invited two outsiders to play on their baseball team. One's smart and one's big. They're brought-in talent. *Ringers*."

Ringers. The word sounded shiny and dangerous as a switchblade.

Baseball means everything on the island, where each village has a team. Kinnakeet is mad to win. So are we. I spied Otto cresting a dune. "Otto's at Buxton Woods."

The woods are dark and swampy—a herpetologist's paradise. They're flush with deer and raccoons, birds and frogs. And a-slither with snakes—some deadly poison, others pink-bellied and bite-happy. "I knew it. Tommy Wilkins *does* have a hideout in the woods," I murmured.

I gave the broad Pamlico Sound, on the other side of our narrow island, a sweep. A sloop with red sails sliced through the bright blue water. "It's Papa!" I shouted, snapping my spyglass closed. "Papa's home!"

CHAPTER 2

DANGER KNOCKS

We sprinted downstairs and out into the blinding afternoon sun. "Wait," Neb called. "The Matchstick Alert!"

The Matchstick Alert is a state-of-the-art security technique borrowed from *Dime Novel #16: Danger Knocks*. As the firm's tallest member, I hold a matchstick high on the door jamb and Neb tugs the door closed. If the matchstick's there when we return, headquarters is secure. If it's not there, we've got trouble.

"Alert set," he said, pulling the door closed. "You two warn Faye about Otto, and I'll get Babylon. We'll ride to the dock."

Neb and Rain love riding his pony, Babylon. I hate it.

I squinted across the ocean. Far offshore, something glinted, and a shiver skated my spine. "I saw that flash from headquarters. Somebody's watching us. I feel it."

"You *feel* it? That's not very scientific," Rain said, reading the sea. "Porpoises," she said as three graceful, gray-blue creatures rolled in the water, their broad backs glinting.

"U-fish," Neb teased.

"Porpoises are mammals. Race you!" I said, and we took off.

We blasted past Neb's picket fence and across the compound of whitewashed buildings. Neb veered toward his pony, Babylon, who grazed beyond the clothesline. Rain and me pounded up the steps, startling the cat. We zipped across the porch and skidded into the parlor. Faye and the sisters walked around the room like teenage zombies, books balanced on their heads. "Eerie," Rain whispered.

Faye let her book slide off, and caught it in one hand. "We're walking like movie stars, kiddos. You should try it." She frowned. "You look like something a gull hacked up."

I glanced in the mirror. Rain and me both washed our hair before school. Hers hung in accordion waves just past her shoulders. Mine hovered around my head like an orange cumulus cloud. My hair's a perfect hygrometer. I know how humid it is by how big my hair gets. Sometimes I tell people I have a head for science, but so far nobody gets it.

Fact: Faye's movie-star pretty. Hair the color of cedar bark, violet eyes. She looks sweet, but then, so do crabapples. "Why are you wearing Papa's shirt?" she demanded.

"It's my lab jacket. Listen—"

"You think *that* looks like a lab jacket?" She grinned. "You slay me, kiddo."

"Faye, Otto plans to blackmail you," Rain interrupted.

Rain cuts through chitchat like a shark through a school of fish.

"Blackmail?" Neb's sisters let their books fall. Ruth, who's tall and bony, put her hands on her hips and glared at me.

Naomi, who's short and island smart, spoke up. "Otto's black-mailing *Faye? Why?*"

"Guess," I said. People will guess things they'd never flat-out tell you.

Faye went red. "Did that little rat follow Reed and me to the edge of Buxton Woods last night? I *thought* I heard somebody."

I tried to look horrified—which I was. We try to be quieter than that. "It's more like extortion than blackmail. Otto's fishing for protection money," I said. "Don't take his bait."

Faye snorted. "That twit's hitting *me* for cash? Thanks for the heads-up, doll babies."

Doll babies? Sometimes I wonder if Faye and I are related.

Neb clip-clopped past the window on Babylon's back, and Rain and I sped to the door. "Hey, Hollywood," I said. "One more thing. Papa's home," I said, and slammed the door.

Faye isn't the only one who knows how to make an exit.

Rain hopped onto Babylon's bare back, light as a grasshopper. I hurled myself across the pony's shaggy rump and grabbed the back of Rain's sweater to keep from sliding off. Neb and Rain ride like water flows. I ride like a kid born to hunch over a microscope with a pencil clenched between her teeth. I hung on as Babylon followed the footpath across the dunes, to the village where old wooden houses line the shady, white-sand street.

"There's Papa's sloop!" I shouted, sliding to a graceless heap in the grass by Grand's store. The store sits at the heart of the village with its back to the water, a little warehouse and two fuel tanks to one side. I ran to Grand's rickety dock, which stitches its way into the sound, as Neb tied his pony and left her to graze.

Papa had dropped anchor a hundred yards from shore. I lifted my spyglass. He stood square-shouldered and trim on the deck of the *Miss Ada*, giving orders to his crew—a red-faced white man named Onslow Banks, and a dark-skinned Black man from Pea Island, Richard Oscar. Together they let the sloop's red sails fall gracefully to the deck.

The Pamlico Sound, the nation's largest, is mostly too shallow for big boats. Grand had already sent two smaller barges—called lighters—to *lighter* Papa's goods from the sloop. Trouble rolled ashore in the very first load. "Fifteen barrels of flour?" Grand yelped. "And ten rolls of *black* cloth? Are we expecting a plague?"

Grand whipped off his spindly gold glasses and raked his fingers through his white hair, standing it up like meringue. I could see him counting beneath his breath. He says it calms him. "Take it to the warehouse, gentlemen," he said. "I'll sort it out later."

The odd parade of goods continued: candy but little sugar, garden seeds, box after box of fishhooks, coffee, and peanut butter. Mountains of canned goods, fresh apples, gallons of gasoline, bags of animal feed in pretty flowered sacks just right for making feed-sack dresses and blouses. "We'll never sell this much gas," Grand said. "Your father has lost his mind."

At last, Papa rowed ashore in his skiff. As he stepped to the dock and pushed back his sun-streaked brown hair, I charged down the dock and leaped into his arms. My toes barely grazed the dock's rough boards as he swung me around. He plopped me down and kissed the top of my head as Rain sprinted up. "Rain," he said, scooping her into a hug. "How are you? How's your mother, how are the cats?"

Before she could answer, Neb clomped into place and gave Papa the Boy Scout salute. "Neb," Papa said. He snapped to attention and fired off a three-finger salute. "At ease, Scout." Neb was the most at-ease boy I knew until his daddy got sick. Now he's tight as a new clothesline. Without the Boy Scout Handbook, I think his life would fly apart.

Papa smiled—something he does so much, his tanned face shows pale laugh lines around his brown eyes. "I know I've only been gone a few weeks, but I swear you're *all* taller. Any word from the FBI yet?"

"Any day now, sir," Neb said. "It's only been—"

"Six months and two days," Rain said. She recited:

Dear FBI,
The Dime Novel Kids of Hatteras Island welcome a
prime assignment.
Alphabetically yours,
Neb, Rain, and Stick

Rain has a memory like flypaper. Everything sticks.

"It will come," he said, studying the jumble of boxes in his skiff. "Any new cases?"

"We're closing in on the notorious Tommy-Gun Wilkins," I said. "Citizen's arrest, like in *Dime Novel #54: Polly Pounces.*"

Papa's eyes went serious. "A citizen's arrest? Let's talk that over first," he said, waving to Faye, who strolled toward the dock. Faye's too proud to run.

"Plus we got an around the clock watch on the postmistress," I added.

"Miss Agnes?" Papa said. "Any crime, or just general bad taste in men?"

Fact: Postmistress Agnes Wainwright circles Grand like a buzzard circles carrion. "Grand's too good for her, but it's more than that," I said, lowering my voice. "Miss Agnes is suspicious. She won't let us into her house despite our charm. She prowls while the village sleeps, and hangs up laundry when it's not even wash day."

"Shocking," he said. "Glad you're on it. Let's see, I know there's something for you Dimes somewhere." He leaped nimbly aboard his skiff, opened a new blue-green satchel, and snagged a small, bright-colored box. "Paints for my favorite artist," he said, handing them to Rain. "Neb, I saw this in Norfolk—a balsa slide, for your Boy Scout neckerchief. The blank face should be easy to carve. Bear, bobcat . . . whatever you like."

Even Neb's hair seemed to wilt. "Thank you for this . . . chunk of wood, sir."

Papa grinned. "Your dad's the best decoy carver on the island. Ask him to show you," he said. "How's your mother?"

Neb's lip quivered. I spoke up before he had to. "She's gloomier than usual, with Mr. Mac sicker than usual," I said, and Neb nodded his thanks to me. Neb's so angry about his father being sick, he's even stopped speaking to God.

"I'm sorry, Neb," Papa said, placing a hand on Neb's shoulder. Neb's face righted itself like a ship on a pitching sea. Papa glanced at Otto and his goons, who'd slumped on the shore like a pack of hyenas. "How's Otto?"

"Greedy and mean."

"Same as always, then. Too bad."

"James Lawson!" Grand shouted from the other end of the dock. He slammed his clipboard against his leg and stalked toward us. He's wiry, Grand, and bowlegged as a pair of parentheses. "Explain yourself!"

"I'm in trouble," Papa said. "You'll have to wait until supper for your gift, Genius. Do me a favor? Tell your mother I'll be home soon as I can. Lord knows I need a bath and a shave," he said, rubbing the reddish stubble on his face. "And Stick . . . or is it Sarah now?"

"It's Stick," I said, very firm.

Papa's dark eyes went warm. He says I'll get tired of being called Stick one day. I say never. Stick's a wild-card name, a name for a girl who makes her own rules. "Stick, please tell your mother I can't wait to see her."

As we ran to Babylon, Papa's voice boomed out: "Titus, I know this isn't what you expected, but I can explain."

"Wonder what that's about," I muttered.

"The war," Rain said.

"The war's not coming here," Neb said, fear sharpening his tone.

"It is," she said. "Mama Jonah says she feels it coming like a rising storm."

"Mama," I shouted, letting the back door slam at my heels.

I sprinted through the kitchen to our living room. Faye says its white-and-blue-checked linoleum tiles and over-stuffed furniture are fuddy-duddy. I say she's a snob.

Mama peeked in from our library. "Stick, what's wrong?" Mama's a perfection of ordinary except for her eyes, which are rare and violet like Faye's, and her smarts, which are sharp as my own. If Papa's our sail and fate's our wind, Mama's the ballast holding us steady.

"Papa's home," I said, and her smile made her square face beautiful. "He wants a bath and a shave, and he can't wait to see you."

She sprang into action, as usual. There's not an ounce of sit-down in her. I followed her into the kitchen. "I'll bring the bathtub in off the back porch," she said, her eyes bright. "What shall we have for a welcome home supper?"

My chief rooster, Galileo, crowed in the backyard.

Bad timing.

I glanced out the window as my hens sprinted toward Galileo, eager for the bug feast he'd announced beneath our fig tree. "Not chicken," I said, very quick. "Chicken would ruin my genetics experiments, and the hawks are bad enough already." A hawk will wipe out a flock of chickens, if you let it. "See, I'm crossing my Rhode Island Reds and white leghorns to—"

She held up her hand. "Jonah brought us a mess of flounder this morning. We'll fry them up and make some slaw."

"And butterbeans," I said, checking the shelves over our windows. The stout jars of last summer's canned vegetables stood warm and inviting. .

"And cornbread," she added. "Your papa can smell it cooking while he bathes. Pump some water please, ma'am, and put it on the stove for his bath. And bring some clothes down for him. Then set the dining room table." She smiled, her eyes dancing. "When Faye comes in, ask her to help you. Papa can help me in the kitchen."

Papa's home.

I don't know what love smells like, but I'd bet on fried fish, cornbread, and butterbeans.

An hour later, Papa's foot hit the back porch floor exactly the way it does—*ba-BAM*—same way every time, a way that means he's home and all's right with the world.

I strolled into our dining room carrying a small jar of inky water, and three tiny flowers. "What the heck is *that*?" Faye demanded, placing a fork by a plate. "A bouquet from the dead?"

"They're crocuses," I said, setting my makeshift vase on the table.

"They look like death in a jelly jar."

"I put black ink in the water to highlight their capillaries. They're my latest science project. Papa will want to see it."

Fact: I'm the only kid on the island who does freelance science projects.

"You are too strange," she muttered, and then went misty. "One day, I'll set the table like they do at the White House so we'll know which fork to use when the president invites us, once I'm a movie star and you're a famous scientist. If girls can *be* famous scientists."

"Madame Curie," I replied.

She raised her eyebrows. "Excuse me?" The things Faye doesn't know could fill an encyclopedia.

At the table that night, we went full-blown ritual. Grand said grace. Mama passed the fish. Faye and me gave our school reports. A's and B's for Faye, who's miraculously above average. "All A's for me except a D in spelling," I said.

Papa raised his eyebrows. "D?"

"Spelling wastes brain space," I explained. "We *do* own a dictionary."

Fact: Mama buys books at shipwreck auctions. We own two walls full of shipwrecked books, and add our own books as we create them. Only the library at the Pea Island Coast Guard Station rivals ours.

So far I've penned one book on the medicinal plants I collect for Mama. Rain's seminal work, *Portraits of Island Cats*,

Volume 1, sits next to mine. Neb avoids books, except the 1915 Boy Scout Handbook he checked out last year. The Universe Encyclopedias—complete except for Volume K—loom large in my own life. Encyclopedias hold every scrap of knowledge known to man and womankind.

"Work on that D, Stick," Papa said, loading his plate. "I'd love to see you claw your way up to average if you can," he added, giving me a wicked grin. "How was Christmas?"

"Fine," Mama said. Christmas means eating nice foods, going to church, and visiting family and friends—not like the hubbub Christmas on the mainland. (See *Dime Novel #75: Santa's Gang of Little Thieves.*) "You next," Mama said. "What's the news out in the world?"

His smile died. "Nothing fit for the dinner table, I guess. What's the story on those poor petunias?" he asked, glancing at my centerpiece.

"They're crocuses," I said. "There *has* to be news. Mama doesn't like me to listen to the radio news without her there to explain, but I'm hearing rumors of U-boats and war."

He peppered his butterbeans. He peppered them again. He's stalling, I thought.

"James?" Mama said, worry washing her smile away.

He sighed. "From Boston to home—we saw men enlisting by the truckload, military bases going up. The government's rationing goods, so people can only buy a little at a time."

"What?" Faye yelped. "Since when can the government tell *us* what to buy?"

"Since we're at war," he said. "They're already rationing

cars and sugar. They'll retool the car factories to make military vehicles. Maybe even airplanes. The military will need more sugar. And they use sugarcane to make explosives," he said, and Mama's fork clattered to her plate. "I'm betting they'll ration other things too. Candy. Nylons, shoes, rubber. Gasoline. Oh, I brought you a newspaper, Titus, for the store."

Grand posts important stories on the store's wall, for the village to read.

"Thanks. And I was wrong about the gas," Grand said. "Agnes already bought ten gallons for her old Buick. Don't ask me why. She never drives it. Three apples too."

The skin across my shoulders tingled. *Miss Agnes bought gasoline?* On an island with next to no roads? "How did *she* know gas would be rationed?"

Grand frowned. "Didn't say she *did* know. Don't start, Stick. There's nothing suspicious about Agnes. You just don't like her."

"Nothing suspicious? She showed up out of the blue, she has no known people—"

He put his fork down. "You're afraid she'll steal me. So what if she does? You can borrow me back. You could at least *try* to be friendly."

"The trick to business is knowing what people need before they know it themselves," Papa interrupted, looking at Mama. "Prices will skyrocket, Ada. For everything. That's why I have to leave in the morning."

"Tomorrow morning?" she said. Even the crocuses looked stunned.

"You can't!" I said, my voice going too high. "We need you on a consultation basis. Tommy's a one-man crime ring, you haven't seen Rain's new art, and Otto's stealing Neb's dinner and trying to shake us down!"

Faye elbowed in. "Don't worry, kiddo," she said. "I'll speak to Tommy about his repulsive little brother. Tommy's shooting pool with Reed Sunday night. I'll snag him then." When Faye's nice to me, she generally has an ulterior motive. Wait for it, I thought. "I'll probably have to stay out later than usual to see it through. Say, eleven?"

Mama was so rattled, she nodded.

The war isn't even here, and already it's got its hands all over my life. Papa's never looked so worried or left so soon. Mama's never looked so pale. I pictured *Dime Novel #132: Eye of the Storm,* and tried to find a still place in my whirlwind feelings. Reed's shooting pool, I thought, breathing deep. Reed spins steady as the earth beneath my feet.

Mama cleared her throat. "No," she said.

The word hung on the air like smoke.

Papa blinked like a confused owl. "No? No what?"

"There's more to life than business, James," she said. "There's me. And Faye, and Stick, and Titus. You may not leave after one meal at my table, not after you've been gone so long. Especially not with a war coming."

Papa captains his ship and Mama captains our home, but I'd never heard them cross at a command level. The table went so quiet, I could hear my heartbeat. Papa took a deep breath and looked at Grand. "As I was saying, Titus, I plan to be here a few more days. I'll set sail first thing . . . Sunday morning?" he said, crooking an eyebrow at Mama. Papa is the only captain on the island who sails on Sundays.

"Agreed," she said, relaxing.

My world went a little less catawampus. "Excellent," I said. "Faye, what time?"

"You're babbling again," she replied.

"Reed and Tommy Wilkins. What time do they shoot pool Sunday night?"

She sighed. "Eight o'clock, if Grand doesn't mind."

"Done," he muttered. "Just act like you have good sense."

Fact: It's illegal to open a store on Sunday, but shooting pool isn't the same as open.

Sunday's the perfect time to stake out Tommy Wilkins, a cold-blooded chameleon of a teenager. Put him in a church, he's the color of the choir. Put him by a pool table, he goes an ugly shade of slick. Let him walk by an unlocked warehouse, he's the color of stolen.

"Thanks for stepping up, Faye," Papa said. "Stick, remember: No citizen's arrest until we talk. And your gift's on the back porch." He grinned at Faye. "Yours too."

Gifts. Incredibly, Faye didn't bite.

"Papa," she said, "are the Germans coming to our island?" Papa's eyes lost their light, and fear spidered through me like lightning across the sky.

Is Otto right? Are U-boats coming? *Are they here?*

"Your mother and I have made our plans. You don't need

to worry. If we need to, we'll move inland to Cousin Leah's place, in Tarboro."

"*Tarboro?* We can't go inland. We're not *woodsers*," I said. "You can't even smell the sea there! What about Rain and Neb? And Miss Jonah? And what about my chickens? I can't leave them to the hawks and raccoons!"

"If we go, we'll invite Rain's family. And Neb," Mama said, very firm. She looked at Papa. "But I won't go unless we have to, James. People depend on me. Two of my ladies have babies coming, and Mac's sicker than he lets on."

Fact: Mama's a healer by nature and by trade. People come looking for her when someone's being born or dying, and everything in between.

"Agreed," Papa said, and squeezed my hand. "Nothing changes an economy faster than war, Genius. This may be my last *safe* chance to sail. Just one more trip, and I'll be home so long, you'll get sick of me. Faye, if you'd pass the cornbread?"

Just like that? The war's here, Papa's going—and pass the cornbread?

Normal settles my fear the way baking soda neutralizes acid. I said the first normal thing I could think of: "Faye likes us to call her Hollywood these days."

"Hollywood," Papa said, trying it on. He winked at Mama. "I like it."

Faye swerved to his flattery like a shark to chum. "I'm trying to get a stage name going," she said. "Kids my age picked it up like crazy. The old and the dimwitted are a challenge."

"They always are," Papa said, giving Grand a fake-sad look. "It's pitiful, really."

Papa's the funniest man I know. "Mental sharpness declines with age," I added, shaking my head. I love double-teasing with Papa.

"Refocus," Faye said. "We're talking about me." She dimpled up and tilted her head thirty degrees to the right, like a Hollywood starlet. She practices in the mirror. She does a nice Katharine Hepburn too—hands on hips, I-dare-you-to stare. "I'm auditioning for the school play," she added, and Papa's smile made the room happy clear to the curtains.

I butted in before Faye could go into her audition piece. If I hear the balcony scene from *Romeo and Juliet* one more time, I may heave. "Papa, all day, I've felt somebody watching from the sea. And I've seen glints on the water. Otto says U-boats sit out there. But—"

"Don't let that pompous little wart get to you," Grand warned.

"Yes, sir." Grand's a shrewd judge of character, if you don't count being head-over-heels for Miss Agnes.

"Wartime jitters, I expect, Genius," Papa said. "Settle down."

"I *am* settled. Observation is the first step in scientific investigation. As a scientist, I *know* what I saw."

"Stick, we're fine," he said, his voice going harsh. The table fell silent. I felt like a bird with nowhere to land. Papa's never harsh, unless you count my one science project gone bad, when I accidentally glued Faye's hair to her mattress.

"I'm sorry, Stick," Papa said. "I guess I'm the one with jitters. I'll ask around, see if anyone else saw something unusual."

"A war," Faye murmured. "I guess we'll . . ." Her voice faded away.

"We'll do what we always do, only better," Grand said.

Grand has been in a war. They called it The War to End All Wars—apparently a premature conclusion—but a plan from him definitely beats a guess from Faye. Even so, questions raced around inside me like squirrels in a barrel.

Will the Germans come? Will they knock on our door? Sit at this table?

Someone rapped at the back door.

I jumped, hanging my heart on the ceiling. "Nazis," I gasped. "They're here."

CHAPTER 3

A SCREAMING TURN

Another rap. "Hello to the house, anybody home?"

"That's Reed!" Faye said.

I thundered to the back door, burning off my fear. Hypothesis: As a species, we're wired to run when scared. (See *T. rex*, Universe Encyclopedia, Volume T.)

"Hey, shortcake. How's life?" Reed asked, the back door open behind him. Only bad news and strangers use the front door.

"Papa's leaving Sunday and a war's coming," I said, trying to look professional. "We Dime Novel Kids will stake out Tommy Wilkins when you two shoot pool on Sunday. And you're in time for fig cake." He swept his cap off and smoothed his hair, which is black as raven wings. "New baseball cap?" I asked, my nerves settling.

"Your Papa brought a few over for the team."

Faye says Reed has General Good Looks. Blue eyes, quick smile, and a barely crooked nose from a fight he almost won. He stands five-eleven—tall for the island. He's strong from pulling nets. Tonight he smelled like cedar—which meant he was building a new boat.

"You started building my skiff yet?" I teased. "The *SS Science*."

He grinned, flashing dimples deep enough to back a Ford into. "I'll build you a sister-in-law boat if Faye marries me, Stick, but don't hold your breath. I suspect Hollywood Faye Lawson has bigger fish to fry." He turned to the white-and-black wrinkle-faced dog on the stoop. "At ease, Schooner."

Schooner heaved a sigh and sat, one back leg curled beneath his stocky body, one stuck out. Reed named him Schooner for the graceful two-masted boats that work our waters. Sadly, even walking down a dock makes Schooner seasick. He's a landlubber from his blunt nose to his black-tipped tail. Schooner grinned at me. He has enough jowls for three dogs.

"Mama," I called, "can Schooner come in? He looks like Sir Winston Churchill, a man I know you admire." Mama's silent *No* sang out loud and clear.

"Sorry, Schooner. I'll bring you some cornbread," I promised, and hesitated. "Reed, is Schooner gaining weight? He looks a little . . . uncorseted in the midsection."

"Yeah, reckon I need to tell the schoolkids not to feed him."

I've never seen kids feeding him, I thought as I led Reed to our table.

"Evening," he said, beaming around the room. "How's everybody?"

If Faye had bigger fish to fry, she didn't show it. "Better, now that you're here," she said, giving him the thirty-degree tilt.

Papa's liked Reed for Faye since way before Reed quit-u-ated high school. Quit-u-ating is as good as graduating on the island, where a high school diploma's mostly good for folding and slipping under the short leg of a rocky table. He sat down easy as coming home.

"How's the baseball team looking?" Papa asked. Reed pitches for Buxton.

"I'd say good, but the Oden twins in Kinnakeet enlisted and the team's brought in a couple of Ringers to replace them. Won't know our chances until I see them play."

"Ringers?" Papa said, frowning. *"Bought* talent? That's low."

"I saw them this afternoon," I said, passing the cake around. "On *our* beach." I tested the waters: "Possible spies."

Reed snorted. "Sorry, Sherlock. They're American head to toe. One from Richmond, one from Louisiana. They mostly stay at their aunt's cottage, way up the beach. Nobody's paying them. They just like to play." He leaned toward Papa. "Captain Lawson, what's the war news?"

The war news.

The words spun through my belly like a tornado of glass. I grabbed my cake and a piece of cornbread and ran for Schooner and my gift, on the back porch.

The next morning I met Rain by our gate. "Tell Miss Pope I'm taking a few days off from school," I said, and she nodded, her eyes shining. She likes Papa near as much as I do.

I spent a sweet day with Papa. He toured headquarters, and helped me set up my freelance science project, *Stick's Shockingly Modern Pickled Eggs*, at the store. On his second day, filled with showers, he listened to Faye's audition piece for the school play, and kept his arm close around Mama.

"Time moves slow when it rains," I said at supper that night.

"You're bananas," Faye replied. "Time's time and humidity frizzes my hair. Yours too, you're just too hopeless to notice. Mama, can't you do something about her?"

Papa smiled. "Stick's fine. Leave her alone."

Life felt so regular, I almost forgot about the war.

The next day, as I left HQ, life took a swerve that would alter two human lives, three if you count Schooner. As in *Dime Novel #85: A Screaming Turn*, change strolled by dressed in ordinary clothes: tan work pants and a borrowed suit jacket stretched a little too tight across the shoulders. "Hey Reed!" I shouted, pounding down the path. "Wait up!"

Reed turned. He'd slicked his hair down, and shaved close. I studied his black suit jacket. My heart dropped. "Who died?"

"Nobody. But I did make a little effort. Thanks for noticing."

"Faye isn't home, if that's who you dressed up for. She's with Neb's sisters, planning what to do if the Germans land."

He snorted. "This war's turning life upside down, and it's not even here yet. Guys leaving, Ringers showing up to play ball, girls acting . . . different."

"You don't look right," I said.

"Nervous, maybe." *Nervous? Reed's never nervous.*

"You're a First Law of Motion Man," I said, trying to settle him down. "Sir Isaac Newton's first law of motion says objects in motion keep moving in a straight line unless something knocks them off course. That's you. You like to go the way you're going."

"Yes ma'am, I do." Schooner bolted ahead and flung his pudgy body into the air to snap at a rising gull. He landed with a gray feather on his lip. "Listen, Stick, is your father in a good mood? I need to talk to him about something important. It's private."

"It can't be that private if you're asking me for help. He looked happy enough last I saw him. Race you," I said, and took off like wildfire.

I am an arrow of a runner—sleek, curveless, nose to the target. Reed has longer legs, but the tight jacket slowed his arm-action. We pulled up at our gate at the same time.

"Hold it," Reed panted. He'd gone gray as old dishwater.

Mama says people show stress in different parts of the body. Faye's stomach goes first. For me, it's my ears. Sadly, for Reed, it's his skin—the body's largest organ. He put his hands on his knees. "Stick, does your father like me?"

"Since when do you care who likes you?"

He caressed Schooner's ears and straightened up. "How do I look?"

"You look strange if nobody died."

"Will you ask your dad if he'll see me? And if he says yes will you sorta . . . disappear?"

"Papa, I'm home!" I shouted, blasting through the back door.

Papa stood shaving at the sink, his suspenders off his broad, dimpled shoulders. I hurled myself into his arms. The war disappeared, Otto disappeared. Unfortunately, so did Reed.

"Hey, Genius," Papa said, kissing the top of my head. "How are Rain and Neb?"

"Fine. We're gearing up for war, soon as we arrest Tommy," I said, and sat down to watch him shave. I love the soapy brush against his face, the glide of the straight razor along his jawline, the swipe of suds. "We'll be *Spy Catchers*—as in *Dime Novel #59*."

Schooner barked on the front porch. Right. Reed.

"Papa, Reed's here," I said as Mama strolled in. "He's slicked his hair and dressed funny. He wants to talk to you. He says it's important."

"Slick hair," he said, glancing at Mama. "Sounds like business."

"Ask him to take a seat in the library," Mama told me, stirring a pot of tonic on the stove. Papa pushed his nose a little to the left and shaved in quick downstrokes over his lip. He has fine lips, thin and shaped just so. I have Papa's lips, which Faye says is a waste.

Mama smiled, and suddenly I realized how much I'd missed her smile. "Air the library out a little, Stick. And don't break the knickknacks."

I shot to the front room, raised the window a tad, and ushered Reed in. "Have a seat. You can borrow a book if you want. I put the ones Rain and me wrote at eye level—prime shopping space. Don't break the knickknacks." I went for pleasant chat, which Mama says relaxes guests. "I've never seen you sweat like that. There are two kinds of sweat glands. It smells like you've activated your *stress* glands. Want me to take your jacket?"

He shook his head and closed his eyes, and I sprinted for the door.

In a flash, I stood outside beneath the open window. The dried hydrangea canes rustled as I pushed them aside to peep over the windowsill. Papa strolled in, hand outstretched. "Reed," Papa boomed, toweling the last whisper of suds off his face. "How are you?"

"Fine," Reed said, popping to his feet and pumping Papa's hand. "Just fine."

They stood a heartbeat longer than felt right. "Stick says you have business to discuss."

"Yes, sir. I mean, no," he said, and Papa sat across from him. "That is . . . nice room. I've never been in here. Lots of . . . books," he added. "Mr. Lawson, I don't make a lot of money, but I fish, and build a couple boats a year."

"I see," Papa said in a tone that said he didn't.

"I'd make Faye a good husband," he said as Mama padded past the door. She stopped dead. "I'd treat her right. You have my word." A person's word is everything on the island.

Papa looked toward the door. "Ada, I believe Reed wants to marry Faye."

Mama shot into the room. *"Marry Faye?* She's only sixteen!" The look she gave Reed said, *This had better not be a baby issue*, plain as day.

"There's no hurry, I promise," he said, going red. "It's just, with the war coming . . ."

Something bumped my leg. Schooner dropped a pinecone at my feet and peered up at me, his eyes dancing and his tongue lolling. He thrashed his tail against the hydrangea reeds. "Go away," I whispered. He wagged harder. "Shhh!" I grabbed the pinecone, rose, and hurled it across the yard. A tingle skittered up the back of my neck. *Danger.*

Mama raised the window. "Sarah Stickley Lawson, get in this house."

"No thank you," I said, rising to my full five-foot-three. "Hydrangea blossoms change color depending on the pH of the soil. As a scientist, I need soil samples and—"

"You were eavesdropping. Don't make it worse by lying," Mama replied.

Fish rot. Fact: Mama hates eavesdropping unless she's the one doing it.

I revised my strategy on my way to the parlor. "Thank you for inviting me. Did I miss anything important?" I asked, taking a seat. "Reed?"

He ignored me. "Miss Ada, Faye's sixteen—old enough to decide for herself. But I'd love to have your blessing before I ask."

Fact: Some truths are best unsaid.

Mama put her hands on her hips. "Faye's too young to get married. Besides, Faye's set on Hollywood."

Papa laughed. "Ada, that's a girl's dream. Surely he could ask. She can always say no."

A silence fell over the room. "Whether Faye goes to Hollywood or marries Reed, I'd enjoy having my own room," I offered. "If that helps at all."

"It doesn't," Reed said. "Miss Ada, couldn't I just ask?"

Mama looked at him the way she looks at a hand of playing cards. "Only if you're interested in a very long engagement. If she's interested too, we'll discuss it. Together. Faye hasn't finished high school. I expect to see her in college."

"College?" I gasped. *"Faye?"*

Reed smiled so sudden, I thought his face might split. "Yes, ma'am. There's a dance club up the beach she wants to see. The Oceanside. I'll ask her there." He shook Papa's hand and gave Mama a hug. "Stick? You and Schooner can be my best men—if things go my way." The subtleties sometimes escape Reed.

"Thanks, Reed, I'll walk you out," I said, heading for the door.

"Sarah Stickley Lawson, *freeze*," Mama said.

All three names. *Again.* Disaster.

I smiled. "I thought that went well," I said as Reed shot out the door. "Faye's too young, but if you'd said no and it got back to her, she'd elope with Reed tomorrow out of spite."

Papa winked at me. Mama didn't.

"Stick, if you like peeping through windows so much, you can wash ours. And since you eavesdropped on *Faye's* business, you can work for her for one full day."

"Give an entire day of my life to *Faye?*"

I looked at Papa. No help. Like I said, Mama rules at home, Papa at sea. I rule nothing but the curiosity buzzing through my head. Trying to tame it is like trying to stand on the back of a wild island pony as it gallops down the shore.

• • •

I washed windows for two days, sunup to supper. Rain and Neb tore in on the second day. "You're lucky you know us," he announced. "We've tracked the Ringers to their lair. Bedrolls, flashlights, and more Vienna sausage cans than you can shake a stick at."

Vienna sausage. "They have money, then."

"And binoculars," Rain added. "Nice ones."

I stopped scrubbing. "Why would baseball players carry binoculars? And who gave them permission to camp on *our* beach?"

"Why *wouldn't* they have binoculars?" Rain asked, swishing a rag in my pot of vinegar water. "You have a spyglass." She attacked a window speck. "Nobody needs permission to camp in the dunes. God owns that land free and clear."

Rain gives everybody the benefit of the doubt, maybe because she rarely gets one.

"They *could* be spies," Neb said. "I say we run them off. Life Rule #31: *When you have a chance to be a hero, be one.* Seeing me as a hero will do Daddy good."

I peeked out the window, at the empty boat landing by our apple tree, and the dark blue sound beyond. Mama was nowhere in sight. "I'm in. But how do we do it?"

"A Get Lost note," Neb said. "It's good for Reed's baseball team, and if the Ringers *are* spies, we might save the island. The FBI will like that. Daddy will too."

I scrambled for my composition book, and tore out the first blank page. "Help me." I glanced out the window. "Quick. Here comes Faye."

Neb started us off: *"Attention Ringers, You're in our territory. Get lost."*

Rain finished it: *"Love, Anonymous."*

"Too hard to spell," I muttered.

"Right. *Love, The Great Unknowns. PS: We are watching you.*"

I quick-folded the paper. "Leave this in their camp," I said. "Don't get caught."

They bolted as Faye sashayed in. "What are *you* doing, Genius?"

"Washing windows," I said. *And maybe saving the island.*

Saturday I touched up the windows to Mama's nitpicky satisfaction, but that meant time spent with Papa and that made it gold. "We sailed north last trip," he said. "This time I'll load up over in Manteo and sell my way south, then buy for the store as I head home."

I hesitated. "Is the war as bad as it sounds?"

"War's always bad as it sounds," he said, rubbing a streak. "If your mother says the word, move inland. I'll find you. How's your weather journal coming?"

A few years ago, Papa brought Faye and me leather journals from Charleston. My collection of raw data now spans years. She scrawled *Dairy* across her diary's cover. Only Faye could misspell her own title. "I can read the clouds good as anybody, and my journal proves it," I said. "It will get me in a university one day."

"And I want to see you there."

Fact: University science programs rarely accept women.

He changed direction. "What makes you think Tommy needs arresting?"

"I don't think it, I know it. Things walk off when he's around. He's dripping cash. He slips into Buxton Woods twice a week. *We* say he's stashing loot there and boating across the sound at night, to hawk it in Manteo. We figure the rise in the heart of the bog is his hideout."

"Stay away from those woods, Stick. I mean it. If you catch Tommy red-handed going in or coming out with stolen goods, Grand will handle the arrest."

Of course. Everything seems clearer when I see it through Papa's eyes.

"Anything else I need to know?" he asked.

I stopped to consider. We'd covered war, my life's work, citizen's arrest. "If Grand marries Miss Agnes, I'll throw myself off the lighthouse balcony."

"Me first," he said, and I laughed like I can't laugh when he's away.

"I wish you'd never leave me."

"Just one more trip, Genius, and I'll be home so long, you'll hate to see me walk through the door. I'll send postcards so you know where I am."

"Deal," I said.

Of course, some deals don't pan out. They don't pan out at all.

CHAPTER 4

DANGER TAKES A SECOND LOOK

January 18, 1942

Papa set sail Sunday morning. Mama herded Rain, Faye, and me up the shell-lined walk to our white clapboard church, which sits with its back to the water. A ragged trail winds to the sound, to the Revival Spot. Rain and me will be up for baptism at next year's tent revival. Neb has gone agnostic—a Greek term meaning *I flat-out don't know anymore.*

Faye looked at Rain and me. "Pull up your socks, both of you," she said.

We ignored her.

"*Please,* girls," Mama said. Mama's settled when Papa's gone and settled when he's home, but the sailing-away days leave her frayed. I pulled up my socks and watched Papa's red sails disappear over the horizon.

As the church door bumped shut behind us, Rain and me blinked like moles, adjusting our eyes—a trick from *Dime Novel #76: Danger Takes a Second Look.* The white plaster walls and pine pulpit took shape. Mama and Faye headed for our pew, on the right. "Find Miss Agnes's signature rooster hat," I whispered. "We'll stake her out while the reverend preaches."

Rain went up on her toes. The door opened behind us and a woman slammed into me.

"For mercy's sake," Miss Agnes snapped, straightening her hat. "Watch where you're going." She glared at me, her fold-up glasses down on her beaky nose.

Miss Agnes is a rectangular woman, solid and sharp-cornered as a new brick—a fact she conceals with avalanches of frills. She wears her short, dark hair in tense curls, and her eyebrows thin over her black, glittery eyes. She watches our village like a hawk watches a chicken yard. "Stand up straight," she said, leveling my shoulders. "Is Titus here?"

Please.

"Grand enjoys a private breakfast with my late grandmother most Sundays, at her gravesite beneath our apple tree," I whispered. "That's where he first kissed her and where they fell in love. She was lush as a just ripened apple and he was dashing in his glory. She's been gone years now, but he still adores her. You could join them, I guess. But it would go against social norms."

"Two's company, three's a crowd," Rain whispered.

"Lord save me from children like you," she said, her eyes narrowing.

"Shhhh," someone shushed from a couple pews away. As Miss Agnes slung her purse over her arm, its gold clasp popped open. A scrap of paper and a dirty handkerchief drifted to the floor as she sailed down the aisle.

"Rain, wait," I whispered, picking up the paper and kicking

the hanky beneath a pew. On the paper, a row of numbers in a flowery hand: *21212ish latest.*

"What is it?" she asked.

"Repetitive prime numbers, more or less," I replied. "We'll study them at headquarters while we search for U-boats and the Ringers."

As we settled in by Mama, Otto's mom stage-whispered across the church. "Pray for our boys in uniform. Imagine how their mothers feel."

I elbowed Mama. "Who do German mothers pray to?" Sometimes my questions make her smile. Not today. She closed her eyes and I knew she was praying for Papa.

Otto and Tommy settled on the front row, pious as monks. It's odd, their daddy preaching and those two dwelling in a half-baked purgatory of cruelty and petty theft. Papa says preachers love to find the lost, and Otto and Tommy want him to find them. I say they take after their scheming mother, and being a preacher's kid offers dang good cover.

After church, Rain, Faye, and me walked home, leaving Mama to chat. Reed chugged up in his rattletrap pickup. "Hey Hollywood," he said. "You're looking beautiful. You girls too."

An afterthought compliment. Still. "Thanks," I said.

"I'm scouting Kinnakeet's team this afternoon. The Ringers are playing."

Faye frowned. "Ringers?" The things that escape her could fill a prison yard.

"Players that play for any team, theirs or not," Rain said. She loves baseball because if you're good you're good—no matter what. She's a hawk-eye for talent, and Reed knows it.

"I'm in," I said. He smiled, but even Faye knew it was Rain he wanted.

"I'll come," Rain said, and Reed popped his blue baseball cap on her head. Mercifully, he had no cap for me. Rain looks cute with a cap perched on her curls. Hats make my orange hair stick out like clown hair.

"Give us three shakes to change," Faye told him, and I tore inside to slip into corduroys and Papa's white shirt—aka my lab jacket—longing for one last hug good-bye.

Reed parked behind a dune. "There," he said, pointing. The team had marked off a diamond on a wide sand flat. The Ringers swung bats to loosen their shoulders. Pale, slick Tommy Wilkins talked with a guy by first base. The guy paid him, put something in his pocket, and trotted onto the field. "What was that?" I muttered. "We need to get closer."

We sped across the sand and up a dune behind center field as Reed dragged Faye along. We peered over the dune. The blond Ringer snagged a hot grounder and fired it to first, graceful as dancing. "Quick feet and good hands," Rain said. The first baseman hurled the ball to the big guy, who juggled the ball and caught it. "The blond has a nice arm. They traded up there."

"They'll use him at second, I expect," Reed said.

"Shortstop," she replied as the big guy hurled the ball over the pitcher's head.

Reed frowned. "Don't know why they have *him*. Must be a two-fer."

We saw why when the big guy stepped up to bat. He spit, pointed at the pitcher, and unleashed a string of curse words. "Excellent ugly mouth," Rain murmured as the pitcher zinged a fastball over the plate. The big guy swung, corkscrewing knees, hips, shoulders. *Whack!*

"Dang," Reed said. "That guy's a machine."

"No. An artist," she said. "No wasted lines or motion, perfect smack against the ball." She looked up at Reed. "Better luck next season."

Another pitch. *Thwack!*

"I got it!" Blondie cried. He stared up at the ball as he raced across center field and straight up the back of our dune. We ducked as he sprang into the air, bobbling the ball. For one perfect moment he hung there, silhouetted like an angel against the sky. Then he looked down into our upturned faces. He yelped and landed in a crumpled heap at our feet.

Rain caught the ball and dropped it in his glove. He laughed.

"You're out, Ralph!" he shouted, and his teammates beyond the dune cheered.

My world-class observation skills kicked in as he sat up, spitting sand: wavy blond hair, hazel eyes. Delicate moon-shaped scar at the tip of his chin. He wore chinos and a half-tucked green shirt. I guessed him at five-foot-ten when uncrumpled. Maybe a size eight shoe.

He popped to his feet neat as toast, and brushed off his britches. "Carl Miller," he drawled, smiling all around. "Forgive me for dropping in unannounced." Rain, Faye, and me laughed. "Come watch us practice if you want," he said. "We're pretty good."

"No thanks. I hear you're camping on our beach," Reed said. *Neb must have told him.*

"We were, until our neighbors asked us to leave." Carl had a mainland drawl. Islanders talk crisper. "See you around, I hope," he said, and chugged up the dune.

"Carl Miller knows we're casing him," Rain said, still smiling. *She likes him,* I thought. "He's sporty," she added, "like a sleek little cat with honey-and-molasses eyes."

Faye sighed. She hates baseball, which is not about her. "That's not fair, bringing in Ringers, even if they are cute." She glanced at Reed. "Which I'm not saying he is. Want to drive up the beach? There's a club I'd love to see. It's Sunday and it won't be open, but . . ."

Reed shook his head. "Not today, Hollywood. I've seen all I can stand to see."

Rain and me climbed in the back of the truck. She wore Reed's jacket, which smelled faintly of fish. "Faye and Reed want to be alone," I told Rain, turning up the sleeves of Papa's white shirt. "Reed wants to marry her."

"She won't do it," Rain said, then smiled. "The Ringers really *do* love to play ball. They're American head to toe, like Reed told you."

"They might still be spies," I said. "Baseball's easy to learn."

We rested against the cab as Reed wound between dunes, to the solid sand at the edge of the sea. "Mama Jonah's scared, like she used to be," Rain said out of nowhere.

Without thinking, I looked to the sea, for U-boats. Maybe they've left, I thought. Maybe we're safe again. "If the war comes, you can go inland with us. Both of you," I said. Sometimes I want her to grow faster so I know she's safe, out on the wild edge of the world.

She leaned against me. "Tell me my story," she said, her voice trusting.

Hearing her story soothes Rain the way science settles me. I've told it a million times by now. "Your mother came ashore on a Tuesday, her petticoats and blond hair tumbling like pale conchs in the gray-blue sea," I began. "This was years ago, when I was two. If Mama hadn't seen her, your mother would have rolled back out to sea and under, but we did see her. Mama stood me by the tideline and said, 'You stand here and I mean it.' I watched her wade into the sea.

"The first wave rocked her sideways. On the second wave, your mother slammed into mine and Mama went half down. Then she grabbed ahold, and dragged her ashore. Miss Jonah groaned and tented up her knees, and Mama put her hand on her belly and looked at the sky and said, 'Lord Jesus, you get down here *now*. Please. I need you.'"

Rain nodded. "Assertive but polite. The way Mama Jonah tells me."

"Mama said push, and there you were in Mama's hands, all wrinkle and wail, and the waves swirled close and the sky cried and your mother looked at the sky and said a word that sounded like one we knew. 'Good enough,' Mama said. 'Welcome to the world, baby Rain.'"

"And Mama Jonah?"

"We brought you both home, but your mama fought the indoors, so scared she couldn't see. We set you up in the arbor on the porch. Your mama never said a word. The sea had swallowed her life, Mama said, and given it back to her. We called her Jonah because of the Bible story, because she was swallowed, and then spit from the sea."

Rain yawned. "Good," she said. "Come home with me. We'll have fish for supper." We always have fish at Rain's house. Miss Jonah fishes like she hears the fish gossip.

Near Rain's place, we pounded on the truck's roof and Reed rolled to a squeaky stop. We hopped down, and Rain handed back his coat. "Mama Jonah," she shouted, scampering down the beach. "Stick and Rain are home. We met a Ringer!"

Rain's house is like Rain: One of a kind.

She lives in a giant wine cask tossed from a ship by the same storm that brought Miss Jonah here. Like I said, it's long as Reed's pickup truck and tall enough to walk around in. It lies on its side, catawampus to the sea, nestled between two dunes neat and steady as a baby in her mother's arm. It's one of the seven wonders of the island, behind the lighthouse, wild ponies, Neb's three-seater outhouse, wandering inlets, hurricanes, and our endless blanket of stars.

Inside, Miss Jonah's delicate needlework decorates the curved walls, and a garland of candy wrappers hangs over the window. Rain's wild art covers every remaining inch of wall-space, most on paper, her portrait of her father painted straight into the grain of the wood.

Fact: Rain's father is a puzzle of a man with most of the pieces still gone. The pieces Rain owns, she gathered from Miss Jonah's dreams and from scouring Volume G. (See *genetics, dominant traits.*) Example: Miss Jonah's white and Rain's a warm always-tan, so Rain gives her father dark skin. Miss Jonah's eyes are crystal blue and Rain's golden brown. She colors his eyes dark brown and gives him a tumble of curls, darker than hers. Miss Jonah's feet arch so high her footprints look like question marks in the sand. Rain's feet are wide and sure, so she gives her father wide feet.

Her dream is to know his face.

I looked around the camp. A fire pit, a stack of driftwood. A whalebone Neb and Babylon pulled up for a sofa. Pots and pans. A canopy decorated with ribbons, a straight-back chair, and a bucket of water. Candles rested by a net, a goat grazed on the dune.

Miss Jonah's forgotten her life before she washed ashore, but her hands remember how to embroider a pillowcase, make a candle, milk a goat. Mama says those are First Life skills. She trades them to keep this life spinning. She swayed toward us now, graceful in her gray skirt and blue sweater, her blond hair up, her pale skin freckled. She's slender and tough as seagrass.

She stooped to check her lines and I checked the sea for danger. Nothing.

Later I'd wish I'd looked harder.

She strolled up with three fat flounder flipping on the line. "Hope you like fish," she said, holding up her catch, and we laughed. Everybody likes fish. "Spend the night, Stick," she said, her faint accent clinging like fog to her words. "You can study the wind and the sea."

"I can't tonight—we got a stakeout at the store. Tommy Wilkins."

She swung the string of fish to me. Secret: She ties scraps of color to her lines, to tease fish onto her hook. "You two clean these and I'll build a fire. Be careful with my knives."

If I'd known then what I know now, I'd have cleaned the fish slower, loved the sound of the waves longer. I'd have savored my meal, and loved the sparkle of our sea. Instead I ate fast, thanked Miss Jonah, and ran to HQ. I gave our beloved sea one last scan, and opened my weather journal: *Sunday, January 18, 1942. 69 F. Hair at half-mast = moderate humidity. Winds out of the E at 12 mph. Papa left today on calm seas.*

If I'd known it was the last normal day in my life, I'd have taken better notes.

CHAPTER 5

THE END OF THE WORLD

At eight p.m., we found Neb balanced on the rim of a rain barrel, peeping through the store's window. "Tommy Wilkins looks smooth as goose slick," he reported. "How does he get his hair to lie down like that? It's practically a helmet."

"Brylcreem," I said. "Grand sells it, but I can make you something close for free. There's no point in being a scientist if you can't make your own hair goo."

"No," he said, very quick. "Don't touch my hair."

Fact: You can get a hundred science projects right, but stick Faye's hair to the mattress just once, and that's the project people remember.

Neb climbed down.

"Let's go. Act normal," I said, lifting my elbows to air the armpits of my white lab jacket. The walk over had left me sticky.

"Rules of engagement?" he asked. Neb's good long as he knows the rules.

"Saunter in, keep your eyes peeled, stay on your toes," Rain suggested.

We sauntered across the front porch, Neb with his hands in his pockets, Rain whistling, me looking aloof and brilliant.

Reed gave me a wink as we made our entrance. As a potential sister-in-law, I winked back. He stretched across the pool table, cue stick in hand. "Hate to run the table on you, son, but here goes." He drew a bead on the barest edge of the yellow one ball, hiding behind the eight.

"Be careful," Neb warned. "If the cue ball kisses the eight ball, you lose." Neb knows the rules to every game ever invented. It's annoying.

Reed glanced at his quarter on the table's rail—an hour's pay if you work hard. He straightened up and chalked his cue stick again as I slipped behind the counter. Behind me rose floor-to-ceiling shelves stocked with fishing gear, Dixie Crystal Sugar, Red Band Flour, Bull Durham Tobacco. Silvery buckets of lard stood like tin soldiers on the bottom shelf. On the counter by our cash register sat my freelance science project: *Stick's Shockingly Modern Pickled Eggs*. I slid the candy counter open. "Heads up," I said, tossing Mary Janes to Neb and Rain.

Tommy hitched his pleated britches near to his ribs. "Where's *my* candy? I wish your mama would teach you some manners."

"Mama's taught Rain and me plenty of manners. We don't like to waste them."

"No candy? How about a pickled egg, then?"

A test subject! Every cell in my body shrieked with joy. "Maybe," I said, very cool.

My mind backtracked to Papa and me setting up my

experiment. "Normally you shell the eggs *before* you pickle them," I'd explained. "Not me. I say the vinegar will dissolve the shells and leave perfect pickled eggs, saving untold woman-hours. Only . . . somebody has to taste them." I'd hesitated. "Is it ethical to test on an unsuspecting subject?"

"I'd say cross the ethics bridge when you come to it," he'd said.

Now here I stood, at the foot of the bridge.

"Give him an egg," whispered Neb, who has suffered more for science than most.

Tommy ran his fingers over his hair. It didn't budge. "What are you going to be when you grow up, anyway, Stick?" he asked. "Not a movie star, obviously."

"Stow it, Tommy," Reed told him.

"I'm a scientist," I replied. "I study the universe, including eggs and thieves."

Tommy popped his knuckles. "A girl scientist. That's rich."

That did it.

"You win. Have an egg," I said, unscrewing the lid. "My treat."

Fumes rose from the jar like a venomous fog. I peeped in. My formula had developed a lively brown surface scum. I fished out a slightly puckered, leathery egg. "Let me know what you think," I said, wrapping the egg in a scrap of paper. "In detail." Guilt tapped me on the shoulder. "You might want to start with a little bite."

Tommy lifted the egg to his lips. I held my breath. The door flew open.

"Evening!" Faye sang, sashaying in. Tommy lowered the egg. "Sorry I'm late. New shoes from Papa," Faye said, like that made sense. She wore brown-and-white saddle oxfords, a white sweater, and an emerald-green skirt with an uneven hem.

Faye's learning to sew. It's not pretty.

Neb leaned close. "What did your papa bring *you?*" he whispered.

"Glass test tubes, in a wooden stand. You'll see."

Faye leaned to adjust her bobby socks. "Hey, Tommy. How's Otto?"

"Fine, gorgeous," he said, and popped the entire egg into his mouth.

Neb gasped. Rain grabbed my hand. Faye chatted on. "I hear Otto's stealing kids' midday meals at school." Tommy chewed slower. His eyebrows sank and his forehead furrowed. "I also hear he's shaking people down. I'd hate for him to end up in juvie."

Tommy gulped, and thumped his chest. "That doesn't sound like Otto," he wheezed, his piggy gray eyes watering.

"How's the egg?" I asked, fishing a notepad from my pocket.

He frowned. "The spices are . . . crunchy. And weird."

There are no spices. I jotted a note. *After four days in vinegar, eggshells are roughly 80% dissolved. ***Possible data on projectile vomiting to follow.*

"So, Tommy. I hear you're enlisting," Faye continued.

"No way. War doesn't pay, and I like my moo-la," he said, fishing out his wallet and flashing a wad of cash. "I'm betting on the baseball season. Reed, who should I back—you, or Kinnakeet? I met their Ringers. Smart money says they'll cream you," he said, pocketing the wallet. He snorted. "Me. Enlisting. That's rich."

"*Otto* says you're enlisting," I told him. I took a chance: "He also says you're selling something *interesting* at the Kinnakeet baseball practices. We Dimes might like to buy."

"Spill the beans, toots," Rain invited—a line from a dime novel. "We have cash."

"Sorry, *toots*," Tommy said, narrowing his eyes. "I only do business with my own kind. Nothing personal."

Fact: Bigotry's always personal.

"Rain's every kind that matters, whether you see it or not," I said. "And if she's not *your* kind, I'd say that's a compliment to her. We don't need your *putidus* business anyway."

Neb hates Latin without warning. Still, he backed me up: "Ditto that."

Tommy shrugged and turned away.

"*Putidus*," I whispered. "Latin for *stinking*." Rain and Neb nodded.

Fact: Tommy and his mother, Miss Dandee, are the most prejudiced people I know.

Grand says islanders can be plenty prejudiced, but Miss Dandee's maybe worse because she grew up on the mainland, where life echoes patterns of enslavement, even though slavery's been gone over seventy-five years. Then again, Mama grew up on the mainland, and she's not like Miss Dandee.

Papa says when you see the world from a ship's deck, as many islanders do, you widen your point of view—and Miss Dandee never saw farther than the tip of her upturned nose.

Miss Dandee veils her prejudice with thin smiles. Tommy wears his like a gold badge.

"Anyway," Tommy said, "if Otto said *I'm* enlisting, well, little kids get things confused. Don't they, Rain?"

"Everybody gets things confused, including you," she said. She leaned and whispered to me: "Little fish." Code for *Let it go—not worth the fight*. She chooses her battles.

Faye clicked on our huge RCA Victor radio. Glenn Miller's "Chattanooga Choo Choo" swung through the store sassy and quick. She swayed toward Neb like she might dance, and he shot out of reach. Faye and the sisters make him practice dance steps with them. If life was a movie, Neb would be a stunt double for boys they haven't met.

Reed lined up his shot. He banked the cue ball off the rail. It smacked the yellow one ball clean and crisp. The one ball rolled, rolled, rolled . . .

And then came the end of the world.

BOOM!

Faye screamed. We Dimes jumped like throw-away cats, twisting and clawing at the air as the sound slammed down and the dust fell in streamers from the rafters. The window cracked and the tins on the shelves rattled like tap-dance skeletons.

Time went slow.

The clock leaned off its shelf and toppled to the floor. Rain clapped her hands over her ears. Neb ducked. Faye froze, her face the color of oatmeal. "They're here," she whispered.

"Nazis," I gasped.

Reed clattered his cue stick to the table, and time whipped back into place. He shot to the door, Schooner scrambling behind. Tommy followed like a sleepwalker.

Faye shoved us Dimes behind the counter. "Stay here till I come for you," she said. "If I'm not back by midnight, sneak home and hide. All of you. Keep the house dark and lock the doors. Don't open them unless it's Mama or Grand or me." She looked straight into my eyes. "I love you, Sarah Stickley Lawson."

The hair on my arms stood up. Faye never says she loves me.

She blew out the lamps and clattered into the night, leaving the front door gaping. "Repent," Reverend Wilkins shouted, flapping down the street, Otto at his heels. "The Day of Judgment is upon us!" Neb's dark eyes went round as portholes.

Rain stood up. "Judgment Day? *Now?* I don't think so. Do you, Stick?"

"No," I said. "But I'm a scientist and if it is Judgment Day, I want to see it." I grabbed my spyglass, slung its leather cord over my shoulder, and looked at Neb, still crouched behind the counter. The clock at his feet stared up at me, its glass face cracked, its spindly gold hands pointing: 8:29 p.m., January 18, 1942. "Come on, Neb."

Neb shook his head and Rain knelt beside him. "Scaredy cat," she whispered.

"I ain't," he snapped, rising. "A Boy Scout is Loyal, Helpful, Friendly, *Courteous*, Kind, Obedient, Cheerful, Thrifty . . ." He grabbed Tommy's quarter off the pool table. "Brave, Clean, Reverent, and . . . what's the other one? Trustworthy."

The words steadied him up, same as Latin and the periodic table soothe me. "But if this *is* Judgment Day and the devil's waiting down on the beach," he said, "you two keep him busy and give me time to run."

Neb, Rain, and me jumped off the porch and raced for the sea.

"Sarah Stickley Lawson, you children go home," Miss Agnes shouted, scooping her wash off the line. She's the only person in town who hangs laundry on the front porch. *"Stick!"* she shouted shrill as a cicada as she took down a pair of overalls. "Go home this instant!"

We sprinted out of town and up the ragged footpath to the dunes. "Keep to the shadows," I said, taking the steepest path to flank Faye. "Scout position," I panted at the top of the dune. We dropped to our bellies in the cold sand, peering through sea oats at the scene below. Offshore a ship billowed fire into a low-hanging sky.

"The U-boats blew it up," Neb whispered. "Just like Otto said."

I breathed deep. Mama says when you're scared, do

something you know you can do. I opened my spyglass, and zeroed in on Faye. She'd scrambled up a dune to Reed and Schooner. Reed took her hand. In a moment he stepped away, hesitated like a kite on a jittery wind, and came back to kiss her. Then he barreled down the dune, arms windmilling. He turned up the beach in the moonlight, his red shirt flying behind like the loose sail of a lost ship.

"Where's he going?" Rain asked, burrowing closer.

"Coast Guard Station," I said, and panned the sea. "They should have launched rescue skiffs by now."

"Maybe they can't," Neb whispered. "Maybe the Germans went there first."

BLAM!

The tanker exploded, spewing a carpet of oil and flame across the ocean. The ship—black against the burning sea—dipped a smidge lower, hoisting her stern into the air. The sailors lowered half-strung lifeboats. Neb grabbed my spyglass and turned to the shore, where villagers gathered. "There's the sisters. Daddy will stay home, to help survivors. Mama too. *Nazis. Here.* Dear God, help us."

Rain pushed her curls from her face. "I thought you'd gone agnostic."

"I'm over it," he said. "There's the coast guard skiffs!" he cried, and relief washed through me. "And the *Ringers!*"

I grabbed the spyglass. Carl and the slugger stood at the edge of the sea. Carl pointed to a glint of moonlight against metal, out on the waves. "The U-boats are still out there," I said, my heart skipping. The glimmer disappeared.

More villagers trickled down. Miss Jonah with her shawl tight around her. Grand with his shotgun. Mama with her medicine bag.

Suddenly I wanted to see Mama so sharp, it sliced all the way through me. Neb and Rain felt it too. We bolted—Rain to Miss Jonah's side, Neb to the sisters. I veered toward Faye, who stood toe-to-toe with Tommy Wilkins.

"You're a fool," Faye told him. "Reed wasn't running *away*. He was running *to*—to the station. In case the U-boats landed there." Her calm surprised me. Apparently, when you're sixteen and war burns ashore on your world, you go calm as a tidal pool. "Brave's never a waste, Tommy. You should try it sometime."

I ran on, stopping by Mama's side as the ship plunged into the burning sea. She hugged me so hard my ears pounded. We stood on the beach, helpless as moonlight. Nazis, I thought. I'd seen them goose-step across the movie newsreels.

We kept our eyes on the sinking ship, same as we always do. Lots of ships go down here, in the Graveyard of the Atlantic. But not like this. Not wrapped in fire.

Men swept off their hats, and let them flutter. Otto's father prayed. Women made their hands into fists and sent their voices singing, cutting through the dark like lifelines: "Amazing grace, how sweet the sound . . ."

Mama squeezed my shoulder, and I found my breath. "Singing," I said to nobody in particular. "It's something we can do."

• • •

Our song died, and Grand stepped front and center. "Family men, take your folks home. Single men, patrol the beaches. Ada, I expect you'll see to the wounded in the lighthouse compound?" Mama nodded. "Dismissed," he said, and the crowd broke up.

Miss Jonah rushed to us. "Ada, I'll help." Mama smiled and looked at Faye. Mama says Faye has a gift for healing. Faye says if it's a gift, she's not opening it.

"I'll watch the house," Faye said.

Mama's voice came quick and in-charge. "Jonah, we have a few minutes before the first survivors come ashore. I'll settle the children and meet you at the compound. Girls, find Neb."

Rain and I flew down the beach. Neb stood with his back to us, staring at his home, behind the lighthouse. "You're with us," I told him. He whipped around, tears glistening. "You're crying," I said, stunned.

"Am not," he said, wiping his face. "I just hate for Daddy to see his world like this, with him so close to saying goodbye."

"Kiddos, go home," Faye bellowed. "I'm right behind you."

"Like that would make us feel better," Neb muttered, and we turned for home.

Carl Miller ran up, his hair tousled, his eyes wide. "How can we help?"

"They'll need a hand with casualties at the keeper's house," Faye said. "Ask for Mr. Mac. Or Miss Jonah or Miss Ada."

He turned and ran like a boy flying around the bases, heading full-tilt for home.

• • •

Nothing's changed and everything has, I thought, tramping home. Houses stared at us blank-eyed, trees held their breath, the path I'd walked a million times forgot my feet.

"Go to bed," Mama told us, locking our back door. A chill raced down my arms. We never lock our doors. "Faye, get Papa's shotgun. Sit where you can see both doors."

Minutes later, she came to my room. Rain and me shared my pillow. Neb snuggled upside down in our bed, his feet at my elbows, his head at the foot of the bed.

"Stop touching my feet now please," Rain said, kicking at him.

Mama frowned. "Why's that window up? You'll catch your death."

"So we can hear the Nazis coming," Neb said, propping up on one elbow. "We're sleeping in our clothes too, in case we have to fight. Daddy's too sick to fight, but I'm not."

"They aren't coming here," she said.

"Then why's Faye standing guard?" I demanded. "We're old enough for the truth."

Mama strolled to my window, and looked into the gnarled arms of my Emergency Exit Oak. I've been jumping out and shinnying down since third grade. Nobody knows—not even Faye, who sleeps like a lump of cold lard in the bed across the room. Outside, a twig snapped. Mama stepped behind the window casing and peeked out. "Schooner's standing guard," she reported. "And you *are* old enough for the truth."

"Spill the beans, toots," Rain whispered.

Mama raised her eyebrows—normally signaling danger—

but pressed on. "The Germans are hunting ships, not people. But no lights in here, just in case. If Faye shouts *run*, you three fly out this window, climb down that tree, and run to Buxton Woods. Hide until we come for you."

My blood went cold as two days dead. *She knows about my Emergency Exit?* "Jump to the oak?" I said. "Is that even safe?"

Mama kissed Rain and me, ruffled Neb's hair, and closed the door behind her.

"That little maggot Otto's right," Neb whispered. "They're here."

"We'll do what we *know* we can do," I said, and tried to think what that was. We have no *Dime Novel #0: The End of the World*.

"Motto," I said.

We put our fists together beneath the quilts: *"Non tatum sursum"*—don't mess up.

For the first time, Latin didn't help. I felt smaller than I am and so wrong-side-out, my fear fluttered like curtains in the window's breeze.

Papa, I thought, please come home.

CHAPTER 6

CLUES AT DAYBREAK

January 19, 1942

Galileo crowed. A hen squawked. I opened my eyes. *Morning.*

Faye sat bolt upright in her bed and whipped around to stare at me. "I'm in charge, don't push me," she snapped.

Faye's in charge? In what universe?

The night rushed back to me. "Are the Nazis here?" I whispered. "Is Papa back? I thought you were standing guard!"

"I don't know, Papa's not back, and I stood guard until Mama came home."

"Came home? But she's helping the survivors."

"There are no survivors," Faye said, her voice flat. "Not here, anyway, not with that fire."

She pulled on her brown slacks and shrugged into an old sweater. She snagged scuffed boots and tiptoed to the chifforobe. She combed her hair, staring into the mirror. "Dear God, don't you dare let me die in this sweater," she prayed, and eased out the door.

Rain sat up. "Where's she going?"

"To look for Nazis." We padded to the window. Faye walked across the yard, jittery as a dash of water on a hot skillet. "That's her Katharine Hepburn walk," I whispered as she cantilevered Papa's shotgun over her arm.

"Schooner walks like a pudgy John Wayne," Rain said as Schooner eased to Faye's side. At the post office, Faye wheeled toward the door. "No!" Rain cried. "Not Miss Agnes!"

"Dibs on Miss Agnes's Buick if Faye *does* shoot her," Neb said, staggering to his feet. His spiky black hair lay flat on one side, like a dented porcupine. Fact: Neb's wanted an auto ever since Reed told him it's easier to get a date if you've got wheels. On the island, if your foot reaches the brakes, you got a license to drive.

As Faye and Miss Agnes raised the flag, Schooner bolted away, running so hard his rear legs passed his front. I grabbed my spyglass. "Squirrel," I reported as Schooner bellied through a hedge, into Miss Agnes's backyard. He leaped for the squirrel, missed, and stopped to sniff a silvery smudge of ashes. "Miss Agnes burned something last night!"

"Who cares?" Neb muttered, and fell back into bed. "Just five minutes more sleep."

Ever since his daddy got sick, Rain and me humor Neb when it's free. "*I* care," I muttered. "Five minutes sleep and no more."

We crawled into bed. *Nazis. The ocean in flames. Miss Agnes's mysterious smudge of ashes.* I closed my eyes, wishing Tommy and Otto Wilkins were the biggest problems on my horizon, and knowing they never would be again.

• • •

Clunk.

"Somebody's downstairs," I said, sitting up. How long had we been sleeping?

Bonk! "Please God, if that's Germans, let them take Faye and leave us alone."

"That's wrong," Neb said, grabbing his neckerchief off the bedpost. "Faye's a *sister.*"

I looked up to heaven. "I take that back, amen." It wasn't scientific, but it felt like it worked. We snagged our shoes and tiptoed out. At the living room coatrack, I grabbed Papa's olive hunting vest and tugged it over my red sweater.

Fact: The wool vest is warmer than my lab jacket, and smells more like Papa.

Neb padded to the kitchen door. "Entrance from *Dime Novel #7: Clues at Daybreak.*"

"No!" I shouted. Too late. He blasted through the door. Faye screamed. Mama whirled, spatula raised. "Good morning," I said, following him in. "What did we miss?"

"Good looks and good sense," Faye said, sliding a pan of biscuits from the oven and fanning the smoke off them. I went to the sink—we got the only inside hand-pump in the village.

"The Germans sank two more ships last night," she said. "Don't let the smoke on the horizon rattle you."

"Two *more* ships? Where's Papa?"

"He's safe and so are we," Mama said. "I sent word for him to continue on. Your people are fine, Neb. And Rain, your mother is too."

Faye butted in. "Stick, are you wearing Papa's *hunting vest?* Don't you dare set foot outside this house!"

"Scientists need pockets," I said as Neb splashed water on his bent hair.

"The beach isn't fit for children today. It's littered with life jackets and . . ." Faye's voice trailed off as she poured three glasses of milk. "Stay off the beach until I say different."

Until she says different?

She poured coffee for her and Mama. "Since when do *you* drink coffee?" I asked.

"Since now," Faye said, her eyes filling with tears. "Since the sea caught fire. Since strangers blew up my life." She burst into tears.

Neb rolled his eyes, but I knew she wasn't acting. Faye's Hollywood tears flow dainty. She real-cries with her face screwed up and her eyes devil-red. Her nose started running as Mama wrapped her in her arms. Several unappetizing minutes later, Faye snuffled. "Go to school," she said. "Miss Pope's opening late. You still have time."

"No thank you," Rain said.

"Ditto," Neb and me chorused.

Mama sighed. "Let's get breakfast on the table and then we'll see."

Mama moves natural as breathing in the kitchen—like she can feel how food wants to be cooked and how plates hope to be stacked. For Faye, the domestic arts are a running dog fight. Finally Faye plunked her plate of burnt biscuits beside Mama's plate of glistening bacon and perfectly scrambled eggs, and we sat. Mama held out her hands—one to me, one to Faye. "Stick," she said as I took Rain's hand, "would you offer thanks?"

"But Faye's biscuits are burned," I whispered.

She squeezed my hand like she might pinch it off, and my words rushed out: "Thank you for Faye's biscuits and also the nice food. Take care of Papa. Bless all of us except the Nazis—"

Mama broke in. "Keep us safe and teach us peace. Amen."

As I reached for the bacon, the door flew open. Little Tim Scarborough sped in and grabbed a biscuit off my plate. "Miss Ada, come quick," he panted, his freckled face flushed. "A wounded man's rolled ashore. We need you bad."

Mama jumped up as Faye wrapped the two least-burned biscuits and some bacon in a napkin for her. "School," Mama said, pointing to me, Rain, and Neb. And she flew out the door.

To my horror, Faye walked us to school—down the white-sand lane where the trees tunnel their branches together to give us shade, past eight houses and Grand's store, into the heart of the village. "Feels like a hurricane day," Neb said. "Like time blew away." He was right. No boats on the sound, no clothes flapping on the wash lines—not even Miss Agnes's.

Miss Agnes stepped onto the post office porch, a few doors ahead. "Hey Miss Agnes," I called. "If the FBI comes looking for us, send them to the school."

"No," she shouted. "And in case you wonder, a U-boat wouldn't waste a torpedo on a ship small as your papa's." My spirit rose like a kite. "You look cheap in that lipstick, Faye Lawson," she crowed. "Wash it off."

Faye waved. "Sorry, can't hear you!" She looked at us again. "Yes, indeedy," she seethed, "as I hoisted the flag this morning I thought, *Finally, Miss Agnes and I are having a moment together.* Which will matter if Grand marries her."

Miss Agnes as a grandmother. My stomach lurched.

"But did Miss Agnes nice me back? No. She said, 'Are you wearing *lipstick*?' I said, 'I am—*Tangee.* It's a different color on everybody. Try some?'"

"I'll try some," Rain said, looking up at her. "I love color."

"You're too little. And *Miss Agnes* said, 'If God wanted me to look like a clown, He'd have picked up the paintbrush Himself.' *Really.*"

She rocked to a halt at our schoolhouse—two neat rooms, with grades one to three to the right, and four to seven to the left. The tack-on classroom on the back sits empty. The eighth grade quit and the seventh moved in with us.

Kids shuffled up, shoulders slumped.

Papa says courage needs room to breathe. I squared my shoulders. "We'll take it from here. We aren't scared," I said.

"You would be if you had better sense," Faye said, and held out my dented yellow dinner pail. "Dinner for all of you. I'll meet you right here when school lets out."

"Joy," Neb muttered.

"If anything happens, listen to Miss Pope. Follow directions for once, Stick."

Fact: People who follow directions never solve a mystery. Not in science, not in dime novels. And, as it turns out, not in war.

"Dinner pails in the hall, please," Miss Pope called. "Don't run."

I smiled at her. "You'll be surprised to know that in the dime novels, people eat *dinner* in the evening, when we eat *supper*. At noon, when we eat *dinner*, they call it *lunch*."

"Fascinating," she said. "Keep moving. Everybody inside."

Miss Pope's dumpling-shaped and ancient—maybe forty. She wears shiny dresses, gold-rimmed glasses, and fuddy-duddy black lace-up shoes. Her salt-and-pepper hair coils around her head in neat little braids. Today she wore her rhinestone pin from her State Fair Collection.

I placed my pail in the hall, as always, and settled in, drinking in the ordinary: Ordinary windows, ordinary pine floors, ordinary blackboard streaked with chalk dust. Miss Pope nodded to scarecrow-thin Eli Phillips, who stepped outside to ring our huge school bell. You can hear its song clear across the sound. Only one desk sat empty. I raised my hand. "Otto's missing."

"I can see, thank you," she said. "Place your homework on your desks."

Homework? Did the Nazis sizzle her brain as in *Dime Novel #9: Brain Ray City*?

Neb raised his hand. "Excuse me. I thought I might die last night, so I didn't do mine. Can we talk U-boats? They're current events, and—"

"Can we talk U-boats?" one of Otto's goons mimicked under his breath.

Incredibly, Rain unfolded a paper from her pocket and placed it on her desk. "I couldn't sleep last night," she whispered, and Miss Pope strolled over to read Rain's lone homework sentence: "I lullaby my yellow balloon with silvery notes from my blue bassoon."

"Rhyme and color," Rain said, her voice fat and satisfied as Eli ambled back in.

"Rain," Miss Pope said, "where did you learn the word *bassoon?*"

"She eavesdropped up a grade," I said. "You talked musical instruments in seventh last week." With multiple grades in one room, you can listen up a grade if you get bored, and down a grade if you don't remember.

Miss Pope marked her book. "Lovely work, Rain. Extra credit for you."

Eli raised his hand. "Forget bassoons, Miss Pope. When's our navy getting here?"

Nothing ruffles Miss Pope, who has seen Raleigh. "I'm not sure," she admitted. "We'll learn more on the radio news, this evening." She grabbed her umbrella, hooked the handle of our huge world map, and rolled it down like a giant window shade. "But I'm glad to see you taking an interest in current events. As I said last week, we're at war with Germany and Japan."

"Let's start over," Neb urged, leaning forward. "We care about it now."

"This tiny jut of sand is us—Hatteras Island," she said,

tapping a thin elbow of sand jutting into the Atlantic Ocean.

"Not likely," Scrape said. "It's so . . . *small*."

"We *are* small," she said. "We're a tiny part of North Carolina, in the United States—here. Supply ships sail up and down our coast. German U-boats—*submarines*—now sink our ships so we can't help our friends in Britain. Over here," she said, tapping a small island across the sea. "Thanks to Japan's attack on Pearl Harbor, most of our navy's on the bottom of the sea or too crippled to fight. I doubt the navy will be much help, sad to say."

Neb studied the map. "And Hitler's Germany is . . . ?" She tapped a large green country, across the ocean. "We're bigger," he said, relieved.

She picked up a bit of blue chalk. "Yes. But Germany now rules Poland," she said, marking a country north of Germany. "Also Austria. Denmark, Norway, Belgium, the Netherlands, Luxembourg, and . . . France," she said, marking a large country that touches the sea. "And Italy has joined with Germany," she said, marking a boot-shaped country.

"But that's most of Europe," Neb said, going pale. "The Germans have airplanes and tanks and U-boats. All I have is a slingshot."

"Germany and Italy are moving armies into Africa," she added, marking the huge continent. "Hitler's bombing our friend Great Britain. Meanwhile the Japanese are headed for Australia and China, taking countries on the way," she said, coloring them in. "We do have allies—including Great Britain, Russia, China," she said, checking them on the map. "But that's where we stand, children—at war with much of the world."

The door opened behind us, shooting a wedge of sunlight across the room. A fourth-grader shrieked. "We're safe," Miss Pope said. "Settle down."

Otto's stern-faced mother, Miss Dandee, stalked in. *"Miss Pope,"* Miss Dandee snapped, glancing at the map. "Stop scaring these children. Take your seat, son. I'll handle this."

Handle what? We perked up. Otto slipped into his desk and leaned over to brush his shiny black shoes. "Aunt Iris sent new shoes," he muttered.

"Iris is my sister," Miss Dandee said, like: a) we didn't know, and b) we cared. "All my sisters have plant names," she prattled on. "My given name's Dandelion—Dandee for short."

Fact: If we could harness Miss Dandee's lip flap, we could power the island.

"Hey Otto," Neb said, "how's your aunt Poison Ivy?" Even Otto's goons laughed.

"Ivy's fine," Miss Dandee said. "Stand up, son." Otto rose. Even sullen and blushing, Otto glowed beautiful as a bent angel. "Class, from now on, call this young man Mark," she said. "Otto's a German name. Our family is *not* German."

Rain studied him a moment. "That's sad, losing a name. Poor Notto."

"Where's your other boy? Are you calling Tommy something new too?" I asked.

"Tommy's out helping others, I'm sure," she replied.

Helping himself to other people's belongings, I thought.

But somehow the animal thrill of tracking small-time Tommy Wilkins had faded, with death lurking just offshore.

"What do Nazis look like, anyway?" Neb asked, looking anxious.

"Well," Miss Pope said, "many Americans came here from Germany. So, Germans look like many Americans."

Rain frowned. "That won't help in a lineup."

"Oh, for heaven's sake," Miss Dandee said, and stalked out.

"U-boats hold perhaps sixty men, most of them needed to keep the ship alive," Miss Pope said. "We don't have to fear an army coming ashore, Neb. A U-boat won't hold an army."

"But *some* Germans could come," he pressed.

"Perhaps," she admitted, letting the map roll to the top of the board. "A handful of spies. But what do we have that spies could possibly want? Fish? Sand? Gulls?"

Good questions.

I swiveled in my seat to look out the window. The little kids had sprinted outside for early morning recess. The mail boat crossed the sound, headed for the post office.

Maybe Nazis think different than we do, I thought. Maybe they want things we can't imagine. *And maybe somebody's waiting to make them feel welcome.*

Miss Agnes stepped outside to feed her orange cat. She looked up the street, and down. I pondered the mysterious ashes in her backyard, and my personal sandstorm of suspicion hardened into a small pebble in my heart.

• • •

That afternoon, time stretched out velvety as a dozing kitten.

As Miss Pope droned on, I plotted an investigation of Miss Agnes's hideout—her house and yard. Neb tapped out Morse code, from his Boy Scout manual. Rain sketched a map of the island, with angel-cats standing guard. At day's end, Miss Pope rapped on her desk. "Go straight home. Tonight's assignment: Listen to the radio news!"

We walked boldly into our first wartime afternoon, and the first break of the day. "Faye has left us to face the horrors of war alone," I said. "Excellent. I know we've all been focused on the ashes in Miss Agnes's yard. I'd love to hear your thoughts."

"We didn't think about them," Rain said. Still, we turned to study Miss Agnes's rickety old house, a block away. A head-high rose hedge fenced in its backyard. Her front porch clothesline again held the wash she'd taken down last night— overalls, a pink petticoat, red earmuffs, a frilly nightgown.

"Overalls? She wears dresses," I muttered.

Neb frowned. "We can't citizen's arrest her for weird laundry, Stick. You just hate her because she might take Grand away."

"Grand theft in the first degree," Rain agreed. "But a fire *is* curious. I say investigate."

Neb shrugged, and we strolled casually past Miss Agnes's house and zipped around the corner. "Ouch!" he cried, ripping a thorny vine from his sleeve.

"Beware the *Rosa canina*," I said. "Latin for dog roses. Terrible thorns but incredible rose hips. I gather them for Mama's tonics."

Neb whipped around to stare at me, his eyes at half-mast. He looked like a sullen spike-haired lizard. "We *know*. We help you harvest them. Do you have to talk like an encyclopedia? How do we get in without getting caught? That's all I want to know."

"Schooner used J. Edgar's door this morning," Rain said, heading for a narrow tent-shaped opening in the hedge. Miss Agnes's portly orange tabby, Edgar, occupies the title page of Rain's *Portraits of Island Cats*. "Over here."

We skinnied through on bellies and elbows, and surveyed Miss Agnes's yard. Wiregrass, shed, clothesline full of frightening underwear. Rusty red Buick, outhouse, clam rakes. "Why does she have two clotheslines? One here, one on the porch?" Rain whispered.

"Because she's batty," Neb said, kneeling by the ashes. "Paper clip," he said. He flipped through a half-burned notepad. "Pad of grocery and laundry lists. And a charred book spine."

I slid them in my book bag. "But why burn them here?"

Rain tilted her head, eyeing the hip-roofed house. No paint, plank steps, single chimney. One window on each side of the back door. Miss Agnes had pulled the shades on one window. "The house looks like it's winking," she said, winking back.

"Don't do that," Neb snapped. Neb's weird, but straight-arrow weird. He likes his clothes to match and prays for tame hair. Rain opened her sketch pad and drew the yard and ashes.

Miss Agnes's voice trumpeted to us. "Edgar! Snack time! Gato-gato-kitty!"

"She's coming!" Neb said, his eyes going glassy. "Run!"

We rolled through the hedge and pounded down the street. The closed sign in the post office window *plus* the open door meant Miss Agnes had gone but would soon be back. "Come on," I said, leading the way. "We got maybe five minutes to search for anything . . . spyish."

Edgar galloped toward Rain. "Hey Edgar, you're missing your snack," Rain whispered, scooping him into her arms. His purr filled the tiny room. "What's *gato* mean?" she whispered.

I stepped behind the counter, to the in-box. "Rain, keep an eye out for Miss Agnes," I said, searching the mail.

"Stick! That's *illegal*," Neb cried. *"Dime Novel #21: Stamp My Heart Fragile,* says—"

"Nothing from the FBI," I reported, and turned to the out-box. "What's *this?*"

Neb went pale. "A *different* federal offense?"

I lifted an envelope with a typed address: "To MRS. CALEDONIA yVETTELIA ROBERTSON, DOLL SURGEON, NEW yORK, NEW yORK. From Miss Agnes. And here's a package going to the same address." I picked up the long box. The contents shifted, and clicked.

"You broke it," Neb said.

"Did not," I said, putting it back quick, just in case. I picked up another letter.

"DROP IT!" Miss Agnes bellowed from the door. "What the Sam Hill are you doing?"

Rain froze, her face snuggled in Edgar's fur.

"Stick," she whispered. "Miss Agnes is back."

CHAPTER 7

NOW YOU SEE US, NOW YOU DON'T

Miss Agnes glared like the hot side of the sun.

Think, Genius. Think fast. "Grand sends his love," I said. "He adores your rooster hat. You should wear it more often."

She plopped a scarred leather briefcase on the floor and snatched the letter from my hand. "You're the smartest kids on the island, yet I catch you in a silly flap and seal operation."

A flap and seal operation—a term we know from *Dime Novel #53: A Spy Talks.* But how does she know it? I tried to look stupid. "I don't know what—"

"Don't play stupid with me," she snapped. "It means lifting the flap on an envelope, reading the letter, and resealing the envelope. Post office lingo—and a felony." She turned her gaze to Neb. "I never figured you for *this*, Nebuchadnezzar Alfonzo MacKenzie."

"I wish you wouldn't call me that," Neb said, going pink. He hates his name. "We didn't flap and seal, Scout's honor. Tell her, Stick."

Miss Agnes stared at me. A sickly silence fell over us.

Normally I spin an alibi easy as a spider spins silk, but as Miss Agnes tapped her claw-like fingers on the countertop, my flair for fast talk went to dust.

Neb edged toward the door. Rain blocked him. "Miss Agnes, it looks like Edgar knocked over the out-box and Stick picked up the mail for you," she said—a perfect use of Life Rule #1: *If you must lie, use true details to avoid slip-ups.*

Fact: Of the three of us, Rain apparently runs coolest under wartime pressure.

Miss Agnes kicked her leather case, spinning it behind the counter. "Get out," she said, and we bolted. "Leave my cat!" she screeched, and Rain let Edgar spill from her arms.

"*Who* was that letter addressed to?" Neb asked as we ran toward HQ.

"To Caledonia Yvettelia Robertson, in New York," Rain said.

"That's a horrible name." Neb adores names odder than his own.

I looked back at the PO. "What on earth does Grand see in her?"

"Miss Agnes is like her hedge," Rain said. "He sees thorns and the promise of roses."

Moments later we rounded the dune. The sight of the ocean punched me like a fist to the belly. Our sea had gone gray with oil and grief. The waves churned ashore so heavy, they could barely lift their faces to the sky. Up and down the beach, men searched for washed-ashore sailors. Orange life jackets and half-burned trash littered the tideline. The lost ship's watery grave burned orange and low, sending black smoke to the sky.

"The clouds' hearts are breaking," Rain whispered.

Rain keeps a fine line between what's living and what isn't.

We turned to the nearest unbroken thing in sight: the lighthouse. Our headquarters stood on its granite pedestal, its serene white-and black-pattern spiraling to the clouds. We darted around heavy pools of thick black oil, and scampered up the steps.

Our matchstick lay on the floor. "Someone's been here!" Neb said.

"Intruders. And they may still be inside," I whispered.

In the lighthouse, I blinked fast, adjusting my eyes to the dark. Light from three narrow windows high over the door and four windows opposite stabbed the dark like golden swords.

Upstairs, something moved. A sudden, unscientific dread filled my soul. "Take cover."

We darted beneath the stairs and peered up at the circle of daylight topping the tower. Something rustled. The blood left Neb's face. "Spies," he whispered. He pointed to the door, and pumped his elbows like running.

I shook my head and pointed up. So did Rain.

We tiptoed up the spiral stairs and slowly raised our eyes to floor level. "No," Rain whispered. Our chairs lay on their backs, one with a broken leg. Our desk spewed notes, crayons, ropes for practice knots. One of Rain's masterpieces lay on the floor.

A mouse shot by, and I screamed. *"Mus,"* I said, letting the Latin calm my thundering heart. "Neb, did you leave food up here again?"

"No," he said, looking guilty. "I definitely probably don't think so."

Rain rushed to her painting. "Why would somebody hurt my art?"

"Good question. Neb, you take rodent patrol. Rain, we'll investigate."

"No," Neb said, crossing his arms. "Nowhere in the Boy Scout Handbook does it say boys catch the mice. Catch your own rodents, Stick."

The mouse shot beneath the desk and I jumped to our apple crate. Understanding slid across Neb's face. "Scared of the dark, scared of mice," he said. "What kind of scientist are you? What else are you afraid of?"

Plenty, I thought. Snakes, lightning, puberty, death.

"Nothing," I said. "Many scientists suffer from *musophobia*."

"We're two hundred feet up," Rain said. "A ground mouse can't smell food left up here. And it wouldn't climb two hundred fifty-seven steps just for fun. Somebody brought it here." She grabbed a collection jar. "Here, little mouse, come to Rain." She herded the mouse into the jar, and trotted downstairs.

Fact: Rain possesses outstanding interspecies communication skills.

Neb jumped. "Is that another mouse?"

"Cut it out," I said, and he cackled. He peeped behind our dime novels.

"Our money's still here." He sniffed. "What's that smell?" Neb has a nose like a bloodhound. "It's your mom's elderberry cough tonic. Of course, everybody uses that."

"*Islanders* use it, Neb. Nazis don't. We got ransacked by an islander." I strolled to my Curious Plant Collection. One jar lay on its side, open. "My skin guck's gone." I glanced into Neb's baffled eyes. "Mama made acne paste for Faye and I grabbed some for us. Just in case."

"Be prepared," he murmured. "Good. So. We're looking for a pimple-faced coughing mouse-lover. It doesn't add up."

"Nothing adds up until you know the math."

I turned to examine our beach. Neb stepped beside me and our breathing fell into rhythm. Neb's electricity fits mine exactly—maybe because I've been feeling it all my life. For the first time since the Germans set our sea on fire, I settled into my skin.

Down below, Reed's pickup puttered along the tideline. Faye hopped out, snagged an oily life jacket from the surf, and slung it in the back of the truck. Not exactly a starlet move. The Ringers walked in the opposite direction. They darted into the sea and guided a raft ashore.

"Any suspects in mind?" Neb asked.

"Miss Agnes? Otto? The Ringers?"

Neb sighed. "Otto sat in school with us. The Ringers were helping down on the beach. Maybe you're right to suspect Miss Agnes so hard," he said as Rain topped the stairs. "She *could* have wrecked HQ during school. And who didn't come to the beach last night? Who put gas in a car she doesn't drive? Who sees every letter that comes to the island and every letter that leaves? Miss Agnes."

"All circumstantial," Rain said. "Besides, Miss Agnes loves Grand and Grand loves us."

"Spies fall in love," he said. "And sometimes they only say they did. Maybe she needs Grand for something . . . nefarious. Like *Dime Novel #31: For Better or Much, Much Worse.*"

The hair on the back of my neck stood up. *Nefarious*, from the Latin word *nefarius*. Meaning dead wrong.

Neb neatly splinted our chair's broken leg, and set it up again. "I say we stake her out strong. If it's not her, we move on. If it *is* her, we trap her—even if it breaks Grand's heart."

A silence fell inside me. With war at our door and Grand's heart on the line, the stakes suddenly felt higher.

"We don't want him to accidentally marry a spy," he said, watching my face. "*Plus,* if we catch a spy, we get the FBI's attention. President Roosevelt's too. *Maybe even his wife's.*"

Neb doesn't look it, but he's wily. I glanced at my self-autographed photo of First Lady Eleanor Roosevelt, who will one day invite me to the White House. "Right. I'm in," I said, scooping my papers back into my desk drawer. "Rain?"

Rain taped her *Cats in Jubilation* back on the lighthouse wall. "I say we focus on our intruder first."

"Who could have been Miss Agnes," he pointed out.

"Or not," she said. "Thieves are like mice. If they find a nibble, they come back for a feast. We need a trap. I like the one from *Dime Novel #75: Ghostly Footprints*. I believe it will prove Miss Agnes *didn't* ransack our place. But I say we set the trap and see."

"That's fair," I said, and Neb nodded. "Meet at the store this evening for supplies—and the radio news."

"The news," he said, going dreamy. "*We* might personally be unknown even to those who know us, but after tonight's news, our island will be famous."

Neb wasn't the only one thinking that way.

By 6:30 p.m., villagers had packed the store, eager for the once-a-day broadcast. I could hear the jangled nerves in the howdy-do chitchat—a little too loud, a tad high-pitched. Neb strolled in with the sisters, Ruth and Naomi. Rain shot inside as her mother stood on the porch greeting her friends. Miss Jonah hates a closed-in space.

Grand scooped up a bag of flour and taped it closed. "Don't see why you need it."

"To catch a spy," I said as he hurried off to referee a fight at the checkerboard.

Otto swaggered in behind his daddy. "Saw your mom outside, Rain," he said. "She's *unique*," he added, sharpening the word into a weapon.

"All of God's children are unique," Reverend Wilkins said. "Evening, Rain." He likes Rain and her mom. "Jesus says to welcome strangers," he tells Otto, but Otto's not buying it.

"What's that?" Otto asked, looking at our flour sack. "Forget it, I don't care. In a minute, the world will know what's happened here. The navy will come, maybe build a base." He shot his father a nervous look. "Listen, I hope you misfits didn't misunderstand me the other day."

"You mean when you tried to shake us down for protection money?" I asked.

"Is that how you took it? Look. We're on the same team now. Right?" *Now that you realize you can't actually protect anybody,* I thought. "We're all Americans," he said as Rain walked up. "Well, all except Jonah."

Rain's eyebrow crooked up—face code for *Now what?* "We're Americans," she said.

"Forgive and forget." Otto stuck out his hand. It seemed suspicious, but maybe Grand's right: Maybe war changes things. Rain shrugged, I nodded, and Neb shook his hand. Girls and women don't shake hands on the island, but according to our dime novels, city women do.

Tommy barreled in. Polished shoes, nice slacks and shirt and . . . a tie? My eyes traveled its length. I nudged Rain as Otto headed for Tommy.

Rain gasped. "That's Mr. Olsen's missing tie pin!"

I rushed to Grand. "We got Tommy red-handed with stolen goods. Citizen's arrest," I whispered. I pointed to Tommy and mouthed the words *Got you.*

Tommy smirked. "Attention," he called, sounding like his daddy. The crowd rustled still. "Friends, you're the first to know: I'm joining the navy. Wish me luck."

"What?" Otto gasped.

"No need to reward me," Tommy said. "A guy down on the docks was so grateful, he gave me a tie pin. Said he found it." He took it off. "Stick, I'll leave it to you to figure out who lost it. That's your speed." He tossed the pin on the pool table.

Fish rot. Outplayed by Tommy Wilkins.

"I'll miss this little place," he said. He shook his father's hand. "Otto, take care of things. Please pray for me, all of you. I'll pray for you."

"Liar," I whispered as the place erupted. "He never prayed for anything except more."

"You don't know his prayers," Rain said, very sharp. "I'd unthink that."

Unthink it? Like thoughts are fish line you can reel back in?

Otto trailed Tommy out as a truckload of older kids pulled up. They swaggered in—most of them from our world, and two from another.

The Ringers!

Andy Gray peeled off his jacket. "Hey everybody, this is Carl Miller, from Richmond." Carl bobbed his head and smiled. "The big guy's his cousin Ralph, from the Louisiana bayous. Some of you met them. They helped with the rest of us after that ship went down last night."

"Evening, everybody," Carl said, like he'd known us all our lives.

I zeroed in on Carl's slope-shouldered cousin—Ralph. Six feet tall. Strong. Thin brown hair, green eyes set in a quasi-reptilian face—triangular, hard cheekbones, flat stare. His shoes—maybe a size fourteen—looked huge beside Carl's. The Ringers wore identical wristwatches, khakis, and scuffed brown belts.

The room went quiet. Grand had disappeared in back; Faye seemed frozen.

As the lone coherent family member, I stepped forward. "Welcome. I'm Stick, part-owner of this island-famous business establishment."

"So *you're* Stick," Carl said, giving me a curious look. "Good to know."

Good to know? Why? Has somebody been talking about me?

"You boys go back where you came from," Reed interrupted, elbowing past me.

"Uh-oh," Rain whispered.

Faye came to life. "Hold on, Reed. I've got this," she said. "Welcome, Carl. You too, Ralph. Any friend of the Kinnakeet gang is a friend of ours—until baseball season starts anyway, and then we'll pound you into the ground."

Carl grinned. "Says who?"

"Says me—Hollywood Faye Lawson."

"I've got a dollar says you're wrong, Hollywood," he said.

The crowd laughed and I relaxed.

Faye's a lightning rod of a girl. She pulls the electricity out of a moment, sends it shooting out the soles of her saddle oxfords and into the earth. It's a gift.

"Thanks for making us feel at home," Carl said, looking around the store. "I haven't been here since I was a little boy. An older gentleman ran it then."

"That's Grand," I said. "He's in back grabbing more salt."

"Nice fellow, loved to talk about World War I. Quite a hero, as I recall. I remember your island's lighthouse too, Stick. The most beautiful I've ever seen."

"Glad you approve," Faye said, and gave him the thirty-degree tilt. Reed walked over and slid his arm around her waist like he was claiming her. Interesting.

"Listen," Ruth said, "did anybody see lights on the horizon early this morning?" The store went tense. "Just a few quick flashes. I just . . . Could have been a U-boat."

Just like that, the current changed. Fear curled into a blade deep in my stomach.

I took a deep breath and held it, picturing the first elements of the periodic table: *hydrogen, helium, lithium, beryllium* . . . The blade faded away.

"The coast guard, maybe, looking for survivors," Faye said, her voice edged with doubt.

Carl shrugged. "If it's Nazis, they can go straight to the bottom of the sea."

The chitchat shifted gears again. Miss Agnes squeezed in at the last second, goosing people aside. "*Must* you people smoke?" she demanded, swiping at the blue cigarette haze.

"Stick," Grand said, putting the salt up. "Crack a window for Miss Agnes."

I squirted through the crowd and raised a window. Outside, moonlight glinted off the roofs and silvery oaks. I leaned out the window. "Miss Jonah, we'll crank up the radio for you."

"Thank you, Stick." She settled her cloak and sat on the porch rail.

Inside, Reed took over. "*We'll* be top story tonight," he said. "Hope they say how many U-boats lurk out there, and when help's coming."

Miss Agnes snorted. "Why would they? U-boats sit on top of the sea at night, with their antennas up, listening."

"She's right," Carl said. "Why give our plans away?"

"Germans are as eager for news as we are, and mad for American jazz," Miss Agnes added, sizing Carl up and moving on to Ralph. "Our government won't tip them off."

"*Mad for jazz?* How does she know?" Neb whispered.

At five till seven, Faye made a beeline for the cabinet radio—the only big radio on this end of the island. It runs off our wall of Delco batteries, in the warehouse, same as our lights. Radio signals shift with the clouds. You never know if a clipped New York accent will bank in, or a Southern drawl. Reed calls it the Crapshoot Radio System.

Faye zeroed in. "Hush! Here's New York."

"*Tonight in sports news,*" the newscaster began. "*In Chicago, the Cubs will not—I repeat WILL NOT—light up Wrigley Field for night games, as planned, announcing today they would donate the building materials associated with the project to the war effort.*"

"Afraid of enemy bombers, I guess. Here come the *real* headlines. We'll be up first," Faye said, and we craned closer. Only we weren't up first.

Or second.

Or third.

We weren't up at all. My hopes plummeted graceless as a sack of rocks. Faye clicked off the radio and the store went still.

"They invisible-ized us," Rain said. "Like *Dime Novel #3: Now You See Us, Now You Don't.*"

Reverend Wilkins walked to the door. "When your right hand offends you, cut it off," he said, his voice sad. He walked away.

Neb's eyes went big. "*Cut your hand off?* Aren't things bad enough without that?"

"Bible verse," Miss Agnes said. "He means the government doesn't like the news from our island, so it's cutting us off. Censoring our news. They don't want Mainland America to know the U-boats have arrived. America's scared enough after Pearl Harbor."

Faye shook her head like a dazed boxer. "Then . . . we're on our own."

Miss Agnes eyed her. "You're smarter than you look."

"Faye's smart, she just likes to hide it," I said, crossing my fingers behind my back. I looked at Grand. Somehow the news had made him older. "Grand? What can we do?"

"Plenty," Miss Agnes said. "Put blackout curtains over

your windows, so Nazi bombers and U-boats can't find you. Keep your eyeballs peeled. Locate your backbone—Stick, you'll have no problem with that." Surprisingly, her compliment felt good. "And don't whine. I hate a whiner. There's a civilian defense meeting in a few weeks. Be there."

"Civilian defense wants men and boys," Mr. Aikens called.

"Our world has changed. You'd be wise to change with it," she said, and walked out.

Grand crossed to the door to watch Miss Agnes stalk away like a long-legged, over-ruffled bird. (See *emu*, Volume E.) "That Aggie," Grand said, smiling. "She's a spitfire."

CHAPTER 8

A TIME FOR HEROES

The next morning—*52 degrees F, gusty winds*—Neb rode Babylon to school and left her grazing by the bell. The morning smelled salty and rich as the black mud etching the sound. "The Matchstick Alert held last night," he reported, swinging his dinner pail. "And I dusted our downstairs floor with flour—just enough to pick up footprints."

"The trap is set. Now we wait," Rain said, plunking down at her desk.

Wait we did. The days crawled by odd as a five-legged lizard—a mix of almost-regular and not-quite-right. Many ships sailed by, but the *Norvana* went down on the 21st as I flunked spelling again. (See *coincidence*, Volume C.) On the 24th, the *Empire Gem* and the *Venore* sank.

The sea burned, bodies washed ashore, oil smothered the waves. No one came to help.

"Helpless," Neb said. He wasn't the only one who felt it. Children went silent or deafening loud. Adults went ashen or high-blood-pressure red.

"I feel it too," I told Mama at supper. "I read the clouds but they feel strange and distant. Like the Nazis stole our sky."

"We'll get our bearings," she said. "You'll see."

"Worry about something your own size," Faye suggested,

snagging a piece of lacy cornbread. "What's Otto up to these days?"

Otto. "He never leaves his seat, but every blessed day—presto—Neb's dinner's in Otto's dinner pail. Like Otto's some kind of malevolent Houdini."

Faye shrugged. "You're the genius, kiddo. Figure it out."

Grand says even a blind hog finds an acorn sometimes, and Faye had stumbled on a good idea. We put our stake-out of Miss Agnes on hold and shifted focus to mean-spirited Otto. With a solvable problem, life found its scale.

On Monday, February 2, as I left school, Miss Agnes bellowed out the post office door. "You, Stick! Postcard!" Papa's scrawl grinned at me: *Genius, leaving Wilmington for Charleston. PS: We invented the first submarine in Charleston in 1830. Bad idea? Love, Papa*

I bolted home. "Mama!"

Old Miss Evans slumped at the kitchen table. Lately neighbors dropped by with odd pains. "Can't shake this headache, Ada." "Look at this rash?" "Feels like my prayers bounce off the ceiling instead of rising up to God." Over and over, Mama made a salve, a balm, a packet of tea. People paid with a mess of fish, an armload of collards, meat from their smokehouse.

"We *have* to stop worrying," Mama said at supper. "We'll scare ourselves to death."

"Little Hudson Aikens broke out in hives today," I said, spearing a bit of sausage. "He's first grade. He never worries."

"He feels our worry. I'll send a salve to school with you.

Tell him not to eat it." She buttered a biscuit. "On second thought, I'll take it to his mother."

Fact: Mama's salve contains arsenic—a poison that smells like almonds. (Volume A.) Like many substances and some people, a small dose will cure you, a large dose will do you in.

"We can't just sit here," Faye said, passing the collards. "I hear spies come ashore in Wilmington to buy vegetables. They even go to the movies. Last week, a dead Nazi washed ashore with a movie ticket in his pocket." She leaned toward us. "He went to see *The Man from Dakota*, which is mad." She waited for the horror to set in. "It's not even that good."

"That's your conclusion? *He should have waited for a better movie?* Here's something more uplifting to think about," I said, tossing Papa's postcard on the table.

Mama grabbed it, her eyes shining. It felt good, bringing home a smile.

"By the way, we Dimes are pitching in on the war effort," I said. "Rain's watching the sea. Neb's studying Morse code. I'm researching ways to dissolve oil. Too many creatures can't survive an oily sea."

"Kerosene dissolves oil," Faye muttered, taking Papa's card.

"You can't pour kerosene on a sea gull."

Even with the bit about the sea gull, our work sounded drab. I could hear Papa's voice: *Spice it up, Genius.* "As you know, we have driven the notorious Tommy-Gun Wilkins off the island, but as you may *not* know, I've decided to major in Undercover Meteorology. The study of the relationship of weather to spy-craft."

Fact: I just invented *Undercover Meteorology.*

I zipped mentally through *Dime Novel #87: Book of Spies,* for espionage terms: "Of course we're on the lookout for *bona fides*—aka fake papers. Rain's a gem there, with her art background. Codes—Neb's a natural," I said, warming to the subject. "And I'd love to have a *music box*—a shortwave radio. I'm pretty sure I can make one if I can get the parts. In fact—"

"Nix the tall tales, kiddo," Faye said. "Use your so-called genius for something good."

Invisible-ized by my own sister.

"We'll be on a major stakeout starting Monday," I replied, very cool. "Don't wait up."

"Stake out Miss Agnes today?" Rain said Monday morning. Babylon plodded beside us, Neb riding bareback as always, his schoolbooks and dinner pail clunking with each step.

"I know a strong stakeout was my idea, but I can't," Neb said. "Daddy's coming home from Norfolk. From the doctor's. We're hoping for a good report."

Rain and me skidded to a halt. "You didn't tell us he'd gone," I said.

Fact: When an islander goes all the way to Norfolk for a doctor, it's bad.

"I forgot," he mumbled. As a Boy Scout, Neb almost never

lies. Without practice, he's pathetic. "I can stake out Miss Agnes on Tuesday, if you like."

The rest of the day, he didn't say one blessed word about Mr. Mac. On Tuesday, he again stayed mum. After school, we bellied through Miss Agnes's rose hedge and hid. At dusk, a light blinked on in the room with the pulled shades.

"Bingo," Neb whispered.

We crept to the window. Me and Neb dropped to our hands and knees. Rain kicked off her Mary Janes and hopped on our backs like a circus rider, her toes digging into my shoulders as she peeped through a rip in the shade. "She's typing," she whispered. "Her desk's a mess. Cigarettes, lighter, lipstick . . ."

"She doesn't smoke," I said. "And she hates lipstick."

"Here she comes!" Rain cried, leaping down and rolling beneath the house. Neb and I rolled beside her as the window shade rattled up, shooting a rectangle of light across the yard.

"Who's there?" Miss Agnes called, heaving the window open. "Show yourself!"

Plump, orange Edgar stalked into the window's light, a mouse dangling from his mouth. *Mus!* My heart jumped.

Neb clamped his hand over my mouth.

"Gato, gato, gato," Miss Agnes said, her voice going syrupy. "Was you making a big noise? Good kitty boy, catching bad mousie." I felt Neb shudder. He's hated baby talk since we were babies. "Nighty-night, kitty-gato." She closed the window and pulled the shade.

"Gato, gato, gato? Is she speaking in tongues?" Neb whispered.

I shoved his hand from my mouth, and spit grass. "I looked it up the other day. It's Spanish, maybe. Or Portuguese. It means *cat.* Languages exist in families. See—"

"Stop it. I asked a yes or no question."

"Edgar's bilingual," Rain mused. "Interesting. Still, Neb's right. Oversharing can grate." I let it roll off. "Come on. We were lucky today, but we'll never be this lucky again."

She called it. Our luck went belly up at four p.m. the next day, just after Miss Agnes drove the Buick to the post office. "That's it. Let's pack it up," I said.

"No," Neb muttered, his voice going leaden. He sighed. "I might as well tell you. The doctor didn't say much good to Daddy except that miracles do happen. The best miracle would be him getting well. Second-best would be me making something of myself while he's here to see it." He looked at us. "Spy-catching is my best glory bet. *Please.* Follow that car."

It was a spectacularly bad idea—I could feel it somewhere near my liver in a place the Universe Encyclopedia leaves undefined. But you do what you can when a friend's heart is breaking. "Good thinking," I lied.

We darted across the street and stepped behind the PO's oleander bush—scientific name *nerium oleander.* Oleander's the Faye of the plant world: decorative and deadly poison.

A bitter wind whipped across the sound, shivering us like reeds.

"*What?*" I said, staring at a new clothesline. "A *third* clothesline? At the *PO?*" We eyed the oil-stained hanky, red earmuffs, pink robe, a second pair of earmuffs.

"How many ears does she *have?*" Neb said. "Never mind. Remember *Dime Novel #86: A Time for Heroes.* Infiltrate."

We eased inside the old car, Neb settling behind the wheel. He adjusted the rearview mirror and examined the faded red ceiling liner Miss Agnes had thumbtacked in place. I opened the glove compartment and pulled out an old photo. "Miss Agnes has a sister," he said, leaning close. "What's she doing in a jungle?"

I checked the date. "This thing's ten years old. That's a young Miss Agnes, in her pre-frill days. When she had . . . blond hair?"

Rain leaned over the seat. "And cheekbones."

I flipped the photo over. "Someone's sketched a map. The village, the ferry, the lighthouse. And an X at the north end of the island." I put it back as Schooner ambled by wearing a baseball cap with slits cut out for his ears.

Schooner in a baseball cap? We turned to watch. Rookie mistake. Something meaty slammed against my window. "Get out!" Miss Agnes shrieked. She slapped the window again.

Squid spit.

Faye says attitude shapes reality. It seems unlikely, but at that moment, attitude was all I had. "Act like we own this car," I whispered. Neb draped one hand over the steering wheel and smoothed his cocklebur hair with the other. Rain took out her sketch pad. I rolled my window down. "Afternoon, Miss Agnes. We're on stakeout. Any tips? We value your opinion. Did I mention that Grand loves your rooster hat? We do too."

"Follow me, Miss Nosy Pants," she snapped, and stormed toward the store.

"Joy," Neb sighed, piling out of the car. "Public humiliation. I can't get enough of it."

Near the store, I gave the Split-up Signal. Rain strolled left, Neb slunk right. I trailed Miss Agnes inside. "Don't let the heat out, kiddo," Faye sang from behind the counter.

Faye makes two dollars a week for keeping the store spick-and-span. Since the attack, she's been doing part of Grand's work too. Mama says the thought of another war depresses him. Lately he oversleeps, and doesn't change his shirt.

"Afternoon, Agnes," Grand said, his face brightening. "What can I do you for?"

"A bottle of cough syrup," she said, nodding to Mama's elderberry tonic—the same tonic Neb sniffed out in HQ, after the break-in.

"Anything else?" Grand asked, and gave her a wink.

"Oh my God, he's flirting," Faye muttered, shivering.

"First," Miss Agnes said, fluffing her frills, "you can promise you'll take ration stamps seriously when they arrive. I'd hate to see you go to prison this late in life."

Grand's blue eyes sparkled. He propped his elbow on the counter and his chin on his fist, and smiled like a movie star. "Would you miss me, Agnes?"

She went pink. "Second, you can tell me why your grand-child's following me."

"Is she? Faye, stop following Agnes. You're old enough to know better."

"Not *Faye*," Miss Agnes said, placing three apples on the counter. "Sarah Stickley."

I glanced at the side windows. Rain peered in one, Neb in the other. They're standing on the rims of our rain barrels, I thought. I pointed to the door. Something splashed.

"I'm a busy woman, Titus. I have mail to distribute, and with ships going down and rumors of spies all along the coast, I don't have time for Stick's tomfoolery."

"What rumors of spies? How do you know?" I asked.

She whirled on me like a lace tornado. "I'm the *postmis-tress*. I know everything about this island—except why you're following me. Titus, I want her punished."

"Consider it done," he said, very calm.

Grand's only punished me once, three years ago, back when we could swim in the ocean. We Dimes had splashed out deeper than Grand had said we could go. A riptide dragged us flailing and screaming out to sea. Grand shouted for help and started to us. Papa pushed him aside, tore off his shirt, and dived beneath the breakers.

Papa's arms knifed through the water as Grand stood helpless onshore. By the time Papa reached us, Neb and me were crying like babies and Rain was shivering like a cold rat terrier, the water lapping at her ears. "Stay together. We'll be fine," he said, giving Rain a boost. "Lie back in the water. We'll float out on the current and let it tug us down the beach. Nothing to it. Don't fight the current." He sang to us as the current swept us out. When we could barely see the lighthouse, the current turned to run along the shore. Finally, near the tip of the island, it turned again, to push us in. Papa swam with the current, nudging us ahead of him.

It was close, I know now. Too close.

If the current's icy fingers had clutched us an instant longer before it turned to shore, we'd have missed the island entirely and been swept out to sea. Grand knew it then. He helped Papa drag us ashore, collapsed, and sat in the sand crying like a little boy.

Seeing Grand cry punished me to forever and back, and he knows it.

"Hello," Neb said, strolling in. "I'm sorry you found us working for the public good while cleaning the Buick for you." He kicked off his wet shoe. "Mr. Grand, Mama sent money for that ugly yellow gingham she bought. I'm praying she doesn't make me a shirt."

Neb's mother is to fashion as a killing frost is to tomatoes.

Grand pulled out his ledger and flipped to Miss Irma's IOU page. "Ugly yellow gingham. . . . Here it is." He grabbed his knife, sliced the note from the page and slid the receipt to Neb. Then he smiled at Miss Agnes. "Will the apples and cough syrup be all, my dear?"

The words *my dear* worked on her like hot on butter. Her hand drifted to her collar. "Blackout fabric for six windows, delivered to my porch, please. Titus, dear."

"We'll deliver it for free if you let us inside," I offered.

Her dewy smile withered. "I'd rather strangle myself with my own stockings," she replied. "I'll take the apples and tonic with me, Titus. Please put them on my tab."

"Wait. You said fabric for *six* windows," Rain said. "Your house has eight."

Miss Agnes closed her eyes. "Fabric for *six* standard windows, Titus." Rain's right, I thought. Miss Agnes has eight windows, and nothing's standard about her house.

"I make curtains," Faye offered. "Thirty cents a window, if you supply the material."

"Done. Anything on the radio *this* week, Titus? About us?" Miss Agnes asked, and he shook his head. For one blink, her beady eyes looked sad. "We're expendable, then."

"We most certainly are not," Faye snapped. "We're the front line. I'll defend this island myself if I have to."

"You?" Miss Agnes said. "What are you going to do? *Lipstick* the Germans to death?" She slammed the door behind her.

"I hate her," I said.

"Well, stop it," Grand said. "She's better than you think." He looked younger and stronger, standing up for her. Suddenly I liked Miss Agnes a little more.

It soon passed.

CHAPTER 9

IF THE SHOE FITS

February 12, 1942

On Saturday, February 12, our careers screamed into high gear. "The Matchstick Alert!" Rain gasped, snagging the fallen matchstick from our granite steps. "Someone's been here!"

"Or they're still here," Neb said, and gulped.

"Time for heroes," she whispered.

We shouldered the heavy door open, sending a slow wedge of light through the dark. A set of footprints started across our flour-dusted floor, and then carefully backed out.

Rain squinted. "Whoever it was whisked most of the footprints away—with a jacket, maybe. Something metal made this mark. A zipper." She darted beneath the stairs. "Or this brass button," she said, holding it up.

Neb knelt to study the lone clear footprint left in our trap. "It's too big for Otto or Miss Agnes." He frowned. "The Ringers, maybe?"

I shook my head. "Ralph wears size huge and Carl has a dainty foot. That's in between. Let's check outside. Maybe we can track him down."

The tracks led to a tidal pool—and disappeared. "He's not *in* the pool, but he didn't wade out . . . How do you explain *that?*" Neb muttered.

"An angel taking flight?" Rain guessed. Sometimes I'm not sure when she's kidding.

HQ sat just as we'd left it. I put my lab jacket on and checked my weather instruments. Neb trotted down to measure the print.

"According to the chart in *Dime Novel #74: If the Shoe Fits*, our intruder wears a man's size eleven," he said moments later.

Rain shook the brass button she'd recovered from beneath the steps. "Sounds like a broken heart," she said, and picked up the note Miss Agnes had dropped in church, the day Papa sailed away: *21212ish latest.* "These numbers *have* to be a clue. So we have three clues: the note, the button, the footprint. But no clue how to use them." She glanced at Neb's neckerchief and gasped. "What happened? Did Schooner chew that up?"

He beamed. "My neckerchief slide? I didn't think you'd ever notice. I carved it. Daddy showed me a few tricks. Give me your honest opinion. Go on. You can't hurt my feelings."

Fact: Neb's feelings are first to get hurt, every time.

Rain turned away. He leaned in, holding the slide toward me: a blobbish head, this-way-that-way teeth, a possible mane. Papa says fate favors the bold. I went bold. "Manes are hair and only mammals have hair. A lion. The mane and teeth are a tip-off."

"What?" Neb screeched. "It's a *porpoise*. He's *smiling*. That's water splashing around him, not a *mane*. When it comes to art, Stick, you're a good scientist."

"A porpoise," Rain said, very smooth. "I can see that."

Double fish rot.

I grabbed my spyglass and turned to the window, avoiding Neb's accusing eyes. "Bus is stuck again," I announced as the passengers filed out. They rocked the bus as its wheels spun, spewing sand. "There's Naomi and Ruth."

"They're going to visit Aunt Bernice," Neb said. "*They* saw a porpoise. Eventually." As the passengers struggled, the Ringers strolled from the dunes. Ralph pushed in beside Ruth and put his shoulder against the back of the bus. Carl nestled in by Naomi.

"Neb, do the sisters know the Ringers?"

"Everybody knows them by now. They helped on the beach the night of the attack. Ralph helped unload a boat and only took a couple fish for pay. Carl helped Old Miss Edna weave a net the other day, just to learn how. You got to like a guy who helps a widow."

"Nobody's *that* good," I muttered.

Neb studied his neckerchief slide in our mirror. "I carved a porpoise because they're frolicking and playful, like me," he said. We stared at him, stunned. He smiled. "But I could change it, if you think it's too . . . liony."

"Never second-guess yourself," I replied.

As the bus lunged forward, the Ringers piled on with the sisters. I turned my spyglass to the sparkling sound. "Hey! Sam's coming over on the mail boat. *He's got passengers!*"

I zeroed in hard. I know everybody on the island by shape, voice, and in some unfortunate cases, smell. "Definite strangers," I reported, hanging Papa's shirt on its hook.

"*Non tatum sursum,*" Neb shouted, and we charged for the stairs.

"Ahoy, Neb!" Sam shouted, and tossed a line. Two strangers sat in the back of the boat, the woman tall and proud, the man slumped and pale green.

Neb snugged the boat against the dock. The man lurched onto the pier, leaned over, and put his hands on his knees. Sam, who's Black, waited for the dark-haired woman to hold out a hand. He took it, and she stepped ashore like she knew how. "Thank you, Sam," she said, her accent strange and interesting.

Sam nodded. "Twenty cents for you and your brother."

He's handsome, Sam, at ease on water and on land. He's the only Black property owner this end of the island, and the only Black mail carrier I know. Most Black people left the island after the Civil War. Sam's grandparents came back with enough money to buy a house.

As the woman opened her change purse, I took in her plaid cloak, pleated skirt, and neat blouse. *Definitely not Sears and Roebuck.* Sam put ashore a pile of suitcases. "Hey Sam, what's the news?" Neb asked, grabbing a couple wooden thingamajigs Sam swung his way.

"Our ships are sitting ducks out there, Neb, that's the news."

Sam stepped to the dock and hurried along, swinging the mail sack.

Rain smiled at the travelers. "Welcome. I'm Rain. This is Stick and Neb."

"Julia Cornwall and my brother Dirk," the woman said. She stuck out her hand like a man, only with her wrist bent pretty. I'd never seen a woman shake hands, but I knew how. Like all great literature, dime novels take you places and teach you things—how to shake hands, answer telephones, fall in love. I shook her hand smart as a whip. So did Rain and Neb.

Dirk belched. "I'm afraid Dirk's seasick," she said. We took a cool step back.

"Hello, Dirk. I see Miss Julia got the looks in the family," Neb said, very friendly.

Mama says ninety percent of all true things are best unspoken. This would be one example. Still, I could see Neb's point. Dirk looked like a tall, sickly catfish, his thin, pale mustache etching his upper lip, his wide-set eyes and broad face moist from sickness.

"You'll feel better if you upchuck," Neb said. "Watch your shoes." He turned to Julia. "Carry your bags for three dollars, and we'll tote the doo-hicks for free."

Sam hurried back with the mail sack, leaped into the skiff, and cast off. He smiled at Rain. "Nice seeing you, girl."

"You too, Mr. Sam," she said.

"Nice carving, Neb," he called as he poled away. "Otter?"

"Porpoise," Neb shouted.

Julia stooped to look at Neb's carving. "Lovely," she said, and rose to study our village of ramshackle buildings and abandoned fish houses. Honestly, if I didn't live here, I'd keep going. Her gaze stopped at Miss Agnes's odd clothesline, behind the post office. She skimmed the peculiar assortment of laundry like she could read it.

"Three dollars is fine," she said, smiling. "Where's your hotel?"

Our hotel?

"Ocracoke Island maybe," Neb said. "You got a half-day walk to catch the ferry you already missed. Or I can rent you a room. Two beds. Five dollars a night."

Five dollars?

That's robbery, but Neb's folks need the money and the sisters can sleep at our house. Besides, on the island we have a love/hate relationship with tourists: Love their cash, hate that they can't just mail it in.

The strangers looked at each other like a couple of worried dogs. "I'll throw in breakfast," Neb added, and she nodded. "This way," he said as we gathered their things.

Miss Agnes stepped out of the PO and put a hand on her frilly hip as we started forward. "Miss Agnes isn't right in the head," I whispered. "Don't make eye contact."

Miss Agnes stepped in front of Julia. "How do you do? Agnes Wainwright. The weather turns cartwheels this time of day."

Julia looked Miss Agnes in the eye. "We are artists, but we've never painted wind."

"I have," Rain said, looking puzzled. "I could teach you."

"I've got a cottage for rent," Miss Agnes said. "Five dollars a week, if you're interested."

Fact: Miss Agnes's cottage was Jake Harker's fishing shack until she traded him a washing machine for it two years ago. We Dimes cleaned it up nice for her, but nobody stays in that shack but rats.

"Thank you," Julia said. "Neb, I believe the cottage suits us best."

Miss Agnes cranked her face into a possible smile. "I don't know what these scamps told you, but don't pay them more than ten cents for carrying your things."

"I hate her," Neb whispered.

"I heard that," Miss Agnes snapped, and sped ahead to her shack in the shadow of the water tower. We Dimes slowed to the travelers' pace and I invented a new rule. Life Rule #32. *Interrogate when it seems natural.*

"You have an accent," I said.

"It's pretty," Rain added.

"Are you from Germany?" Neb asked.

Fact: Blunt is the best shortcut God ever made.

"I'm from Austria," Julia said. "Be careful with our easels, Neb."

"Austria," he said, adjusting the easels on his shoulder. "I've always wanted to see your national beast, the kangaroo."

I winced.

"Kangaroos live in Australia, Neb. I'm from *Austria*. In Europe."

Up ahead, Miss Agnes unlocked the shack's front door. *Since when does that dump have a lock?* Rain beamed at Julia. "Austria's the pink country beside Germany. We saw it on Miss Pope's map. Germany swallowed it."

The sadness in Julia's eyes near stopped my heart.

"Yes," she said. "Hitler's Germany has swallowed many countries and many, many lives. I live in Montreal now, like Dirk. We booked passage to your island last year, before . . ."

"Before the war came here," Neb said, and she sighed a yes. We stepped onto the shack's porch and I peeked inside. We'd cleaned the place stem to stern, but I braced for the trio of dented lard buckets we'd set around the rusty woodstove, for chairs. I gasped.

"When did it get pretty inside?" Rain whispered.

Excellent question. Miss Agnes had hung Faye's black-out curtains at the windows, placed three wooden chairs around the polished stove, and popped a photo of long-nosed President Franklin D. Roosevelt over the mantel. On a little table sat three apples.

The hair on the back of my neck stood up. Miss Agnes had bought three apples every few days since the first ship went down. She knew the Artists were coming!

Three chairs. Three apples . . . Three spies?

Life Rule #33: *Stay close to your suspects.* "We're excellent island guides," I said. "We'll trade our services for art lessons. Neb and I are remedial but Rain's a genius."

"We can get you free tickets to baseball games, if you stay that long," Neb added. "We have Ringers on display." Brilliant. There are no tickets. You show up and spread a blanket.

The thick tangle of vines beneath the water tower rustled and Julia's hand went fast to her handbag. J. Edgar swaggered from the tangle. "Julia, this is Edgar," Rain said, and Julia relaxed. "He hunts the thicket beneath the water tower."

Neb propped the easels on the porch and sniffed the air. "What's that smell?" he asked, and sniffed again. "Miss Julia, do you smell sort of . . . spicy?"

"Ignore him," I told Julia, but she already had. Her gaze drifted inside the little house, where Miss Agnes shoved open the black curtains.

"Perhaps we *will* need guides," Julia said. "I'd like to climb your famous lighthouse, and sketch your wild ponies. I hear you have a mysterious woman living in a giant wine cask by the sea. Do you know her?"

Neb and me looked at Rain. "We've met," Rain said, very cautious.

"Leave our bags on the porch," Julia said, tugging three, new one-dollar bills from her skirt pocket. "I believe we said three dollars. A deal's a deal," she whispered, tucking the crisp bills in my hand. She winked. "But don't tell your postmistress."

She stepped inside with Miss Agnes and Dirk, and firmly closed the door.

As we walked away, Rain looked back. "How did she know Miss Agnes is the postmistress? Miss Agnes never said it. And neither did we."

A patch of skin between my shoulder blades tingled.

"*Wind turning cartwheels? Painting the wind?* That's code," Neb added. "And I bet those three apples are a signal too."

I pictured the scrap of dropped paper in our clue box: *21212ish latest.* My stomach dropped. "Today's February 12—or 2/12." I looked up, at the sun. "And it's noonish. 2-12-12ish."

We went so quiet, I could hear our shoes squeak against the sand.

"Stay calm," Neb said, panic edging his voice. "Whatever you do, don't lose your wits. Our true shot at FBI fame has arrived."

CHAPTER 10

TWIN OF DARKNESS

Mid-February 1942

Fame turned out to be a moving target. Miss Agnes kept the Artists hopping, taking them here, touring them there—and giving us a chance to open a satellite HQ in the tent of briars and vines draping the space beneath the water tower.

"Great view of the Artists' Shack," Neb said as we set up Miss Agnes's lard buckets. "Now all we need is a way to buddy up to them. Think, you two. Think!"

While we thought, ships went down offshore and life regained its shape—wash days on Mondays, church on Sundays, baseball now and then, school five days a week. We learned not to walk up quiet behind people already rattled.

Fact: With Tommy Wilkins at boot camp, valuables still disappeared. Miss Pope's snow globe. Reed's screwdriver. Dirk's gold wristwatch.

"Maybe Tommy *wasn't* the thief," Neb said, looking worried.

"He *was*," Rain told him.

"Rain's right," I said. "This is Otto peeling Tommy's small-potatoes empire."

At school, where Neb's dinner pail turned up empty day

after day, Miss Pope reacted to the stress of war by going hyper-normal. "Looking normal makes us feel normal," she said. "When you feel normal, you act normal. When you act normal, you *are* normal."

I raised my hand. "Excuse me, there's no evidence to support that hypothesis."

"Thank you, Stick, take out your spelling books."

"Invisible-ized," Rain whispered. "Now you see me—*poof*."

Meanwhile, Faye's life made a U-turn—and so did our case. "I'm putting the brakes on my Hollywood debut," Faye announced at supper one Monday. "Too many European actresses have flooded Hollywood. Hedy Lamarr, Luise Rainer, and lots of others, all fleeing Hitler's war. I'm now planning a debut of a *different* nature."

"Smart," I said, but the sadness in her violet eyes left my heart desolate.

"Keep your eye on February twenty-sixth," she added, slapping lima beans on her plate. "I call it Faye Day. A day that will make history."

I smiled at Grand. "The Romans built rooms just for throwing up in, on occasions like this. See *vomitorium*. Volume V." He didn't smile back. "What's wrong?"

"War news," he said, glancing at Mama. "We've started rounding up Japanese Americans, and putting them in camps."

"Why?" I demanded. "What did they do?"

"Nothing." He sighed. "People are afraid after Japan's surprise attack on Pearl Harbor last December. They're extending that fear to Japanese Americans—which is flat-out wrong." He rose. "Excuse me, Ada. I don't have much appetite."

"Finish eating, Stick," Mama said as he walked away. "He'll be okay. We all will."

As it turned out, Faye Day *would* make island history, but not the way Faye had planned.

At five p.m., we Dimes caught a massive break. "Miss Agnes has a migraine," Rain reported as she and Neb ran up with her water bucket. "The Artists are alone!"

"Stakeout. Seven p.m. to midnight," I said. "Meet at HQ-B in two hours. Dress stealthy. Wear black, as in *Dime Novel #77: Twin of Darkness.*"

"No. Naomi says I look better in brown," Neb said, pumping Rain's water bucket full. "Black washes me out. I want to impress Julia. But yes to midnight."

"You miss the point, but excellent," I replied.

"Dark clothes make me sad," Rain said. "Mama Jonah's made me a new blue feed-sack dress with white embroidery. I'll wear my white socks and red Mary Janes. Yes to midnight."

Life's simpler in dime novels, where everyone looks good in black.

I rushed inside and pounded upstairs. "You still owe me a day's labor for eavesdropping," Faye called. "I want some of that time starting at six."

Rot. "I can't. I'm on future FBI business."

"Dress nice and do something about your hair," she

responded. "I'm throwing a debut party at the store. You're my setup crew. The party's for teenagers only, so you have to leave when it starts. Don't humiliate yourself by forcing me to go to Mama on this."

A little before six, I smoothed my black sweater and tried to smush my cumulous-cloud hair into a specific shape. I visualized the cover of *Dime Novel #86: A Night to Remember,* and sailed downstairs to my first teenage party. "Great blouse, Faye, love the sleeves. This week's sewing effort paid off," I said.

She pushed up the long sleeve. "Thanks. How do you get your hair to *do* that? You look like a tangerine lollipop." She shrugged. "Never mind. Let's go."

Halfway to the store, she screeched to a halt. "Shoot. I left my cookies."

"I'll get them," I said, and sprinted back. By the time I made it to the store, hid *my* half of the cookies, and blasted in with her half, Faye had lit the store's kerosene lamps.

"Love the lamplight," I said, setting her plate on the counter. "It's romantic and it softens the look of acne." I glanced at the clock. 6:25 p.m. Thirty-five minutes until meet-up time. "What can I do?"

"Close the curtains before the Nazis blow us to smithereens."

Reed's truck chugged up, and he strolled in, Schooner at his heels sporting a red bow tie Faye had made from a scrap of cloth. Reed wore a soft blue shirt and khakis. Fact: It's odd when your dog dresses better than you, but this is the year of everything different.

"Evening, ladies," Reed said. "You staying to dance, short-cake?"

"Stick's the setup crew," Faye said. "Reed, this is huge, hosting our first dance as a couple." Reed's eyes lit up. He's crazy about her, I thought. But why? "I want everything nice. Stick—get those putrid eggs off the counter."

"What's the hurry?" Reed asked, grinning. "Tommy Wilkins is back from basic training. He might want one." He muscled a bucket of lard behind the counter as Faye took the lid off the pickle barrel and sniffed. The sharp brine-and-vinegar scent rumbled my stomach. Reed shouldered her aside, closed the barrel, tipped it on one edge, and arced it across the floor.

"Dance with me like that, and I'll be a happy woman," Faye teased, spreading a tablecloth over the pool table. Fact: Faye will be lucky to get three dances out of Reed, but she dances with everybody who asks her and Reed never minds.

Outside, someone landed flat-footed on the porch. Tommy Wilkins stepped in, looking trim and sharp in a navy uniform. He tucked his white sailor's hat beneath his arm. *"Almost* Seaman First Class Thomas Wilkins, reporting for duty," he said, grinning.

"Well, look at you," Faye said. "That uniform's quill."

"Hollywood talk. It means she likes it," I explained. Tommy scratched Schooner's head. Schooner curled his lip and growled. Some things, a uniform can't fix.

Tommy looked around. "This place brings back memories."

"You've only been gone a few weeks," I said. I checked the clock—6:35 p.m.

"Basic training is a different world, Tangerine Girl."

"Don't call her that," Faye said.

Tommy propped a shiny black shoe on a chair and leaned forward, crossing his forearms over his knee. For an instant, he looked handsome. His words made him ugly again. "Reed, you should sign up. Not going makes you seem . . . less than. Juicy Fruit, Stick?" he asked, opening a pack of gum. "You may not see more until war's end. Otto tells me Scrape's chewing pine sap. Of course, Otto doesn't have to worry about that. Not with me around."

I glanced at the slender, foil-wrapped slice of temptation. My mouth flooded. *Take it*, the devil whispered. *Don't you dare*, my pride snapped. "No thanks," I said.

"Where's everybody, gorgeous?" Tommy asked. He nudged his sleeve up to flash a gold watch. "Oh. Guess I'm early. Little gift from Otto. Nice, huh? He did some odd jobs to earn the money, I imagine."

I glanced at his arm. *Dirk's* gold watch stared up at me. One mystery solved.

"Otto with a job *would* be odd," I muttered.

Tommy shrugged. "Don't think Otto likes you much either. Or the kids you pal around with. You should be careful." He clicked the radio on. "Who's coming to dance with *me*?"

"Ruth and Naomi love to dance," Faye said. She scattered a bag of cornmeal and gave it a glide as Tommy coaxed a tune in and heaved himself to his two left feet.

"I'm not kidding, Reed," Tommy said, snagging a Pepsi. "Be a man. Sign up."

Reed smiled. "Somebody has to keep the ladies happy while you're off playing soldier."

"I'm not *playing* soldier," Tommy snapped, sliding a nickel across the counter. "I ship out in a few weeks. Can't say where," he added, calmer. "Can't even tell Otto."

For one breath, my world lost its spin.

Obnoxious Tommy Wilkins is going to war, I thought, and a piece of my world broke loose. A real war, far from our invisible island. Tommy's getting a fresh deal—new people, new places, new possibilities, I thought. From here on, he can be whoever he decides to be.

Somehow the knowing left a ghost standing in the middle of the store, showing off a stolen watch and a navy uniform, and drinking an ice-cold Pepsi Cola.

At 6:44, Ruth and Naomi stepped in, dressed to the nines. Or what passes for the nines on the island. More like four and a half, if you're comparing them to Faye's magazines. Pencil skirts made in home ec. class, and yellow-and-white gingham blouses. "Hey Stick, thought you were meeting Neb at HQ-B, whatever that means," Naomi said.

"Roger that," I said as the gang from Kinnakeet rolled up on a flat-bed truck. Carl Miller bustled in with the rest, moving easy and happy in the thick of it. Ralph lingered in the door like a little kid, not making eye contact. (See *introvert*, Volume I.)

"Take your shoes off at the door if you've been to the beach," I called. "No oil allowed."

The chatter picked up and in a blink, Faye's friends packed the store—with the enlisted boys like gaps in a snaggle-toothed smile. "Have some cookies," Faye said, placing her plate on the pool table. "Fair warning: I made them myself." She whipped the dishtowel off her plate. *"What the heck?* I made more cookies than that."

"With your cooking, fewer could be a blessing," I said, and the room laughed. "Pepsis and Cheerwines are a nickel," I added. "Honor system. You know where the drink box is."

Carl mingled, while Ralph pretended to examine Mama's tonic bottles. Mama says to always make people feel welcome. "Hey Ralph, have a cookie if you want."

The slow of his Louisiana drawl almost slammed my brain into reverse. "No thanks, bébé," he said. I glanced at the clock. 7:08 p.m. The stress of trying to be on time left, and I became one with total lateness. Relief washed over me like a warm tide. (See *Zen*, Volume Z.)

"I'm Stick, a pre-famous scientist and future FBI selectee. What's your story?"

"Me? I babysit pretty boy over there. We're like Wednesday and Thursday, one right behind the other. He's the social butterfly. I'm more like a praying mantis or something."

Weird. I searched for a graceful reply. "I, too, enjoy entomology," I said. He frowned. "The study of insects," I added. We helped ourselves to a long silence.

"Your dog's fat," he finally said, glancing at Schooner. "Must eat beaucoup scraps."

Fortunately, Faye hopped on a chair. "Attention, ladies,"

she called. "You're invited to the *debut* of the island's security club. My house, Saturday at ten. Teenagers only."

"Here's Count Basie's hit," the radio announcer said. *"'One O'Clock Jump.'"* Folks pranced onto the floor in twos and threes.

"We better get used to dancing alone," Faye murmured, watching Naomi and Ruth step onto the dance floor as Tommy loped hopelessly behind them. "Stick, we said you could stay until the party started. It's started."

"How about the next dance, Faye?" Carl called across the room.

Before she could say *sure*, Reed scooped into her like wind into a sail. "Find your own girl, buddy," he said. "Faye dances with *me*."

"Reed's *jealous?*" Rain asked a few minutes later, her face clouding. "Sad." We sat in HQ-B, on the old lard buckets. "What else?" She took a cookie from my plate.

"Faye's debuting a girl's security group but we're out. Carl dances like Fred Astaire, Ralph dances like a cement mixer, and like I said, Otto gave *Dirk's* stolen watch to *Tommy*."

Neb peeped through the vines. "We better get a move on if we're visiting Julia. Rain and me can only stay another hour."

"Another hour? We said midnight!" Annoyance rocked me like a choppy sea. If I ever have high blood pressure, it will be because of Rain and Neb. We darted to the Artists' Shack, where the blackout curtains didn't quite reach the window-sill.

"Thank goodness Faye can't sew straight," I whispered,

and peeped inside. Julia wore a shimmery red dress. Dirk, in a black suit, hunched over a table, sketching.

"Julia looks like a mermaid," Rain whispered. She pulled her socks up. "Excuse me," she said, taking Neb's cookie and putting it back on the plate. "Follow me please. Now."

She walked bold as a rooster's crow to the Artists' door and knocked. Julia opened it. "Cookies from the Dime Novel Kids. You look like a mermaid," Rain said. "May we come in?"

Neb clicked his heels and gave an odd little bow. In the distance, a car backfired. A vehicle with cat-eye headlights purred toward us and sputtered to a halt.

"Close that door!" a woman snapped. "You'll get us all killed!"

Miss Agnes!

Dirk blew out the lamp, stepped out, and locked the door. "Thank you for the use of your car, Agnes." His catfish smile sent goose bumps tiptoeing up the back of my neck.

She tossed him the keys. "I deflated the tires so you can drive in sand, and taped over the headlights so U-boats can't shoot you. Stay on the firm sand below the high tide line."

"You're letting them borrow *the Buick?*" I said. "You don't let *anybody* touch that car."

"There's a map in the glove compartment," she said. "You want the Oceanside Club."

The Oceanside Club. Where Reed wants to take Faye.

Dirk swung his briefcase into the car and looked at the sky. "Your stars dazzle me. So elegant, so unexpected." He slipped behind the wheel. "Won't you come, Aggie?"

"Next time, perhaps," she said, and the Buick puttered away. Miss Agnes swung toward us, her ruffles menacing in the moonlight. "Stay away from them. Don't even talk to them."

"Why not?"

"Because I said so."

I like to stand my ground, but it's hard on an island where the sand moves with wind and tide. *"Because I said so is no reason, Aggie."* Rain and Neb took a quick step away from me. I had gone too far. "I mean, Miss Agnes."

She lowered her face to mine, her breath reeking of mullet. "Go. Away." She stalked off as Edgar slunk from beneath the oleander and followed.

"What's the Oceanside Club?" Rain asked.

"A dance place, up in Nags Head. Faye says it's quill. That means great."

"Mama says the club is sin city," Neb said, frowning. "Why would Julia go to sin city?"

"To dance?" Rain guessed. Rain would give Satan the benefit of the doubt.

Neb studied the Artists' Shack. "Did you bring our Lock-Picking Kit?"

I felt in my hair for Faye's bobby pin, which can open any lock on the island. Miss Agnes stood on her porch, staring at us. Edgar sat beside her, tail swishing. "Another time," I said, patting the pin back into place. "Let's go practice our spy lingo. Who's in?"

Three figures sauntered toward us, quiet as velvet.

"Never mind who's *in*," Neb said as Miss Agnes slammed her door. "Who's *that?*"

CHAPTER 11

TROUBLE TRAVELS IN THREES

"Notto!" Rain gasped, pulling us into the shadows.

Otto and his goons slunk up like a trio of gangsters in *Dime Novel #71: Trouble Travels in Threes*. "Check the door," Otto said. "A little art will impress Tommy out of his mind."

Scrape crept onto the porch and tried the door. "Locked," he whispered, and tried a window. "What kind of people lock their *windows?*"

Miss Agnes charged to the center of our street. "Who's there?" she bellowed. Scrape dove off the porch and rolled beneath a shrub. "Stick?" she called. "Is that you?"

"Yes," Otto said, making his voice high. "It's me, you old hag. Stick Lawson."

"It is not!" Neb shouted. "It's Otto!"

"Liar Neb!" Miss Agnes screeched.

Otto lowered his voice and looked our way. "Kraut lovers, hiding in the dark," he sneered. "Fade, boys," he commanded. Otto and Jersey stepped into the deep shadows. Scrape scrambled up and followed, leaving something glittering in the sand.

Rain scooped it up. "Miss Pope's missing brooch," she whispered.

I looked toward Miss Agnes's house. Wash fluttered on her front clothesline: a man's hat, an undershirt, two life jackets. Miss Agnes stood silhouetted in her window's light. "We've learned our lesson. We'll never do that again," I yelled. She stalked inside and slammed the door.

"The perfect escape," Neb whispered as we headed for the lighthouse.

Just outside the village, where live oaks crouch with their backs to the wind, Otto stepped from the shadows. From the jut of his chin to the clench of his fists, everything about him said *fight*. "Rain, Rain, your mama's a spy," he sang. "Come here to snoop, come here to die."

Rain went tense as a snarl of wire. "We're not spies, Notto."

"At least *you* speak English. What's Jonah speak? *Kraut?*"

"Kraut isn't a language, it's a cabbage," I said. "Ask Grand. He learned it in *his* war. Miss Jonah's as American as anybody that ever washed ashore here."

His goons eased close. Jersey's stocky and dull as a rusty butter knife. Scrape's a head taller than Otto, but walks hunched, like a dog expecting to be kicked. I kept my eyes on Otto.

"You're outnumbered," Otto said. "Three guys against two girls and a Neb."

"Us against you," I said. "Even odds."

Even odds was a stretch. Scrape and Jersey have flunked sixth grade twice. They're big. Neb's foot-slow, but has lightning hands. Rain's fearless as the sea. Me, I'm cunning, with whiplash leg-reach. And we have a secret weapon: We're not afraid to lose.

Fact: When you're not afraid to lose, anything can happen.

Otto eased forward, and I put up my hands. I wiggled my fingers because it's strange, and smiled because it's creepy. Strange and creepy scares kids.

Otto's eyes flickered. "Where'd your mama come from, Rain? Germany? What about your daddy? What was *he*?" he sneered. "Too bad he's not here to save you."

"He's here," Rain said, very even. "Same as yours."

Otto lunged for her hair. Rain blocked his hand.

"Don't touch her," Neb shouted.

"Nebby has a girlfriend. I say Jonah's a spy. Everybody knows what to do with spies."

My stomach lurched. Papa's voice whispered to me. *Use those brains, Genius.*

"She's no spy, and I can prove it," I said. "Rain, how old are you?"

Rain looked at me like I'd gone mad. "Ten."

"So your mother came here . . . when? 1931? 1932? *Before* Germany elected Hitler."

Scrape whistled. "They *elected* that guy?"

"Hitler didn't even *have* spies when she came. And even if Miss Jonah *was* a spy, what would she tell him? How many fish she caught?"

Scrape chuckled, and fear shot through Otto's beautiful blue eyes. What a waste of beautiful blue.

"Shut up, Scrape," Otto said, and popped his knuckles the way Tommy does.

So that's it. If Tommy's fighting, Otto is too. "Did we

call you *Otto?*" I said. "Hey Scrape, Miss Dandee changed Otto's name, remember? Otto's a German name—his grand-daddy's name. Seems funny, you accusing Rain's people when *you* own the German blood, Otto."

"Shut up, freak," Otto growled. "One on one—Neb and me."

"One on one, you and *me*," I countered, and started wiggling like seaweed in a gentle sea, letting my arms and neck wobble. Like I said, weird scares people.

"Quit it, Stick," Neb said as Otto peeled off his red jacket. Neb took off his neckerchief, and handed it to Rain. Jersey drew a circle in a patch of moonlight—their fighting ring.

"Little fish," Rain whispered to Neb. "Let it go. Fall down, and he'll leave."

Neb shook his head. He's never taken a fall in his life. He stepped up, raised his fists, and put his weight on his strong leg.

The two boys circled, Otto bouncing on his toes like a boxer, Neb solid.

Otto faked a grab and Jersey cheered. Neb swiped and Otto jabbed, catching Neb on the jaw. Neb shook his head like a bull and Otto rushed low. Neb danced back and clubbed his ear.

Otto's howl pierced the sky, and he attacked in a flurry of punches. Jersey cheered again as Neb staggered back, a cut opening over his eye.

"Stop, Otto," Scrape said. "Neb can't see."

Otto swiped Neb's leg. Neb stumbled back, arms flailing. Rain grabbed his arm, softening his fall. He sat in the sand, his head in his hands, blood dripping between his fingers. "Kraut lover," Otto snarled, kicking sand at him. "You Dimes, go to the devil."

"No thank you, Notto," Rain said. "You run ahead without us."

Otto lunged at her. Rain and me went back-to-back, fists raised.

"Cut it out!" a man shouted, stepping into our ring of moonlight. Carl Miller grabbed Otto's arm. "What's wrong with you?" He frowned. "Hey. Aren't you the preacher's kid?"

Otto scowled. He hides behind his father like shade behind a tree. But force him into the open and the sunshine swallows him alive.

Suddenly I liked Carl Miller maybe thirty percent.

Scrape stepped up. "Who the heck are you?"

Carl smiled and held out his hand, very handsome. "Carl Miller, the Ringer playing for Kinnakeet. You?"

Scrape gave Carl's hand a quick shake. "Clarence Fulcher. People call me Scrape."

"Scrape? Why's that?"

"Because his folks just scrape by," Otto said, leering. "Gave him the name myself, years ago. Pretty funny, right?"

Carl looked at Otto like he was something you wouldn't want to track in from the chicken house. "Not to me, I guess. Nice to meet you, Clarence," he said, and Scrape nodded.

"Jersey," Jersey said, stepping up. "People call me Jersey because it's my name."

Carl's smile never wavered. "Nice to meet you, Jersey. You

boys are kind of . . . big to be beating up kids. Except for you, Otto."

"Butt out, stranger," Otto snapped. "We don't need Jonah here, and we don't need you."

"We've known Miss Jonah forever and *everybody* knows Carl by now," I said. "They're not strangers. They have as much right to be here as you do."

Otto spit. "Tell your mother to watch herself, Rain. *We're* watching her. And we're watching you too, Carl Miller."

Carl shook his head as Otto and his goons walked away. "I hate a bully. Well, nice seeing you, Stick. And meeting you, Rain. Neb." Carl looked like a friendly stick of dynamite standing there in the moonlight, strong and trim.

"You know our names," Rain said, smiling.

"Baseball players talk, you know. About your investigations, your . . . individuality."

"You mean you gossip about our weirdness," I said, and he laughed.

"There's more than one way to see a thing. I see a famous scientist, a famous artist, and a famous . . . Neb. How's your detective work going?" He handed Neb a handkerchief, for his eye. "Me, I figure Otto's gang is robbing everybody. But I can't figure the Artists, or why the postmistress's sticking so close to them." He looked sheepish. "I'm trying to figure how your island works. Plants, people, animals . . ."

"Stick wrote a book on the plants we collect for Miss Ada. I drew the art. It's in Miss Ada's library," Rain said.

"Love to see it sometime." *Maybe I like Carl forty percent.*

"You have curiosity," she said. "Mama Jonah says that's the first ingredient in everything good. Art, science, code breaking."

He grinned. "I have plenty of curiosity. Too much, my father says. I like to satisfy it myself instead of asking lazy questions like that slouch Dirk. He came to us with a ton the other day. How deep's the inlet? How deep's the sound? Do we have patrol boats? Lazy."

Interesting. "Thanks for the tip," I said.

"Here's a tip for *you*," Rain said. "You steal second base better than anybody I've ever seen. But you know what God says." She whispered: "Thou shalt not steal."

Carl stared at her a moment and then laughed wild and free. "I think God loves me every minute of the day whether I'm stealing second base or not," he said, grinning.

Maybe I like him fifty percent. Make it fifty-one, putting him in the positive.

"We owe you for helping us tonight," I said. "Mama cooks a good Sunday dinner and I plate a nice pickle. Our house is the two-story on the edge of town. Do you like butterbeans?"

"Love them. Thanks, Stick. I'll take you up on that one day."

Maybe he's not so bad, I thought as he walked away, whistling. *I might even like him sixty percent.* One thing's for sure: He showed up right on time.

Neb and me walked on with Rain, our Internal Danger Scans on high alert.

As Neb peeled off for home, Miss Jonah's soft voice drifted across the dunes: "The wind's howl, the angels' song, the porpoises laughing me home ..."

"What's she talking about?" I whispered.

"Our story," Rain said, very matter-of-fact. "Hers starts different than mine."

I headed back to the party and peeked through the window. Carl stood with Naomi. "My father wants me to enlist," he was saying. "That's why I left home—to figure out what *I* want. I'd enlist now, only my grandmother may not be with us much longer ..."

Ralph sat in the corner, flipping peanuts into the air and catching them in his mouth.

When the party broke up, I followed Carl and Ralph, for practice. They skirted Rain's place and headed into the dunes. "You broke up their fight?" Ralph drawled as they spread their bedrolls. "Well, ain't you the hero. Uncle Yaeger will be proud," he said as they stretched out.

Who's Uncle Yaeger?

"Beaucoup stars, pretty boy," Ralph added.

Carl yawned. "That's the Milky Way, cuz. A river alive with billions of stars."

Maybe I like Carl seventy percent.

As he fell asleep, Ralph sang an old Sunday school tune under his breath, his huge feet wagging in time with the music. "This little light of mine, I'm gonna let it shine . . ."

I turned to catch a glimpse of a woman watching us across the dunes. Miss Agnes? Julia?

Poof. She was gone.

An hour later I scampered up the Emergency Exit Oak, swung through my bedroom window, and landed light as a cat. Faye sat up in her bed and ripped her sleep mask off. "Where have you been? What are you doing with that cookie plate?"

"Shhhhh," I said. "I thought you'd be asleep."

"Shut the window. It's freezing in here."

Faye's bad moods curdle milk, but she always leaves the window open if I'm not home. I lowered the window, slipped into a nightgown, and headed toward my bed. As my eyes adjusted to the dark, I reached for my namesake invention—the Stick-O-Matic.

Fact: As a scientist, I know dark's the mere absence of light. As a creature whose senses have evolved over eons to register danger, I know to the depths of my soul that the pool of dark beneath my bed is pure evil. At night, it twines its long, thin fingers in my bedsprings, licks its pale lips, and waits for me. I grabbed a box of matches and slid it open.

"You're chicken squirt," she whispered. "Afraid of the dark."

"I am not," I lied. "*Nyctophobia* is common among geniuses my age."

"I understand," she said, her voice going sweet—a sure sign of treachery. "There's that split second after you blow out a candle and lean out of bed to set it on the nightstand. The moment a madman from beyond time could reach from beneath your bed . . ." She let her voice hang in the dark between us. *"And grab your bony arm!"*

"Stop it!" I said, my voice going high. "I hate you."

I swiped the match against the box, and lit the Stick-O-Matic's candle, which sits in a pie pan of water on my night-stand. Gently, I settled a Mason jar upside down over the candle, on spacers just tall enough to keep the jar's rim from touching the pan. I hurled myself into bed and pulled the quilts to my chin as the flame slowly burned the oxygen in the jar, creating a vacuum. The water rose, the flame consumed the dwindling oxygen. The candle blinked out.

Fact: The Stick-O-Matic is genius. Every kid on the planet will want one.

"I'll patent that and make a fortune one day," I whispered. "I'm glad Reed's truck finally started, after the dance. Tell him to check the carburetor. Are you going to the baseball game Sunday? What about the civil defense meeting when it rolls around? I am."

"Stop spying on me, you freak," she snapped, but already I was drifting away.

• • •

"I can't go," I told Rain on Sunday morning. "Mama's grounded me for flunking spelling. Neb can't go either. Our first home game, and we're both out. You go for all of us."

She reported at supper. "Ralph's a slugger, and Carl steals bases better than Otto steals a silver dollar. Kinnakeet won. Reed didn't say a word, just walked off the field."

"Carl's cute," Faye said, taking a fish cake.

"Can't judge a book by its cover," Grand said.

"Feel free to judge me by mine," she invited, and Grand laughed like he used to.

I changed the subject. "Miss Agnes has the Artists over for supper every night. That's out of character. She doesn't even let Grand in."

"Leave her alone," Grand grumbled. "And me too, while you're at it."

When we made applesauce from the last apples in Grand's barrel the next weekend, I set aside the three best ones. "We're bribing our way into Miss Agnes's house, even if it means total humiliation," I told Rain and Neb.

"How would that be any different from usual?" Neb muttered.

We knocked on Miss Agnes's door at seven p.m.

"Yes?" she said, peeping out. "Oh. You. Go away."

Julia and Dirk sat on a sagging sofa with their coats buttoned up. Someone had placed wood and twigs in the fireplace, but no one had struck a match.

"Are those cookies?" Julia called, leaning forward on the sofa.

"Apples," I said. "Your favorite."

Neb smiled. "I'm a Boy Scout. I could start a fire for you, if you'd like."

"We could bring wood from the backyard," I offered.

Miss Agnes's eyes went dangerous. "How do you know I have firewood out back?"

A slipup—rare with geniuses but not unheard of.

"Most people do, plus Neb's psychic," I said. "He dreamed it." Julia smiled at Neb and he leaned into the room, smoothing his hair. Fact: Neb's the least psychic person I know. Intuition could swarm his ears like mosquitoes and he'd never hear the whine.

"Julia, I rode my pony over in case you want to meet her," he said.

"Shoo," Miss Agnes replied, shoving him out the door. She glanced at his neckerchief. "Nice porpoise," she added, and locked the door.

"Porpoise!" he cried. "She got it!" He beamed at us. "Who would think she has such a good eye for art? How did I do with Julia? Do you think she likes me?"

"Julia may have been *mesmerized*, I didn't have a clear look," I said, passing the apples around. "Great word. In the 1700s a scientist named Mesmer theorized—"

"Stop it, Stick," Neb said, adjusting his neckerchief.

"Why lay a fire and not light it?" Rain asked, frowning. "It's chilly tonight. And if Miss Agnes's chimney works, why did she burn papers in the backyard?"

"Maybe it *doesn't* work. But then why lay a fire?" Neb

asked, carrying his apple to Babylon. "Here you go, Baby."
They both hopped on Baby's back. "Let's go to HQ and re-figure our clues."

Fact: I love Babylon and hate riding her.

I worry about her back with the three of us up there, and I worry about cracking my teeth. At my age, I have less than a one percent chance of growing a third set of choppers. (See *hyperdontia*, Volume H.) "You go ahead," I said. "I'll meet you."

At HQ, I lit a candle and Neb opened the cigar box marked *CLUES*. Inside lay the paper clip and half-burned notepad from Miss Agnes's yard. I flipped through the pad. "Postage rates, grocery lists, ship schedules. A list: jacket, kimono, lingerie, mittens."

"What's a kimono?" Neb asked.

"A robe, maybe, but I'm not sure. I'm missing Volume K."

Neb grabbed the brass button from our box. He held it to his ear and shook it. It rattled.

"That list is alphabetical," Rain said as he tapped the button against the floor. He bit it and frowned like a puzzled chipmunk. "Jacket, kimono, lingerie, mittens. Maybe Miss Agnes alphabetizes her outfits?" she guessed. "That could explain her color combinations."

Neb gave the button a twist. "Rot," he muttered, and twisted it backwards.

The button opened, splitting neatly in half. "It's back-threaded," he said, looking stunned. He tilted it to the candlelight. "A compass!" He looked at us, his eyes wide. "We really *are* geniuses! All of us! I knew it! Who hides a compass in a button?" He leaned forward, eyes glowing. "This is *proof* of spies. It could mean a parade, fame—just what Daddy needs."

We sat a moment, inhaling the heady aroma of pre-fame.

"But whose button is it?" Rain asked. "Miss Agnes doesn't wear brass buttons. Julia doesn't. Dirk? Carl? Ralph?"

"We can check out the Ringers easy," I said. "I know exactly where they camp."

CHAPTER 12

LOW LIFE IN HIGH PLACES

We soon got our chance. On Monday we watched from a distance as Carl and Ralph hopped the Island Bus, heading north. "They're wearing zip-up jackets. Not a button in sight. Gone to see Carl's grandmother, maybe," I said, closing my spyglass.

"The coast is clear then," Rain said. "Let's upend their camp."

Upend it, we did. Bedrolls, binoculars, duffel bags full of drab clothes. No brass buttons. "Hey! Here's the note we sent when we first saw them camping on the beach," Neb said.

Rain recited: *"Attention Ringers, You're in our territory. Get lost. Love, the Great Unknowns. PS: We are watching you."*

"Only . . . holy moly, how could we make a mistake like *that?*" he gasped, staring at the paper. He handed me the note. At the top, in bold handwriting. A name.

MY NAME! In *my* handwriting!

I rubbed my finger over the dark gray letters. They smeared.

Neb leaned close and sniffed. "Smells like wood smoke."

"Hate to interrupt your snooping, kids," Carl said, strolling into camp, "but I forgot my binoculars." He looked around the camp. "Find anything interesting?"

"Just that note," Rain said as a blush walked up my neck.

He laughed. "I picked up the ashes trick from a coworker on Richmond's docks. He loved Sherlock Holmes, maybe that's where he learned it. Can't say." He strolled to the cold campfire, pinched up some ashes, and scattered them across the bottom of the page. A math problem materialized as the ashes filled the imprints.

"This is my math homework from weeks ago," I said.

"Actually, you did your homework on the page *over* this one. Your pencil left an impression and my ashes filled it in." He grabbed his binoculars. "Feel free to borrow the trick. Tell me, what do you know about the postmistress?"

"She plans to marry Grand," Rain said.

"Ouch. Sympathies, Stick." *Maybe I like Carl seventy-five percent.* "Never mind, then," he said as the bus blew its horn. "Ralph and I are going bird-watching, up on Pea Island. Canada geese, ducks. Maybe even a swan."

As Carl trotted off, gulls wheeled over us. "*Laughing* gulls. I hate them," Neb said.

"Try not to take nature personally, Neb," Rain said, hopping up and brushing the sand from her hands. "I say we join up with Carl Miller. He's smart, and he's a good snoop. He doesn't get mad easy or he'd be mad with us. He has a good heart or Schooner wouldn't like him. And there's not a brass button anywhere in this camp. I say we put him on our ally list."

"What about Ralph?" Neb asked.

Rain shrugged. "Ralph's a different bird."

Thursday after school, we caught two breaks. First, a post-card from Papa: *The war held us up but we're starting home. Love you, Genius. Guess who.*

Second break: The Artists gave Miss Agnes the Big Slip.

"Dirk's painting a portrait of the lighthouse," Rain announced, staring out our window.

Neb looked up from his practice knots. "*Everybody* paints the lighthouse. Babylon and me posed a thousand times. We're famous, except for our names and faces."

I grabbed the spyglass as a thunderhead's blue-gray shadow raced across the ocean and down the beach. I zeroed in as Julia strolled up to Miss Jonah and held out her hand. Miss Jonah reached out, her wrist crooked pretty just like Julia's. "Since when does your mama shake hands?"

Rain shrugged. "I don't know. Women don't shake hands on the island."

"Well, she just shook hands with Julia, and I want to know why."

We caught Julia as she strolled back, sidestepping splotches of black oil, and swishing a wide-brimmed hat. "Rain," she said, smiling. "Aggie said your mother lives in a magical house, and she's right. It's charming." Julia looked like a portrait—hair up, skirt blowing, a dangly silver bracelet on her arm. "Your mother is as beautiful as you are. Where does she come from?"

"The sea."

"Shipwrecked, as Aggie said," Julia mused, taking Rain's hand.

"Shipwrecks happen," Neb said, wedging into the conversation. He shouldered me aside, to walk by Julia. "My great-grandpa washed ashore like a good-looking chunk of driftwood. Naturally Great-Grandma took him in."

She laughed. "Rain, your mother looks familiar. Is your father . . ."

The question was bogus as a tin nickel. If Miss Agnes told her Miss Jonah lived in a *magical* house by the sea—and I doubt that word ever passed Miss Agnes's acid lips—she also told her Rain's father remains unknown. "You ask too many questions," I said.

"Odd thing for a scientist to say. Honestly, Jonah's just so . . . striking. And I'm so . . ."

"Nosy," I said. "We saw you shake hands. Women don't shake hands on the island."

"*You* shook hands with me," she said.

"We're unique. We read a lot."

"Well, women shake hands in my world, and you're right: I *am* nosy," she admitted. "I enjoy all kinds of investigations. Something we may have in common, Stick. And since you're curious, Jonah and I shook hands just to say hello."

Shaking hands must be another First Life skill, then—like

embroidery and milking a goat—something Miss Jonah's hands remember.

Julia looked at Rain. "I wish I knew more about your mother. Which ship . . ."

"This is all I have," Rain said, tugging the necklace from her blouse and showing her ring. "My father gave it to Mama Jonah for me. Do you know him? Or Mama Jonah?"

Julia examined the heavy ring and its engraving. "A man's ring. *M*," she said.

"Merlin?" Neb guessed. "Mickey?"

"I'm sorry, Rain. I don't know, but I'll think about it."

I changed the subject. "Why do you spend all your evenings at Miss Agnes's house?"

"Because she invites us," Julia said, and I felt suddenly small. Miss Agnes, who has the social skills of a barracuda, had outdone us in hospitality. "Your lighthouse is magnificent," she said, and Neb puffed up like he'd built it himself.

"It's our headquarters," he told her. "The tallest brick lighthouse in the United States—1.25 million bricks, 257 steps. We're upstairs. In the penthouse." *Penthouse*, a term from *Dime Novel #8: Low Life in High Places.*

"But how do you fit around its giant light?"

"I'm surprised Miss Agnes didn't tell you," I said. "The ocean undercut the lighthouse years ago, and the Feds abandoned it. The old light's gone. They use an electric light in a rinky-dink tower by the woods. The rinky-dink guides ships at night and the lighthouse's spiraled pattern guides them by day."

"Then the ocean danced away, leaving the lighthouse for us," Rain said.

"It's nice inside," Neb added. "My Boy Scout knots, Stick's test tubes, Rain's art."

Julia gave him a smile that would toast a biscuit. "Really? May I come in?"

My partners looked at me, their eyes voting yes. I hesitated. Invite a probable spy into HQ? I considered Life Rule #32: *Interrogate when it seems natural.* "We've been meaning to invite you over," I said, and led the way to our door.

Julia loved HQ. The posters, our dime novels, my science gear. "I hope to remove oil from our sea water," I explained. "I'm in my early stages of theoretical exploration."

"That means she's thinking about it," Neb said as she strolled to Rain's art.

Rain rose to stand by her work, hands clasped behind her back, face still. Julia studied the colors shrieking across the page, the people walking with bodies front-ways and faces sideways. Jesus—the only one with His head on right—floated over all Rain's worlds, calming seas and beaming as cats danced, tails swishing. Sometimes He walked on water, olive-skinned, unafraid of the storm. Sometimes He lifted broken ships and carried them to shore on His shoulders. Even in storms, the sun always found Him.

"These are beautiful," Julia said, her voice soft. "So strong.

Such a unique voice. What happened here?" she asked, running her finger across the tear on Rain's *Cats in Jubilation*.

"Notto," Rain said, and Julia turned to her, eyebrows raised.

Neb stepped in. "Other people call him Otto, but his mother calls him Mark. Bet you can't guess my entire name."

"Oh, *Otto*," Julia said. "That angry little boy destroyed this beautiful art?"

"We taped it back together," Neb said. "Miss Pope owns Scotch tape, a new invention. She lets a select few use it," he said, and she smiled.

"You're very talented, Rain. Did you teach yourself?" Rain nodded. "Amazing." She looked at Rain the way a fisherman looks at the sea. Like it might be filled with a million fishes and all the answers to every question you never asked. "I'd love to paint with you, Rain."

"Yes, thank you. Tomorrow after school," she said.

Julia laughed. "Wonderful. All of you come. My place." She inspected the beach one last time. "Do you ever see the Ringers from up here?"

"Not likely," I said before Neb could say yes. "Why?"

"Just nosy. See you tomorrow, my dear Dimes," she said, and headed for the stairs.

"Her dear Dimes," Neb said, peering dreamily out our window as she walked away. "I don't think anybody ever called us that. My dear Dimes."

I punched his arm. "She's a possible spy, Neb. Life Rule #2: *Never give your heart to a suspect.*"

"Right," he said, watching Julia stroll down the beach. "That was close."

A couple hours later, the wind shifted. Thunderheads rolled ashore like a tantrum: *March 8. 58 degrees F, wind from the NE at 25 mph. Barometric pressure rising.*

"Art lessons," I said. "Excellent cover. We can search the shack."

"No thank you," Rain said. "Art means more than spies."

As the storm lashed our windows, Neb hammered in a new hole in his belt.

"Even with you two sharing your biscuits with me, I'm losing weight. If I get any skinnier, I'll turn wrong-side-out," he said. "Beats me how Otto gets my dinner every day."

"Stick and I have a surprise," Rain said, corralling her crayons. "A Top Secret Weapon from Stick's Curious Plant Collection," she continued, selecting a jar of small, withered fruits. "A shocking addition to a ham biscuit."

Rain's a genius!

Neb leaned over the fruits, sniffing for clues. "Prunes? Baby figs?"

"Persimmons," I said. "We picked them green—back before the end of the world." Frost-kissed persimmons are sweet. Green, they'd make the devil squeal.

"Do they dry up bitter too?" he asked. I looked away and he gasped. "You haven't tested them! What kind of scientist are you?"

"The kind that doesn't experiment on herself," I replied as he popped a persimmon in his mouth. He chomped down once, twice . . . and rocked back like a storm trooper had kicked him in the chest. He puckered his face and pounded his feet on the floor.

I went soothing, like Mama when I throw up. "Green persimmons are full of tannic acid," I murmured. "That odd feeling in your mouth is your tongue slime clotting. Volume T."

Neb spit the persimmon across the room. "I'll take three. What do you want for them?"

"A baby cat from under your smokehouse," Rain said, before I could say *Nothing*.

"Soon as he's big enough," he said. "I'll let you know before I unleash this weapon on Otto. I want perfect timing. Revenge can blow up in your face faster than cartoon dynamite."

Already the sky had cleared. Our sky mostly cries like Faye: loud and done.

"I gotta go," he said. "Civilian defense meeting tonight. Boys only."

"The meeting Miss Agnes mentioned the night we *didn't* make the radio news?" I said. *"Boys only? We'll see about that,"* I said, and the three of us headed for the door.

CHAPTER 13

STORM'S RESTLESS HEART

Rain and me bolted into the kitchen as Mama poured a bowl of oysters into a pot simmering on the stove. Faye glanced up. "Good grief, Stick. Your *hair*," she said.

"Seventy percent humidity," I reported. "Nature styles me, as in *Dime Novel #84: Storm's Restless Heart*."

Grand slammed the door. "Agnes drives me mad," he said, stalking in. "Going here, flitting there. She acts like those Artists mean more to her than I do."

Faye stopped dealing our plates around. "You're jealous," she said. "Unappealing. Rain? Stick? Help me with supper. I'm in a hurry."

I darted to the silverware drawer. "We are too. We got a civilian defense meeting."

She looked at me like I'd dropped in from Mars. Which I'd love to do one day. "Sorry kiddo. I'll be too busy to babysit you two. Stay here, and cut paper dolls out of the Sears and Roebuck catalog. Try to develop a feel for fashion."

Rain crossed her eyes at me slow as two ships passing at sea.

"They say the meeting's for men and boys, but my security team's going," Faye said, taking the cornbread from the oven. "Nothing personal, Grand, but we can't leave our safety to little boys and doddering old men."

Grand snorted. "Why would I take that personal?"

Fact: Grand may be old, but normally he has more bounce-back than a new bedspring.

Mama took the lid off her pot, and steam wrapped the room in aromas old as time: oysters, potatoes, onions, bacon. Faye cut the bread. I grabbed the butter from the icebox and Rain ran for the pepper.

Rain and me always pull our own weight.

As we dried the supper plates, Rain glanced out our window. "Third-grader alert." Roy Powell's a string bean, but he's good with a boat. He beached his skiff and shot across the yard, scattering my chickens. He banged on the door.

"Miss Ada? Mama says the baby's coming!"

Mama grabbed her satchel. "Stick, listen to Faye. She's in charge."

"Wouldn't it be better to leave the *smart* one in charge?" I asked.

Mama gave me The Look—the flat-lipped stare that smothers all life from a room. "Yes ma'am," I muttered, and she strolled out the door calm as the inside of an oyster shell. Mama says calm's the first step to handling any emergency. She talks calm as she walks, which is one reason people listen to her.

"Wasn't Roy loitering by the dinner pails yesterday?" Rain asked.

I ran to the door. "Hey Roy," I shouted. "How much to rob somebody's dinner pail?"

"Can't say," he said, backpedaling across the yard. "Ask Hudson Aikens." *Little Hudson Aikens? The angel-faced first-grader?* Mama hopped in the skiff and shoved off.

"No," Faye said before we could ask to go. "You're not going."

Some people are not good with power. Hitler, Faye, and Mussolini come to mind. But the ocean's a good teacher: Sometimes you roll out before you roll in. "Let's go to my room, Rain," I said. "We got homework."

Minutes later, we stood at my bedroom window watching Faye and Grand stroll over to Old Miss Evans's house. Miss Evans shifted her porch chair and eagle-eyed in on our house. "Faye's posted a guard on us," I said. "We'll go out the *other* window and sneak along the edge of the sound. Not yet, not yet . . . *Now,*" I said as Faye turned toward the church. We charged across the room to my Emergency Exit Oak.

Rain scrambled onto the sill and sprang like a flying squirrel. I jumped behind her, loving the scratch of the bark as I slid down and dropped beside her. I spanked the tingle off my hands. "Keep low, and try not to rile the yard dogs."

Across from the church, we hid behind a shrub. "We'll wait until the meeting's nearly started, so Faye can't send us out."

Old men and boys scuffed up the walk, past ballast stones painted white. Neb eased by with Mr. Mac, who looked thin and brittle as a bundle of twigs. "I don't care what Faye says,"

Mr. Mac said as Carl peeped around the church corner. "Your sisters can't come."

We eased over to Carl. "Hey," I said. "I thought you'd gone bird-watching."

"Ralph got bored." He frowned. "What are you doing here? Isn't it just for guys?"

"We're going in," I said. "That's the kind of girls we are."

"The kind I admire," he said, smiling. *Maybe I like him eighty percent.*

We turned as Ruth and Naomi headed up the walk. Ruth walked like she meant business—chin forward, arms swinging. Naomi slumped. "But Ruth," Naomi said, her voice shaking, "Daddy said *not* to come."

"Faye's right. We have to think for ourselves," Ruth said. "The men will leave and then what? You can do this, Naomi." The sisters walked up to the church door. Naomi made a quick U-turn and sped back down the steps. Ruth followed her onto the street, still coaxing.

"See you later, toots," Rain told Carl, and we headed for the door.

We scooted into the dim sanctuary and darted to the side, behind a deacon's bench. The place was thick with men's voices. Old Man Tyson, who has the face of a garter snake, had practically fallen out of his pew, trying to stare Faye down.

Faye and Grand sat in our family pew, on the right. Neb

and his dad sat on the left. Otto sat on the front row like a preacher's pet, whispering with Scrape and Jersey.

Rain and me flattened against the wall as the sisters stepped inside. "Don't be scared," Ruth told Naomi, firm. "Look straight ahead, and walk like you have a right." They strolled down the center aisle, pale but determined, and perched beside Faye.

"Here's two more that don't know their place," Old Man Tyson said, very loud. "*Some* girls don't know how to be girls."

"We know perfectly well, thank you," Faye said.

"You don't or you wouldn't be here," he snapped. "Surprised you didn't drag that Jonah in here with you. She's worn out her welcome, if you ask me. Her and her little creamy too," he said, and Rain and I both gasped. I'd never heard Mr. Tyson talk like that before.

How can a soft, sweet word like *creamy* bite like barbed wire?

"Don't you call her that," I murmured, afraid of giving us away.

He stayed focused on Faye, who stood arms akimbo. (See Volume A.) "Mr. Tyson," she said, "nobody asked you about Miss Jonah *or* Rain, and I don't think God would appreciate that kind of talk, especially in His house."

"True!" Rain said, loud. Faye turned toward us, horrified. We ducked.

Grand glared at his old friend. "Own the island now, do you? Get to say who lives on it?" A few men laughed. "Jonah's true as anybody I ever met, and Rain's a glory of a girl. They're my family, both of them. I'll thank you to leave them be."

Rain stayed quiet, but I felt the pain rolling off of her. Suddenly I hated Mr. Tyson from the white of his hair to the scuff of his boots.

Fact: It pays to know who people are, even if you hate who they turn out to be.

Reed stepped inside. "Hey," he said, his voice low. "What are *you two* doing here?"

"Learning more than expected," I said. "When are you asking Faye to marry you?"

"Soon."

A handsome man in a smart navy uniform stepped onto our little stage. The crowd rumbled itself still and Reed headed for his seat. "Thank you for coming," the man said. "I'm Captain Ed Davis, representing the Office of Civilian Defense tonight."

Davis stood maybe six feet tall, and slender. Short brown hair, olive complexion, dark eyes. His gaze settled on Faye. "I came to talk to the men this evening, especially those over forty-five. And boys under sixteen."

"Now," I whispered, and Rain and me darted down the side aisle to settle in by Neb.

"If you ladies and little girls would excuse us, we'll get down to business," Davis said, giving Faye a nod. The crowd muttered. Ruth and Naomi sat still as stone.

I stood, Rain bobbing up at my side. "Excuse me," I said.

"*No!*" Faye shout-whispered. "*You two! Sit down!*"

"Excuse us now *please!*" Rain said, stomping her foot, and the church went quiet.

"How do you do," I said, my voice ringing out like Mama taught me. "I'm Sarah Stickley Lawson. You may call me Stick. These are my friends Rain and Neb," I said. Neb rose to slump beside us. "Could you please tell me who was second in command of the Office of Civilian Defense until she moved on to better things?"

The captain frowned.

"First Lady Eleanor Roosevelt," I said. "I saw it in Grand's newspaper. If she can be in this, we don't see why we can't be."

"God invites *all* of us to church," Rain said, shooting a glance at Mr. Tyson. "Nobody outranks God and Eleanor Roosevelt."

Faye and the sisters rose. "They make a good point, Captain Davis," Faye said.

Captain Davis's face went the color of a steamed lobster.

A woman's voice rang out from the back of the church. "These girls are annoying but correct. They pull their own weight. Let them stay."

Miss Agnes!

"Dang," Neb whispered as Miss Agnes sailed down the aisle like a battleship of lace, her rooster hat gleaming.

Grand rose to meet her. "Agnes is right," he said. "These girls' lives are at risk too, and they're able. A man would be a fool to throw away half his resources."

Captain Davis looked around, sensing the currents. "Exactly what I should have said," he told us, his face finding a lesser shade of red. "Welcome, everyone. Let's get started."

An hour later, my heart had turned to lead. *Faye's right*, I thought. *We're on our own.*

"The military's building bases on the mainland," Davis said. "Camp Lejeune. Fort Bragg. Camp Davis. Etcetera."

I raised my hand. "*Etcetera* is Latin for *and the rest*."

"Stop it, Stick," Grand said. "Captain Davis, those bases are miles away. Put a base here. The Nazis come so close, they can steal the eggs out from under our hens."

Davis's smile sagged. "Expect mines in the *major* inlets, and nets across major rivers to keep the U-boats from coming in. But not here. In an emergency, Norfolk will respond."

"But that's hours away!" Faye said. "Will the Germans land here?"

Davis looked around, sizing us up. Or looking for a quick escape. "I hope not."

"Will a U-boat sink a fishing boat?" Carl asked from the back pew. I turned, smiling. My smile died. Dirk stood cloaked in the shadows, his catfish gaze steady.

What's he doing here?

"I doubt they'd waste a torpedo on a fishing boat," Davis said. "But most U-boats have an 88-millimeter gun on deck. U-boats do surface, usually at night, and that gun's sixteen-pound shells can do a lot of damage. I'd fish the sound. It's too shallow for U-boats. Men twenty-one and older can expect a letter from the draft board. Men eighteen and over can enlist," he said, glancing at Reed.

"You gentlemen over forty-five and you boys under sixteen, welcome to Civilian Defense. These airplane spotter's cards will get you started," he said, ripping open a carton. "They're like regular playing cards, only each shows an airplane's profile. The cards marked *Allies* are friends. The ones marked *Axis* are trying to kill you. When you see an *Axis* plane fly over—that's Germany, Japan, and Italy—phone it in."

Grand snorted. "How? You have telephones in that box?"

"The store near the ferry landing has a telephone," Davis said as Otto jumped up and grabbed three packs. "So do coast guard stations, including the one at Chicoma . . . Chicoma . . ." He pulled a slip of paper from his pocket and glanced at it.

"Chicamacomico," I said. "It's an Algonquin word. So are *raccoon* and *persimmon*." The study of languages (Volume L) fascinates me. Oddly, among islanders, I am alone in this.

"What about us?" Faye asked. "What can the women do?"

"Women eighteen and over can enlist as nurses or secretaries."

"I'm sixteen," she said. *"I'll* watch for airplanes."

"Thank you, Miss . . ." he said, handing the last pack of cards to Neb.

"Hollywood Faye Lawson."

"Stick's sister," he guessed. "You can plant a victory garden, and can your vegetables to free up other food for the military.

You can make blackout curtains. Nylon will be rationed. You could do without nylons . . ." he said, his voice trailing away.

"Uh-oh," Rain whispered.

Faye hissed like Mama's pressure cooker. "*Nylons?* We *always* plant a garden, and we *always* can what we don't eat or give away. We've *made* curtains. You would too, if the Germans could practically look through your windows. We want to *help*. Not pickle cucumbers. Who's going to protect this island when our men enlist and the Nazis come? *You?*"

"I'll do my best," Davis said. "Other questions?"

I raised my hand. "Rain and me didn't get spotter cards."

"We're out, girls," he said firmly. "Thank you for coming. Meeting adjourned."

"*Poof,*" Rain whispered. "Strange," she added, watching Mr. Mac scoot Neb to the door. "Mr. Mac usually likes to stay and talk. Maybe he feels puny today."

We squirmed through the crowd to Faye, who shot Captain Davis a glare that would sink a battleship. "What a twerp. I hope our paths never cross again," she said.

Only, our paths did cross.

They crossed hard enough to fill three graves deep in the heart of Buxton Woods and to send lives spinning to the stars.

The next morning, Saturday, March 14, Mama packed a dinner pail as Rain and me finished the dishes. "Rain, tell me about your art classes," Mama invited. Unlike adults who ask and ignore your answer, Mama really listens.

"They're good, Miss Ada, now that it's just Julia and me."

My ego sagged like last summer's hammock. Neb and me had gone to art with Rain twice. Watching Rain and Julia was like listening to musicians hum. Same flow, different song. Rain paints wild, with her heart wide-open. Julia paints careful and neat. They painted together like sky paints sea, different and alike at the same time.

"Maybe this blue instead," Julia had told her the first day we painted together.

Rain tried it. "Very nice," she murmured, and Julia had smiled.

Now I smiled at Mama. "Neb and I possess negative artistic talent," I said. "Our results can be summed up in two words: *dirty paper*. Rain's taking lessons on her own."

Mama looked at her, very thoughtful. "And what do you think of Julia?"

"She's a great artist but so sad. Hitler swallowed her people."

Mama froze, a cheese biscuit halfway to her dinner pail. *"Swallowed her people? What do you mean?"*

"One day when Julia went for bread, Hitler's soldiers took her family. It happened on a Thursday with a hint of snow. She came home with a pretty braided bread, and they were gone."

Mama went pale. "Gone where?"

Rain looked away. "She doesn't like to say. It makes her cry."

Mama took a deep breath and stared outside at my young

roosters, who have started fighting to rule the flock. "I'm taking the bus up to the Pea Island Coast Guard Station today," she finally said. "I'll be back by dark."

Fact: The Pea Island Station is the nation's first Black station. Its Black captain and crew would hold every courage award there is, if the Feds gave awards to Black men. My family and Rain's say it isn't right, not recognizing them. Others disagree. "Stick," Mama said, grabbing her medicine bag, "work with Faye today. You owe her eight more hours."

"Eight hours? But I've learned my lesson," I cried. "I'll never eavesdrop again."

The lie hung on the air like a sour-breathed fog.

"Eight hours, any way she dices them," Mama said. "Rain, Mr. Oden dropped off a quart of string beans to thank me for bandaging his hand. Take them home with you, please, and invite your mother to come see me when she has time. I miss her."

Unlike Neb, Rain hears the unspoken. "Thank you," she said, heading for the door.

"Yoo-hoo!" Miss Agnes called. She stepped into the room and folded her face into a somewhat pleasant expression. Rain skidded to a halt, holding the beans before her like a shield.

"Morning, Agnes," Mama said. "Stick, go find Grand for Miss Agnes."

"No need," Miss Agnes said. She stood a moment, awkward in polka dots.

"Do you have a postcard from Papa?" I asked, my heart beating faster.

"Don't be silly. The post office doesn't deliver mail."

Her hand darted into her skirt pocket. "Here," she said. "I thought these playing cards might do until I locate spotter cards. Keep them *very* dry or they'll curl up on you."

Miss Agnes, being nice?

"You two are braver than I was at your age, I expect," she said. She frowned. "It's a gift."

"Thank you," we said, and she hurried away.

Mama blinked rapid-fire. "She's never been quite so . . . pleasant."

"It's the war," I said, putting the cards by the window. "Grand's right. War changes everything."

Maybe not *everything*. Moments later, I looked into Faye's violet eyes. "Clean my side of the room, polish my shoes, and iron my blouse," she said. "Get some giddy-up in your get-along, Stick."

"Wouldn't you rather have a leisurely picnic? I could make a basket."

She handed me a mass of blue wrinkles. "Starch in the collar, don't scorch it. We meet the security club at two o'clock. Target practice. Move it."

"Target practice? But I'm a pacifist, more or less," I told her. "I don't like guns. I may even be a conscientious objector. Volume C. I must decline your invitation."

"We are in a *war*, Stick. What part of that hasn't sunk in? Get moving."

A couple hours later, with Faye's side of the room clean enough for surgery, I headed down to iron her blouse smooth. "Done," I shouted, and hit the kitchen, stomach rumbling.

She handed me two plates. "We'll have leftovers from the icebox. I'll take a cup of oyster stew, with cabbage and a smidge of fish. Make sure you pick the bones out of my fish. Hurry. You haven't started my shoes and I need you to search the trash pile for targets. Be careful. I don't have time for you to get snake-bit."

By two o'clock, I hated Faye at a cellular level.

An hour later, I followed Faye, Neb's sisters, and two Kinnakeet girls to the edge of Buxton Woods, Faye tripping along in her polished shoes, me dragging a burlap sack of cans. "Set the targets up over there, Stick," she said, nodding to a log. "And toe a line in the dirt for us. I don't want to mess up my shoes."

Faye and Neb's sisters stepped up to the line with their fathers' shotguns. I hurried to a safe spot behind them and stuffed my fingers in my ears. Faye's a crackerjack shot, thanks to Papa. Ruth and Naomi shot wild, then settled in. The girls from Kinnakeet, who shot second, were a hazard.

An hour later, I handed Faye the last shotgun shells in her bag. "These shells cost a fortune. You should take up a collection," I whispered.

She glanced at the sisters. *Right. Neb's sisters can't pay.*

I gasped. "You're shooting up your Hollywood money!"

"Mind your own beeswax," she muttered, passing the

shells around. She smiled at the Kinnakeet twins. "You're shooting low, ladies. Steady your guns against that tree limb."

I set up the targets and scampered to safety. *Blam blam.* The targets sat untouched.

"But I aimed dead at it," Margaret Bond said, going red. *She's giving up,* I thought.

"Nice try," I said. "You're six inches low every time. Lead sinks as it flies. Gravity—"

"Thanks, Stick," Faye said, passing out the last two shells. "One more time, girls. Aim high." *Blam!* The cans backflipped off the rails. We cheered. "Great job," Faye said. "Good call, Stick. We'll meet next week. Stick, don't forget to pick up the cans."

That night I settled into bed, exhausted from cooking supper and rolling Faye's hair. As I poured water into the Stick-O-Matic, Faye lifted her eye mask. "So, what do you think?"

What do I think?

"I think a million things a day," I said. "What do I think as a reformed eavesdropper or your sister or a scientist or—"

"As a genius," she said. "What do you think about the security club?"

I took longer than needed to light the candle. Faye never asks my opinion. It felt like stepping into a new world without knowing if I could step back. "*You* shoot great, and you're a natural leader. People listen to you. The sisters are fine *now* but under stress—say if Nazis land . . . Maybe you could do breathing exercises with them, to help them learn to settle in."

Faye propped up on her elbow. "Really, Stick. They already know how to breathe."

I went remedial. "It's called meditation. Volume M. The Kinnakeet girls are willing. I'd say you need a strategy." Her puzzled silence washed over me. "So, if *lots* of Germans roar ashore, you're outnumbered and you need one plan." She nodded in the Stick-O-Matic's soft candlelight, setting faint shadows dancing on the wall behind her. "Maybe you hide, shoot, and run. If only a few Nazis come ashore, you want a different plan. It's always better to have a strategy you don't need than to need a strategy you don't have."

"Right. Thanks," she said, and yawned. "You still need to do something about that hair."

Some things are eternal. The spin of the universe, the ocean's dance, Faye's obsession with the orange protein sprouting from my scalp. "I'm going to sleep before the light dies," I said, and closed my eyes, breathing steady to keep the pool of fear trapped beneath my bed.

CHAPTER 14

GUILT FORGETS MY NAME

Mid-March 1942

Fact: By mid-March, war was as everyday as scrambled eggs.

Between March 11 and March 19, the waters near our island became a killing field. The *Caribsea*, the *Ario*, the *E.M. Clark*, the *Kassandra Louloudis*, and an Australian tanker went down one by one. On March 19, U-boats sent three ships to watery graves: the *Liberator*, the *W.E. Hutton*, and the *Papoose*. We knew the sounds by heart: the *boom* of the torpedo strike, the *blam* of the ship's boiler exploding.

Then came Thursday, March 26—a day of cold revenge, and hot chaos.

"The sisters like Faye's club," Neb said as we walked to school that morning. "They got attitude all of a sudden. I'm a little bit scared of them."

"The fish have attitude too," Rain said. "The water worlds have split into the worlds of fish and of U-boats." She wiggled her head, and I knew she was shaking out a drawing.

Neb kicked a stick down the road. "Don't talk abnormal," he said as Schooner waddled up and fell in with us. "Think regular. Example: There's Reed's boat, out on the sound."

Reed fishes when the moon and tides agree. He poles into the sound, his boat full of woven nets. Setting them's easy. Hauling them in full of fish isn't, but it pays when he trucks his iced catch to the end of the island to sell.

On March 26, gas-powered and man-powered boats criss-crossed the water with Reed's, like any other spring day. We waved to Eli Phillips, who'd quit school to help his daddy fish. Eli always rang the school bell.

Miss Pope would miss him before the end of the day.

"This morning, I unleash our secret weapon," Neb said, swinging his dinner pail. His dark eyes danced. *"Revenge of the green persimmons. Notto, beware."*

We greeted Miss Pope like angels, and set our dinner pails in the hall. "Has anyone seen my glass paperweight?" she asked. "I'm offering a reward."

Otto smirked. "A reward? How much?"

"Return it and find out," she said.

She knows he took it, I thought.

At noon Neb opened his dinner pail, and fake-yelped when he found it empty. Otto and his goons laughed, and carried their pails to the oak. Otto opened *his* dinner pail. "Ham biscuits!" he crowed. "Just like Neb's mother makes!" He took a huge bite, chewed twice, and swallowed.

Neb gasped. "I didn't know he'd actually *swallow* it."

Otto clutched at his throat as Rain and me divided our collard-and-cornbread sandwiches into thirds and shared with Neb. A crowd gathered around Otto. Scrape frowned at Neb.

"Scrape knows I did it," Neb whispered. "Run!"

"He knows nothing," Rain said. "Look innocent and eat."

Ten minutes later, Otto staggered to Miss Pope's desk, his eyes watering. He plunked his pail down with most of Neb's biscuits inside. She looked up from her mullet stew and dabbed her fingertips with a napkin. "Yes?"

"Otto may be dying," I said, trailing Otto in. As Mama's daughter, I carry a certain weight in medical matters. "Stick out your tongue, Otto." Incredibly, he did. "A white, gunky *lingua*. Sad."

Otto's beautiful blue eyes filled with tears. "What's a lin . . ."

"*Lingua*. Latin for *tongue*," Miss Pope said. "Stop it, Stick."

"Yes, ma'am," I said, checking to see if I felt shame. Nothing. Just as in *Dime Novel #79: Guilt Forgets My Name*. "It could be worse, I guess. It could be rabies, which is fatal in ninety-nine percent of all cases. Children Otto's age are at risk."

The class gasped. "Poor Notto," Rain said as Otto doubled over, clutching his belly.

Miss Pope plucked a bit of dried persimmon from Otto's pail. "What's this?"

"Don't know," Otto gasped, rocking back and forth.

"Of course you know. It's inside *your* ham biscuit."

I stepped up. "Mama says half of curing is knowing the illness. If we knew what that was, we might be able to save him."

"Ask Neb," Otto moaned. "It's *his* biscuit."

Miss Pope slid her glasses down her nose. "Neb? Why is your biscuit in Otto's pail?"

"Good question," Neb said. "My meal has disappeared every day since Thanksgiving. I'm not sure *how* it ended up in Otto's dinner pail."

"I have a theory," I said, and walked to the door. "The Dimes call first-grader Hudson Aikens," I boomed—a line from *Dime Novel #31: Witness for the Prosecution.*

Hudson crept in. "Tell me," I said, "did anyone ask you to rob Neb's dinner pail?"

He pointed. "Otto said, put Neb's food in Otto's pail at little-kid recess. Forever."

Of course. Little kids' recess—before ours, when our classroom door's always closed. "Otto said he'd keep Jersey from picking on me if I did. I'm sorry, Neb."

"They won't bother you again. Run along," Miss Pope said, and he shot out of the room. "Otto, explain. Your mother sends you to school with a full dinner pail every day."

"I feed it to Schooner," Hudson shouted from the hallway. Miss Pope tossed her napkin to her desk and glared at Otto. Finally, I thought, Otto's going to get what he deserves.

But Fate and a U-boat had other plans.

BOOM!

The schoolhouse lurched and tilted. Desks slid. Little kids howled like wolves. Miss Pope sprang to her feet. "Get in the hall! Crouch against the wall. Cover your heads!"

We flew into the hall. Otto clutched his belly. "I need the outhouse," he whimpered.

BLAM! Window glass flew through the air like a flock of broken birds.

Miss Pope moaned and pulled a glass dagger from her leg. "Be calm," she called, her voice thin as reeds. "Wait for my signal." Silence fell like a dare. Rain clutched her ring. "Father, Father, Father," she murmured, and whispered a nonsense lullaby. Neb tapped his fingers against the floor. Morse code. *SOS, SOS.*

"Wait," Miss Pope said, opening the door. The world held its breath. The birdsong died. The trees looked like they wanted to run.

We waited. My thighs burned. Someone behind me threw up—probably Otto. Blood trickled down Miss Pope's plump calf, into her fuddy-duddy shoe.

She turned to us, her round face pale. "Now! Run!" We thundered for the door.

Miss Pope flew to the school bell and grabbed the rope. I looked over my shoulder once as I ran. If I live to be a million, I'll still see Miss Pope, eyes squinched, glasses dangling from one ear. She clung to the rope, riding up to hang an instant, and coming down to bend her knees and ride up again, the brass bell near turning flips.

On the sound, boats had turned for shore. Women snatched their children off the street.

Mama met us near the store, pale and frantic. "Inside! Now!"

"Grand!" I shouted as Schooner skidded through the door behind us.

"Right here, Junebug," he said, scooping me into a hug. He

hasn't called me Junebug since I was knee-high. "We're fine," he said, his voice the twin of Papa's. "Ship ran too close to shore, I expect, and those buzzards took her anyway. Settle down."

Mama stood at the window, her arm around Rain's shoulders as Miss Agnes and Julia ran toward the shore. "Where are *they* going?" Mama murmured. *Where, indeed?*

Grand slid open the candy door, and miraculously pulled out three pieces of red taffy.

"I've been saving these for a day like today," he said, and looked at Mama, his blue eyes sharp beneath his white brows. "I'll walk Neb home a little later and invite Jonah for supper, if that suits you, Ada."

Mama's face had gone white as marble. She nodded and rested her forehead on the windowpane. I opened my taffy. Its soft sweetness rushed through me. *Chew slow,* I thought, savoring the sweet river of red.

This may be the last red taffy in the whole wide world.

That afternoon, Faye dumped her books on the kitchen table.

"Thank goodness," Mama said, hugging her. "The Germans torpedoed a ship too close to shore. We're fine. Thank heavens you're home."

"They blew up the school with us in it," Rain added.

"I got here soon as I could. I'm setting the dining room table tonight," Faye said, her hands fluttering through her schoolbook like startled birds. "Like they do it at the White House.

We'll need a salad—a scrap of cabbage will work. Bread. Fish, meat, vegetables. And dessert—last night's fig cake. Iced tea and water. I said I'd do this and I will. It *matters*."

She didn't say the rest, but we felt it: *This may be my last chance.*

"Stick, you and Rain help me in the kitchen," Mama said. "Faye, set a place for Jonah."

An hour later, Faye stood studying her schoolbook. She'd gone calm as the cabinets she'd emptied.

"What are all these forks and plates for?" I asked.

Grand and Miss Jonah walked in as Faye pointed to the fork at the far left of the plate. "Fish fork, dinner fork, salad fork. Plate and soup bowl. Dinner knife, fish knife, soup spoon. Bread plate. We get a couple of glasses . . ."

I picked up a renegade fork. "And this?"

"Oh fuzz, I don't know," Faye muttered. Miss Jonah took the fork, placed it horizontal over the plate, and headed for the kitchen. Faye's eyes went big. "She's right, it's the dessert fork. How would she know *that?*"

"A First Life skill," I said. "Something her hands remember."

Grand broke the news the next day: "The community doesn't have the heart or money to fix that building. School's out. Miss Pope is packing," he said. "Ada, nobody would fault you for leaving too."

For a moment, Mama looked alone, and shorter than I

remembered. She squared her shoulders. "We'll stay. For now." She went back to her work like nothing had changed.

But something had changed. Over the next days I caught her looking more and more to the horizon. She's as lonesome for those red sails as I am, I thought. Red sails and open arms.

Papa, please come home.

CHAPTER 15

THE WIDOW WEARS WHITE

March 30, 1942

With school out, our spy-catching hit overdrive.

Monday morning, we strolled into the PO. I smiled at Miss Agnes. "Good morning."

"Nothing from your papa, please go," she replied.

"Thanks," I said. "We need a quasi-professional courtesy. *Quasi*. Latin for *almost*. You have connections." I caught a flicker of a smile. *She's proud of her connections*, I thought. "We're trailing the Ringers. Carl Miller checks out. We seek background on Ralph. Last name unknown."

She looked up, her eyes sharp. "Ralph Perdu. *Perdu*. French for *lost*."

I gasped. *Miss Agnes and I share an interest in languages?*

I steadied myself. "We request personal background, rap sheet, whatever's available to a person of your high professional status."

"We have no status," Neb said, like she might have overlooked that.

She drummed her fingertips on the countertop. "What's in it for me?"

"Fish?" Rain offered, and Miss Agnes shook her head.

"Dance lessons?" Neb said. He closed his eyes. "Say no, say no, say no," he whispered.

"No," she replied. "I want a week without seeing you in here, unless I send word that a postcard from your papa has arrived. Where is he, anyway?"

"I figure him around Savannah. The war keeps waylaying him."

She nodded, quick as a hawk. "That's my offer. I'll inquire about Ralph Perdu in exchange for one week's peace. Take it or leave it."

"We'll take it," Rain said, and we closed the door behind us. "I'm going to Julia's for art. I'm *hoping* for no distractions," she said, and flew away like her Mary Janes wore wings.

"Did she call us distracting?" Neb asked, frowning. "Because I'm not seeing it."

I changed the subject. "How's Mr. Mac?" I asked. "You all left the civilian defense meeting so fast the other day, I didn't get a chance to speak to him."

He blinked away sudden tears. "He's just watching his time spin away. He doesn't even try to stay anymore. But come play cards at my house next Saturday. He'll be glad to see you."

Saturday night, we settled in for cards in Neb's fussy parlor. Sadly, we were not alone.

"This is a heck of a thing for a Saturday night and a good-time girl like me," Faye announced, putting a record on the

Victrola. "Reduced to *practicing* dance steps while Reed goes fishing. But cheer up, ladies. Once we learn this step, we'll try on the wigs I borrowed from the school's drama closet."

Neb shuffled his spotter cards. "I hate Nazis," he said. "Of course, they *did* blow up the school. I appreciate that. Still."

Neb's prickly when out of sorts. I took a stab at comfort. "Your mother would skin us alive if she knew we were playing poker in here," I whispered, and his scowl softened.

Hypothesis: Deep inside, Neb's an outlaw waiting to blossom.

Rain studied her cards and laid them face-down. "These are ugly."

True. My cards showed the black silhouettes of two German airplanes and an Italian one, plus two American airplanes. Not as pretty as diamonds and hearts, but not ugly enough to wreck Rain's mood. "What's wrong?"

"Julia's silver bracelet went missing." Her eyes filled with tears. "She told me at art. She didn't say I took it, but she almost did. She said she'd been given *certain information.*"

My temper went lava. "Otto. That bottom-feeder stole it and he's blaming you."

"The important thing is, she *believed* him," Rain said. "You two stopped in for water. You could have taken it. Otto brought a pie from his mother, and Scrape and Jersey came in too. *They* could have taken it. Julia could have suspected anybody. *She chose me.*"

Neb frowned. "Why would she do that?"

"Why do you think?"

"Oh," Neb said, his voice soft.

Fact: Some people think the pigment in your skin determines the strength of your character. Grand says they're ignorant. I do too. Neb laid his cards face-down on the table. "So that's how she is. I wouldn't marry her now, even if she begged me."

Rain pushed three seashells to the center of our table. "I bet three," she said as Miss Irma swept in, no-nonsense nice and fire-poker thin.

"Nebuchadnezzar," she said, wiping her hands on her apron, "*what* are you doing?"

"Learning aircraft with my spotter cards, Mother."

She scooped up his cards and dropped them like nettles. "To think they ask children . . ." Her voice trailed away. Miss Irma's high-strung as an acrobat's wire ever since the Japanese bombed Pearl Harbor on her birthday. December 7. Even Mama's tonic can't calm an insult like that, especially with Mr. Mac sicker and sicker, cranking her wire tighter and tighter.

"Keep the volume down. Your father's resting," she said, and marched into the kitchen.

"Kiddos, help us move the furniture," Faye said, glancing at the mirror. She could marry a mirror and be happy.

"You're not our boss," I said, but we helped push the furniture to the walls, and rolled up the scatter rugs. Faye stretched a paper pattern across the floor—tan with black footprints printed on it. "Get over here, Neb."

"I don't want to dance."

"Yes you do, you just don't know it. You can be a boy and we'll be girls."

"You don't have to name me a boy, I *am* a boy," Neb said.

"This old dance is the rage again. Hit it, Naomi."

Naomi dropped the needle on an old Cab Calloway song, "Jumpin' Jive." The music strutted across the room and we moved with it. A knock at the door stopped us cold.

"Everybody relax. Nazis don't knock," Ruth joked. She flung open the door and put on her smooth company voice. "Well, Captain Davis! What a surprise. Come in."

Captain Davis? From the civilian defense meeting?

He whisked off his cap and stepped inside. "I . . . I guess you're not the only one who's surprised," he said, gazing around the room. "Ladies. Neb." His gaze moved from the sofa, to the Victrola, to the old wedding portrait on the wall. "You *live* here," he said, sounding dazed.

"Of course we do," Ruth said. "What can we do for you?"

He looked at Neb. "Neb, is your father here?"

Neb stepped up. "He's resting. What's wrong? Have the Germans landed?"

"There you have it," Faye said. "Three practically grown women and the military guy's talking to a skinny twelve-year-old just because he's a boy."

"Oh," Davis said, his voice going cool. "Hi, Faye."

Miss Irma walked in, drying her hands. "*Captain Davis?*" she said, her voice sharp.

"We told her about you," Neb said. "We were just studying my cards. You can count on us. All *three* of us."

Captain Davis looked at Miss Irma, and then at Ruth and Naomi. "You live here," he said again like he was shell-shocked. "All of you."

Miss Irma's smile didn't touch her eyes. "Neb, get your father," she said, and he shot out of the room. "Girls, set the furniture to rights. Naomi, get Captain Davis something to drink." Naomi flew away before Captain Davis could say no.

"Let me help with the furniture, then," he said.

A little later, Neb's father eased in wearing his navy-blue lighthouse keeper's uniform. It hung on him like an old suit on a bent hanger. "Captain Davis," Mr. Mac said. "I'm Noah Mackenzie, but people call me Mac. Have a seat."

"Thank you, sir. I'm here to . . ." Captain Davis said, and his voice faded away. He looked from Ruth, who waited steady as moonlight, to Naomi, who fidgeted. He changed tack. "You have a beautiful home, Miss Irma."

"Thank you," she said, sitting and folding her hands on her lap. Mr. Mac lit his pipe. Mama says he's reckless, smoking with his breathing like it is. Neb hates it and Rain and me hate it too. Neb needs a father more than any boy we know.

"You're wondering why we're here," Mr. Mac said.

"Yes sir, I am. I thought this compound was shuttered. The

U.S. Lighthouse Service would be surprised to learn it has guests."

"Possession is nine-tenths of the law," Faye fired back—a line from a movie. I was pretty sure she didn't know what it meant, but I backed her up.

"This place would fall apart without Mr. Mac," I said. "You should thank him."

Davis unfolded a paper. "The thing is, sir, I have orders to make this my headquarters."

"This is our home," Ruth said, rising. "You people abandoned it."

"But it's not your *house*," he said, calm as a bowl of chowder. "Weren't you reassigned, sir?"

Mr. Mac exhaled a cloud of blue smoke. "This cough. Some know-nothing in a white coat gave me some X-rays and a bottle of pills, and cut me loose."

Davis turned his hat in his hands. "And they didn't restaff the place. Why would they? The light had been moved out. They didn't need a keeper of a lost light."

"Captain Davis," Faye said, "if you think you're throwing my best friends out—"

"I'm *trying* to think of a way we can all get what we need," he interrupted. "How many buildings are still standing, Mr. Mac? The keeper's house and lighthouse, obviously."

"The men's dormitory out back. A smokehouse, a shed," he said.

"And the only three-seater outhouse on the island," Neb added. He's outhouse proud.

Davis tapped his hat against his knee. "Mr. Mac, my orders are to set up here, and establish community ties. I hate to be blunt, but I'll be shipping bodies to Norfolk as they wash ashore, establishing radio communications, and handling POWs as we pick them up."

A flashfire of fear shot through me. "Prisoners of war? Here?"

Mr. Mac nodded like POWs were everyday. "How many of you are there?"

"Just me, for now."

"To do all that?" I said. I figured him the way Grand considers a barter. "As a rule," I said, "we hate outsiders. But we could like you if we wanted to. We got friends all over the island. In churches, at school, at the store."

"My father's lighthouse brought a lot of men home from the sea," Naomi added. "People don't forget a thing like that."

"We could put in a good word for you—if we wanted to," I said.

Davis grinned. "Message received. Mr. Mac, what's in that old dorm out back?"

"A few bunks, a couple desks. We've handled shipwrecks here forever. We use the dorm for survivors, and to sort washed-ashore items. The old smokehouse becomes our morgue. You're welcome to build on our system. The island's ready to help, I imagine."

Davis nodded. "Thanks. I could set up in the dorm. I'd planned to hire a cook. But if someone invited me to Sunday dinner from time to time—"

"You're invited every day," Ruth said, quick as a whip. "Monday's wash day all over the island. Your things would be no trouble."

The tension left his shoulders. "And I'd rather hand over my money to you folks than to strangers. That arrangement helps me and you. Until they send more men, anyway."

"You won't need more men. We've formed a security club," Faye said.

"Faye's Brigade," I said, giving it a name on the spot. "My sister's a natural leader. Even when she's backwards, people follow her. They'll outshoot any man you got. Including you."

Ruth nodded, very game. Naomi's mouth fell open.

"I welcome all the help I can get," he said, and my spirit soared like an osprey. He swatted it down like a mosquito: "I'll set up in the lighthouse tomorrow morning."

The lighthouse?

"Sadly, that's off-limits to you," I said. "You may have the dorm. The lighthouse is our headquarters."

Davis's face went neutral. "I need the lighthouse."

"I'm sorry, the answer is no."

He shifted gears. "You kids seem like the kind of people I'd like to have on my team."

Neb smiled at Captain Davis, his eyes glowing. *That's one vote for Davis,* I thought.

"I could make do with half the space upstairs," Davis added.

"Jesus says to share," Rain said. Two votes for Davis.

Faye jumped in. "Sharing office space would be an honor

for the Dime Novel Kids," she told me. "Nobody else on the island partners with the military."

Captain Davis's eyebrows flew up. "The *Dime Novel* Kids? I love dime novels. Not many people appreciate them."

A likely trick. "What's your favorite?"

"Dime Novel #21," he said, very prompt. *"The Widow Wears White."*

"Mercy," Miss Irma said, her hand fluttering to her throat.

I looked Captain Davis up and down. Not a bad view, really. He was old—probably twenty-eight—but in military-good shape. "We'd need something official," I said. "Medals would be good."

"Deal," he said. "We'll divide the lighthouse tomorrow morning."

"Regrets. Tomorrow's Sunday. And we're busy Monday morning."

"Monday afternoon then. That's the last open spot on my calendar."

"Deal," Neb said, holding out his hand. Captain Davis gave it a quick shake. Rain and me held out our hands too—the first island girls to take up the art of the handshake.

CHAPTER 16

HEELS OF LAST RESORT

Monday morning, Mama peeped in my room. "Comb your hair and invite Rain and Neb in for breakfast. They're by the gate, practicing looking casual. Neb's act needs work."

She strolled in. My official U.S. Weather Bureau Station folder lay open on my bed. In it, I archive Papa's old postcards. She picked up a favorite: a photo of the Statue of Liberty. She ran her finger across Papa's scrawl, kissed the top of my head, and gave me a hug. "I miss him too," she said.

"I'll put the folder back in the library when I come down," I promised, and she smiled and sailed out the door.

Mama likes to run a tight ship.

After breakfast, Mama snapped my dinner pail closed. "Be back by dark. If there's trouble—"

"I know," I said, slinging my spyglass over my shoulder. "Run home unless there's gunfire, and then lay low." I kissed her good-bye and we pounded out the door.

"What's our plan?" Rain asked as I hurled a rock at the hawk perched in our apple tree. We hurried into the village, passing the PO at a brisk trot.

"To find out who Julia really is, and figure out who stole her bracelet."

"Speak of the devil," Neb muttered.

Julia strolled toward us with a long cardboard tube tucked beneath her arm. She swerved to Rain. "Rain, I'm sorry. Please forgive me. You are the *last* person who would steal from me. I'm sure I lost that bracelet. I feel like such a . . ."

"Loser?" I suggested, and she glared at me.

Julia went eye-to-eye with Rain. "I'm so sorry, Rain. Can you forgive me?"

Miss Jonah teaches Rain to forgive anybody who apologizes from the heart, but Rain never forgets. Neb and me remember with her.

"Little fish?" Neb asked. Rain shook her head. *She's not letting this one go,* I thought. Still, she let Julia take her hand.

"What's in the tube?" Neb asked, falling into step with Julia.

"Watercolors. We roll our art and mail it home to Canada. Aggie's swamped at the PO today. Once I mail this, I'm heading to the beach to paint with Dirk. Join us, Rain?"

"Not today," Rain said.

Neb kicked at a stick. "Seems like Dirk would be tired of painting the lighthouse."

Julia smiled. "The lighthouse sells. It's famous all over the world." She stepped onto the porch, tracking damp footprints—one leaving a crescent-moon print across the heel. Julia quickly wiped her feet, smearing the odd print.

"Leave her be," Miss Agnes snapped at us from the PO doorway. "And no, the FBI hasn't written. Neither has your father. Go away." She slammed the door—and locked it.

"Invisible-ized by a fellow woman," Rain said as Schooner ambled from beneath a fig tree. "Hey, boy. You're looking trim now that you're not eating Otto's food."

Neb looked at Rain. "What are you thinking? About Julia, I mean."

Rain tapped her chin. "I'm thinking Julia didn't mean to hurt me, but she did. And I'm thinking Julia's headed for the beach after she finishes here, and Dirk's already down there, and he always carries a meal. And I'm thinking I'm tired of pussyfooting around with those two. Follow me, please," she added, and just like that, we were on the prowl.

Two blinks later, Rain and Neb formed a human shield as I jiggled our bobby pin in the lock on Julia's back door. *Click.* The door swung open. Neb sniffed. "Cabbage and onions and . . . *gun powder?*" he guessed, as we snuck into the kitchen.

"Not gunpowder. Scorched garlic," I replied.

Thanks to Mama's herb and vegetable gardens, I can identify most any plant by taste, look, and smell. Thanks to Faye's cooking, I know what almost everything smells like burnt.

We crept on, past a tower of plates on the old table.

I peeked into a bedroom. Dirk's dark suit hung like a long, molted skin on the wall peg. His shiny wingtips sat by the dresser. "Neb, you search Dirk's room in case of underwear. Rain and me got Julia's room."

"Why do boys get the bad jobs? Kill the bug, check the mouse trap, touch the underwear." He fussed his way into

Dirk's room as we pushed into Julia's: sagging bed neatly made, chest of drawers, hazy mirror. Clothes on pegs, shoes by a stack of luggage.

I placed my spyglass on the desk. "You check the clothes. I got the luggage."

"No thank you," Rain replied. "Touching people's clothes makes me feel cloudy inside."

Rain looks like a cherub but she's stubborn as a bloodstain.

"Roger that," I said. "You check the luggage. I got the clothes." I patted down the clothes, and turned to the chest of drawers. My fingers closed around a sketchbook. I thumbed through: "Here's a sketch of Miss Jonah!"

"Julia's brilliant," she said, glancing at it. She laid a burgundy passport and a clutter of receipts on the desk. "A brilliant artist, a brilliant liar. Here are her bona fides. Her fake papers. The suitcases are empty except the little one. These PO receipts sat on top of everything else." She put the receipts on the desk. "Julia said they mail their art to Canada. These receipts say New York and Miami. She's even lying about that."

Neb burst in. "Dirk has fake names: Philipe Barbosa, Ernst Yung, Eddy Spitz. And passports from Brazil, Germany, the United States . . ."

Something clunked on the front porch. "Can't believe I forgot our food," Dirk said from the porch.

Fish rot.

Rain scooped the passport and receipts into the little suitcase and hurled it in place. Neb raised the window. We tumbled out like a cup full of monkeys, landing in a heap on the grass. Neb grabbed the window's crosspiece, and slid the window down.

I peeked over the windowsill. *No!* My spyglass stared back at me from the desk!

Panic winged through me like a murder of frightened crows. "Grab that mop and bucket," I said, pointing. "We're going undercover. Now."

"Clean our floors? Why?" Dirk asked, slouching in the doorway.

Neb lowered his voice. "Man to man? It's bugs—a boy job, but Rain and Stick can handle it. Please show Julia out. I don't want her to see this."

I peeked around Dirk, into the front room. Julia stood there barefoot, a pair of flat-soled shoes dangling from her fingertips. "I think these shoes will be better for the sand," she said.

Rain scooted around Dirk, into the room. "Thank you for liking my art, Julia," Rain said. "Where are your palmetto bugs?"

Palmetto bugs. Brilliant.

"Eurycotis floridana," I said. "Like roaches but bigger. One lays fourteen to sixteen eggs a week. Time is of the essence." Julia stared at us, her green eyes calculating. *She's not going for it,* I thought. "There's one!" I shouted, pointing behind her. Rain screamed.

Julia bolted, slamming the front door behind her.

"Pull the curtains and stomp," I whispered. Rain high-stepped around the front room as I sprinted into the bedroom and slipped my spyglass in my bucket. "I'll get the passports," I whispered, shoving the bucket at Neb.

"No," Neb said. "It's the first thing they'll look for. Let's get out of here."

A flash later, we stepped onto the porch. "Thanks," I told the Artists as Neb strolled away with the bucket. "In case of insects, come directly to us. The postmistress suffers from *entomophobia*—an irrational fear of bugs. We hope to keep her from full-blown phobia."

We'd almost made it to the lighthouse when I took the bucket from Neb. It was heavier than expected. Sadly, I didn't ask why. Instead, I turned to Rain. "Something's bothering me."

"The origin of life again?" she guessed. "The mechanics of time?"

"No. You said the PO receipts sat on top of things in the little suitcase. On top of *what?*"

"Money," she said. "The little suitcase is full of ten-dollar bills."

"A suitcase full of ten-dollar bills? Why?" Neb said, pacing HQ's floor.

"Because a wallet couldn't hold that much cash," Rain said.

I read the clouds and made my notes. "Quarter inch of precip last night. Winds out of the east," I muttered.

"Who cares?" he asked. "We *could* question Julia, but how can we without admitting we broke in?"

Downstairs, the door scraped open. "Hello?" *Captain Davis.*

"Halt," I shouted, smoothing my lab jacket. "What's the password?"

"I'm coming up," Davis shouted.

"Enter," Rain shouted back.

"We'll keep the ocean side of the office," I whispered. "It's the best lookout for weather and U-boats." They nodded as Davis started up at a brisk trot—rookie mistake. He stepped into HQ, panting. He looked around, waiting for his breathing to settle.

"We're safe from out-of-shape Germans, anyway," he said. "They'd die halfway up."

"Welcome to your side of the lighthouse," I said, pointing to the sound side of our space. He strolled the room, admiring Rain's art and Papa's latest postcards. He leaned in to admire Neb's neckerchief slide. "Nice—"

"Porpoise," we said in unison.

Captain Davis opened the steel door leading to the rusty balcony. He took a cautious step out, and a quick step back in. "I'll take the ocean side of the room."

He's smarter than he looks, I thought. "The sound side has a better view."

"And I'm glad for you to have it. Let's move your things. Then I'll fetch mine."

An hour later, our half of headquarters was shipshape. "You helped us, now we'll help you. Turnabout's fair play," Neb told him. "Where's your stuff?"

Davis flashed a smile. "Thanks. I like that about you Dimes."
Recognition feels good, even from a pushy Fed. It took two trips
to lug in Davis's stuff: electrical gadgetry, a swivel office chair
with a ripped cushion. A UNC poster, a box of charts, and what
turned out to be a shortwave radio when he put it together.

Rain taped his charts up for him. "Those are the ugly airplanes from Neb's cards," she said. "We know them by heart—
all three of us."

Davis sprawled in his chair. "The more eyes, the better,"
he said, reaching into the last box. He lifted out four warm
Pepsis, and an opener. "Thanks for your help," he said, prying
up the lids. He handed a bottle to Rain and one to me, then to
Neb. We Dimes clamped our lips over the bottles, to catch the
warm fizz. He didn't.

"You brought four drinks," I said, covering for Neb as fizz
spouted from his nose. "You knew we'd help you move in."

"I hoped so. You can see quite a bit from here," he added,
looking out over the island. "Seen anything I need to know?
What do you know about those Artists?"

What *do* we know? They have fake passports, I thought.
They lie about mailing their work to Canada. They associate
with Miss Agnes, whose status remains unknown. And they
own a suitcase stuffed with ten-dollar bills. But why would
we share our hard-earned information with an unproven
roommate?

I smiled at Davis. "They're from Canada," I said.

He set binoculars on his desk. "You can use these up here,
but never touch the radio."

"Feel free to use our spyglass," I countered. "Make sure you don't track any oil into headquarters, and set the Matchstick Alert when you leave."

"Matchstick high in the door?" *He's savvy,* I thought. "Deal. Dimes, please rise." He pulled three star-shaped pins from his pocket. "With deep appreciation for your lighthouse maintenance, your love of dime novels, and your willingness to admit a scurvy dog like me, I present these stars of excellence." He went down the row, pinning them to our collars.

He stepped back and saluted us. We saluted in reply, Rain and me going military, Neb whipping off a Boy Scout salute. "Congratulations, Dimes. Now, if you'll excuse me, I have work to do," he said, sitting. "Remember: Don't touch the radio."

From honorees to evictees, just like that?

Rain gave him her angel smile. "Is that a U-boat?" she asked, pointing over his shoulder. Davis grabbed his binoculars and swiveled in his government-issue office chair.

We touched his radio and shot down the stairs.

That evening, as my family finished supper, Rain strolled in with Neb, who clutched a lumpy pillowcase. She smiled at Mama. "May Neb and I visit with Stick in private? We need all hands on deck now, please."

What the helium?

Mama laughed. "Stick, you're excused."

The three of us tore upstairs to my room. "What's wrong?"

"Emergency meeting," Rain said. We sat cross-legged on

my bed, our knees practically touching. She looked at Neb. "Show her."

Neb went sullen. He upended his pillowcase, dumping Julia's shoes onto my bedspread.

"Tell her," Rain demanded.

Neb sighed. "I confiscated Julia's shoes when we went back to get your spyglass."

I stared at him in horror. "You knew not to take the passports, but you took her *shoes?*"

"I didn't think it through," he said, his voice pleading. "I was there, the shoes were there, they'd made that odd print, I had a bucket." He sighed. "She'll suspect we took them. We were there when her shoes walked off without her."

Rain's eyes filled with tears. "I don't want her to think I'm a thief."

"I'm sorry, Rain," Neb said, his voice quivering.

I threw my arm around Rain and we stared at Julia's brown shoes, at their neat trim, their two-inch heels. *Very sophisticated.*

Rain turned the left shoe over: normal as baby teeth. Then the right shoe. "The shoe with the crescent heel," she said. I hopped up, snagged Faye's comb, and tapped the heel. "It sounds hollow," she said, and gave it a deft twist. It swung open. A capsule rolled onto my quilt.

"A white capsule with a red band," Rain whispered. "Identical to the one in *Dime Novel #22: Heels of Last Resort.*"

"A suicide pill, then. Certain death," Neb added as Faye flew in.

We froze, Rain holding the open shoe, me holding Faye's comb, Neb holding the pillowcase. The suicide pill lay between us. Faye took in the scene. "Who said you could use my comb?" she demanded, grabbing it. "Listen, girls, I'd hoped to fix your hair next Saturday, but I'm going to the island's snazziest club. With Reed. Little place called the Oceanside Club."

"That's good," Rain said. "I already like my hair."

"Me too," I said, and Faye snorted.

"Who cares about the Oceanside Club?" asked Neb.

Faye frowned. "Everybody who's anybody, porcupine head."

How can Faye be sixteen and insult like a third-grader? I gave her a smile. "Porcupine head. Neb's hair is *quill*, get it?"

She didn't get it. "The Oceanside," she said, and shot out the door.

I turned back to the suicide pill. "Is there anything else in that heel?"

Rain shook her head. "*Spies* carry suicide pills," she said. "And fake passports. And maybe suitcases full of cash. But how could Julia be a spy after Nazis stole her people?"

"*What?*" Neb said.

"It slipped out one day while we painted together with our hearts wide-open," Rain said. "She said not to mention it to Dirk. It makes him too sad."

"Right," Neb said. "Only how does that all line up?"

"I don't know yet," I said, "but by now Julia knows *one* of us stole these shoes, but not why. We have to put them back or blow our cover."

"What cover?" Neb said.

"We're genius spy-catchers, traveling incognito as us," Rain explained.

I scooped the pill back into the shoe and closed the crescent heel. "Why would a boy swipe a woman's footwear?" I hurried on before Neb could guess. "He'd do it because he's in love. Love makes people stupid. Example: Reed's asking Faye to marry him at the Oceanside."

Neb whistled. I opened my drawer, snagged paper and pencil, and scrawled a quick note. "Neb, copy this over. Change the wording to reflect your personal style." Neb has no writing style but I try to be generous. I took out Faye's shoe polish as he read my note.

He shook his head. "I don't know."

"Do it. Do it now. Please," Rain demanded, and he picked up the pencil.

He read the words out as he copied them: "Dear Miss Julia, I polished your shoes," he muttered as I smeared polish on Julia's left shoe. "Please marry me. Neb." He cleared his throat and looked from Rain to me. "I'm over her, but . . . Do you actually think this will work? The age difference might kill Mother."

Rain put her head in her hands. "It will never work, Neb," she said. "But it *will* explain why you took the shoes."

I stuffed Julia's shoes in the pillowcase. "Let these dry, buff them to a high sheen, and place them on Julia's porch with your note," I told Neb. "Don't let her see you."

"Right," he said, relaxing. "What can go wrong?"

CHAPTER 17

THE CREATURE IN US ALL

It's amazing how many things can go wrong in one skinny day.

Take the next day, for example. "Today we find a way inside Miss Agnes's lair if we have to bust a window to do it," I said, lugging Mama's cleaning supplies along. "We need to know who she is, and how she's connected to the Artists."

"She could be a Nazi, like Dirk," Neb said. "Or something confusing, like Julia."

"She's no Nazi," Rain said, smoothing her dress—blue with tiny stars.

A breeze sailed across the sound, wrapping us in the soft, round scent of salt water and the sharp, clean smell of pines. Schooner fell in beside us, his head down. He burped. "Seasick again," Rain said, rubbing his ears. "He probably walked out on the dock."

Fact: It's sad, being a landlubber on an island.

"Look smart," I continued. "If Miss Agnes mentions Julia's shoes, we never heard of them. Be charming." We pushed inside the tiny post office. Miss Agnes stood behind the counter, the Sears and Roebuck catalog open to the men's suspenders page, the sunlight glinting off her frilly dress's lacy white collar. She looked up, letting her glasses slide down her nose.

"Felicitations," I said, smiling. "It smells nice in here. Did you dab vanilla behind your ears? Faye says boys love it. Old men might too."

Fact: Grand is allergic to vanilla.

"It's you. Nothing from your papa today," she said, and my heart fell. "Go away."

"We can't," Rain replied. "We're being punished."

Miss Agnes closed her catalog and smiled, and I hung my head. "Mama says I got to ask you if you want us to wash your windows, inside and out. It's free until we learn our lesson."

She licked her thin lips. "What did you do this time and how did you get caught?"

"Free child labor," Rain said. "Take it or leave it, please."

"I'll take it. Outside only. Don't go in my house. Don't mess with my laundry. And don't touch the Buick *ever*, you little pests."

It would be our last cordial conversation with Miss Agnes for many days.

Schooner collapsed beneath Miss Agnes's scraggly cedar as we set up on the front porch. "Case the joint through the windows," I whispered, adjusting my stepladder.

Neb poured vinegar in our wash water. "No can do. She has curtains."

As we washed one salt-misted window and moved to the next, I studied her odd front-porch wash line. "Remember the list of clothes we found behind Miss Agnes's house?"

"Of course," Rain said. "Jacket, kimono, lingerie. Alphabetical."

"Look at her clothesline. What do you see?"

"A man's hat," Neb reported. "And—" He gasped and went beet-red.

"Good grief. You have sisters. You've seen *underwear* before," I told him.

He looked away. "Not such . . . excited, frilly underwear. Nobody should ever see that."

"A hat, underwear, and two life jackets," Rain added. "Maybe she rinsed the salt water off the life jackets and hung them up to dry?"

Neb studied the clothesline: "The *first* letters of the clothes on her list were alphabetical. It could be code. Put the initials of these clothes together, what do you have? Hat, underwear, life jacket, life jacket. *H-u-l-l.*" His face fell. "Hull?"

Rain scrubbed at a fly speck. "That hat's a *fedora.* Her clothesline says *FULL.*"

Neb beamed. "Exactly!" he said.

"It spells full *now*," I said, my blood surging. "But Miss Agnes changed it just after the Artists showed up. What hung on the PO clothesline the day they first arrived, with Sam?"

"A hanky, red earmuffs, a frilly robe, and an evening gown," Rain said. "*H* for *hanky, E* for *earmuffs, R* for *robe,* and *E* for *evening gown. H-e-r-e.*"

"A message guiding the Artists in! And with the shack full, it's now signaling she has no vacancy," Neb said as we moved our gear to the side of the house.

I grinned. "*Fedora.* Rain, you're a genius."

Neb pressed his hair flat. "*And?*"

"And you are too," I told him.

He glowed as he wedged his ladder between the side of the house and an overgrown hedge. "That's a tough code, and *we* broke it. The FBI can't ignore that." He scaled his ladder, turned, and slapped at the shrub. "This shrub's a hazard."

Up we went, Neb high on his ladder, me on Mama's medium stepladder, Rain on the ground. We heard Julia and Dirk before we saw them.

"We *can't* miss this, *sister* dear. Timing's everything," Dirk said, his voice sharp as Papa's razor.

"I realize that, I just—"

"Stop wasting time on those ridiculous island kids and pay attention to business."

"What business?" Neb whispered. He leaned, peeping around the privet.

"Use your head," Dirk said. "Our man's on a life-and-death schedule."

"What man?" Neb muttered. He leaned more, sticking his foot out for balance.

"This drop spells success or failure for the entire East Coast," Dirk continued. "Today we talk Aggie into taking us to the new naval base on Ocracoke Island—to update our info. And we need her Buick for our trip to the Oceanside Club, Saturday night. Here. Take this."

"Take what?" Neb whispered, leaning even more.

The ladder slipped.

Time slowed.

Neb's brown eyes went helpless and wild.

His ladder shot out from under him and he fell, swiping at the shrubbery like a cat batting at moths. He crashed at Julia's feet, sprigs of greenery clenched in his hands and teeth.

Think fast, Genius. I landed flat-footed beside Neb and went into a scientific crouch.

Life Rule #34: *Look like you know what you're doing, especially if you don't.*

"Step back, Artists," I said as Rain struggled to my side. "Science needs room to breathe." Rain gently shook a branch from between Neb's teeth. "Thanks for your willingness to sacrifice your body for science, Neb. Based on my calculations, gravity's in full force."

"Hello, Julia," Neb replied, gazing at her. He looked at Dirk. "Dirk," he said, very cool.

Julia looked at him the way Faye eyes a pimple. "Thank you for polishing my shoes, Neb, but I must decline your proposal. Excuse us, children."

She hooked her arm in Dirk's and sashayed on.

"She called me a child," Neb said as Rain and I sat him up. "It's over between us. I've moved on, and now she has too."

Neb had regained his color by the time we passed our ladders over Miss Agnes's wall of thorns and belly-crawled through Edgar's door into the backyard. Snatches of voices floated to us from the front yard. Julia's, Dirk's, Miss Agnes's. Car doors slammed. The Buick backfired its way down our main street.

"They're gone," Neb said. "Did you bring our Door Opening Kit?"

I plucked Faye's bobby pin from my hair and went to work. The back door squeaked open and we stole inside. "Dang, it's musty," Neb whispered, closing the door.

We sniffed the air for sensory clues—a technique featured in *Dime Novel #95: The Creature in Us All*. We crept across the musty hall, to the office door. "Locked," I reported.

I jimmied the lock and the door scraped open. I darted to the window and slowly lifted the shade. A dusty light crept across the room—up the side of Miss Agnes's cluttered oak desk, across a Royal typewriter, over a half sandwich covered in pale mold—possibly *Penicillium* (Volume P). My hand slipped. The shade flapped itself crazy at the top of the window, and sunlight bolted to shelves beyond the desk.

Three sets of glassy eyes stared at us. A scream pierced the dusty silence.

"Stick! Hush!" Rain cried, strolling to the shelf. "They're just dolls." Fact: Many scientists have a fear of dolls.

Neb checked the typewriter. "Dolls and an unfinished letter." He read:

```
MRS. CALEDONIA yVETTELIA ROBERTSON
DOLL SURGEON,
NEW yORK, NEW yORK.
DEAR CAL,
THAnKS FOR HELPING EMMy. HER EyE'S GOOD
```

```
AS new. I THINK IT GIVES HER PERSONALITy.
HERE's ANOTHER DOLLy WHo nEEDS yOUR HELP. I
FOUND THIS BABE-IN-ARmS IN A JUNK STOrE IN
greeNVILLE, N.C. AS YOU CAn SEE, HEr HAIRs HAvE
FALLEN OUT. pITY.
THANKS AND DO SEND ME
```

"Her hairs have fallen out? That's terrible grammar. Send her what?" I asked as a fly buzzed my head. I slapped at it.

"I don't know. That's where she stops."

"She means this doll. It's bald," Rain said, cradling a porcelain doll. *Click.* The doll's eyes closed. Rain sat her up. *Click.* The doll's eyes flew open.

"That's the sound Miss Agnes's package made in the PO, the day you felonied the mail," Neb said. A nest of yellow doll hair rested on the desk. He nudged it with a pen. "Looks like she balded the doll herself. Weird."

No weirder than using *felony* and *bald* as verbs, I thought.

Neb rolled in a fresh sheet of paper and tried the typewriter keys, one by one. "Only the *y* actually sticks," he reported, frowning. "She made the other letters lowercase herself. She could have used capital letters if she'd wanted to. This is code, or I'll eat it."

In the distance, a car backfired. And then again, closer. Schooner barked a warning.

"They're coming back! Retreat!" I grabbed the carbon copy of Miss Agnes's letter and stuffed it in my pocket as Rain sprang for the window shade.

"Go, go, go," Neb whispered, holding the door open.

"Sorry, Dirk, forgot my hat," Miss Agnes bellowed from the front door. "Won't be a minute." She slammed the door. "This way, Julia," she said as we squeezed into the closet, leaving the door ajar. "I have news of your family," she said, her voice soft. "We now know they were moved from Austria to Poland." Julia gasped. "But that's *all* we know. They may have escaped the train, they could have been taken *through* Poland to . . . well, I don't know where."

"Of course," Julia said, her voice wobbling.

"We mustn't lose hope." Outside, Dirk blew the horn. Miss Agnes's voice came quick. "Here. Take this lipstick. I won't use it—wrong pocket litter. Just open, point, boom. It shoots one bullet," she said, swiping at a fly.

They started toward the door as Dirk blew the horn again. "My *brother* can be obnoxious. Don't forget your hat," Julia said, and then snorted when she saw it. "What happened to *that?*"

"Edgar," Miss Agnes said, smoothing its feathers back into place. She laughed a real laugh, one I'd never heard before. Light and carefree, happy as a hiking song. "Where's my hat pin? Be careful, the tip's poison." She locked the office door, and their voices died away.

"Miss Agnes has a poison pin and a lipstick that shoots bullets?" I said.

"Just one bullet," Neb said, like that made it better. "What's *pocket litter?*"

"Little things spies carry, to make them fit in," Rain replied.

"Movie tickets, receipts for art supplies. Things like that. It's in *Dime Novel #53: A Spy Talks*."

Neb tiptoed to the door. "Sounds like Julia doesn't like her brother."

"Dirk's not her brother," Rain said. "He's too rude. And if he was a brother, Miss Agnes would share family information with him too. He may not even know Julia's family got stolen."

"Good points. I wonder what they're *really* doing, working together . . ." I shook my head. "This way," I said. "I've been thinking about Miss Agnes's chimney."

The parlor smelled of lamp oil and mothballs. I knelt at the fireplace and reached up into the flue. Together, we lowered a small black case to the floor. I clicked it open. A jumble of dials and wires stared up at me. "A shortwave radio," I gasped. "No wonder she didn't light a fire."

"Or invite Grand to visit," Rain said.

"Hands up, thieves!" Miss Agnes shouted behind us.

We whipped around, raising our sooty hands.

She stood in the doorway, her white lace collar glowing in the dim light as she lifted a tiny camera to her eye. "Smile," she said. *Immortalized at the lowest moment in our professional lives.* Still, Faye says there's nothing a smile won't improve. We smiled. *CLICK.*

"What are you doing in my house?"

"Nothing," we chorused.

Outside, Dirk bounced on his horn. Neb edged for the door. "This has been nice, but it sounds like Dirk's in a hurry. We don't want to keep you."

She grabbed the front of his shirt and twisted it tight, lifting him to his toes. "Why are you here? What do you want?"

Neb pried her fingers open one by one. "What do I want? In the long run, I'd say I want a family, but of course I need a mate first. My prospects are momentarily slim, but Daddy would feel better if my future was settled, due to his health. Rain and Stick are like sisters, so they're out. I think we can agree there. So that's the long run. Short run, we want to be famous. Famous scientist, famous artist, famous Neb. And there's our FBI ambitions. You?"

Miss Agnes pushed him away and sank onto her sofa, hissing, her long legs splayed beneath her skirt. "I give up on you three. So choose: I can shoot you or recruit you."

A bluff. Not even Miss Agnes would shoot us.

"Or," she said, going crafty, "with the photo in this little camera, I can send you to jail."

Neb swallowed hard. "Recruit us, I guess. Maybe. There's a rumor going around that you're a Nazi, and if that's it, we're out."

Finally. One of us had said it to her face.

Miss Agnes glared like she could incinerate us. "Don't be ridiculous," she said, nodding to a burgundy love seat. "I'm American as apple pie. Your grandfather wouldn't have me otherwise. Neither would the post office. Sit."

We sat. "The only apple native to North America is the crab-apple," I said, my voice cold. "But please present your terms."

"As postmistress, I'm head of the local Post Office Special Operations unit, a secret government organization charged with investigating the suspicious on this island."

Is she kidding? "Post Office Special Ops? Never heard of

it," I said. But if true, the poisoned hat pin and loaded lipstick make sense, I thought.

"I never heard of *you* until I met you, but alas, here you are," she said. "You three are *always* in my way. Since I can't get rid of you, you may join me—as my underlings. Code names: Red Dime, Bristly Dime, Little Dime," she said pointing to each of us in turn.

"Thanks, but we're aiming higher," Neb said. "The FBI."

She narrowed her predator eyes. "Join me, or I report you to Captain Ed Davis for breaking and entering, and off you go to a juvenile detention center in Raleigh."

"We're in," Neb said, and Rain and I nodded. "What do we do?"

"You'll watch the Ringers. For some reason, they don't cozy up to me. Find out what they're *really* doing on this island. Because they didn't come to play baseball. Submit a report every other week. In triplicate—standard PO procedure. You may ask one question."

"Why are you hiding a shortwave in your chimney and who are Julia and Dirk?" I read the glint in her eyes. "That was a compound interrogative—technically, one question."

"If you feel confused, it's probably Latin," Neb told her.

Miss Agnes ignored him. "I hid the radio in case of invasion. The Germans will take the lighthouse first—highest spot on the island. And Davis's radio with it." *Probably true*, I thought. "And I don't know who Julia and Dirk are." A *lie*. Outside, Dirk bounced on his horn like he could lasso Miss Agnes with its sound and drag her to the car. "You are dismissed."

At the doorway, I turned. "How did you know we were in here?"

"You let flies into my office, Red Dime. Rookie mistake." As we slunk to the back door, I heard her low, soft voice: "Gato gato gato. Where are you?" Edgar shot down the hall.

"That's just wrong, a bilingual cat," Neb fumed as we crossed the backyard. "I can barely do English." He sighed as we neared the rose hedge. "Now we're underlings. To the person we hate most next to Hitler."

"We are not," I snapped. "Remember what Eleanor Roosevelt says. 'No one can make you feel inferior without your consent.' We're in a jam, is all."

Rain tilted her head the way she does when a new drawing's falling into place. "The *important* thing is, Julia and Dirk are going to the Oceanside this Saturday on the biggest mission of Dirk's life, and we need to see who he's meeting. And to see if Reed proposes to Faye."

Rain has a way with a summary.

"We'll go incognito, from the Latin word meaning *unknown*," I said. "Dress mature."

"How mature?" Neb asked.

"Gussy up, Bristly Dime," Rain said. "We want to blend."

"Use the alibi from *Dime Novel #45: Triangle of Lies*," I added as Neb crawled out Edgar's little door in the hedge. "It's never let us down."

Sadly, there's a first time for everything.

CHAPTER 18

TRIANGLE OF LIES

April 4, 1942

Saturday afternoon, we darted across Reed's backyard and rolled into the bed of his pickup truck. Schooner bounded in behind us, his yellow gingham bow tie gleaming. "What good does it do to dress nice when we have to ride with Schooner? He stinks," Neb muttered.

Neb wore his navy-blue sweater, and pressed shorts. "Can you tell I singed these a little?" he asked, showing his cuff. "How do I look?" he asked, trying to mash his hair down.

I took in his crumpled shirt, his spiky hair, his scorched shorts. "Good," I said.

Rain wore her pink-flowered dress with a wide red belt. I'd borrowed Faye's shoulder bag of drama club disguises, and a waist-nipped blouse to go with my blue school skirt.

I peeked over the truck's side, at the unpainted house Reed inherited from his parents last summer. A nearly finished skiff sat on sawhorses by the truck. A lean-to slouched at water's edge.

Faye will live here if she marries Reed, I thought, admiring the rushes along the curved shoreline and the snowy white egrets hunting in the shallows. I'll see her only for Sunday dinner, and after the babies come, not even then. Slowly, she will become a stranger to me.

"What is it?" Rain asked. "You look happy."

"Get down," I whispered.

Reed's back door swung open and I yanked a seaweed-scented burlap sheet over our heads. Neb retched. "Breathe through your mouth," I whispered as Schooner—outside the tarp—plunked down on my arm.

"Hey Schooner, ready to ride? Good guy," Reed said, and Schooner thumped his tail against Neb's face. I peeped out. Faye looked Doris Day good—sweet and perky.

"Faye, hold on. I want to ask you something," Reed said.

"You don't need to ask me," she teased. "*Yes*, I want to dance, and no, I don't mind if you step on my feet." She gasped. "Reed! You're gray as cement!"

"Hollywood Faye Lawson," he rasped, "will you marry me?"

Rain inhaled sharp. I didn't need to look to know Neb was trying to reduce himself to his essential elements. This is it, I thought. Faye's caught in a crosscurrent of dreams. Her dream since fifth grade—marrying Reed—against her dream of Hollywood.

"You're not going away. You'd never leave your family in danger," he said. "And I'll make you happy, Faye. I swear I will."

"Does anybody else wish they could close their ears?" Neb whispered.

"Did you hear that?" Faye said. Schooner barked, and she laughed. "For a minute, I thought Schooner said something."

She's stalling, I thought. When she spoke again her voice

tiptoed careful and slow. "Like Grand says, war changes things. I guess I need time to think."

Time to think. A line from a movie. Fact: Faye's never taken time to think in her life. She paused, and I knew she gave him the thirty-degree tilt. "Give me time. Come on. I don't want to miss the dancing."

That's Faye in a nutshell. Hollywood or Hatteras Island, she never wants to miss the dancing.

Four stinking-dog hours later, the truck careened into an oyster-shell parking lot. Reed cut the engine, and slammed his door. "Thirsty, Schooner?" he asked, and water gurgled from a bottle. "Stay, boy. Hollywood Faye Lawson? Ready for the time of your life?"

As their voices faded, Neb threw off the burlap sheet. "I hate myself, I stink so bad."

I sat up, gulping fresh air. Four hours is a long time to breathe in what other people breathe out. I cased the long building by the sea, its soft, yellowish light haloed against the evening sky, its bright windows shining.

"It looks like a fairy tale," Rain whispered.

"They don't believe in blackout curtains, that's for sure. Get down!" Neb cried as a buzz of women sashayed past, perfuming the night. They beelined across the parking lot and up the steps, to a side porch. Neb vaulted over the side. "Wait here." He wound his way through the cars. A minute later, he ran back with a fancy spray bottle. "Close your eyes," he instructed. He spritzed us, and then himself. Schooner sneezed. "It's perfume. I hate it, but it's better than smelling like a dog," he said, and darted away to return the scent.

Rain hopped out of the truck, light as a cricket. "Bathroom," she said.

"A place this swank has bathrooms inside," I told her, and her face lit up. It's Rain's dream to see indoor plumbing—a popular feature in dime novels. I saw it when we visited Tarboro, on the mainland. "Can you wait?" She shook her head. "Then we'll go between the cars." I grabbed Faye's shoulder bag. "Girls, this way. Neb, that way. You can admire the indoor plumbing once we're inside." I scanned for Miss Agnes's Buick. "Then we find the Artists. This may be our best chance to impress the FBI."

Twenty minutes later, as we hid behind the scraggly shrubs at the club's side door, a car backfired. "Finally," Neb muttered, lowering a branch and peering out.

Julia and Dirk tooled up in Miss Agnes's Buick and strolled across the parking lot, Dirk swinging a briefcase. Julia stopped to adjust Dirk's tie as a pack of sailors headed for the door. "How will we know your contact?" Julia asked.

"Easy," Dirk said, heading inside. "He's wearing a green suit."

We ducked as two men strolled in from the beach. "Try to smile, cuz," one drawled as they trotted up the wooden steps carrying a paper bag. The door swept shut behind them.

"Carl Miller!" I whispered. "And Ralph! We can scout them for Miss Agnes. Now we just need a way in." We shot onto the side porch and peered through the window. The bar stood elbow-deep in sailors and women in pretty dresses. Two women in aprons cleared tables. Across the room, light shot across the bar and a man entered carrying a box.

"A back door! Let's go!"

As we neared the back exit, a car rumbled up. "Duck!" I said. On the black car's only blue door, in fancy letters: *the Dream Makers*. Four hound-dog-skinny guys—three white and one Black—rolled out. They smoothed their suits and straightened their thin ties. "I *guess* this is it," one of the white guys said, popping the trunk. "It's lit up enough to invite the Germans in for a drink, but a gig's a gig. Grab your things. Arnie, the piano is set up inside."

The Black man, Arnie, nodded. "Hope so. Can't make music out of thin air."

Science's cue to enter.

I stepped from the shrubs. "Actually, Arnie, music is *always* made of air—vibrating air. If the vibrations' overtones and frequencies are compatible, the music sounds good." They stared at me. "Volume M." My smile wilted in the silence. "For *music*."

Neb stepped from the shrubs. "Welcome. The manager sent us to carry your things."

Arnie frowned. "Thanks, but musical instruments cost. We'll carry them. How many of you live in that shrub, anyway? Come on, Dream Makers. Let's roll."

"Wait!" I cried, and, in a moment of desperation, went with the truth. "We're the Dime Novel Kids on the trail of spies. The fate of the country plus our future careers with the FBI may be on the line. We must infiltrate, and you are our cover. Give me a horn."

Arnie laughed. "Great story. See you later, crazy cats."

Rain stepped from the shrubbery and grabbed Arnie's hand. She looked up at him, her brown eyes pleading. "I have to use the bathroom, crazy cat. Now. Please."

Arnie led Rain through the employees' digs, past the line of Delco batteries that powered the lights, into the dim heart of the club. Neb and me followed, slipping behind a large potted plant inside the door. "Potty's over there, shug," Arnie told her, and Rain disappeared behind a door marked *Ladies*. I pulled down a large, artificial leaf.

"*Planta artificialis*," I whispered. "A total misuse of science."

Neb lowered a fake limb. "Thanks, Arnie. We owe you."

"Indeed." Arnie frowned. "You smell like a girl. You should try a different aftershave."

Neb went pink as the Dream Makers walked away to set up their instruments. "Arnie thinks I shave," he crowed, looking delighted. "Where's Julia? She might think I shave too."

"Nobody thinks you shave. Julia's over there, talking to sailors. We need to get closer." I eyed a stack of trays at the end of the bar.

Life Rule #3: *When undercover, blend.*

I herded Neb into a dark alcove. "We can't blend with hair like ours." I opened Faye's shoulder bag of drama club disguises and rummaged through. "Put this on," I said, handing him an old-man wig—short gray hair curly as a sheep's wool. I pressed a fake mustache on his face and he slipped on horn-rimmed glasses. "You look like a round-faced, withered old man," I said.

"Thank you. Now you."

Moments later, I fluffed my platinum-blond wig and selected a pair of dark glasses. I ambled to the bar and snagged two black aprons, praying my disguise would work. It did. We slipped our aprons on. From the *Ladies* room, I heard a toilet flush. Again. And again. Rain was enjoying the indoor plumbing.

"Bus tables and eavesdrop," I said as Arnie took the stage.

"Evening, everyone," Arnie said, "we're the Dream Makers. Welcome to our dream. Here's a Duke Ellington tune, 'Take the A Train.'"

Faye dragged Reed to the dance floor as a soft wave of music washed over us. Two songs later, Arnie started a slow one. As Faye and Reed wrapped around each other like a couple of lovesick squid, the front door opened and a man in a shiny green suit sauntered in.

"There's our man," Neb whispered as Dirk ushered the man to a side table.

The man in green wore his black hair parted hard in the center, accenting the pallor of his heart-shaped face. His wolf-blue eyes shot needles of ice through my veins. Every cell in my body wanted to run. Instead, I slipped nearer, balancing my tray.

"They're all here, Mr. Green," Dirk said. He glanced at me. "Get lost, cookie."

Cookie? I bumped his elbow, sloshing his drink, and drifted away to case the club.

Faye had stopped dancing and put her hands on her hips. *She's angry*, I thought. Reed had gone red—not good. Julia danced with a sailor. Carl Miller spun a distant postcard rack, chose a card, and took a pencil from his pocket to scribble on it. I tried not to think of Papa.

Fact: It's tricky, casing spies *and* the Ringers, *plus* Faye's so-called love life. With Faye stalled out and Dirk and Mr. Green huddling over a map, I zeroed in on the Ringers. I headed for the bar with a tray of dirty glasses as Ralph picked up his drink.

"That's two bits, buddy," the bartender said.

"I've got it. I'll take this card too," Carl said, and forked over a five. "Keep the change. Listen," he said when Ralph strolled away, "can you turn the club's lights down? They backlight our transport ships. Makes them easy targets for U-boats."

"I like the lights, bud," the bartender growled, and Carl's smile faded. He slipped the card in his pocket and headed for Julia's table as I pelted over to Neb. "I can't get close to Dirk and Mr. Green. You try," I said.

He smoothed his mustache. "In a minute. Here comes Rain. She'll never recognize us."

Rain breezed up. "Hi Neb. Hi Stick. Where's my disguise?"

I scooped the bag from under the table and handed it over without instruction—one of my many mistakes of the evening. Rain took off for the ladies' room to try one on.

I wasn't the only one making mistakes. Over at their table, Faye jerked her hand from Reed's. *"I told you. I need time."*

"Fine." Reed stalked out the door and down to the beach.

"What just happened?" Neb asked, watching them.

"Reed's a First Law of Motion Man, knocked off course by Faye's lack of enthusiasm for his proposal," I said.

"Speak English," Neb demanded.

Fact: It's hard being a steel-nerved investigator, a scientist, and a loving sister at the same time. "Faye's sad. Ask her to dance," I said, giving Neb a little push. "She won't guess it's you."

"Sorry," he said as Carl walked over to Faye. "I'm casing Mr. Green."

As I wiped off a table, I scoped the room: Julia sat down with a navy man on the other side of the room. Over at Dirk's table, Mr. Green slid a fat envelope from his jacket pocket. We slipped their way. "It works out," Dirk said, taking the envelope. "You'll see."

Neb edged closer. Dirk glared at him. "Beat it, you old geezer," he growled.

We beat it. *"What* works out?" Neb whispered, looking worried.

"Your guess is as good as mine," I said, loading up with

glasses at the next table. "I'm heading for Carl and Faye. See if you can find Rain."

Carl and Faye sipped Pepsis at the bar.

"Hey, there's the Artists," Faye said as Carl slid another fiver to the barkeeper. "You won't believe this, but my kid sister thinks they're spies. Do you have any sisters or . . ."

"Spies? Really?" He squinted at Julia. "I have a little brother," he told her, pulling the postcard from his pocket. "He'll love this photo of your lighthouse."

A postcard. For one flash, I saw Papa's smiling eyes.

Fact: I miss Papa like cloud misses sky.

At eleven o'clock, with the club packed, Mr. Green headed for the men's room. Rain lowered a limb of the *planta artificialis* and peeped out.

I tried to keep my voice neutral. "You picked the bald wig cap."

"Trouble at your six o'clock," she whispered, looking like a human lightbulb.

"Carl Miller!" Reed shouted. I turned to see him barreling toward Faye, his hands curled into fists. "Stay away from my girl—"

The sky exploded. A silent blast of orange and white lit the windows. We ducked. *Boom!* The soundwave hit, buckling the wall and shoving Reed like a puppet. Sailors scrambled to their feet and sprinted for the door, Reed in their midst.

"Turn out the lights!" Carl shouted.

"We got it!" I shouted, running for the back room. "Meet up on the side porch," I said as I disconnected the wall of Delco batteries. I felt my way along the wall, into the club. People crowded the doors, pushing, shoving. *Blam!* The ship's boiler exploded.

"Faye!" I shouted. She looked my way, tripped, and fell face-first into the crowd.

I elbowed my way to her and grabbed her arm. "Get up!" I cried as Carl snagged her other arm. We jerked her to her feet and dragged her to the deck. I darted back inside.

Where's Dirk? Where's Mr. Green?

I fought my way through the crowd to grab Dirk's briefcase. His hand clamped mine. "Thief!" he shouted as Mr. Green dropped something and bent to find it. I corkscrewed my body, wrenching the briefcase away.

Pop! The case opened, spewing cash and papers like confetti. My right foot landed on a passport and skidded out from under me. I fell into a screaming split and rolled beneath a table. Dirk raked papers into his briefcase, and I reached out and scooped an armful of evidence into my blouse: papers, a book, something round and smooth.

In the distance, sirens wailed. Mr. Green bolted into the throng and Dirk grabbed my wrist. Behind me, someone hooked my blouse and slid me away from him. "Run, Stick," Julia said as Dirk shot toward the door. "Get out of here. Now!"

• • •

Outside, Faye leaned against the porch rail. Neb and Rain stood in shadows. I waited for Faye to speak. She didn't. "You look like something a gull hacked up," I offered.

She whirled on me. "Who the spit are you? Leave me alone!"

My disguise. Apparently only artists see through it.

Rain and Neb stepped forward—a curly-haired old man and a lightbulb in a pink-flowered dress. We peeled off our wigs. I smiled, loving the rise of my hair in the humid air.

Faye retched. Like I said, her stomach's the first organ in her body to show stress.

Carl strode up. "What are you kids doing here? Faye, are you okay?"

"Faye's stressed. We're tracking spies," Rain said as Mr. Green shot by in a red Ford. She went up on her toes to study the car.

Faye closed her eyes. "My life can't *get* any worse than this." But it did. Reed took the porch steps two at a time. *He's still off course*, I thought, watching his eyes.

"I better go," Carl said, patting his pockets. He frowned. "Lost my postcard. Oh well. Great seeing you all. Reed." He held out his hand.

Reed ignored it. Not me.

"War changes things," I said, shaking Carl's hand. "You never know if you'll have another chance to say goodbye."

CHAPTER 19

DANGEROUS AS THEY COME

Four hours later, I sat up in the back of the truck and stretched.

Sunrise softened the eastern sky. Over the western horizon hovered Venus—second planet from the sun, temperature roughly 900 degrees F. (Volume V.) The morning air smelled salty and fishy-sweet, and the rolling boom of the waves soothed me.

"Wake up," I said, nudging Rain and Neb. "It's light enough to check our haul."

Fact: Nothing sleeps better than the back of a humming pickup truck.

Rain awakened slow and soft. Neb woke up like a startled ferret, his dark eyes blinking, his hair bent in the shape of the spare tire's curve. I emptied our evidence bag.

"What did we get?" Neb asked, sitting up.

"A bundle of twenty-dollar bills, probably from Mr. Green," I said, holding it up. "Dirk and Julia only carry tens. This is maybe one hundred twenties, equaling two thousand dollars."

Neb's eyes went wide. "Two thousand dollars? We could buy a couple of cars with that! Or retire from jobs we never even had! Is there at least a finder's fee or . . ."

Temptation tapped me on the shoulder. I spoke fast, before it could whisper in my ear: "This is evidence that might help save the people we love," I said.

"Sorry," he mumbled. "The greedy side of my brain wakes up first." He reached into the pile of loot. "Hey, here's a postcard from Carl, to somebody named Fritz."

"Carl's little brother. He dropped it in the stampede," I said as Rain took the card and studied it. I looked across the ocean, trying not to think of Papa's postcards.

Fact: It's hard *not* to think in one part of your brain, and be a genius in others.

Rain opened a passport. "Dirk's bona fides—a German passport with a Nazi stamp."

Neb opened the sketchbook. "Tourist drawings," he said, and turned a page.

"And a list of names," I added, scanning it. *Was there something else?* I ran my hand around the bottom of the bag. "That's it," I said.

Rain looked from Neb to me, her brown eyes serious. "Cash, a German passport, a list of names, sketches. And Mr. Green—who's dangerous as they come, as in *Dime Novel #89: Dangerous As They Come*. This is too big for us," she said. "Real ships are going down. Fathers are dying—sons and brothers too. This is proof that Dirk's connected to something big. If Dirk finds out *we* have it—"

"He doesn't know," I said quickly. "He couldn't see through our disguises—mine *or* Neb's. Only artists could. You and Julia."

"Julia's with Dirk," Neb said, flipping a page. "She'll tell him, first and last."

"She won't," Rain said as Schooner rested his head on my leg.

"Maybe not," I said, "but I don't want to bet our lives on it. I want to be known to the FBI, but I don't want us holding on to this stuff. I don't want our parents holding it either."

I glanced over my shoulder as the lighthouse came into view, tiny against unending sand and rolling sea. We're probably three miles away from HQ, I thought, eyeing the tower.

"We could give it to Miss Agnes," Neb said. "She's federal."

I shook my head. "I still don't trust her. Also, she hates us," I said.

"She likes Rain and me a little. I can tell," he said. "But how does this all sort out? We know Julia and Miss Agnes are working together, but so are Julia and Dirk. Which, thinking sideways, means Miss Agnes and Dirk are working together too."

"If a=b and b=c then a=c," I agreed, feeling my science-juice kicking in. "I think that's from *Euclid*, Volume E. But don't quote me."

"Believe me, I won't," Neb muttered.

Rain stretched and shook the sleep from her curls. "There's more than one way to see things," she said. "I say if Dirk=c, he's the only c on the island. My heart says Miss Agnes is good even if she *is* blackmailing us into helping her. And Julia's good deep inside too, but confusing. Like surface splash on calm, deep water."

"So where does that leave us?" Neb sighed.

"Mama Jonah says when you're not sure, you trust a little and see what happens."

Neb studied a sketch. "Turning this haul over to Miss Agnes is trusting a lot," he said.

I closed my eyes, searching for options. *Papa, I wish you were here.*

Rain spoke up. "Captain Davis is federal. The U.S. Navy."

"Brilliant," I said, opening my eyes. "You too," I told Neb before he could go insecure. "I say we go to Trust a Little Mode with Miss Agnes. And we read Captain Davis in as an underling, and give the evidence to him. *Normally* we'd keep it, and the glory," I added.

"Only this is too big and we're scared," Rain murmured, closing her eyes and leaning her head back to catch the morning sun on her face.

"And this is war," I said. "War changes everything."

Moments later, Neb looked up from Dirk's sketches. "You don't think Faye will tell Daddy we were at the club, do you?"

Fish rot. Of course she will.

I tapped on the truck's back windshield. Faye rolled her window down, and I stuck my head in smile-first. "Don't tell anybody we were at the Oceanside," I said.

"Why *wouldn't* I tell, Miss Spy Britches?"

"Because we know your secret. We'll trade silence for silence."

Faye hissed like an angry goose. "Deal." She rolled her window up.

"What's her secret?" Neb whispered as I settled back into the bed of the truck.

"We don't know," Rain said, her eyes still closed.

I tapped again. Faye rolled her window down. "Bathroom break, please."

"Stop breathing on me," she replied. "Can't you wait?"

"Bathroom break? You got it, shortcake," Reed said, leaning across her and giving me a smile. *He looks like he's back on course,* I thought. Maybe Faye said she'd marry him.

As Faye and Reed wandered into the dunes, I pulled Neb and Rain into a quick huddle by the sea. "Is everybody sure of our alibi?"

Rain yawned. "I do better with a picture, please."

We knelt in the sand and I mapped out our homes. "Rain, I told Mama I was spending the night at your house," I said, drawing an arrow from my house to hers. "And Neb said he was spending the night at my house," I said, and I drew an arrow from his house to mine. I smiled at Rain. "And *you* told Miss Jonah you were sleeping over at Neb's. Right?"

"Almost," she said, and my bladder screamed. "I don't lie to Mama Jonah. My father wouldn't like it. I told her I was spending the night with you and Neb. Not a lie, because here we are."

Fact: Rain feels her father's wishes clear as I feel Papa's. I sense Papa's wishes from knowing him every heartbeat of my life. Rain knows her father's through Miss Jonah, and from the secret place that sings art to her.

"Excellent," I said. "The point is, nobody expects us home yet. Keep a low profile. We'll ask Reed to let us off at HQ," I finished, and we ran into the dunes for a bathroom break.

"Headquarters," Neb said as the truck pulled away again. "Genius move."

Reed's brakes squealed as he stopped at the lighthouse. Captain Davis walked toward us. "Morning," he said with a tired smile. "Your folks are looking for you."

"Which folks?" Neb asked. He gives off a certain odor when scared. "Looking for who, exactly?"

"All of you," he said. "Agnes is trying to soothe them."

Miss Agnes? My scientific poise exploded into a confetti of anxiety.

"Faye," Davis said, "I'm surprised at you, taking these kids out like this."

"I *didn't*. I'm bringing them back," she said. "Not that it's any of *your* beeswax."

"Everything on this island is my beeswax," he said. He tapped on the truck's roof and Reed ground the clutch and lurched toward home.

"Trapped like a *mus*," Neb said. He'd gone white as rice.

"*Mus* means mouse. You're trapped like a *rattus*." I waited to see if the Latin might soothe me. It didn't. "We need a new plan. Fast."

By the time we turned onto our sand street, we had one. "Plan A, we'll say we have urgent business with Davis, and get out as fast as we can. Plan B, we admit we were trailing Dirk, a spy. Plan C, we'll turn over the sketchbook to the parents but nothing else," I said as Neb turned its pages. "And we'll unload our other evidence on Captain Davis as soon as we can.

"This could turn out to be a positive development," I said, trying to think how. "This is a perfect opportunity to find out if Miss Agnes is *really* on our side."

Neb gasped as the truck rocked to a halt by the garden gate. "Holy Toledo," he said staring at the sketchbook. "This is code!"

Code? Now?

I ripped out the page. "Pocket this," I said, shoving it in his hand and stuffing the book in our bag. "Walk tall and do not worry. Our plan cannot fail."

Moments later, our plan failed.

"Sunrise!" Mama shrilled, stepping out on the porch. "Where on earth have you been?"

We froze. Schooner rolled his eyes up at me as Grand and Miss Agnes followed Mama out, Grand's face lined with worry, Miss Agnes's rooster hat glimmering. Mr. Mac trailed them, worn and tired as last year's stockings.

I went for a blanket pardon. "We're sorry," I said. "We didn't mean to worry you."

"You mean you didn't mean to get caught," Mama said, her voice like ice.

"That kind of goes hand in hand," Neb admitted, sliding his hands into his pockets. "How did you find out we . . ."

Miss Jonah stepped from the arbor at the end of the porch. "I dreamed about Rain's father. I looked for her at the lighthouse, then at Neb's, then here. Where *were* you?"

We wheeled and pointed at Reed. "With him."

"Miss Ada, I can explain," Reed said, sounding like someone was trying to strangle him with his own vocal cords. "The kids, uh, snuggled in with Schooner. Then a U-boat torpedoed a ship and I ran to help and now we're home."

An impressive summary, highlighting only positives.

"Neb, why?" Mr. Mac demanded. "Your mother is worried sick."

"Neb was a hero in this," I said. Fact: Mama will ground me from here to kingdom come, but Neb's daddy punishes hard. Rain mostly gets off free.

I unleashed Plan A. "Sorry, but we have a meeting with Captain Davis. We'll fill you in on the *unclassified* details once we return." We turned neatly and headed down the walk.

"Halt," Miss Jonah said. "On the porch. Now. Please."

"We're carrion," Neb muttered as we trudged up the steps.

I looked at Mama. The disappointment in her beautiful eyes sank my heart to the floor and stood on it with both feet. Still I pushed on: Plan B. "Dirk is a spy and we can prove it. Miss Agnes? Care to share what you know?" I settled my gaze on her.

All right, Aggie. Back us up. You know who Dirk is.

"Dirk? A spy?" Miss Agnes said, adjusting her frills. "Hard to imagine."

Traitor! From the Latin tradere, *meaning* to hand over.

We rolled smoothly into Plan C. Rain opened our bag, pulled out Dirk's sketchbook, and placed the bag on the floor. "Evidence from the Oceanside. Dirk's sketches of the lighthouse," she began, showing it the way Miss Pope shows a picture book. As she turned the page, I slid our evidence bag behind me with my foot. "The water tower," she said, and Neb scooted the bag into the vines overhanging the porch. "Dirk lacks genius. The shadows are off. Sad," she said.

She turned the page and Grand leaned in, his blue suspenders gleaming. "You don't wear suspenders," I said.

"I do now," he replied, and Miss Agnes smiled. "That's Norfolk's Naval Yard," he said.

"And the Hatteras Ferry," Mr. Mac said, frowning.

Faye stepped closer. "And the Coast Guard Station."

My stomach dropped. *This is better evidence than we'd realized.* "Sketches of potential targets," I said as a hawk landed in the apple tree, scattering my chickens.

"Potential targets, my left hoof," Miss Agnes said. "These are sketches for paintings. Give me that book. If Dirk really *were* a dangerous spy, you could have been killed."

Rain clasped the sketchbook to her chest now and backed away. Miss Agnes patted her skirt pocket. "Where's the photograph of you three? I'm sure your parents will want to see it."

Rain forked over the sketchbook.

"I hope your photo doesn't show any background clutter,"

I said. Like a shortwave radio, I thought. She raised her eyebrows, and then she raised the stakes.

"Titus," she said to Grand, "won't you come by for pie this evening?"

Grand went pink and nodded. She's calling my bluff, I thought. She'll have everything in that house normal as dust before he gets there.

"Neb, your mother's waiting," Mr. Mac said. "Break me a switch."

"Yes sir." Neb plodded to our fig tree and broke a three-foot shoot. Mr. Mac switches Neb until he cries, and he's too stubborn to cry fast—even though I told him a hundred times.

Mr. Mac held the switch toward Mama. "Ada? Children need consequences."

"I prefer other consequences." She looked at me. "Two weeks labor in the victory garden. *Minimum.*"

Clearly stress had clouded her mind. "We don't have a victory garden," I said, very gentle.

"We will when you're finished. Make it twice the size of last year's garden. Include my herbs. And fence it in. Your chickens pecked my cantaloupes to death last year."

"What time does Stick start?" Miss Jonah asked.

"Seven o'clock every morning until it's done, with Sundays off for church," Mama said as Neb and Mr. Mac walked away.

"You too, Rain," Miss Jonah said. "Seven o'clock Monday. Here." She strolled off.

Rain scooped up our evidence bag, now minus the sketch pad, and ran to catch up, our bag bouncing against her hip.

The sun rose over our weedy little garden plot. My rooster crowed. "That went well," I said. "According to my research, the last frost date for our area is April tenth. I'd say we should wait at least until then to—"

"You'll start tomorrow morning. Go set the table for breakfast," Mama said.

"Yes ma'am." I watched Neb slow his step to match his dad's. Mr. Mac dropped his switch. "Mama, how much time does Mr. Mac have?"

"Ask the angels," she said, her voice tired. "Reed and Faye, I want to talk to you."

"Titus," Miss Agnes said, very royal. "I need to check on Edgar. Despite Stick's folly, it's been a pleasure."

"Thank you for the suspenders, my dear," he said. "They're dandy."

As she steamed toward the gate, the hawk launched itself from the apple tree, folded its wings, and dove like a heat-seeking missile. At the last moment it spread its wings and thrust its razor-sharp talons forward.

Thwack!

The hawk flapped away, the rooster hat clutched in its claws.

Miss Agnes patted her hair into place, and marched on without looking back.

"Never much liked that hat anyway," Grand said, and we headed inside to breakfast.

CHAPTER 20

NO ESCAPE

April weather is like Faye—freakishly temperamental. Rain and me started out in jackets on Monday, and ended up in short sleeves before noon. "We're getting blisters from chopping wire grass," I said when we came in at noon to eat. "We'd better quit for today."

Mama smeared aloe on our hands and plucked two pairs of work gloves from a drawer.

"Like *Dime Novel #81: No Escape*," Rain said, nudging her curls from her face.

All afternoon we chopped weeds. "Think we'll ever finish?" Rain asked, stretching.

I looked at the little bit we'd done, and the so much to go. "When we're old women, maybe. Where did you hide our evidence?"

"I snuck out while Mama Jonah slept," she said, "and buried it at the turn-off to our place. I don't like to sneak on Mama Jonah. And I don't like to hold on to that evidence."

"Me neither," I said. "We'll get it to Davis pronto." But pronto was slow in coming.

After two days, we'd raked the garden plot neat. "Mama, we're going to HQ," I said. "Captain Davis is practically expecting us."

"No ma'am, you certainly are not," she replied. "You know where the compost is. Take your time turning it in. Use the well-aged chicken manure for the corn. Don't inhale the dust."

Trapped.

We planted corn the old way to satisfy Grand: "Space the hills thirty-four inches apart. Four kernels per hill," he said. "One for the earth, one for the crow; one to thin and one to grow."

"That's not science," Faye teased, strolling by. "That's poppycock."

"It's generations of observation, and observation is the first step in scientific experimentation," I said. "Where are *you* going?"

"Make-up ball game," she said, flouncing away. "Too bad *you* two can't make it. We haven't seen Carl and Ralph since the Oceanside Club, so Reed figures we have a chance today."

"If you see Captain Davis, ask him to stop by," I shouted after her.

He didn't. But Julia did, a sun hat shading her pretty face. "Hello there," she said, stopping by the garden fence. "Don't suppose you've seen Agnes's cat? He's gone missing."

"Missing?" Rain gasped. "Edgar's not cut out for the wild."

She nodded, taking in Rain's neat garden layout. "Lovely design."

"Thank you. We're planting everything that will grow," Rain said. "Collards, tomatoes, beans, okra, cabbages. Miss Ada's herbs. Grand's corn. Beets for Mama Jonah."

Life Novel Rule #32. *Interrogate when it seems natural.*

"Mama likes cantaloupes," I said. "We could plant something for you and Dirk if you're staying that long. Are you? We can plant something for Mr. Green too, even though he seems carnivorous. Who is he, anyway? What's he doing here?"

Julia's face went cool. "He's a business associate."

"I noticed you stayed away from him. That seems smart." I shrugged. "Thanks for helping me at the Oceanside the other night. It was a close call," I said, picking up my hoe.

"Speaking of the club," she said, very easy, "I believe you took some things of Dirk's. Get them and I'll return them for you."

"I saw a list of names, but I lost track of it in the club. Miss Agnes took the sketchbook. She might share."

Julia looked at me like she could read my soul. "Dirk's not as sweet as he used to be. I don't want him coming here looking for the things that belong to him."

Dirk? Here? A chill walked my spine.

"If you change your mind, you know where I am," she said. "Well, I need to stop by Aggie's. Her heart's broken without Edgar." She popped her sun hat on Rain's head. "I hope we can paint together again one day, Rain," she said, and strolled away.

"If you see Captain Davis, tell him to drop by," I called after her.

"She won't," Rain said, adjusting the brim of her new hat.

"We have to act, Stick, before Dirk comes around and that evidence takes us down."

Dirk. Here.

For the rest of the day, Rain and me jumped at every shadow, every rustle, nervous as two tambourines on a rattletrap tailgate. Everybody who walked past looked like Dirk until they didn't. Every voice sounded like his until it wasn't.

By day's end, we'd frayed our own nerves. "I'm calling an Emergency Midnight Meeting tonight, with Davis, at HQ," I said. "Can you get word to Neb?"

"I'll try. I can run by his place on my way home, but I can't stay long. Mama Jonah will be looking for me," Rain said. "I'm under house arrest, same as you."

That night, as Faye snored like a living gargoyle (See Volume G), I sprang from my windowsill and slid down the Emergency Exit Oak. Rain and Neb were waiting at HQ. So was Captain Davis. "Sorry I'm late—Faye kept snorting herself awake," I said, taking my seat.

Captain Davis finished lighting the candles. He wore chinos, bedroom slippers, and a pale blue pajama top buttoned wrong. "This better be good, Dimes," he said. "A guy like me needs his beauty sleep."

"It *is* good—for you," I said as Rain opened our bag. "You're the first military man to be offered an assignment by the Dime Novel Kids. Your mission? To make sure our evidence ends up in the right hands. Do you accept?"

"You'd be an underling," Neb warned.

"Story of my life," Davis replied. "Agnes mentioned you finding a sketchbook."

Neb frowned. "You're in cahoots with Miss Agnes?"

"I'm in cahoots with myself, the U.S. Navy, and apparently you," he said. "What's up?"

"We believe the sketchbook Miss Agnes took from us holds Dirk's drawings of potential targets. Dirk works with a dangerous Mr. Green," I said, leaning forward. "He's big."

"Even Julia's afraid of him," Rain added.

Neb nodded. "Dirk and Green are Nazi spies, and we have proof."

"*Nazi spies?*" Davis said, his eyebrows rising as Rain pulled Dirk's passport from the bag and placed it on Davis's desk.

"Dirk's German bona fides." She reached into the sack again. "A bundle of cash and a list of men's names, probably from Mr. Green—possibly fellow spies."

I took the bag and ran my hand along the inside. I thought I'd picked up something else at the club, but the bag was empty. "Neb?" I said.

"We also have this code from the sketchbook," Neb said, rising. "It was a booger to decipher."

Captain Davis sat up straight. "Code?"

"May I introduce Neb, head of our Internal Decoding Department," I said.

Neb gave Davis a modest smile. "It's a one-to-one code, easy to decipher once you catch on. It says *operation thunderstruck torch boot-toe elbow clock tba.*"

Davis sat up, all signs of sleepiness erased. *"Operation thunderstruck torch boot-toe elbow clock tba,"* he said. "Mysterious. Thanks, Dimes. I'll take it from here," he said, reaching for the passport and cash.

I clamped my hand on his. "One moment. We want information in return."

He leaned back, his chair squeaking. "What kind of information?"

"Who is Miss Agnes? Who is Julia? Julia seems nice. She makes mistakes but apologizes from the heart." I paused. "But she too has bogus identification papers."

"Who can we trust?" Rain asked, her voice soft. "It's hard, not knowing."

Davis raked his fingers through his tousled hair. "Agnes I trust, but I honestly can't tell you why. Julia is an enigma to me—a complete mystery. I'll keep an eye on her. Dirk I wouldn't trust with a pile of toenail clippings. Anything else you can tell me about this Mr. Green?"

"He looks like Dracula in a green suit, but with regular teeth," Neb said.

"Green and Dirk were huddled over a map at the Oceanside," I said. "Dirk went total bootlicker, he was cozying up so hard. And he said, *everything is there.* Mr. Green handed him a fat envelope." I hesitated. "That may not be cause and effect," I added. "But it all happened."

"He escaped in a red 1940 Ford Deluxe, license number NY 7954," Rain added.

Davis scribbled the number down. "I'll radio this number in

tonight and drive your other evidence to Norfolk in the morning. If you're right about Dirk, my guess is my higher-ups will want to leave him in place until he makes a move. I'll let Julia and Dirk know you and your families are under my protection. By the way, Dirk and Ralph have buddied up. Any thoughts?"

"No, but I like knowing you're paying attention," Rain said.

Captain Davis is curious about the Ringers too, I thought. Same as Miss Agnes. "We don't want our information shared with Miss Agnes," I added. "Not yet."

"I'll do what I can."

"And if you locate Green, we'd like to know." I glanced at Rain, who dipped her head toward the door. "Give Rain and me time to slip into the moonlight before you blow out these candles. Many spy-catchers are afraid of the dark."

The next day, we finally caught a break. "Mama," I said, "Neb's here. Can I go to the post office with him? Papa's postcard is *so* late. Maybe Miss Agnes overlooked it."

The light left her eyes—a sure sign of worry. "One hour off for good behavior. Not a moment more."

We dropped our hoes and ran.

"What do you think of Post Office Special Ops?" Neb asked as we approached the PO.

"I don't know," I admitted. "But Miss Agnes still has that photo. I say we play along. Trust a little."

Neb nodded. "I have something to show you two, after this," he said.

Miss Agnes glanced up from her work as we thundered through the door. "Good," she said. "You've brought your report. And before you ask, no postcards. I'm sorry."

No postcard—and I totally forgot her stupid report.

"Here's our report, in triplicate," Neb said. Incredibly, he pulled it from his pocket:

REPORT FROM THE DIMES. We went to the Oceanside Club and put on disguises. Dirk met with Mr. Green, who ran away during the U-boat attack. We only got a sketchbook and you took that. We hope Edgar comes home. Maybe he has found a girlfriend.

Yours truly, Neb and the Dimes

"Nicely done, Bristly Dime," she said.

"Sorry about your rooster hat," I lied, lifting a clump of feathers to her counter. "The hawk left this by the garden." I hesitated. "As head of the Post Office Special Ops, you *could* have backed us up the other day, on the porch," I said.

"As head of POSO, I can't tip my hand, Red Dime," she said, and nudged the hat carcass with her pen. "Turnabout's fair play, though," she said, and opened her briefcase. A mouse—*a mouse!*—scampered from behind it.

I breathed steady until my panic faded.

That's *how a mouse invaded HQ the day after the U-boat attack. It rode up our 257 steps with Miss Agnes!*

Miss Agnes's eyes went misty as she shooed the rodent

away. "Edgar used to bring his rodent catches into the PO and let them go. He made the place his own little game preserve. So cute. There's a reward for finding Edgar, you know." She slid a paper from her briefcase and cleared her throat. "Well. I've located Ralph Perdu's background. No small feat."

"Excellent," Rain murmured. "Edgar will be proud."

Miss Agnes read: Ralph Perdu. Nineteen years old. From Bayou, Louisiana, raised by German and French immigrant parents. Speaks German, French, and English. Sentenced to twelve years for attempted murder in 1937 and released in 1940.

She looked up. "And now he's here. Lucky us."

Neb whistled. *"Attempted murder?* Who did he try to kill?"

She folded the paper. "Someone who got on his nerves, I assume. Ralph Perdu's dangerous. Watch out for him, underlings. Anything to add before you go?"

"We hear Dirk's spending time with Ralph. That's bad news squared," I said.

"And we'll try to find Edgar," Neb promised.

"Thank you," she said. "Dismissed. Stick," she said when we reached the door. "I'm sorry your father's postcards have stopped coming. I know you're worried. Titus is too."

Grand's worried?

"Thank you," I said. I walked slowly across the porch, my head high, my heart beating like I was running a hundred miles an hour.

• • •

Neb walked with us back to the victory garden while I tried to calm my hammering heart. "Otto's been busy. He swiped Mr. Gray's prize fishing lures," he said, perching on the garden bench. "And the code from Miss Agnes's typewriter was easier to break than Dirk's code."

Rain and I sat beside him as he spread the carbon copy on his knee. "See, the *Y* on her typewriter's busted and can only make little *Y*s. But most of these lowercase letters are on purpose." He whipped a crumpled paper from his pocket. "When you eliminate the *little Y*s except one and write out the rest, you get: *any news on mr green rsvp.*"

A chill zipped across my shoulders. "*Mr. Green?* So Miss Agnes knew about him."

Mama stepped onto the back porch and gave us the *Back to Work* look.

Neb rose and hovered a moment, like a bee unwilling to fly. I tried to smile. "Don't worry about the postcards. Papa's okay," I said. "The mail's jammed up, that's all."

Papa's postcards stayed jammed up. As the days passed, Mama went pale. Still, she gave us occasional time off for good behavior. Twice we carried water to Miss Jonah's. Once we followed Julia to Miss Agnes's. And once, we walked past the Artists' Shack to find Dirk on the porch, holding a stick-broom, staring at its handle.

Knowing we were under Captain Davis's protection made me bold. "There's no instructions, if that's what you're looking for," I called to him. "The straw goes on the floor and the stick's a vertical lever. One hand creates thrust and the other's the fulcrum."

He glared at me, his catfish eyes cold. "Scram, kid. Or you'll be sorry you know me."

We scrammed. We planted, hoed, baby-talked seedlings. Like Mama, I wore a brave face as my hopes of postcards faded and my weather journal went garden-brained:

April 15, Finally! The USS Roper *sank our first U-boat, just off Bodie Island, to our north. No survivors. Dry winds from the west. The baby cabbages look limp.*

April 17, Winds from the south. Word is Julia and Dirk visited a new military base near Jacksonville, NC. No sign of Edgar. A storm pounded the collards flat.

Friday April 24, 70 degrees F. We're done! The garden's beautiful. Papa will love it.

They say God took seven days to create the world and everything in it. It took Rain and me three times as long to create a quarter-acre garden. But in fairness, God didn't have Mama nitpicking His every move. We leaned our hoes against the fence and bolted for dinner—and straight into trouble's arms.

"Shoes at the door," Mama called as we pounded up the steps. We kicked off our shoes and eased into the kitchen, blinking. "Mama, I'd like to plant a few peas for genetics experiments," I said. "Papa will love it and there's space, I just—"

"*Sarah*," Mama said, and I froze. *Sarah Stickley Lawson* means I'm in hot trouble. *Sarah* means cold trouble—the *be careful* variety. "Say hello to Miss Dandee," Mama said.

Otto's mom. She must have come to the front door, as trouble usually does.

"Hey Miss Dandee," Rain and me chorused. "How are you?"

"Better than you, I'm sure. *Mark* says you're being punished for grand theft."

Mama frowned. "Mark? Oh, Otto. They most certainly are not."

"By the by," Miss Dandee said as we washed our hands, "he asked me to tell you girls he'll drop in. He's lonely. His brother Tommy has shipped out to . . . Well, it's top secret. Even in his sleep, poor Mark holds on to the silver dollar Tommy gave him, the little love."

"That's sad," Rain said.

It *was* sad—Tommy tossing him a silver coin after Otto went to all the trouble of stealing him a nice watch. Miss Dandee shifted her purse. "Mark cooked dinner for us the other night. Can you imagine? He sliced *onions* with his bare hands. People surprise you."

"That is a surprise," I said. Fact: Manual labor repels Otto like sulfur repels snakes.

She looked at Rain. "I hear *you're* doing well at Sunday school," she said, like that would be a shock too.

"Sure she is," I told her. "Rain's the smartest kid in our class—ask Reverend Wilkins. She's a wiz on Bible stories and she knows the books of the Bible—*in order.*" Otto spouts books in random order, like a string of firecrackers going off. "I expect Rain and me will get baptized at revival this summer. Sprinkling's fine, but I hear dunking's a sure spiritual bet."

"There," Mama said, like my words proved her point. "Another excellent reason to invite Jonah to church."

Miss Jonah? Sitting inside a stuffy building? Is Mama delirious?

"Jonah's one of us," Mama continued, nodding me and Rain to the plate rack.

Miss Dandee sniffed. "We have too many foreigners on this island, if you ask me. Dirk, Julia, Jonah. Besides, Jonah's English is . . . lacking. I don't think she'd enjoy our church."

Rain frowned. "Her English is good if you talk to her."

"That's right," I said. "Besides, according to Universe Encyclopedia Volume J, Jesus didn't speak English. He probably spoke—"

"*Sarah*, don't forget the silverware," Mama interrupted.

Sarah again. I hurried the plates and silverware to the table, hoping to look well trained. I like to reflect well on Mama when I can.

"Ada, you miss my point. What do we know about Jonah, *really*?" Miss Dandee said, like Rain wasn't standing right there. "All we know is *somebody* put her on the beach and she gave birth to this . . . child," she said, flicking her glance over Rain.

Rain looked at her, shocked. "*God* put Mama Jonah on the beach. Your husband Reverend Wilkins says being saved from a shipwreck and tumbled ashore is impressive. Most people get born here or come on the ferry."

"Rain's right," Mama said. "We *could* ask the reverend for his thoughts."

Miss Dandee's mouth puckered like a drawstring purse. Reverend Wilkins likes Miss Jonah and Rain, and she knows it. He traded Miss Jonah a goat for a bucket of fish years ago, to get her milk business started. Now she keeps Mama stocked with goat milk for newborns and old people with delicate stomachs.

Reverend Wilkins believes in loving strangers until they're not strangers anymore.

Miss Dandee dropped her veil of kindness like a hand- ful of dirty handkerchiefs. "Don't twist my words, Ada. We welcome everybody to our church, even Sam and his family, and he's *Black*. We work together, pray together. We're all the same on the island."

"We're not all the same," Rain said. "Mr. Sam's children can't go to our school. He lives in a house *outside* the vil- lage because he and his family aren't welcome inside the village after dark. And everybody calls you *Miss* Dandee, but people call him Sam when he's old as you are."

I gasped. When did Rain get so bold? And I've been calling him *Sam* all my life!

"Well, I'm sure Sam wouldn't want it any other way," Miss Dandee snapped. "My point is, we welcome every *true-blue* American. I'm sorry. Jonah simply doesn't belong."

"How can she not belong in the only world she's got?" I demanded.

Miss Dandee ignored me. "Not to *mention* the fact that we don't know the first thing about the child's father."

"The *child's* name is Rain," Mama said, her voice going a dangerous shade of polite. "She's standing right here. And we know quite a bit about her father. We know he was an honorable man. Smart, talented, capable—"

"Don't be ridiculous," Miss Dandee said. "How would you know that?"

"Who else would a woman like Jonah marry?" Mama asked. "Besides, the proof is standing before your eyes," she said, touching Rain's shoulder. Rain stood taller.

"Stick," Mama said, "please get the door for Miss Dandee."

Miss Dandee rose like a fury as I darted for the door. Halfway there, she turned to Rain. "I hear your mother *borrowed* my pearl necklace. Return it. The very idea."

"She didn't borrow it unless you lent it," I said. "Ask Otto where it is."

Someone stomped across the porch and we jumped. Scrape's father stood in the doorway, his hat in his rough hands. "Miss Ada," he said. "Come quick. It's my boy, Clarence."

"Scrape?" Rain said.

"Somebody's poisoned him. I think he's dying."

CHAPTER 21

POISON'S PERFUME

Scrape's father bolted to his shove-boat as Miss Dandee stormed across the yard. Mama looked at me. "You two eat your dinner, and find Jonah. Bring her here if she'll come and if she won't, stay with her. Where's Faye?"

"At the store," I said. "Why is Miss Dandee acting so mean? What's *happened*?"

"I'll send Faye to help you and be home when I can." She grabbed her blue-green medicine satchel. "We'll talk then. Do what I say."

Faye caught up with us near Rain's. "Mama told me about Scrape," she panted. She leaned over, clutching her side. "Jeez. Who names a kid Scrape?"

Rain looked at her. "Mama Jonah didn't poison Scrape."

"Of course not," Faye said, shocked.

"Miss Dandee will say she did," Rain said. Soon as the words hit the air, I knew they were true. "She's already lying about us. And Stick, I'm not getting baptized with you. Mama Jonah can't stand for me to go underwater. You have to go to heaven by yourself."

"Stop it," Faye said. "We're all going to heaven if I have to drive us there myself. Hurry, you two. I want to get this settled."

We found Miss Jonah sewing, the line of her chair stark

against the curve of the dunes. "Please sit," she said, nodding to her driftwood furniture. "We'll have a storm tonight."

"I concur. Barometric pressure must be falling like a drunk gull," I said, and she laughed. She gets my humor, same as Papa.

"Miss Jonah, Mama says please stay at our house tonight," Faye said.

Miss Jonah smiled. "No thank you. We're fine here."

"Come to breakfast, then," Faye said. "You and Rain. We'll all go church." She went blunt. "Miss Jonah, you have to. People think someone's helping the U-boats sink our ships, and there's rumors of spies up and down the coast."

Like Dirk, I thought.

"You're the only one living out here," Faye went on. "You keep a fire while the rest of us black out our windows. Mama wants people to see you in church—like the rest of us island-ers. *Please.* She says it's important."

Miss Jonah dropped her sewing. "You think I'm a *spy?*"

"Of course not, but Miss Dandee and her boy Otto do, and you know how they are," Faye said, and changed tack. "Miss Jonah, did you sell Scrape's daddy some fish?"

"No. Otto bought four nice grouper a few days ago, but that's all the fish I've sold. What's wrong?"

Four grouper to Otto, who cooked for his parents. Four big fish for three people.

"Scrape's sick and people are looking for somebody to blame," Faye said, and Miss Jonah looked suddenly tired in a way sleep can't fix. She rose and walked to the sea.

"I don't think she understands," Faye said, watching her.

"Of course she understands," I said. "She's shipwrecked, not stupid."

Miss Jonah stood, staring at the waves like they might talk to her.

"Her heart's exploding," Rain said, her voice sad. "But explosions end. We'll be there tomorrow—for breakfast and for church. I promise."

Faye returned to Miss Jonah and Rain's near dark, as the sky mumbled and lightning outlined distant clouds. Miss Jonah had welcomed me to spend the night.

Fact: Miss Jonah treats me like I'm hers, same as Mama treats Rain.

"Scrape's worse," Faye said. "His fever's so high, he's seeing stars. His stomach's sick, his heart wobbles. Mama wrapped him in collard leaves to break the fever—like *that* will help."

"It *will* help," I interrupted. "Collard leaves are huge and thick, and hold their weight in water. They're natural cold compresses."

"You don't believe that."

"I'm a scientist," I said. "I believe everything that's true."

"You're bananas. Listen, kiddos. I told people Miss Jonah didn't give Scrape the fish that made him sick, but Otto swears she did. Miss Dandee's stirring people up, and Mama's afraid they'll come here. Reed and I will stand watch in the dunes. If we see them, I'll call out and you three run to the lighthouse and block the door. I don't think you'll need to, but it's better to have a plan you don't need than to need a plan you don't have. Strategy, kiddo. You taught me that."

She was actually listening?

"Right," I said, but fear whirled inside me like a tornado of razors. "Did you say his *heart* wobbles? Did somebody put a sauce on that fish? Did it smell a little like almonds?"

"I think so. Why?"

"Tell Mama somebody stole my white acne ointment. It's important."

"You're worried about acne? *Now?*" She squinted at my nose. "Where?"

"*Tell her,*" I said. "Run. Scrape's father is right: He's been poisoned."

Rain gasped. "As in *Dime Novel #87: Poison's Perfume,*" she said.

While Scrape fought for his life, Rain and me dressed the fish from Miss Jonah's pail, and she fried them in her cast iron spider. After supper, we strung up a tarp to hide her fire from the sea, and spread our scraps in the dunes for the cats and raccoons to eat.

I stopped outside Rain's door, every sense focused. Rain frowned at me. "Faye's never been in here and she's curious," I explained. "I'm soaking in details for her."

"No. You're listening for trouble," she said.

Rain knows me like sea knows salt.

Inside, I took in the art—Rain's firecracker dance of colors. Miss Jonah's delicate needlepoint. "Let's play school," Rain said, lighting a candle. We sat on her crinkly straw mattress and her kitten curled in her lap, purring, while the handsome jigsaw portrait of her father looked down. "I'm Miss Pope. Spell *house*."

I detest spelling. "*H-O-U-S-E*, house," I said as the kitten hopped down.

Outside, Miss Jonah stirred her fire, sending up an ember shower. People *could* see it as a signal to U-boats, I thought. But she's kept a fire long as she's been here. Everybody knows that—only nobody knows who to trust anymore, nobody knows who's safe.

Fact: The war's wearing us down. Fear seeps through us like cold through thin.

"I hope Miss Jonah sleeps inside tonight," I said, very tactful.

"She will. She'll leave the door open to catch a breath of stars."

After a while, Rain and me went out to help smother the fire, and to brush our teeth with sassafras sticks. We squatted together and watered the dunes, and scurried back in. We crawled into bed—her head at one end of her mattress, mine at the other, and drifted toward sleep.

A half hour later, Miss Jonah spread her mattress and lay with her head at the door, watching the storm clouds gobble the stars.

• • •

Miss Jonah's scream shredded the night.

Rain scrambled up and flew to her mother. "Mama, Mama, shhh, shhh," Rain said, folding herself against her mother and trapping her arms. "It's Baby Rain, Baby Rain. Shhh, shhhhh."

Miss Jonah sobbed and went silent, her and Rain rocking like they were both mothers, both babies. Odd words from a forgotten world fluttered by like a scatter of lost leaves. Then a mumble of English: "Ship rolls, angels call. Strong hands push me through." And she fell asleep again, breathing soft as a newborn.

Rain and me slipped out and sat on her whalebone sofa. Rain pulled her knees to her chin, tense as Neb's spinning top just before he slings it across the floor.

When you're scared, do something you know you can do.

"Play school again?" I said. "Twelve times seventeen," I said, like Miss Pope. Fact: Sometimes I think God pegged the universe together with numbers.

"Twelve times seventeen makes two aught four," Rain whispered. She scratched the numbers in the sand and circled the answer. "Two hundred four."

"Very good," I said as the ocean's waves drum-rolled down the beach. I took a chance: "Whose strong hands?" I asked.

"My father's," she said. "Mama Jonah dreams them most nights now."

Miss Jonah's dreams tax Rain and excite her at the same time. I see it in her eyes.

"Miss Dandee's lying about Mama Jonah," she said.

"She's a wicked old busybody," I said, slipping my arm around her shoulders. Rain walks big along the edge of our world. Sometimes I forget she's only ten. "Miss Dandee's a liar, same as Otto. People know that."

"I'll draw my father's hands soon," Rain said, going stronger. "Maybe even his face." She leaned down and traced her foot in the sand. "I have my father's feet," she said like she'd never said it before. "I know how to stand in the world."

"You do," is all I said. We sat together easy and familiar as the roar of the waves against the beach.

Lightning flashed closer. "Lightning melts sand into glass," I added. Then, very casual: "I'd hate to see what it would do to us."

As we ran for Rain's door, I waved to the dunes on the off chance Faye might see. From deep in the dark some kind of mutant monkey-bird screeched back.

Rain gasped. "What was that?"

The monkey-bird screeched again and my heart melted. "It's Faye, trying to blend into nature."

"Weird," she whispered.

Still, I thought, Faye really *is* watching over us, just like she said she would.

Next morning, Faye knocked against the side of Rain's house. "Scrape's up. I told Mama what you said, and she shouted *Of course!* and told his mother to steam him a peck of oysters."

"Brilliant. Oysters are full of zinc, a natural antidote for arsenic—an ingredient in Mama's ointment. If the oysters cured Scrape, somebody poisoned him. Maybe Otto."

"Otto? But Scrape's his *friend*."

"Otto doesn't have friends," I said. "He has followers."

"Come inside, monkey-bird," Rain invited from the doorway.

"*Monkey-bird?*" Faye whispered. "Rain's so weird." But I could tell it pleased her to be invited into Rain's home at last. She stepped in, looked around, and gasped. "It's like the set of an A-list movie. Striking and beautiful and . . . totally abnormal in the keenest possible way."

"A movie?" I looked at Rain. "She means that as a compliment."

But Rain was studying Faye like Neb studies a code. "Some days I'd like a movie-star plot for my life, where Mama Jonah remembers and my father lives in our box-shaped house. But then I'd be a different girl."

Faye gave Rain's home one last peep. "I love the girl you are," she said, and Rain smiled. "Listen kiddos, I've got to wash my hair. Come to breakfast. *All three of you*. It matters."

An hour later, as Faye brutalized a dozen eggs, Rain and I set a table on the porch. Mama's keeping Miss Jonah outside as long as she can, I thought. Mama called on me to say grace. "Thank you for food and friends. Watch over us and keep Papa safe. Amen."

As we washed dishes, disaster: I knocked Miss Agnes's playing cards into the dishwater.

"Stick," Mama said as we fished them out, "run and get Miss Jonah's shawl from her house. We'll meet you at church."

Two side-cramps later, I tore around Rain's Dune to find Carl and Ralph at the edge of the sea, Ralph with his pants legs rolled up, bowlegged and prissy as he picked his way across the shells. "I don't see why Yaeger cares about this danged lighthouse," he said, stepping into ankle-deep water and dancing back. "What the heck?"

"It's oil, from the sunken tankers," I said. "Who's Yaeger?"

Carl found his smile first. "A friend. Where are you off to this morning?"

"Rain's place. Her mother needs her shawl, for church." I glanced at Ralph's oily feet. "Kerosene will take that off. Grand's at the store. He's officially closed but tell him I sent you."

"Thanks," Ralph said. "Why are you out here all alone?"

"Why *wouldn't* I be out here all alone? It's *my* island."

I heard Mama's voice in my mind: *Make visitors feel welcome.* "Thanks for helping us at the club, Carl." I hesitated, trying to drum up chitchat. "You smell good."

He grinned. "It's aftershave—Old Spice, from Norfolk. And you're welcome. Is your whole family going to church, or what?"

"You mean is *Faye* going," I said. "She is. She rolled her hair, which is naturally flat as a board. Reed only goes on Easter. You can walk me in if you want."

"Don't mind if I do. Ralph, care to join us?"

"I'm not much of a choir boy, cuz. You go ahead. I'm going to Dirk's." Ralph winked at me the way a lizard winks at a fly. He sloped away whistling an old Sunday school song—"This Little Light of Mine."

"As a scientist, I assure you it's hard to quantify creepy," I said. "But if creepy was cash, Ralph would be loaded. Miss Agnes says he did time for attempted murder."

Carl looked at me like I'd bit him. "How would she know?"

"She's postal," I explained.

He shrugged. "Ralph made a mistake and did his time. I hope people won't make things hard for him. His mother and mine are sisters, and tight as a pair of new shoes."

I glanced at Rain's place. "What time is it?"

Carl's gold wristwatch lay face-down on his arm. "Oops. Got dressed in the dark," he mumbled, and flipped it face-up. "Ten thirty."

"*Rot*. I hope you're in good shape, because we have to run."

Carl turned out to be in *excellent* shape. We snagged the shawl and sprinted to the church with minutes to spare. "Your church is beautiful," he said. "What are those?" he asked, nodding to the pile of stones by the door.

"Ballast stones from old ships. The reverend makes us kids paint them to work off sins. Neb, Rain, and me whitewashed most of them. Otto gets off free."

Stern-faced Mr. Aikens nodded us through the open door and I scanned the room. Miss Agnes and Julia perched up front. Miss Dandee is going to sling a fit with two "foreigners" in the house, I thought as Rain waved from the back pew.

I handed Miss Jonah her shawl and tugged Carl to Mama and Faye. "Mama," I whispered, "this is Carl Miller, who saved my life during a recent practically fatal U-boat attack. I invited him for Sunday dinner. Carl, my mother Ada Lawson, healer and person of standing."

Mama blinked fast and tried to smile.

"How do you do, Mrs. Lawson," Carl said, and then smiled at Faye. "Hello, Faye."

"Well, Carl Miller," Faye said, giving him the thirty-degree tilt. "What a surprise."

Only, I thought, it wasn't a surprise at all.

Miss Jonah bolted at the end of the service, Mama and Rain at her side. Faye and me strolled out with Carl.

"Why is that Jonah woman in my church?" Mr. Tyson snapped.

Rain looked back over her shoulder. "This isn't *your* church," I said to him, my temper walking up the back of my neck. "God welcomes all his children."

Rain gave me a nod. We walked on, Mr. Tyson's cold stare boring into my back.

The oaks along the sandy street laced their fingers over-head to create a shady tunnel. "Hope you're hungry, Carl," Faye said. "Reverend Wilkins went on a little long today. He's still wound up about one of our ships sinking a U-boat. His son's in the navy."

"Which U-boat?" Carl asked, his voice off-key.

"The *Roper* sank the U-85," I said. "Back in April, while I was doing hard time in the garden. None of the German sailors survived. Captain Davis took the bodies up to Norfolk. Word is some of the Germans wore street clothes and carried U.S. dollars. I have my sources," I added, very mysterious.

"Let me guess. Neb told you," Faye said, and Carl laughed.

"The U-85. I guess I heard that. Your hair looks nice, Faye," he said, and winked at me.

Faye swung her curls. "Natural curls are hard to tame, but I try."

Seeing my home through Carl's eyes warmed me to my core—the Emergency Exit Oak bowing low along the front walk, our neat garden, Mama's cannas standing like a scarlet choir around the outhouse. My chickens clucked beneath the fig tree while our skiff nosed the shore. "Paradise," Carl said as Rain scampered out to meet us.

"Mama Jonah's been inside enough for one day," she told me as her mom sailed toward us. "We're heading home. Stick, I spread your playing cards on the windowsill to dry."

Then came surprise number one in an afternoon of three surprises.

Carl held out his hand. "Miss Jonah, I'm Carl Miller. My

little brother would give a red yo-yo and two salamanders to live in a house like yours."

She smiled and shook his hand the way she'd shaken Julia's, on the beach. "A pleasure," she said, and strolled away. That handshake is definitely a First Life skill, I thought.

Surprise number two: Carl trailed Mama into the kitchen. "I miss my mother's kitchen, Mrs. Lawson. I'm your man for anything that doesn't require talent or skill."

Mama's chill melted like ice cream in July. "Spoon up the sweet pickles, then."

When we settled around the table and bowed our heads, Carl bowed his too. But he watched Faye from beneath his lashes as Grand prayed, and I had a feeling he prayed for more than baked chicken and oyster stuffing.

The third surprise came as Mama rose to cut the custard pie.

"Anybody home?"

"Reed!" Faye's eyes glazed over—a sure sign of brain stall.

Reed strolled in as I hopped up to help Mama. "Reed, you remember Carl Miller," I said.

"Nothing wrong with my memory, shortcake." He pulled up a chair by Faye's.

"I invited him for Sunday dinner. He went to Norfolk the other day," I said, placing the first slice of pie at Carl's place, and the second at Reed's. "He's wearing the latest aftershave."

"How are things in Norfolk?" Grand asked, leaning toward him.

"Hopping, sir," Carl said, relaxing. "The base is growing

gangbusters. They probably have twenty-five thousand men stationed there—and that's not counting the sailors on the ships."

"Good target for U-boats, I imagine," Grand said as I gave him a piece of pie.

Carl shook his head. "Bay's so full of mines, they look like jellyfish at low tide. At high tide, our boys turn the mines off so ships can pass. You have to stay in the channel, though. The *E.H. Blum* strayed off course, exploded, and sank"—he snapped his fingers—"just like that."

My heart went faint. What if Papa's ship drifted in Savannah? Or Charleston?

Grand listened, calm as the blink before dawn. He's smart, I thought. He knows how the world works. *He* can answer a question simmering inside me—but later, in private.

"The old forts have rearmed too," Carl continued. "It's a suicide mission for a U-boat."

"Suicide's just right for some scutters," Reed said. "How'd you wind up being a Ringer, Carl? Me, I play for my home team or I don't play. Not a traitor's bone in my body. Fact is, some people don't think you came here to play baseball at all."

He's been talking to Miss Agnes, I thought. She trusts the Ringers far as she can pitch them.

Carl let Reed's insult roll over him like a wave over a porpoise. "Baseball brought me here, but other things call me back," he said, smiling at Faye. "I love this place. Anyway, baseball's just a game, Reed. I don't care which side I'm on, as long as I get to play."

Later, I'd think that was an odd thing to say. At the time, I let the taste of Mama's pie dizzy its way through me, and wondered how Faye would handle two boyfriends sitting at the same table.

That night, I slipped down the hall and knocked at Grand's door. "Come in," he called.

I took in Grand's room—the mahogany furniture, the photos of Grandmother, the photo of his buddies from World War I, him standing with his friends, baby-faced and eager.

"I'm too old to dillydally," he said, his eyes smiling.

"I've done something wrong and I don't know how to fix it," I said, perching on a chair. "Normally I'd ask Mama, but she's stretched thin lately, with Papa gone."

"You've hooked me," he said, grinning Papa's grin.

"It's Sam Ellis, who pilots the mail boat. I've always called him Sam. Just plain Sam. I never even thought about calling him *Mr.* Sam, even though he has children old as I am. And even though I say *Miss* Dandee. And I don't even like her."

Grand nodded. "Dandee is a pill. So?"

"So, it's not right. I didn't even realize I was doing it until Rain said it out loud. I don't know why I didn't see it for myself, the way I call him just Sam."

"You didn't see it because you didn't know there was anything to look at," he said, leaning back in his chair and hooking his thumbs in his suspenders. "Prejudice is a snake. It can lie by your foot forever without you seeing it, but once you see it, you can't take your eyes off it. You didn't see it because we *all* call him Sam."

"All the *white* people do, which is my point. Now that I know I'm wrong, do I start calling him Mr. Sam, or apologize, or keep calling him Sam since we're used to it or . . . what?"

Grand studied me a second. "What would you do if he was white?"

"I don't know. I guess I'd apologize and ask what he'd like."

"There you go," he said. "But ask him in private, and respect his answer. Sam Ellis is a smart man. He owns his house, and holds down a job a lot of white men wouldn't mind having. Some folks think he's risen high enough. He may not want you to call him Mr. Sam. It only takes a feather to tip a scale, and it only takes a feather to put a target on a man's back."

Or a woman's, I thought, thinking of Miss Dandee's ugly rumors about Miss Jonah.

"Thanks. I'll ask him next time I see him. By the way, I hate your new suspenders," I added, very tactful. "They seem . . . wrong."

"You hate them because Agnes gave them to me. Let it go, Stick. I have plenty of love for both of you."

The words rushed from me like water over a busted dam. "Grand, I know her house looked right to you and I know she's sweet when you're around. Only—"

He laughed. "Agnes is rarely sweet. I like that about her. Everybody has secrets, Stick. People learn each other by finding out what those secrets are."

"What do you think Carl Miller's secrets are?"

"Carl? I'm not sure yet," he admitted. "War's brought an odd mix to the island. But I know this: I like Carl Miller. That Dirk that hangs around Agnes's house? I wouldn't give him credit on a can of pork and beans." He yawned and I headed for the door.

"Stick," he said, turning me around. "I admire a person who acts on what she learns about herself. Your papa does too." *Papa.* My eyes flooded and Grand crossed to me in two quick steps. He wrapped me in a hug tight and strong as cable around a spool.

"It's okay. Stick, I miss him too," he said, rocking me side to side as I cried. He wiped my tears with the sides of his thumbs, and I hugged him again.

"I still hate the suspenders," I said, and closed the door behind me.

The next morning, my words tumbled out before Sam's foot hit the dock. When I rambled to a halt, he gave me a quick nod.

"Thank you, Stick," he said. He looked at the village, sitting with its back to us. "I'd appreciate it if you'd call me Sam, the way you always have. But I won't forget you offered."

"Thanks," I said, and hesitated. "Anything in that mail sack for me?"

"Not that I saw. But ask Miss Agnes. She'll know."

• • •

Despite Grand's kind words and Mama's calm face, by Wednesday afternoon, I couldn't stifle the cold dread growing in me. "Something's happened," I told Neb and Rain. "I feel it."

Friday night, I sat down to supper, closed my eyes, and inhaled the sharp orange scent of mashed rutabagas and the soft, warm smell of chicken stew.

I didn't feel Change's slow walk up our street and across our yard.

"How's Captain Davis as an associate?" Grand asked, helping himself to rutabagas.

"He's usually gone, a trait I admire. He's busy transporting POWs and the bodies that wash ashore." And chasing down our clues from the Oceanside, I thought. "Pass the cornbread, please?"

Someone rapped at the front door. We froze.

The front door. Trouble.

"Let me, Ada," Grand said, but already his face looked ten years older.

"We'll both go," Mama said. She rose, and steadied herself against the table. The two of them walked to the door, me and Faye bobbing in their wake. My heart pounded as Grand opened the door. Mr. Mac stood at attention, in his dress blues.

"Ada," Mr. Mac said, and took off his white hat.

"No," Mama whispered, and Faye rushed to slip her arm around her.

Mr. Mac studied the air just over Mama's head. "Davis got

word over the radio. James's sloop went down near Wilmington. Onslow Banks's body washed ashore at Cape Fear. James and his other crewman, Richard Oscar, remain missing."

A cushion of air swallowed me.

"You're wrong," I said. My voice sounded tinny and distant. "He's almost home."

Mr. Mac stepped closer, reeking of tobacco smoke. "A squall hit Frying Pan Shoals a few days ago—some of the most dangerous water I've ever seen."

"You're *wrong*," I said again. "Papa's navigated those shoals a hundred times. Even if the *Miss Ada* did go down, he swims like a fish. He's not lost. Why aren't you out looking for him instead of coming over here and scaring Mama half to death?"

"The coast guard's *been* looking," he said, putting his hand on my arm. He made his voice gentle. "They found his skiff and map chest, Sarah."

"DON'T YOU CALL ME SARAH," I shouted. "That's for later. That's for Papa and me."

I charged the door. I ran to outpace time, my fear shoving me across dunes, to the greedy sea. "Give him back!" I shouted. "Give him back now!"

Papa. The word pressed into my heart like a foot into sand.

Papa, please come home.

The next few days moved like a movie half off the track—stalling, shooting forward, clacking by at a slant. I no longer cared about U-boats. Or Otto. Or spies.

Each morning I woke up safe in my old world. Three heart-beats later I lost Papa all over again and a tsunami of sorrow crashed over me, dragging me under.

We moved through life like ghosts. Grand opened the store, but when Otto stole a jar of Brylcreem, *Scrape* made Otto pay. Mama set Mary Beasley's broken arm, but when her father paid with a washtub of clams, she left without them. Faye met the world like she was chiseled from stone, but at home she cried for hours when her curls wilted and fell.

Me, I spent my days at HQ, reading the clouds, and look-ing for Papa. I scanned for red sails, and reminded myself to breathe. I measured the push of wind and heat of day, and recorded them in handwriting that didn't look like mine.

Neb wrote our next report to Miss Agnes, lining up the carbon paper to make three neat copies.

REPORT FROM THE DIMES. Carl Miller's back. He seems okay to us. Twice I've seen Ralph and Dirk in a skiff, checking water depths in the sound together. Once, Dirk threw up. Julia stopped by Stick's to offer her condolences and an apple pie. We're wondering why you haven't dropped in with comfort food.
Yours Truly, Neb and the Dimes.

Rain stuck to me like pine sap over the next days. Neb barely looked into my eyes. "What?" I asked. "You've walked every step of my life with me, and now you don't know me?"

"I'm sorry," he said, studying my shoes. "I look at Daddy

and then I look into your eyes and I can't stand to know what's coming, and how it will hurt." His chin quivered. "I'm not a scientist, not an artist. I'm just Neb, son of the keeper of the light. Who will I be without him? How will I know how to live?"

The silence stretched out long and aching.

"We'll watch Rain," I said. "She's been doing it all her life."

At home, I went to the encyclopedias for comfort, but didn't know which volume to pull. A for *Alone*? L for *Lost*? H for *Help*? The answer must lie in Volume K, I thought, the volume missing from our shelf.

"I hate my life," I said one afternoon, closing my weather journal.

"No you don't, and thank you for never saying that again," Rain said. "Your heart hurts. Mine does too. Neb's too. But nobody's hurts like yours right now."

She handed me a new picture. "Here's golden Jesus walking across water with your papa on His shoulders like a little boy, while the fish barrel-roll in the sky. Here's the lighthouse, and Neb's pony praying on the sands, and my father's brown eyes watching over us." She traced her finger across a blast of purple and orange. "This is your heart praying for its explosion to stop."

She had nailed it.

I lived in perpetual explosion—not at the spark of ignition, not at the place of impact. Somewhere helpless and flying apart and in between.

She sat close. "Holding the world together when our hearts explode is harder than a fish learning to fly, but fish learn and we do too," she said, leaning against me. She felt warm and soft and sad. Rain's known this all her life and I'm feeling it for the first time, I thought. And the tears found my eyes.

Fact: As time passed, the explosion ended, and the pieces fell to earth one by one.

On Monday, with Faye and Grand at the store, someone knocked at the front door. Again. Mama went white as alabaster. She rose like a sleepwalker, and swung open the door.

Miss Dandee stood dressed in black, holding a sweet potato pie.

I was so glad she wasn't an officer, I hugged her. She went board-stiff, shoved the pie into my hands, and sailed to the parlor's sofa. "My dear Ada," she said—a lie, right off the bat. "This would be so much easier if we had a body. I think I speak for everyone when I say it's time to plan a memorial service. We all loved James, but—"

"We still love him and he loves us," I said. "And you don't speak for anybody."

"Stick, hush," Mama said. "Thank you, Dandee, but we're waiting for James to come home." She took Miss Dandee's elbow, and led her to the door.

"I'm only trying to help," Miss Dandee said.

"No you're not," I shouted.

"Stick!" Mama said. "Dandee, I apologize. Stick's not ... herself." Miss Dandee huffed away, slamming the door behind her. "Stick," Mama said, her voice pale and full of tears. "Dandee's only doing what she knows how to do. And we may have to accept—"

My anguish wrapped itself in a swirl of anger. "Why did you let Papa leave? He would have stayed if you'd asked him. Why didn't Faye? Why didn't Grand?"

Why didn't I?

"Papa would never give up on us," I shouted. "And I won't give up on him."

CHAPTER 22

GRIEF'S AMBUSH

Carl whistled his way into Grand's store a week later. Julia followed him in to browse the canned goods. Fact: Dirk's practically a ghost since we talked to Davis, but Julia pops up most everywhere we go.

"Any word about your father yet?" Carl whispered, and Faye shook her head. Then, louder: "A Pepsi if you have it, Mr. Grand," he said, sliding a nickel across the counter.

"Help yourself, but most anything else, you'll need a government ration stamp. All of us will. Feds . . . blasted meddlers. Making me do their paperwork," Grand seethed.

"Afternoon," Carl said to the old men crowding the checkerboard. They ignored him. He strolled over to me. "Sorry about your dad. How are you?"

Fact: My heart's gone to driftwood, lifeless and bare.

"I'm doing," I said. "Where you been?"

"My grandmother's."

I squinted at the faint mark on his face. "Did she give you that black eye?"

He looked sheepish. "Ralph," he muttered, and sauntered to the newspaper on the wall. "Looks like London's catching it. Don't know how the Brits stand it, bombs raining down every night. They call it the *Blitzkrieg*. The *lightning war.*"

"People stand what they have to," Mr. Gray said. "Why aren't you in the war, Carl Miller?" he demanded, voice sharp as a fishhook. "Something wrong with you?"

Faye says Mr. Gray's rudeness is his most entertaining quality.

"Plenty wrong with me if you ask my dad," Carl said, very easy. "But Uncle Sam says I'm 1-A—top of the line," he added as Rain and Neb blasted in.

"Mama needs cornmeal, please," Neb said. "We just got our ration stamps and we haven't figured out how to use them yet. If you could just let us slide this once . . ."

As Grand ambled off to get his cornmeal, I scanned the candy counter—a desert of empty boxes. "I hate Germans," I said. "They don't know the people in London, they don't know Papa. He would never have left if it wasn't for them."

"Think something different, kiddo," Faye said, her voice soft.

Faye says we change how we feel by changing what we think. For lack of a better idea, I gave it a try. "Carl, you've never seen HQ. I can tour you, if you like." Carl hesitated, watching Faye sweep. "She's playing hard to get," I whispered.

"See you later, Hollywood," he said, and I led him out the door.

"What a view," he said minutes later, strolling to Davis's desk. "What's Davis like?"

"Like me. He's always reading the clouds, only he's looking

for enemy planes instead of weather," I said. "You can touch his radio." He picked up the radio transmitter like he knew how, and then grabbed Davis's binoculars. "You should stop in and talk to him. As the military side of our office, he could come in handy one day."

"Maybe so. You ever see lights out on the ocean?" he asked, scanning offshore.

"Sometimes. Like lonely fireflies," Rain said.

"U-boats," Neb said, practicing his square knots. "What do you think they're like, the Germans sitting out there?"

"I think they're tough. I visited a sub once," Carl said, taking Davis's seat. "I hated it. It's so closed in, I had to stop thinking so I could remember how to breathe. I'm too much of a mammal to live undersea." He scanned a paper on Davis's desk. "I noticed Julia at the store. Faye says you think the Artists are spies."

"We can't comment on an investigation," Neb said, "but Dirk is."

Carl grinned. "Even Ralph says he's up to something—and he admires Dirk. That Miss Agnes, now, *she's* a puzzle."

"She misses Edgar," Rain said. "She's grieving."

"Is her cat still gone?" He sighed. "That's sad. But if I wanted to catch the FBI's eye, I'd stake out Miss Agnes. Shoot, I'd give five bucks to know what she's up to myself."

He's as curious about her as she is about him.

Neb looked up, eyes sparkling. "Cash on the barrelhead?"

Carl shrugged. "Well, it was a figure of speech. But just this once, I guess."

Easy money, I thought, but Rain shook her head. "No thank you. Big risk, puny reward."

"*And* I could do a portrait," Carl said. "Of the three of you."

"You draw?" Rain said, startled. She sized him up. "Cash up front, art at the end," she said. "We'll need time to investigate."

He opened his wallet and slipped out a five. "You know, Ralph mentioned seeing some cats roughing it on the other side of Kinnakeet some time ago. Maybe Edgar found some friends."

"But that would put him ten miles from home!" Neb cried.

Carl hopped up. "I better see if your sister is through playing hard to get," he told me, smiling. But when he turned at the steps, the laughter had left his eyes. "I'm praying for your father, Stick," he added. "I'm praying we all get home."

Fact: Grief is an ambushing son of a gun.

The next day, I stood before a sad-eyed Miss Agnes. "Grand said you wanted to see me," I said as Rain and Sam chatted on the front porch, their voices carrying through the open door. "I'm sorry about Edgar."

"Thank you. I hear Carl Miller visited your headquarters, Red Dime. Why?" she asked quietly. "Did he express an interest in anything unusual? The cards I gave you, perhaps?"

"Why would he care about those cards?"

"I thought you wanted to be an agent, but your heart's not in this. It's your papa, isn't it?" She drummed her fingers against the counter. "Maybe a doll would soothe you."

Then, grief's ambush. As in *Dime Novel #10: Grief's Ambush*.

My world wobbled. Miss Agnes, offering a doll to me—a grieving genius, an FBI applicant, a dedicated scientist and the inventor of Undercover Meteorology *and* the Stick-O-Matic. I pictured the row of glass-eyed dolls in her inner sanctum, one with no hair.

My laughter exploded. I doubled over, trying to catch my breath.

Miss Agnes looked like I'd slapped her.

Rain rocketed in, leaving Sam standing in the door. "Stick," she said. "Stand up." I stared at a spot on the counter, trying to regain control. The laughter rose inside me like a geyser. Each time it receded, I looked at Miss Agnes and erupted again, tears rolling down my face. "Excuse us," Rain said, tugging me to the door. "We have a case."

She pulled me outside, to Neb and Babylon. Sam had just started back to his shove-boat. "Okay, Rain?" he asked.

"Okay, Mr. Sam," she said, her voice soft, and he walked away.

I dried my face. "I thought he didn't want that."

"I've called him that forever. It's different for me. Mama Jonah taught me how. Come on," she told me. "We're searching for Edgar today on the other side of Kinnakeet."

Great. A day-long jostle on Babylon means a sore rump to go with my broken heart.

But surprisingly, the mosey along the sound eased my spirit. "Gato, gato," we called at each shed. Finally, at the tenth lean-to, a faint reply: *"Meow?"*

"Over there," Rain said, running to the lean-to. "Under those nets." We scrabbled the smelly nets away, uncovering the sharp edges of a wire cage. J. Edgar stared up at us, his yellow eyes glassy, his orange fur matted.

"Who'd put him in a *crabpot*?" Rain cried, working the wires loose. "At least they've been feeding him. But not nearly enough."

"Otto's mean enough to do it," I said as she scooped him out.

"No," Rain said, hugging Edgar. "Otto would have ransomed him back to Miss Agnes. Ralph knew where he was. *Ralph* did this. But why?"

We rode back on Babylon, Rain cradling poor, matted Edgar and feeding him the fish from our biscuits. Miss Agnes flew off her porch to meet us. "My baby!" she cried. She wrapped Edgar in a bony hug and burst into tears.

"I didn't know she would cry," Neb said the next day as he shuffled his spotter cards up in HQ. "Thanks for giving me the reward money. Daddy was proud when I brought it home."

Rain nodded, and I elbowed my weather journal aside. Data doesn't mean squat when I can't share it with Papa.

"Hey," Neb said, dealing. "The sisters say Faye and Reed are breaking up."

"Maybe," I said, studying my cards. "I overheard them last night from the fig tree. Reed said if Faye likes Carl so much, he might go out with somebody else," I said, and Neb whistled. "Then Faye said, '*Fine*, see if I care.'" I tossed a matchstick in the pot. "There's not much back-down in Faye anymore."

"She's like you that way," Rain said. "I bet this shiny school of fish," she said, pushing her matchsticks into the pile.

Neb closed his eyes, looking exactly like his mother, only shorter and wearing the wrong hair. "Talk normal, *please*. You bet *six matches*," he said, adding six matches to the pile. I added five matches and he laid down his cards. "Three fours."

Rain smiled. "That beats my shiny fish."

"Three nines," I said, reaching for the pot. A jolt of happiness shot through me, with a shot of guilt right behind. It can't be right, celebrating cards with Papa missing.

"What?" Neb demanded. "You won and you look like you're going to cry."

I heard Faye's voice: *Think something different, kiddo.*

"Let's use my cards, for a change," I said, taking out my deck. "Miss Agnes reminded me of these just yesterday."

Neb scowled. "They look like puffy clown cards."

"I got them wet." I shuffled, bending the cards up and

letting them fall together. The top card flew apart, revealing a papery middle layer lined with faint blue squiggles.

My curiosity jumped. "What the heck?" And for one instant I felt like my old self.

"It's a map," Rain said, studying it. "Or part of one, anyway."

In minutes, we had fifty-two card-size partial maps. Five minutes later, we'd put our puzzle together. "It's a map, but I don't know these towns," Rain said. "Olinda, Salvador, Belem..."

"Why would somebody hide a map in a deck of cards?" I asked.

Neb jumped to his feet. "We can encyclopedia the towns at your place."

"Race you," I said, and we were off. We soon settled into Mama's library. "Neb's right. We need a strategy. Let's look up the names of those towns," I said, passing out Volumes O, S, and B.

"Olinda, Salvador, Belem," Rain reminded us.

Ten minutes later, we gave it up. "They're too small for their own entries," I said. "They sound like romance language words. Maybe Spanish or Portuguese. Neb, you have S. Find out where Spanish is an official language. Rain, we'll take Portuguese."

"Darn," Neb said minutes later. "Spanish is official in twenty-one countries."

"And Portuguese in eight," Rain said. "Portugal, Angola, Brazil..."

"Brazil again," I said, my pulse quickening as I opened Volume B and looked up Brazil.

"There," Rain said, pointing to the map. "The northeast section. Rainforests in one part . . . Maybe Miss Agnes lived there. We saw her rainforest photo, in her car."

"One of Dirk's passports came from Brazil," Neb said. "That can't be a coincidence."

I scanned the article. "And southeastern Brazil has a large German-Brazilian population. Not a large *Nazi* population, but a large group of ethnic Germans. There's a difference."

The excitement of the hunt had cleared grief's cobwebs from my mind—for now, anyway. "But what does Miss Agnes gain by giving us this map?"

"Nothing, maybe," Neb said. "Maybe she's just yanking our chain. For all we know, Miss Agnes may not even *be* Miss Agnes. Which could be a blessing."

Rain frowned. "No. Miss Agnes is Miss Agnes, through and through."

I ferried the encyclopedias back to their shelf. As I jostled them into place, my official U.S. Weather Bureau Station folder toppled to the floor, spewing Papa's old postcards.

Neb scooped up a handful. "I didn't know you kept these."

I fanned them out. "Pen drawings of Savannah and Florida's coast, a watercolor of Charleston. Here's a favorite," I said. "The Statue of Liberty." I flipped it over, and Papa's handwriting stole my breath. I shoved the postcards into the folder and tucked it away.

"Stick," Mama called. "Set the table for supper. Invite Neb and Rain."

"Coming," I shouted. "Can you all stay?"

"No thanks," they said, and headed for the door.

That night, as the Stick-O-Matic flickered out and Faye popped her homemade sleep mask into place, I drifted into a dream—Papa smiling and handing me his old postcards, one by one. The Statue of Liberty, Boston, Baltimore, all the way down to Miami, near the tip of Florida.

He laughed and handed them to me again, starting in New York, and ending in Florida.

At least I see him in my dreams, I thought. Even the sea can't take away my dreams.

"I've got it!" I said the next morning as I blasted into HQ. "I know what the code from Dirk's sketchbook means!" Neb and Rain looked up. So did Captain Davis. "Remember? Operation thunderstruck torch boot-toe elbow clock tba," I said.

I flipped my old postcards onto Davis's desk. "A torch—the Statue of Liberty. In New York. The toe of a boot—Miami, down in Florida. And us," I said, pointing to his wall map. "An elbow of sand, sticking into the Atlantic. *Landing spots for spies.*"

"Operation Thunderstruck," Rain said.

"*Torch, boot-toe, elbow*, with the time to be arranged," Neb added.

"Thanks," Davis said, grabbing his radio transmitter.

"Thank Papa for the postcards too," I said, smiling. "He gave us a little clue."

CHAPTER 23

UNDER COVER OF DARKNESS

June 1942

Time slipped by, pulling summer toward us like a kid pulls a red wagon.

All through May, Mama had looked for Papa every way she could, growing thinner by the day. She sent letters and telegrams. She asked sea captains and strangers. By June, grief's sharp dagger had dulled to a constant butter-knife ache in our lives.

The sinking of our ships slowed, but didn't end. The ocean churned oil. Through it all, Carl came and went, easy and graceful as a sailboat in a steady wind.

Late on the afternoon of June 3, we walked our report in triplicate over to the PO. Miss Agnes, who'd loosened our report schedule, looked up as we stepped inside. Rain wasted no time.

"DIMES REPORT, June 3, by Rain," she announced, and read.

> Dear Miss Agnes, Dirk and Ralph are twins from
> the same heart. The air around them sizzles with

a danger so clear, the sea birds fly the other way around.

"Jeez," Neb whispered. "I've seen those guys watching the sound, but I didn't see *that*."

"Different eyes," Rain replied, and read on:

"What does Ralph want more than anything?" I asked Carl Miller. "Power," Carl said. "Stay away from him, toots, and keep Stick and Neb away too." PS: I'm drawing a portrait of you and Edgar. I call it Madonna and Cat. PPS: Do you have Julia following us? That's not a nice way to treat an underling.
Love, Rain and the Dimes

A silence fell. I counted it down. One Mississippi, two Mississippi, three Mississippi . . .

Fact: Few people can tolerate a four-second silence.

Neb cracked first. "Julia's following us? Why would she do that?"

"Thank you, Rain," Miss Agnes said. "Riveting perspective. Dismissed."

At the door, I turned. "We've always wanted to visit Brazil. Haven't you?" I said, and we left for HQ.

"Don't let me forget Faye's shoulder bag," I said as we bounded up the lighthouse stairs a little later. "She wants to *dye* it, if you can believe that." We set to work—Rain drawing, Neb practicing his knots, me checking my weather instruments and recording my data.

Downstairs something whispered. The wind, I thought, or a land-level mouse.

Rain taped her latest masterpiece, *Angels Reach Down,* to the wall. In it, angels in rainbow colors reached into rough seas as a man's strong brown hands lifted a woman up to them. Beaming porpoises and flying fish cavorted in sea and sky.

Rain tilted her head, examined her work, and nodded. "Very good, Rain J. M. Lawson," she whispered. Then, louder: "It's your turn to report in triplicate, Stick," she said, returning to her supplies. "Here's the carbon paper."

Another whisper of sound, this time on the staircase. I shivered.

Fact: I should know by now to honor my own shivers.

Outside, the sun slipped to the horizon, sending an army of blue-gray shadows across our dunes. I grabbed Faye's bag from beneath my desk and turned it over, shaking out sand and wigs. A thin spool of white paper clattered out and wobbled across the floor. "I *thought* I picked up something else at the Oceanside," I said, scooping it up. "This must have gotten trapped in an inside pocket."

I put a pencil through the spool's center and Neb walked the one-inch-wide paper across HQ, unwinding it. Rain hopped up to study it. "Hieroglyphics on a skinny scroll?" she guessed.

"Hello? Anybody home?" Julia called, stepping into our

headquarters. The shoes with the crescent heels dangled on her fingertips. "My goodness, what's that?"

I shoved the spool behind my back. "Nothing," we said.

She beamed as she looked around our office. "I'd forgotten how much I love this place. Look, I know you have the spool. I heard you talking as I climbed up here."

"In your whispery stocking feet," I said. "Sneaky."

"Dirk lost that spool at the Oceanside, and I need it," she continued. She placed Neb's chair to block the steps and sat down like we'd invited her. "I like you kids. You're smart and talented." She looked at Neb. "And you're capable, and loyal to your people."

"We already know that," Neb said, and she smiled.

"It may not look like it, but we're on the same team," she said. "Trust me. Please."

"Which team is that?" Neb asked. "The Nazis stole your family, so we figure you're not working with them. Is it Post Office Secret Operations, like Miss Agnes?"

Julia's face went lonely as sundown in a graveyard. "The Nazis sent my family to a place called Auschwitz. And you're right—I'll die before I help the Germans. But that's all I can tell you."

"What's on the spool?" I asked. She looked away. "What does Brazil have to do with anything?" I demanded. "We found the map in Miss Agnes's cards."

She laughed. "Agnes bought those cards from, umm, a magician when she was on vacation in Rio. Rio's in Brazil. Maybe that explains the map."

Miss Agnes? On vacation? Doubtful.

"You're a brilliant artist and a terrible liar," Rain said. "I'm sorry, but you're not trusting us and we're not trusting you."

Julia slipped her shoes back on. "Then let me *buy* the scroll," she said, pulling a bundle of tens from her skirt pocket. "Here's a thousand dollars. For art school. For your family, Neb. Stick, I know Ada's been to Wilmington more than once to identify . . . well, to see if . . ."

"To see if a washed-ashore body was Papa." I said it fast, like ripping off a bandage.

"Ships *do* pick up survivors," Julia said. "Your father might need cash to start over. Or your mother might need it to move inland." The sunlight had fled now, and the near-dark breathed against the back of my neck. "No?" she said, the smile leaving her voice. "Fine. Dirk's downstairs. He's dying to come up here. And he will if I call him."

A threat—and a probable bluff. Dirk's not a wait-here kind of guy.

Besides, Davis warned him off.

Dime Novel #25: Under Cover of Darkness tickled my memory.

"Most scientists find it hard to think in the dark," I said, crossing to the Stick-O-Matic and lighting the candle. I placed the Mason jar on top of the spacers in the pan of water.

We still don't know who Julia is, I thought, but we know who Dirk is, and he's not getting this scroll. Julia sat blocking the stairs, waiting for our next move. *Options: I can push her down the spiral stairs—but that might kill her and I'm not risking eternity over Julia. We could fight her—but she might be armed. I glanced at the door to the rickety balcony encircling the lighthouse.*

Rain's gaze followed mine, and she shook her head. I pretended not to see as my plans materialized. *Plan A: I throw the spool off the balcony and hope we get it first. Or, if Julia follows me onto the balcony, Plan B: I run around the lighthouse, build up a lead, and tear back in here and down the stairs. Julia will never catch me—not in those crescent heels.*

I looked at Rain, who slowly shook her head, her eyes wide.

"I'll count to three," Julia said. "Then I call Dirk. One."

But what if he is down there?

"Give it to her," Rain said. "We don't need it."

Heroes don't fold. I figured the distance to the balcony door. Five fast steps, maybe six. The water rose in the Stick-O-Matic as the candle used the oxygen in the jar.

"Two," Julia said. The candle flickered. Only seconds to darkness.

"Stick, we have everything we need," Neb said.

"Don't do it!" Rain said.

"Three," Julia said as the flame died and HQ went dark.

I darted across the room, counting my steps. "Four, five, six . . ."

"No!" Rain screamed as Julia grabbed my arm. Neb plowed into Julia, crashing her to the floor as I lurched outside.

The balcony moaned. *It's rustier than I remembered.*

I edged into faint moonlight, and the glimmer of night's

first bold stars. I slipped along the balcony's inner edge, the lighthouse wall cold against my back.

Me, I thought. A hero.

Julia stepped out behind me. Something cracked, setting off a flutter of bats in my belly. Maybe Rain and Neb were right, I thought, looking back at Julia. But it's too late now.

"Go back," I shouted. "It won't hold both of us."

The metal cracked again and I glanced down. The ocean breathed calm against the shoreline as Rain sprinted down the beach.

Julia took a cautious step back. A bolt popped.

The balcony floor slowly tilted. I planted my right hand on the metal floor for balance as I slid toward the balcony's outer edge and the 250-foot plunge beyond.

Time clicked into slow motion as I slid, slid . . .

I jammed my foot against the floor's lip, stopping my skid. I froze, finding my balance, praying the floor didn't shift again. My heart drummed in my ears, and I forgot how to breathe.

I looked up. Julia stretched down from the doorway, fear straining her face. Our fingertips brushed. "I can't reach you," she said. "Don't move. I'll get help. Do. Not. Move." She disappeared into HQ.

I left my right hand solid on the floor. With my left hand, I clung so hard to the rail, my knuckles went white.

"Hold on, Stick," Neb shouted. "I'm tying my practice ropes together for you. Hold on!"

I barely nodded, afraid of tipping the balcony more.

Breathe, I told myself. Focus. *What's taking Neb so long?* Breathe.

Minutes passed, stretched so hard they felt like hours. From the corner of my eye, I saw three people darting along the beach.

I closed my eyes and focused on the pulse in my ankle, the strength in my hands, the cold of the metal floor. "Here," Neb shouted. "Grab hold."

His rope hit near my foot and bounced off.

"Settle down, Neb. Slow and steady," Neb muttered, rewinding the rope. "Catch it," he shouted, and threw it again. It bounced off the rail by my hand.

Slowly and methodically, he wound the rope back in.

"Here it comes." This time, the rope hit my hand. I grabbed it and fast-grabbed the rail. "Climb up! I got you."

"You don't weigh enough," I shouted. "Tie the rope to Davis's desk, and go for help."

"Help's already here. Rain found me," Carl panted from the doorway. He peered down at me and tried to catch his breath. "Jeez, Neb, what are you people doing?"

"Saving the world," Neb replied, his voice shaking. "It's not going well."

"Pull," I called. "And don't you dare let go."

Minutes later, I sat in Davis's chair, my heart pounding. "Thanks," I whimpered for the third time. I leaned forward, trying to get blood into my head. (See *fainting*, Volume F.)

"Thank Rain," Carl said. "She found me."

"Rain, thank you," I said. "For saving me *and* the scroll."

Rain glared at me. "I don't care about the stupid scroll. For somebody who calls herself a genius, that was a bonehead move."

A bonehead move? Me? I looked at Neb, who nodded.

"I . . . I'm sorry," I said, trying to get my bearings. "I didn't think . . ."

"You did too think. I saw you. We warned you and you did it anyway," she said. Rain put her hands on her hips, like Mama. "You think you're the only one who can have an idea? You're not. I'm smart too, toots, or else Mama Jonah and me would have a hard life on the edge of the world. Neb's smart and able or his daddy would be afraid to leave. If you didn't want Julia to have that stupid scroll, you could have thrown it to me or to Neb. Or set it on fire with the candle. Or *thrown* it out the balcony door. Or tossed it down the stairs. You ignored Life Rule #4: *In times of danger, bet on each other.* You are *not* allowed to throw my sister away, *ever*," she shouted, her voice tearing.

She stalked to her art supplies and took out her crayons, so angry her hand shook.

I looked at Carl and Neb. Both of them looked away from me.

Fact: Dead wrong is darn lonesome.

I walked to Rain's side. For one heartbeat, I fumbled for a lie that might make me sound better. But my world would end if I lied to Rain. "Rain, I'm sorry. It *was* boneheaded. And selfish. And I didn't depend on you and Neb, and you're two of the most dependable people in my life. I'll never make that mistake again, I promise."

She turned and looked me in the eye. "Never risk my people again," she said. "Life doesn't always give another chance."

Later, after we'd clued him in, Carl studied the scroll, candlelight playing across his face. "What *is* this thing?" he asked. "It means a lot to Julia. That's for sure."

"It's some kind of slanty codey doo-hick," Neb said. "My area of expertise."

"Looks like a rod code," Carl said, frowning. "You wrap the paper around a rod like a candy cane, write your message, and unwind it. To interpret it, you wind the paper on the same size rod it was recorded on, and then read it. Or decipher it, depending on how complex it is."

"Right. I was just about to think of that," Neb said. "What kind of rod do we need?"

Carl shrugged. "Whatever the sender and receiver agreed on."

The skin on the back of my neck prickled. "How do *you* know how a rod code works?"

"I saw it in a spy movie," Carl said. "The trick is identifying the rod the sender used."

"I guess so," Neb said, his brown eyes doubtful. "But how on earth will we ever do *that*?"

• • •

The next morning as we walked past the PO, Miss Agnes stared at us like she could vaporize us. "Julia told her about the scroll," I whispered as she grabbed her broom and spanked the sand from the porch.

Neb nodded. "Julia probably left out the part where she threatened to Dirk us, and ran away with Stick dangling like a featherless baby bird on the edge of its nest."

"Julia *did* threaten us," Rain said. "But she ran back to the lighthouse with Carl and me. She stayed by the stairs until you and Carl had almost pulled Stick to safety."

Rain would stick up for El Diablo if she saw even a speck of good in him.

"You're right," Neb said. "I was too busy being heroic to pay her much mind."

"Interesting," I said, trying once again to figure Julia out, and failing. "Still, it's only a matter of time before Miss Agnes blackmails us out of the scroll."

Neb screeched to a halt. "That's it," he said, watching Miss Agnes sweep. "I know how to crack the code!"

Moments later, Captain Davis looked up from his desk. "A *broomstick*?"

Neb quickly ratted Julia out, and filled Davis in on the scroll. "A couple weeks ago we saw Dirk staring at a broomstick like he'd never seen one before," he said, handing

Davis Miss Irma's broomstick. "*I* say he was thinking how to re-create the scroll we'd collected as evidence. Watch." Carefully we spiraled our scroll's paper around the broomstick. Neb turned the broom, studying the paper, and smiled. "Numbers, tiny bubbles, quote marks, decimals, commas, letters . . . These are coordinates—longitude and latitude."

I lined up the coordinates with those on Davis's wall map. "The coordinates mark places in our inlets, and easy landings along our inland coast."

"And some of these numbers tell how deep the water is," Rain added, studying the code. "We've seen Ralph and Dirk out measuring it."

"Locations and water depths—information a landing party needs to invade," Neb said. "Dirk's bringing his Nazi friends here, to our elbow of sand. From here they can go to the mainland and the military bases Dirk's been visiting."

"And to families who don't even know the U-boats are here," Rain added, her voice sad.

"Outstanding work," Davis said. "That's twice in the past twenty-four hours that you Dimes have come up big—*again*." He watched us, waiting and smiling.

Twice in one day?

Neb bit first. "Refresh me. What was the first time?"

"Thought you'd never ask," Davis said. "We picked up your Mr. Green last night. He was too arrogant to ditch his getaway car. Can you believe it? Thanks again, Rain. Excellent work, remembering that license plate. And thanks to all of you for identifying him. We wouldn't have nabbed him without you."

"You're welcome," Rain said. Her voice was calm as pond water, but her eyes glowed.

Davis grabbed his hat. "I'll deliver the spool to Norfolk. You heroes keep a low profile. And let me take care of Julia."

"We're heroes. Daddy's going to love this," Neb whispered.

"Of course," Davis added, "I have to swear you to secrecy until we close the net around Dirk and Julia."

"*Secret* heroes?" Neb said, stunned. "That seems wrong."

"Your dad will know one day, Neb, but not today," Davis said. Neb's brown eyes went so sad, his hair seemed to swoon. "Raise your right hands and swear it."

Rain shook her head. "No thank you. Mama Jonah doesn't like me to swear."

"Promise it, then," he said, and we did. "Don't go out on the balcony, heroes," he said, locking the door and slapping a danger sign on it. He took off for his Jeep at a dead run, our spool tucked beneath his arm.

CHAPTER 24

ILL-STARRED EVENTS

Fact: Being a secret hero is worse than being no hero at all.

While we spent the next days in unfulfilled glory, Faye shifted into high gear. She walked the beach with her Brigade each morning, and ran the store like she meant it. To my surprise, Grand seemed relieved to step aside. I walked up one morning to find Faye teetering on a ladder, nailing a new sign on the store.

HOLLYWOOD

"Good job," Grand said as she scampered down. "I'm proud of you."

"Thanks," she said. "I'm proud of me too."

I turned to see Reed down the way, with Schooner bowlegging along at his side. "Hey Stick, pay you a quarter to bring me a pound of nails," Reed called, and walked away.

Now what?

I found Reed in his shady backyard a half hour later, planing the hull of a new skiff. The smell of his white cedar boards rose heady and sweet against the close salt air. "Here you go," I said, setting the sack of nails in the grass by Schooner's head. "Nice boat."

"Thanks, shortcake," he said. "Think you could handle a boat like this?"

"Of course I can and if I can't, I can learn."

"I'll never get to build you a sister-in-law boat," he said. "But this one's yours if you want her, and if we can reach a deal."

"*If* I want her?" I stared at the graceful, wide-beamed skiff. "I've *always* wanted a boat steady enough for taking water samples. She's beautiful."

Fact: Other boats plod through the water. Reed's sing.

He pushed his hair from his eyes. "Stick, I'm enlisting," he said, and my heart lost its breath. "I'm tired of being second-best to any idiot that puts on a uniform. Faye's heart's changed course. Mine's knocked so far off kilter, I might as well set a new course too. I'm hoping you'll take care of Schooner while I'm away."

Schooner lifted his head at the sound of his name, and then lay back in the grass. He rolled to his back and kicked his back legs, his slender pink belly shining.

"Of course I will," I said, giving Schooner a scratch.

"Thanks. He likes table scraps, but no fish—too many bones. You'll have to convince Miss Ada to let him inside when it's cold. Don't *ever* take him out in a boat."

"Count on me," I said as my bartering skills kicked in. "Now that I think about it, I don't really need a boat, but I guess I could take it off your hands. What you got in mind?"

"You already made the deal. Take Schooner when I leave, and it's yours."

"Thank you," I said, my voice wobbling like a drunk loon. "But I wish you wouldn't . . ."

He scooped me into a hug. "I'll be here a few more weeks. I'll write so you and Schooner know where I am. And I'll be back before you know it."

Familiar words.

He gave me one last squeeze, walked inside, and let the screen door slam behind him.

While I practiced feeling nothing about Papa and Reed (see *grief*, Volume G), I composed my report in triplicate for Miss Agnes.

DIMES REPORT, June X where X is unknown, by Stick. (Papa would get that math joke. I hope you do too.)

Miss Agnes: Carl Miller saved my life thanks to Rain, and we have nothing bad to say about him no matter how suspicious you think he is. Your friend Julia is a menace as Captain Davis now knows. Ralph and Dirk are entwined like a couple of snakes, proving they both like dangerous company. And finally, if you wonder who stole your war poster, it was Otto.
-Stick & the Dimes

Fact: While we focused on saving the world and laying low, Otto lived in a holding pattern of petty crime. Oddly, no one accused him. "They don't want to hurt Reverend Wilkins," Rain said, "or turn Miss Dandee against them."

But war changed Otto's holding pattern to something much more dangerous at ten a.m. on June 20, when a long black car drove off the Hatteras Ferry, crept down the island and along our sand street, and oozed to a stop in front of his family's trim house. Already the heat dripped from the trees like tears and the breeze was breathless still.

We Dimes watched from the store's shady porch. "Who is it?" Rain whispered as two navy men got out, smoothed their uniforms, and walked up the front steps.

"It's bad news, that's who," Neb said as Miss Dandee's door swung open and the men stepped inside. Moments later Miss Dandee wailed like a deer with a splintered leg. Reverend Wilkins flew out of the church and ran for her as Otto slammed out the front door, tears streaming down his face.

That's how I ran when Mr. Mac came about Papa, I thought. "It's Tommy," I said.

By the time the stone-faced sailors climbed into their car, the old men in the store had stepped outside. "Ten-hut," Grand said as the car rolled by, and they saluted. The rest of us put our hands over our hearts. Miss Agnes lowered the flag to half-mast.

Miss Dandee wasted no time.

Two days later, the village, including Julia and Dirk, went to Tommy's funeral. Mama said it mattered even if Miss Dandee and Otto wouldn't remember much, and even if they buried a coffin empty as their hearts.

We saw Carl the next day, on the beach near Babylon's corral.

"Tommy Wilkins is dead," I announced. "His ship got sunk by a U-boat in the North Pacific, where the water's cold as ice."

Neb muscled a salt block into place for Babylon. "I hate U-boats and everybody in them. I hope they all die. If this war lasts long enough, I'll kill them myself."

"Don't say that," Carl said. He sat on the skirt of a dune, Rain beside him.

"Tommy went to war to be a hero," Neb said.

"No he didn't. He went to stay out of jail," I said, and Carl winced. "He knew we were closing in on him. Dead doesn't make you better."

Neb wiped his hands on his pants. "Tommy volunteered first, and *that* made him better. Reed was the best boy on the island until Tommy went away."

Carl waited. It's an art, waiting.

My brain has no waiting gear. I pictured Miss Agnes asking if Carl had seen the cards she gave me. *Why was she so disappointed when I said no?* I took my repaired cards from my pocket, and shuffled. "Julia's keeping her distance since the balcony disaster, but she still doesn't add up," I said. "She even lied about these mystery cards."

Carl looked at me like I'd lost my mind, but I plugged on. "Miss Agnes gave the cards to Rain and me. Each card hid a partial map of Brazil." He whistled. "*Julia* says Miss Agnes bought this deck off of a magician in Rio—a lie."

Curiosity spread across Carl's face like oil across the sea. "Why would Miss Agnes give you cards like that? And why would Julia lie about them?"

"That's what we want to know," Neb said.

Carl grinned. "As I recall, I paid you Dimes five bucks up front for information on Miss Agnes. A look at that map will settle that debt nicely."

"Deal," we said, and led Carl to HQ.

Minutes later, Carl studied our map, a faint frown lining his forehead. "This is the kind of map they give spies dropping into a new area," he said. "You know, parachuting in, coming in by train. I hear parts of Brazil are training zones for Nazi spies." He grinned. "Before you ask, I know because I used to spend my spare time at the National Theatre in Richmond. Salty popcorn and pretty girls. I saw every movie that came to town. Including *Parachute Man.*"

I tried to picture Miss Agnes parachuting into a rainforest with Edgar tucked beneath her arm. Nothing happened.

"Of course," he said, "where Germany's spies go, our spies go. It's a funny kind of dance. Hilarious that she would even have these. Still, why did she give them to *you?*"

"I've been thinking about that," Rain said. "She wanted to make friends. And she was angry that Captain Davis didn't give us spotter cards. Miss Agnes believes in justice. Plus she's impulsive, like Stick."

And she wanted Carl to see them too, I thought.

"Miss Agnes, a force for justice," Carl murmured. "Interesting."

He plucked the paper from the map's lower right corner and held it to the window, squinting. "Most maps have keys in the bottom right-hand corner. If I remember that movie right . . . Can I borrow a candle?"

I lit a candle. Carl held the little square of paper over the flame, moving it back and forth.

We leaned closer, watching. As the paper heated up, ghostly letters slowly appeared on its face. They baked up darker, darker, until words appeared in smoke-brown letters:

PW = orange cat

SOS = Eleanor Eleanor Eleanor.

"This is a lemon juice code, from Volume R," I said. "The heat burns the carbon in the lemon juice, turning it brown. *Password* equals *orange cat*. That's Edgar. And *SOS* equals *Eleanor Eleanor Eleanor*—a cry for help."

"A map of Brazil with a key written in English, for English-speakers," Rain said.

"And with a password like orange cat, we can assume Miss Agnes wrote it herself," Neb said, scratching his head. "Let's see if the map's other papers have secret messages."

They didn't.

Finally Carl snuffed out the candle. "This newfangled spy stuff is amazing."

I laughed. "New? George Washington's spies used lemon juice to send secret messages during the American Revolution. That's why I learned about it in Volume R."

"Amazing," Carl said. "Speaking of spy-craft, Ralph tells me Miss Agnes is meeting the Artists at her place tomorrow afternoon. I'd stake her out myself, but she watches me the way a terrier watches a rat." He laid four five-dollar bills on my desk. "Twenty bucks to tell me what they talk about."

Miss Agnes *thought* he'd be curious about this map, and she was right. Twenty bucks' worth of right. But something felt wrong. "You're awfully curious all of a sudden," I said.

"This map makes me curious as heck," he said, "and I bet it makes you curious too. I'll pay you to satisfy all our curiosities."

"Deal," Neb said, scooping up the fives. "There's nothing wrong with helping a friend," he said, his eyes daring me to disagree. "We can listen at a window, or from a closet, or a stepladder. We can even wear our disguises again, if you want to."

"No disguises," Rain said. "Mine makes it hard for my hair to breathe."

I hesitated. Getting caught would spell disaster, from the Latin *astrum* meaning star, which became the Old Italian *disastro*, meaning ill-starred event. (See Volume D. Also *Dime Novel #43: Ill-Starred Events*.) But we couldn't let Miss Agnes blackmail us forever, my curiosity was on fire, and Neb's folks needed the cash.

"I'm in," I said, squaring my shoulders. "Miss Agnes will never catch us."

• • •

"Gotcha!" Miss Agnes shouted the next afternoon, dragging us from her shrubbery. "How dare you? What did you hear? Why are you skulking?" She marched us to the store and kicked the door open like a lacy storm trooper. "Betrayed by underlings," she bellowed.

Mr. Taylor froze, hand on a checker. Faye stopped stacking the cigarette shelf. Otto put the lid back on the Brylcreem, his eyes glittering.

What happened next proves the whole is greater than the sum of its parts. (*Aristotle*, Volume A.) 1) Miss Agnes twisted Neb's ear—which is not allowed beneath my stars. 2) I shoved Miss Agnes hard. 3) She grabbed my wrist and elbow, and swung me over her bony hip. 4) My feet left the floor and the store whirled around me.

I let out an unscientific yelp as Miss Agnes smoothly lowered me into a pile of cleaning supplies and leaped back into a low side crouch, back straight, her open hands before her.

The store went dead quiet. Someone moved a checker on the checkerboard. "I wouldn't cross Agnes if I was you, Titus," Mr. Taylor said. "King me."

Rain knelt beside me and pushed the mop strings from my face. "I think that was jiu-jitsu, a martial art practiced in Brazil. Volume B," she whispered.

"Stick!" Faye said, yanking me to my feet. "Apologize. Now!"

"*Me* apologize? She practically killed me!"

"Oh, I did not," Miss Agnes said. "I simply won't have

children listening at my windows. And I understand Stick is a repeat offender."

Grand sighed. "I don't know what gets into her sometimes."

"The devil, I'd say," Otto said. "Same as Jonah."

"You," Faye said, pointing to Otto. "Get out."

Otto swaggered out as Carl strolled in. His smile collapsed. "What happened?"

"Agnes, we have more to think about than Stick," Grand said, giving Carl a nod. Nobody even acts different when Carl walks in anymore. "News," he said, and she marched over to the newspaper on the wall, folding her wings like a frilly buzzard. She scanned the paper as Julia meandered in and peeled off for the magazine rack.

Carl reached in the icebox as Miss Agnes read the headline: *"German Spies Captured."*

Carl's Pepsi clanged against the box.

Miss Agnes perched her glasses on her beak. "Washington, D.C., June 25. The FBI announces the capture of two rings of alleged spies. One ring rowed to Long Island, NY, from a U-boat. The other rafted ashore near Miami, Florida. The men, who all lived in the U.S. at one time, were recruited as Nazi spies."

"Julia mailed her art to New York and Miami," Rain whispered. We budged in beside Miss Agnes. The suspects in the photo were all men, all white, all glum. "Mr. Green," Rain whispered, pointing to a pale, dark-haired man with wolf eyes. His stare startled, even in a photo.

Miss Agnes studied him, one beaded slipper tapping.

"The spies in New York carried *$175,000*," I read, picturing Julia's suitcase of money.

"What?" Faye gasped. "What can you buy with that kind of money?"

"Anything you want," Miss Agnes said. "And most anybody. If U-boats put them ashore, they buried their uniforms on the beach. Military personnel captured in uniform become prisoners of war. POWs go to prison. Out of uniform, they're spies—and spies don't live long."

Carl lifted his Pepsi to his lips. His hand shook.

"Upsetting," Miss Agnes said, watching him.

Faye frowned. "Carl? Are you all right?"

Miss Agnes's dark eyes followed him as he walked over to the pool table and rolled the eight ball into a corner pocket. When he turned back to us, his color had found his face. "I'm not all right. They can't do this. I'm enlisting."

I turned and looked for Julia. She was gone.

We didn't see Carl for nearly three weeks—just long enough for the world to fall apart.

Julia and Dirk disappeared the night the photo hit the store wall, leaving no clues behind. Fact: We'd see one of them weeks later, deep in the heart of Buxton Woods. The other, we'd never see again.

News of the captured spies spread like a plague of biting flies, fanning fears on the island. "Spies in New York *and*

Miami," Miss Dandee told Mama the next day as I draped myself over the branch of our oak tree.

Mid-July had baked the air up salt-sticky. I'd already fed the chickens and harvested the tomatoes and cucumbers. Now, near noon, the tree felt cool against my belly. Fact: Trees always stand beneath a parasol of shade, making them smarter than most people.

"We *both* know what lies halfway between New York and Miami. Us," Miss Dandee said. "Why do all these ships go down *here?*" She handed Mama fifty cents for a bottle of tonic. "I say *somebody's* helping them. And we both know who it is."

A shiver danced up my spine. *She means Miss Jonah.*

"These waters have been called the Graveyard of the Atlantic for hundreds of years, and you know it," Mama said. "U-boat captains know our ships have to cross the sandbars with the tides. *That* makes our ships sitting ducks. I hear your gossip about Jonah flying around the village, and I hear Otto's rumors. You are dangers to Jonah and to Rain, and I don't like it."

Miss Dandee *humphed* and bustled off.

That night as we put the dishes away, an owl hooted. Mama jumped. She's different since Papa went missing, I thought. She sits more, startles easier.

"A great horned owl," I said, very soothing. It felt odd, me reassuring her. I stepped outside and shouted. The owl lumbered from the roof of the chicken house, its wings silent in the night air. "He's gone," I said, coming back in.

Mama looked across our yard. The moonlight silvered the

garden and tiptoed across the sound's gentle waves. Then out of nowhere: "How's Otto?"

I pictured Tommy's funeral, and Otto—beautiful and pale and broken, his eyes red from crying. Otto clutched Tommy's silver dollar so hard it made the edges of his fingers white. "He's desperate alone and lost without Tommy, and starving for revenge."

She folded her dishtowel. "It's time to go inland. We'll invite Jonah and Rain. It's dangerous for them here. We'll go to Tarboro. People know me there."

She's giving up on Papa, I thought. She's thinking how to save us by herself. I thought it as loud as I could: *Papa, please come home.* But for the first time, I didn't know if he heard me.

The currents had shifted, and Papa had drifted too far from my fingertips.

The next evening, Rain and me headed for Miss Jonah's, the rich, starchy promise of a fish stew calling us around Rain's Dune as Jonah banged her wooden spoon against the pot. "Sit," she called, her pretty bowls scattered down her log table.

What if I woke up in another life, with no family to remind me who I am? Who would I be? "You all come to my house tonight," I said. (See *impulse,* Volume I.)

Miss Jonah surprised me. "Thank you, Stick. We will enjoy that."

The currents are shifting hard, I thought. Miss Jonah feels it too.

• • •

After that night, Rain and Miss Jonah slept on our porch for three nights running. Then—on Saturday night—the shock of my Post-Papa life.

Islanders packed the store, with Faye's crowd in to shoot pool and the oldsters in for the news—something Mama still forbids unless she's there to explain. Slamming Sammy Simpson, the radio announcer, zinged across the air, crisp and clear. *"And now the news."*

I should leave, I thought. But a scientist doesn't flee from the truth.

Slamming Sammy boomed on: *"Hitler whips Germany into a frenzy as his tanks rumble across Russia."* The broadcast faded into a hodgepodge of voices. A man's high-pitched, rapid-fire voice shot from the radio speaker like sand on a fast wind.

Goose bumps marched across my arms. I pulled Neb outside. "Do the words of Rain's lullabies sound like—"

"Don't say it," he said, looking around. "It's dangerous."

"What's dangerous, Bristly Dime?" Miss Agnes asked, stepping from the shadows.

"Nothing," he said. "I mean, Hitler's talking. *He's* dangerous."

"You're just figuring *that* out? Disappointing. Sometimes I think I should fire the lot of you," she said, and pushed into the store.

The next morning, Carl strolled down the beach, Ralph galumphing by his side. Carl's voice drifted to us on the wind: "Sorry, it's for Captain Davis," he said. "You can use mine."

Ralph snorted, and cut into the dunes.

Wonder what that's about? I thought as I charged Carl, Neb and Rain on my heels. "Hey," I panted. Already the morning's flat, searing heat stuck Papa's white shirt to my back.

"Hey yourself," he said, reading my eyes. "What's wrong? Tell me," he said, and sat cross-legged in the sand. Rain plunked down beside him, her knees pulled up to her chin, her eyes forlorn as a cold campfire.

"We heard Hitler on the radio. The words in Miss Jonah's lullabies sound like his, if you slow his down and subtract the hate," I began, and the story poured out of me.

Rain leaned against his arm, and he closed his eyes.

"You look like you lost something," I told him.

"My little brother leans against me like that sometimes." He smiled at Rain. "Will you sing me a lullaby?" He listened as she sang a sweet flow of words, easy as the wind. "That's beautiful. It's not German. Dutch, maybe, or Danish. Rain, I never asked. How did you and Miss Jonah get here?"

I sat up straight, ready to tell her story, but Rain put her hand on my arm. "Thank you, Stick, I can tell it now," she said, and a sliver of my heart flew away.

Rain took a deep breath: "Mama Jonah came to this life one August morning, her pale petticoats and blond hair swirling and helpless in the gray-blue sea. This was sweetest morning after darkest night, the night her ship bellowed and rolled like a heartsick whale, the night angels reached down, their arms of every color, the night my father pushed Mama Jonah through the porthole into an ocean salty as her tears. And she reached back for him, and he put this in her hand," she said, showing her ring. "Then he folded his hands and drifted back into darkness as the angels pulled her away and the porpoises shared kisses of air with her, leading her here.

"This was back when Stick was two, but even then she walked the shore like a pirate scientist, hunting treasures with Miss Ada, who saw Mama Jonah and ran into the sea. The first wave rocked Miss Ada sideways and the next near took her off her feet, but she grabbed Mama Jonah and floated her to the shallows, where Mama Jonah moaned and grabbed her belly. And Miss Ada looked up into God's sweet eyes and she said, 'You get down here, please. I need you. Now.' And Mama Jonah pushed, and there I lay in Miss Ada's surprised hands, smiling at Stick, who wore her orange hair the way the sun wears rays. The waves rocked me. The dune cats danced for joy, the sky's tears washed my face. And Mama Jonah named me Rain."

Neb, who abhors the unexpected, elbowed in. "I was born in the back bedroom. Mama said it almost killed her."

Carl sat quiet. I watched Rain—the straight of her back, the tilt of her chin, the pride in her eyes. The honor of carrying her story for so long and the sweet shock of handing it back filled my eyes with tears no one saw but Rain. We smiled together and for one moment our hearts touched. And then that moment was gone.

"Thank you for that story, Rain," Carl said. "It's beautiful. Your lullaby too." He looked out at the ocean, and shook his head like the sea was a puzzle he couldn't quite work out. "I think it's safer to hum your lullabies for now. People fear what they don't understand, and if other people hear those words, it might be dangerous—for you and your mother." He looked into her eyes, waiting.

She nodded. "People like Otto and Miss Dandee," she said.

Carl kissed her hand, hopped up, and flipped his wrist-watch over. *Face-down again. Quirky.* "I'm hoping to catch Captain Davis, if I can. Stick, any word from your papa yet?"

My heart nose-dived to my belly. "No, but thank you for saying *yet*."

"Wait," Neb said. "Did you enlist? Because if this is good-bye . . ." The question hung on the air like a ragged flag.

Carl clapped his shoulder. "I talked to Davis about it, but decided to wait."

"I'm glad," Rain said. "You could get lost so cold and deep we'd never find you."

"Reed didn't wait. He enlisted," I said. "Schooner's moving in with me. Faye's *furious*. Grand's throwing a party for Reed Friday week. Everybody's invited. Including you."

"I better pass. Reed and I aren't really buddies," he said, and smiled Rain goodbye. "You're so much like my little brother."

"His *brother*?" Neb said as Carl walked away. "I'm not see-ing it."

"I remind him of Fritz Fischer, 2021 14th Street, Rich-mond, Virginia," Rain replied. "Carl wrote his name on the postcard from the dance club."

Like I said, Rain has a memory like flypaper.

CHAPTER 25

DRESSED TO KILL

August 2, 1942

I strolled into HQ Monday morning. Captain Davis glanced at his wristwatch. "O-seven-hundred," he said, clicking his radio off. "You're up early."

"I'm meeting Neb and Rain here at oh-pretty-soon. How far can your radio broadcast?"

"New York, in good weather. And down to St. Augustine, Florida. I was just telling Norfolk I'm bringing up more cargo." *Cargo.* By now, washed-ashore bodies had become ordinary as a box of nails.

I hesitated. "I hope you'll send out an alert for Papa. He's a survivor from the *Miss Ada.*"

He pushed his hat back. "I've been doing that ever since he went missing—as an unasked favor to an officemate. Besides," he said, "Faye asked me to, your mother did . . ."

"Thanks," I said, and changed the subject before my tears could reach my eyes. "When are you arresting Dirk? I could have locked him up twice by now. And what about Julia?"

He grinned. "Your evidence is being put to good use. Patience is a virtue, Stick."

"Well, I need some fast," I told him, my gaze settling on a bottle of Old Spice by the radio. "Nice of Carl Miller to bring you some aftershave."

"What makes you think Carl brought it?"

Who else could it be? Carl said he was visiting Davis, and he's the only one on the island who wears Old Spice. "I'm a scientist and a detective. I make it my business to know things," I said. I checked my weather instruments. The sky looked bruised and sullen. A nor'easter rolled toward us, kicking the waves to white froth.

I grabbed my spyglass and zeroed in on Neb's place as Ruth and Naomi shuttered the windows—like Faye and I did last evening, after my early forecast. I peered at Davis's quarters. "Your place looks ready for a storm if you don't want anything you own," I reported.

He looked up from his papers, startled.

"Nor'easter coming. Secure what you want. If the water rises, pull the plugs out of the floorboards so your house doesn't float away," I added as Rain clattered up the stairs.

"Mama Jonah says the ocean's gone berserk," she reported.

"Storm forecast by Stick *and* Jonah," Davis said, rising. "Good enough for me."

Neb reported in minutes later. "Mother's worked me to a nub," he said, and tried his social laugh, the one that sounds like a bow-saw rasping against green wood. "Neb to a nub. Get it? The sisters say girls like a man with a sense of humor. Pretty hilarious, right?"

"It's *almost* funny," Rain said, very encouraging.

I scanned the beach beyond Neb's place. "What the helium? There's a huge track up the beach. A long trough between dunes and ocean."

"Sea turtle track?" Neb guessed.

"Too wide." I glanced at the towering bank of navy-blue clouds charging toward us like an invading army. "We can't get there before the storm hits."

"Wrong. Come on, cowgirls," he said. "Let's ride."

Minutes later Rain and Neb leaned into Babylon's canter as I bounced across her rump like a helpless scarecrow. The wind gusted and the temperature dropped. "There!" I shouted.

The five-foot-wide trough ran along the shore and turned straight into the boiling sea. "Ah, sugar," Neb swore as the waves gobbled up the odd print.

Lightning hooked a crooked finger across the sky and thunder slammed down, sending Baby skittering sideways. Rain tipped and Neb grabbed her arm, yanking her onto Babylon's back. I toppled into the sand. "Easy, Babylon. Climb on, Stick!"

I ran a few feet up the skirt of a dune and vaulted onto the pony's rump. (See *miracle*, Volume M.) Lightning flashed and Babylon took off as the storm raced ashore, trampling the waves flat. "Your house," I shouted. "It's closest."

The nor'easter pounded Neb's sturdy brick house way past dark and into the night. "Won't your folks worry about you?" Davis asked, lighting the parlor's kerosene lamp.

"In a storm, every house is your house," I said. "Everybody knows it."

As the storm raged on, we gathered around the table in Miss Irma's sweet-smelling kitchen, listening to Mr. Mac's stories of shipwrecks and rescues. Rain loves those stories. Neb inhaled the sound of his father's voice like he could store it in his bones.

I'd give ten years of my life to hear Papa's voice again.

"I better turn in," I said. I headed for the parlor sofa and fell asleep wondering what treasures the storm might bring, never imagining what dangers might roll ashore with them.

Morning awakened bright and whistle clean. "Let's go see whose house floated away," Neb said, thundering into the parlor in his nightshirt.

"See to the porch furniture," Miss Irma called from the kitchen. "And check around the lighthouse for birds blown off course in the storm. I'll bake us a storm bird pie for supper."

"On it," Neb shouted. "Hurry," he told Rain and me. "Let's treasure hunt before the villagers hit the beach. Nothing brings treasures like a storm."

We dressed and tore outside. Our wide beach stretched before us, a glistening carpet of golden sand and tiny shells. "A conch!" I shouted, racing toward an elegant white swirl.

"A blue bottle!" Rain shouted, scooping it from a tiny pool.

But Neb saw the thing that would change our lives—a tiny red wedge peeking from the sand. "Dibs!" he shouted as we raced up the beach. We fell to our knees and scooped away the sand and bright coquina shells. "A book," he said, his smile collapsing. He lifted the soggy volume and turned the swollen pages, stopping on an image: a thin-faced young man with a pointed beard. In the background, a twist of pipes and dials. "A steamer lost it, maybe."

On the next page, young men huddled on bunks with a narrow table between them. On the next, a kind-faced old woman. Rain tilted her head. "I like the way the artist's light always comes from the side."

Neb sighed. "A book." Back at his house, we propped it open by the stove, like a bird drying its wings.

Papa says treasures find us, more than we find them. Funny that a book found Neb.

I bumped into Carl and Ralph days later, beside a calm sea. I heard them before I saw them. "Breakfast is on me, cuz," Ralph said. "Vienna sausages and crackers from your girlfriend's store. She's taken over."

"She has to," Carl said. "People depend on her."

Who would have guessed we'd ever depend on Faye?

"What's the plan?" Ralph asked, taking half a cigar from his shirt pocket. "Yaeger dropped this." He flicked his thumbnail across a match, trying to strike it. "I thought Alfred would beat me to it, the little rat. But I got there before he could move."

"Alfred doesn't smoke. Maybe Captain Davis can give you a light," Carl said.

Enter, me. "Davis is in Wilmington, checking out a ship's survivors."

"How long have you been lurking there?" Ralph demanded, his face going ugly.

"I'm not *lurking*. I'm hunting treasures. What are *you* two doing? Who's Alfred?"

"Alfred's a neighbor, up the island," Carl said, startled. The air between us went rough, and strange. For one heartbeat, I didn't trust him. He smiled. "Sorry, Stick, you surprised us. To answer your question, Alfred's a friend. And we came for Reed's party."

"That's a lie. You hate Reed," I said, and he laughed.

"I like him better now that he's leaving," he admitted, and the air went smooth again.

"Easy up on Reed. He's a good guy. He's just having a really bad year is all." I looked around—disturbed sand, bent oats. "How did you get—"

"We got off the bus up the beach a ways, and walked down," Ralph said, stuffing the cigar stub in his pocket. "*I* like a party if it has beer. Any suds?"

"Green church punch," I said, hoping it would repel him.

"Love the stuff," Carl kidded as we headed for the shoreline. I laughed. Nobody loves green church punch.

Reed's party had spilled across both porches and into the yard by the time Carl and Ralph showed up. Everybody we liked had come except Miss Jonah, who had a cold. People I *didn't like* came too, including Miss Dandee and Otto. Grand invited Miss Agnes.

Grand wore his best shirt and pants, and his new suspenders. She wore electric-blue frills and a gold lapel pin—a wreath with the letters *POSO* hidden in the leaves.

"Looks like Post Office Special Ops is real," Neb said. "They have their own lapel pins and everything," he said, like that would be actual proof.

"People look even prettier than in *Dime Novel #63: Dressed to Kill*," Rain said. "Hey, there's Carl," she said, and we tore out the door.

"Welcome," I said. "You look good. The pretty food's in the dining room. We're frying fish and hushpuppies in the kitchen. Some of the hushpuppies have illegal sugar sprinkles, but you have to ask."

"Thanks," Carl said. "Ralph, we'll stay an hour. Don't fight with anybody, don't kiss anybody, don't do anything I wouldn't do."

"A Louisiana wake is more fun, cuz," Ralph grumbled.

I took Carl's hand when we neared the steps. "Don't mention Papa when we go inside. Richard Oscar's body washed up on Bald Head Island. He was part of Papa's crew."

Mama's face broke into a wide smile when we walked in. "Carl," she said as her gaze traveled warily to Ralph. Mama has a feel for people. So does Schooner, who sat up in the corner and growled. "Mrs. Lawson, this is my cousin, Ralph," Carl said.

"Welcome, Ralph," she said. "Carl, Faye's in the dining room. So is Reed."

"We just came to wish him well. And present this," he said, handing me a roll of paper.

"Art," Rain said, her voice excited. She unrolled a portrait of the three of us, standing in front of the lighthouse. At our feet, a carpet of shells and seaweed.

"Thank you," I said. "It's beautiful."

Mama looked at Rain. "Rain? What's wrong?"

"Nothing. Thank you, Carl." To me, she sounded like her heart was drowning.

The dining room was packed. Miss Agnes had chatted Grand into a corner, but her gaze locked on Carl. Miss Dandee chatted with a friend. "That woman's a danger to us all," she whispered, and hushed as we sped by.

Reed stood by the china cabinet with his friends. "It's in the paper," he said. "Those spies in New York and Miami? Two got time. The rest got the electric chair."

"Serves them right," Carl said, strolling up. "Reed, I came to wish you luck."

"You've wished it," Reed said, nodding to the door. Reed can be awkward.

I pulled Carl away. "Come have some cake. Everybody chipped in their sugar rations."

We'd set the dining room table island proud: Grandmother's lace tablecloth, roasted pecans, dried fruit. Green punch in a fancy bowl. Faye stood at the table, serving cake. Ralph headed for the back door. "One hour, cuz," Carl warned.

At nine o'clock, Carl nodded goodbye to Davis and to Grand. As Carl thanked Mama for the party, Reed tapped a knife against the side of a glass. "Thank you for coming," he said. "I've been trying to think if anything could make this night better. There's just one thing." He turned to look at my sister. "Faye? Marry me?"

The room went quiet as the inside of a coffin.

"Even *I* know that's wrong," Neb said.

I tried to beam good sense into Reed's mind. (See *telepathy*, Volume T.) Nothing.

"I've told you, Reed," Faye said, "we can talk about it when you come back."

"*When he comes back?*" Miss Dandee snipped. "Reed may not come back."

"He will," I said, very strong.

I looked into Reed's ocean-blue eyes and then turned to Faye. But she was gone.

"That was a train wreck," Neb said, very cheerful. He tossed a hushpuppy into the air and caught it in his teeth. "I could have proposed better than that."

"Stick, you children go outside and play," Mama said.

"We're working on social skills," I said. "We better stay."

"*Now.*" Fact: There is no wiggle room in a one-syllable word.

The back door slammed behind us and I scanned the crowd. Kids playing tag, and Ain't No Bears Out Tonight. We sat on Mama's garden bench, sacrifices to the island's bloodthirsty mosquitos.

A half hour later, the crowd thinned. "Otto and his bunch

is leaving," Neb said, tossing his last baked pecan in the air. It bounced off his forehead.

"Gone to catch a spy," Little Hudson said, walking by.

"Mama Jonah!" Rain bolted across the yard, Neb and me right behind her.

As we neared Rain's Dune, the mob's chant rose and fell with the waves: "Nazi! Nazi!" We ran opposite the crowd's path, circling the dune, to find Miss Jonah silhouetted by her fire, her shawl pulled close. We pelted to her side.

There's maybe twenty people here. Twenty against four.

"Go home, spy, and take your creamy with you," a man shouted.

"Mr. Tyson," Rain breathed, and fear closed around my chest like a fist.

"Stop, friends," Miss Jonah called. "Stop! You know me."

"Mr. Tyson," I shouted, "Miss Jonah's goat milk saved your grandbaby's life. You didn't want her to leave the island then." The mob coiled tight and expanded, like a breathing thing.

"Get out of here, Seaweeds," someone shouted as a man lit a torch.

"I see you, Otto," I shouted. "You too, Jersey. Leave us alone." *Where's Scrape?*

Otto picked up a piece of driftwood. My mouth went dry. "They aren't backing down," I said. *Davis is still at the party. So are Mama and Faye and Grand. Carl's walked away. I looked at the lighthouse. It's too late to run. The crowd will fall on us like wolves.*

Four against a night full. You don't have to be a genius to hate those odds.

"Get off our island," Otto shouted. "We already scared two of you Nazis away. Now you. Wade back into the sea and take your girl with you."

My anger crackled hot as Miss Jonah's campfire. "Nobody here's a Nazi, you ignorant piece of goose slick, and you didn't make Julia and Dirk do anything," I shouted. "Go home."

"Stick Lawson, stand with your own kind," Mr. Tyson barked.

"I *am* standing with my own kind, you bigoted old hypocrite," I yelled.

"Me too," Neb shouted.

"So am I," Rain bellowed. "Leave us alone. Now. Please."

Miss Jonah turned to us. "Stop," she whispered. "You'll make them angrier."

"There's a time for everything under heaven," Rain told her mother. "Reverend Wilkins taught me that. Father would say it too. This is the time to fight or get gobbled up alive."

She took a deep breath. "I have my father's feet," she said, closing her eyes a moment.

"And I'm standing right beside you," I said.

Rain stepped forward, her stance broad and strong. I scooped up a piece of firewood and Neb and me moved forward too. "Triangle defense," I called, my pulse pounding. Neb stepped left and shifted his weight to his strong leg, ready to fight. I stepped right.

Miss Jonah swooped in front of us. "Drop that weapon, now," she whispered to me. "You can't beat fear out of people."

I dropped it as Miss Jonah turned to the villagers, calm now as the heart of a storm. "I am no danger to you. Neither is Rain. I may not know as much as you, but I know this: If you harm one of these children tonight, God will have questions for you. Hard ones." She looked at Otto. "And your father will too."

Otto shrank. The crowd muttered and shifted.

Out of the corner of my eye, I saw a dark figure slip forward, skirting the light. "Get ready," I said, and turned toward the enemy. I grinned to show my teeth as the shadowy figure moved nearer, and wiggled my fingers because it's scary weird.

The figure hissed at me. "Stop it, Stick. You look like an idiot."

Faye!

She stepped up beside us as her Brigade flanked the crowd, shotguns across their chests. "We've been deputized," she shouted. *A lie.* "Go home and we'll forget this happened."

"I won't," Rain said under her breath.

Otto sneered. "You're deputies? Then arrest Jonah. She's a thief. Scrape? Get out here," he said, and Scrape stepped from the shadows behind Rain's house, carrying a sack.

Otto grabbed the sack from him and dumped it at our feet. Everything that had gone missing for weeks glistened in the torchlight—tonic bottles, fishing lures, a straw hat. Julia's silver bracelet, Miss Dandee's pearls, Miss Pope's paperweight.

"This was inside Jonah's house!" Otto shouted, lifting Julia's silver bracelet for the crowd to see.

"It wasn't!" Miss Jonah cried. "That's not true!"

"Jonah's a thief," Otto told the crowd. "And a spy. She lights fires to signal the U-boats that killed my brother. She's a danger to every life on this island. She even poisoned Scrape. Who's next? You?" He looked around the crowd. "You?" The crowd grumbled.

Scrape grabbed Otto's arm. "Otto, stop. You said you just wanted to scare them. That nobody would get hurt."

"Do what I say, or I'll tell your family about you," Otto said. "Nobody will take your word over mine, not even your folks. And your brainless friend Jersey will back me up."

The crowd moved closer. Scrape looked at Miss Jonah, and stepped close to Otto. "My folks trust me. But you won't tell anybody about me, Otto," he said, his voice low. "You know why? Because I'll tell them myself. And Jersey might surprise you."

He looked at the crowd. "Listen to me," he shouted. "Miss Jonah didn't take these things. *I* took them. Me and Jersey and Otto," he said, and the crowd went quiet. Scrape snagged Miss Dandee's pearl necklace, letting it snake over his hand as he held it high in the flickering light. "We stole these things to impress Otto's brother, Tommy."

"Liar," Otto said. "Jersey, tell them!"

Jersey and Scrape locked gazes for a moment. Jersey backed away from Otto and dropped his torch.

"Otto even *poisoned* me and blamed Miss Jonah," Scrape said. "And after Tommy died, he blamed her even harder. For that, and all of this too."

Otto wanted revenge for Tommy's death, I thought. And she was an easy target.

"Go home," Scrape said. "Miss Jonah is innocent. This is all a lie."

The crowd broke into twos and threes, and Otto crumbled like a little kid who'd lost his favorite toy. "Scrape, you'll be sorry for this," Otto said.

"I don't think so," Scrape said. "And my name is *Clarence*. Use it."

Faye put her hand on his shoulder. "Go home," she shouted. "And when you see this young man tomorrow, thank him for keeping you from making the biggest mistake of your life." She didn't sound like a movie star saying a writer's lines. She sounded like herself, through and through.

The moment turned sure as the tide.

Otto side-armed his club into the dunes. "Let's go. They aren't worth it," he said. "Not tonight."

"Not tonight," Faye said. "And not on our watch. Ever."

CHAPTER 26

DOUBLE-CROSS

"**M**iss Jonah," Faye said, "you and Rain stay at our place tonight. Please?" Miss Jonah nodded and Rain ran to gather their things. "Mama will be proud of you, Stick," Faye told me.

"Thanks," I said. "You and the Brigade did great. How did they run home and get their fathers' guns so quick?"

She laughed. "They're sticks. That's why I stationed them far away—so nobody could tell. It pays to know your stage props, kiddo."

"Smart move," I said, grinning. "I'll stand watch from HQ," I added, and Neb nodded. "We have a clear view up and down the beach, and of the path into the village. If the crowd reforms, we'll get word to you."

Faye's eyes narrowed. "Good. I'll post a lookout in the dunes. We can form a relay."

Rain ran up with Miss Jonah's bag. "Mama Jonah, I'd like to stay with Stick and Neb."

Miss Jonah gave her a long hug and suddenly I wanted Mama's hug so sharp, it took my breath. "Faye, tell Mama I'll see her tomorrow," I said.

"I will. You lived up to your whole name tonight, kiddo,"

Faye said. "Sarah Stickley Lawson. I'm proud of you." She and her group faded into the night.

Up in HQ, as Neb smoothed his bedroll and Rain spread her quilts, I stared across our world. "The southern beach is clear. So's the path to the village," I reported, scanning the edge of Buxton Woods. I turned to the northern beach, and the sea beyond. A fire smudged the horizon where a downed ship burned, same as most nights. A light blinked far out over the sea. Two quick blinks and a long. Two quick blinks and a long. "Somebody's out there—on the sea."

"Where?" Neb asked, grabbing the binoculars.

"There. Two quick flashes, and a long."

"Morse code for *U*. Look," he added, pointing to a fainter, yellowish light up the beach. Two quick and a long. "Somebody's signaling back."

I grabbed Davis's flashlight and the three of us raced for the stairs.

As my feet hit the sand, I turned to the dunes and flicked my light toward home. A monkey-bird screeched back. "What the heck?" Neb gasped, crouching.

"It's Faye, standing watch in the dunes," Rain said. "All is well. Let's go."

By the time we made it down the beach, night had swallowed the lights. We knelt as the waves pounded ashore and sent their white fingers swirling across the sand.

Moonlight etched sea and dunes. "Two sets of footprints," I said.

Rain nodded. "Deep ones."

"They were carrying something heavy," Neb said, examining the prints.

An idea scraped its fingernails up my spine. "They carried the same thing they dragged the night we saw the wide track leading into the sea."

Neb's face went tight with worry. "Who carries something heavy to the sea?"

For one moment, my senses let loose of my body and drifted just out of reach. No, I thought. That can't be right. My voice sounded distant and sad: "Who moves in and out among us, easy as the tide? Who left the night we saw that odd track to the sea? Who left us tonight?"

"Oh," Rain said, her voice soft as angel feathers.

At HQ, as Neb scanned the beaches for danger, I opened my journal and searched its pages. An hour later, I closed it. "The days Carl rode into town on the bus, the weather rambled every which way," I reported. "But when he just showed up on the beach, the barometric pressure always registered high the night before—bringing easy seas. And the wind came from the east, pushing things ashore. Like rafts. Hypothesis: Carl and Ralph rowed ashore from a U-boat, just like the spies in New York and Miami."

Fact: Science doesn't care whose heart it breaks.

"Carl's no enemy," Rain said. "He can't be."

"Prove it," I invited.

She crossed her arms. "I'm an artist. I don't have to prove what my heart knows is true."

Downstairs, the door scraped open and my heart lunged like a mad dog on a short chain. "Neb, get the machine gun!" I shouted.

A voice rose urgent and quick. "It's Captain Davis! Don't shoot."

"We don't have a machine gun," Neb called, looking relieved. "Stick made that up."

"Good bluff," Davis said, his grin rising up to us. "I was just walking home from the party. I'm sorry I wasn't around earlier—Faye says you did a great job tonight. Anyway, I saw your Matchstick Alert wasn't set and figured you were here. Like me to set it?"

"Roger Wilco," I called.

"Tell him our suspicions about Carl and Ralph," Neb said, his voice low.

"No!" Rain whispered.

"Night," Davis called, and closed the door.

Rain looked at me, her brown eyes serious. "Circumstantial proof won't cut it, toots. I'm not turning Carl in without *real* proof. We saw tonight what happens when people think you're a spy and you're not. Neb, I need that little red book you found on the beach."

"At breakfast," he promised as Davis's Jeep lights flared to life and he drove away.

I walked over to the Stick-O-Matic, lit the candle, and

lowered the glass jar over it. I strolled to my pallet and lay down as the flame flickered out.

Neb yawned. "Daddy says things always look better in the morning."

But they didn't. In fact, they looked much, much worse.

I awakened to a pearly gray sky, and a horizon streaked in red. I slipped into my lab jacket—and Papa's hug. Rain slept curled up like a kitten. Neb lay flat on his back, his neckerchief straight, his arms and ankles crossed.

I picked up my spyglass. *There!* I zeroed in on a raft struggling toward shore with three men on board. Three men in German uniforms! "Invasion!" I shouted.

Neb lunged to his feet, hit a chair, and hopped over to me, rubbing his shin. He grabbed the binoculars. "That raft's too heavy," he said as a wave crashed over it. The men piled out in chest-deep water. "That's Carl," he said. "And Ralph."

They struggled ashore in the breakers, pulling the raft behind them. Ralph and a stranger lifted the raft over their heads and ran to the dunes as Carl gathered the duffels. Minutes later, they started toward us, still in uniforms but minus the raft. Carl stopped, lifted a pair of binoculars—and looked straight at us.

We fell to the floor. "Did he see us?" Neb whispered.

"I don't know. Wake Rain up. We've got to get out of here."

As we tore downstairs, the door scraped open. We froze.

"In here," Carl said. "It's safe. The kids set the Matchstick

Alert—which you can only do from outside. Nobody's home. Alfred, pass out our street clothes." The stranger stepped into a sliver of soft sunlight from the windows above the door.

The fox-faced man from Neb's little book!

"Do exactly what I say," Carl said as Alfred tossed him a dry shirt.

"Yaeger's orders: Blow up this lighthouse, the water tower, and that rinky-dink light tower by the woods. Ralph, you and Alfred wire the rinky-dink light first and hide the detonator. Then the water tower. It's just for cleaning boats, but Captain Yaeger doesn't know that."

Yaeger. Their U-boat captain. How can this be real? Betrayed, I thought. *Just like* Dime Novel #6: Double-Cross.

"I'll wire the lighthouse," he continued. "We meet in Buxton Woods and wait for dusk. From the water tower, travel SSE. There's a rise where a thief once hid his stash. Rain told me."

Rain gasped. The three men wheeled and peered through the dark. "Who's there?" the fox-faced man asked, his accent thick as a fog bank.

I scrabbled my fingernails against the stair.

"Mice," Carl said. "Neb's been eating in here again."

"I say we meet by the water tower," Ralph said. "It's easier."

"I'm in charge," Carl snapped. "We'll hide in the woods and synchronize our watches. We light up all three targets at once tonight, and hope to escape in the dark and confusion."

"But Yaeger said to be back by noon," Alfred said.

Carl ironed his voice smooth. "We'd be sitting ducks in day-light. Don't worry, Alfred, Yaeger won't leave until we make him famous. If anybody stops you, let Ralph do the talking. He improvises better than you'd think, and your accent will give us away. Ralph, if anything happens to the Dimes, or to Faye—I'll kill you." Carl flipped his watch face-up. It glowed in the dim light. *That's why he wears it face-side down at night! What kind of spy-catcher am I?*

"Get the detonators," Ralph told Alfred, and the two men slipped out.

Carl pulled up his shirt, checked the knife at his waistband. "Knife? *Check*. Pistol? *Check*. Courage?" He closed his eyes. "God in heaven, please help your idiot son find a way home. Amen." He opened the door and stepped outside.

"He's setting the Matchstick Alert," I whispered as the door slowly closed.

"Trapped like rattuses," Neb said, his voice pale.

"*Rattis*," I corrected. "Latin's different with plurals."

"Not grammar! Not now! Carl's going to blow us up!" Neb cried.

"Nobody's blowing anything up until nightfall," I said, breathing myself calm. "All we have to do is stay quiet until he wires this place and leaves. Then we run."

We crept back upstairs. An hour later, Carl slunk along the dunes, buried his duffel, and snuck toward Neb's house. Suddenly, he flattened against a dune.

"Faye's Brigade!" Neb cried. "We're saved!"

We clattered down the stairs.

"Thought so," Ralph said, stepping from the shadows. "There weren't mice on those stairs. There were three little rats."

"But . . . you left with Alfred," Neb said.

"Looks like I slipped back in, doesn't it? Sit down and shut up or I'll snap your little necks." He pointed to Neb. "You. Get me some rope."

"I won't," Neb said. Ralph stepped toward him.

"Because he can't," I said quickly. A lie. "Neb's polio leg is acting up. The rope's upstairs, where he practices his knots. I'll get it."

Ralph narrowed his eyes. "Hurry up, lollipop. And don't try anything smart."

I bounded upstairs, looking for anything that might save us.

"Three ropes!" Ralph shouted. "If I come up, I'll only need two when I come down."

I grabbed one of my glass test tubes—Papa's last gift to me. I shoved it in my pocket and snagged three hanks of rope. "Found it!" I shot to the radio. "I'm coming!" I yelled to cover the click of the transmitter switch. I taped the button down, leaving the channel open. "Don't hurt Neb and Rain!" I shouted into the transmitter. "Please, Ralph! Don't kill them!"

Please, God, let somebody hear, I prayed, and started slowly down the stairs. "Why blow up the lighthouse?" I said loud enough for my voice to reach the radio. "And the rinky-dink tower? And water tower? Why does your U-boat captain even care?"

Neb counted out the stairs beneath his breath as I stepped onto the lighthouse floor.

"Almost sorry you found it," Ralph said, snatching the ropes from my hand. "I looked forward to throwing you off that balcony. Who's first?"

My mind raced. "Let Rain and Neb go and take me hostage. I'm tall enough to be a human shield. And I'm smart. I know every inch of this island. And all of the encyclopedia except Volume K."

"Shut up," Ralph said. "I don't need you to think for me. Not you, not Carl."

"That's right," Rain said, very easy. "Yaeger should have put you in charge." A pouty smile crept across Ralph's broad face. Rain reads people like I read clouds.

"If Yaeger *had* put me in charge, we'd have blown up Norfolk by now. But Norfolk isn't famous enough yet. Norfolk wouldn't buy Yaeger a parade in Berlin."

I played along. "Right," I said. "But this lighthouse will."

"*That's* why you're blowing it up?" Neb said. "Because it's famous? Are you crazy?"

"Ralph's smart," Rain said very quickly. "People know this lighthouse all over the world. Even Hitler knows its black and white swirls, I bet. Maybe *you'll* get the parade, Ralph."

He snapped the rope and stepped toward her. "Sorry you won't be here to read about it."

"No," Neb and I said together, but Rain went calm as a lullaby.

"I need to pray," she said, clutching her father's ring. "God doesn't know I'm coming."

"She's right. Heaven's not like here," Neb said, frantic. "You don't just drop in."

"I'm not ready either," I said. My heart fluttered like a bird dying to fly. "Rain and me haven't been baptized, not in the dunking revival way."

Breathe deep, Genius. Don't come unraveled.

"Give us time," I continued as Ralph finally shifted his gaze from Rain. "I know you will. I've heard you sing that Sunday school song. Besides," I said. "Imagine Carl's face when you tell him we were in here praying when he blew the place up."

Ralph's face went sly and cruel. *Finally. A win for us.*

Neb stepped in. "Man to man, you could just let us go. We won't tell anybody you're here and even if we did, nobody listens to us."

Rain whispered her prayer. "Help Mama Jonah and forgive Ralph and tell my daddy I need him. Amen."

Something broke inside my heart. "Rain's practically a baby," I said. "Let her go."

"Shut up," Ralph said. "Put your hands behind you. You first," he said, and Neb put his hands behind him, his lower lip trembling. Ralph bulldogged his hands. Neb grunted when Ralph pulled the knots tight. He tied my hands next. Then Rain's.

He grabbed a coil of wire from his duffel. He bound Neb and then Rain. He leaned over me, smelling like Vienna sausages, and bound my legs so tight my toes tingled.

"Go to Brazil and forget about the war," Neb said. "We've

got a map that will help you." Ralph yanked Neb's neckerchief from around his neck and stuffed it in his mouth.

"I understand your frustration. Neb can be annoying," I said as Ralph peeled off Neb's shoes and socks. Seeing Neb's toes helpless and naked rearranged every atom in my universe. "I have just one question. Did Carl lose a compass button in here? Because your feet are too big to match the footprint on our floured floor and his are—"

"We stole Reverend Wilkins's shoes, blabbermouth. Carl wore them." He jammed Neb's brown sock in my mouth and the black one in Rain's. Rain gagged.

"I'll set your Matchstick Alert when I go," he said. "Nobody will guess you're in here."

Fish rot, fish rot, fish rot.

He slipped out of the lighthouse, and the fear closed in around us.

CHAPTER 27

NOTHING SWEETER THAN BREATHING

I struggled, the rope biting my wrists. This will never work, I thought.

Life Rule #4: *In times of danger, bet on each other.*

I fell to my side and rolled to Neb. I jutted out my chin, nudging his hands. His fingers spidered across my face and closed around the sock. I pulled my head back, leaving the sock in his hand, and gulped the fresh air. "Rain, over here," I whispered, and she toppled and rolled. I tugged the sock from her mouth and Neb keeled over, and Rain removed his gag.

Fact: There is nothing sweeter than breathing. (See *Dime Novel #11: Nothing Sweeter than Breathing.* Also Volume M, *mammal.*) I bottom-bounced to Neb. "Back-to-back," I said. I closed my eyes and tried to picture the knots on his wrists.

"He tied us up just alike," Neb coached. "Double slip knots pulled tight, and anchored with a square knot. Then an over-hand knot to make sure the others can't be loosened."

"*You* untie them. Look at Rain's hands and work on mine."

A half hour later, he slumped. "I can't," he said, tears crowding his voice.

"I have another idea," I said, "but it might not work."

"If it fails, will it be worse than being tied up in a dynamite death trap?" Rain asked.

"Good point." I fell over and rolled to my stomach, pressing my pocket to the floor. I lifted my thigh and let it fall until Papa's test tube broke in my pocket. *Thank you, Papa.*

"Rain, there's broken glass in my right pocket," I said, rolling to my back. "Pull out a piece and cut Neb's ropes."

Rain went to work. After a forever of Rain and me taking turns, the rope fell free.

"I got it now," Neb said, unwinding the wire from his legs and turning to our knots.

Moments later, we raced upstairs, to the radio, blinking against the bright sunlight streaming through our windows. "Mayday at the Hatteras Lighthouse, mayday. Three German spies plan to blow up the lighthouse tonight. We Dimes will nab them in Buxton Woods at dusk." I hesitated. "The honor of your presence is requested."

"The honor of their presence is requested?" Neb said. "Did the ropes cut off the blood flow to your brain? This isn't an invitation to the White House."

Rain grabbed the transmitter. "This is Rain J. M. Lawson. Send help now. Please."

The sun hung high in the sky as Neb peeked around the base of the lighthouse a little later. "Coast is clear." My cut leg throbbed and my empty stomach rumbled as I set the Matchstick Alert to fool Ralph, in case he came back.

"Looks like Carl did his work, all right," Neb said. Packets of explosives the size of spelling books lined the tower's base. "Is there a dime novel on disconnecting bombs?"

Rain frowned. *"Boom Town* says if you get blown up, you don't hear the boom. *Short Fuse Sally* has nothing," she said as we traced the wires to a little box.

I said a prayer and carefully disconnected the red wire, breaking the circuit.

"I didn't hear a boom," Neb reported. "But we *have* to be alive. Heaven isn't this sandy. Let's disconnect the rinky-dink tower and find Mr. Grand. He'll know what to do."

My hope collapsed. "Grand and Mama left this morning on the early ferry, headed to Wilmington." I swallowed hard. It only takes one government paper to make Papa officially gone from this world or one unexpected ship to bring him home. "Let's find Faye. Keep to the shadows. If Carl or Ralph see us, we're smoke."

We kept to the dunes' curves and the yaupons' shadows as we darted to the rinky-dink tower and disconnected it, and sprinted to the village. The cicadas' faint song rolled over us like a rusty wave as we charged the store. "Faye!" I called, and slammed into the locked door. I rattled the knob. "What the blue blazes? We never lock this door."

I looked down the street. No Faye, no kids. Everybody was out fishing or inside, working. "Let's try the water tower," I said, and we took off.

Miss Agnes opened the PO's door as we flew past. "Where are you going? Stick! What's wrong?"

The PO Special Ops distress signal. I took a chance on her. "ELEANOR, ELEANOR, ELEANOR! Tell Davis we're in Buxton Woods!"

We ducked behind the Artists' Shack, peering at the water tower next door. J. Edgar shot from the thicket beneath the tower. "It's just Edgar. Let's go in," I said.

"No," Rain whispered. "Ralph hurt Edgar once. Edgar will run from him now. Wait."

Good call. Ralph slipped from the brambles' gloom three heartbeats later and turned toward the woods. "Alfred might be in there too," I whispered. Again we waited.

"Something's happened to him," Neb said. "Ralph's killed him, or left him behind. We'll disconnect these explosives and follow Ralph. Where the heck is Faye?"

Work done, we crept to the edge of the woods. "Ralph's in here," I whispered as the cicadas whirred. "Carl and Alfred may be too. Stay low and keep quiet."

Rain gulped. "No thank you. Copperheads come out to hear a cicada's song."

"Copperheads actually come out to *eat* cicadas," I said. "Volume C."

"We have to go in," Neb said. "Here's the scoop. The short, thick snakes—copperheads and water moccasins—will kill you. Long skinny snakes are mostly just rude and bitey." He looked at me. "Are you okay? You look like you're carved out of soap."

"I'm fine," I said, trying not to cry. "Many scientists suffer from a terror of snakes."

"Artists too," Rain whispered as the three of us bumped hands. "*Non tatum sursum.*"

Deeper and deeper into the woods we crept, through saplings and briars, through rotten water onto little islands. We stepped from log to clumps of swamp grass to log.

"What's that?" Rain whispered as something slithered through the brambles.

"Keep walking," I said.

Ahead, something rustled. We froze. The birds and frogs fell silent. We faded into deep shadow as Alfred crept toward us, his face chalky with fear. "Hello?" he whispered. "Carl?"

"Shut up," Ralph growled, stepping from a thicket of reeds just yards ahead.

Thank you, Alfred. Without you, we'd have walked right into Ralph's arms.

"Where's Carl?" Alfred asked. "Where did you go? Somebody's trailing me."

"Nobody's trailing you, dummkopf," Ralph said. He yanked a button from his shirt, unscrewed it counterclockwise, and peered at its tiny compass. "Wonder if they have gators in here."

Neb looked at me, eyes wide. I shook my head.

Ralph glided through the bog. Alfred stumbled after him

like an invading army, leaves crunching, branches snapping, mud slurping at his shoes.

We stood stone still. Finally, a pileated woodpecker cawed like a jungle bird and tree frogs swirled out their song. Something moved at our feet. A thin-bodied black snake glided over Neb's shoe. His face went white as parchment as the snake slithered on.

"According to Volume S," I gasped, "a nonpoisonous pink-bellied water snake just—"

"Shhhh," Rain said. "Move enough for the snakes to hear us."

We crept deeper into the forest, tracking Alfred and Ralph by the quiet of the tree frogs as the branches overhead shadowed the sunlight. We squinted through dim light as Carl stepped from behind a yaupon. "Over here, fellows."

Alfred ran to him like a child. "We ran the rinky-dink wires. But we got separated—"

"Shut it," Ralph said. He spit into a clump of ferns, and a frog jumped, plopping into the bog. "Did you wire the lighthouse, pretty boy? Ready for a little bang and burn?"

"Ready. Now we wait for the safety of dark," he said.

Neb shifted, snapping a twig, and Ralph wheeled toward us.

"Relax, Ralph," Carl said. "These woods are flush with wildlife. Raccoons, deer, rabbits . . ."

Ralph stepped toward us. Another step. Another. *Three more steps and I can touch him.*

"Ralph," Carl said, his voice sharp. "Over here. Now." Ralph snorted, but turned back.

Carl scanned the thin curtains of grapevines and briars. "This way," he said, picking out a narrow deer trail. "This leads to high land." We followed them to Tommy's old campsite at the heart of the woods. "We'll camp here," Carl said. "Stow your gear and—"

"Hands up!" a woman shouted.

Faye's Brigade stepped from behind water oaks and willows. Faye glanced at Carl and Ralph, and leveled her gun at Alfred. "What the heck is going on?"

"Faye," Carl said. "Don't shoot."

The wind rustled and a shaft of afternoon's golden light sliced through the trees' canopy, haloing Alfred's thin face. "He looks like an angel," Rain whispered.

Carl leaned down, and carefully placed his pistol on the ground. "Faye, Alfred's a friend. Alfred? Ralph? Put your guns down." Alfred sank to his knees, fumbled a pistol from his pocket, and laid it in the leaves. He raised his hands over his head.

Not Ralph. Ralph stood stock-still, hand inches from the pistol strapped to his hip. "I don't think so, cuz," he said, his voice cold. "I'm not going back to jail."

"*Back* to jail?" Naomi gasped.

"You," Ruth told Alfred. She motioned with her shotgun barrel. "Empty your pack."

"Faye," Carl said, "please. Wait for Captain Davis."

Ralph scowled. "Why?" He looked at Carl and his face went cunning, and then angry. "So that's how it is. You double-crossing son of a gun."

"Empty the bag," Ruth demanded. Alfred upended his pack, dumping his last wire, and a detonator. "All three of you put your hands behind your heads. Now."

Ralph went for his gun.

We Dimes hit the ground. *Blam-blam!* The gray light shattered and the birds flapped like ragged thunder into the sky. When I opened my eyes, Ralph lay on his back in the clearing, not breathing, with Ruth's and Faye's shotguns trained on him. Naomi sat rocking back and forth, clasping her hand. Alfred lay curled on his side.

"We'll get their guns," I shouted, and Neb rocketed to Naomi.

"Where did you come from?" Faye shrieked.

"Who shot my sister?" Neb yelled.

"Nobody shot me. I fell," Naomi said as a car roared to the edge of the forest and backfired. "I think I sprained my wrist."

"Snake," Alfred said, his voice strained. Slowly, he pointed. A copperhead coiled three feet away, insolent and cold, its triangular head raised, the pattern on its thick back almost invisible in the leaves. Faye aimed and pulled the trigger.

Blam! The snake flew through the air.

"Help me," Alfred gasped, raising his pants leg to show a nasty red bite on his pale calf.

"Snakebite!" Neb said. He whipped off his neckerchief,

tied it around Alfred's leg, grabbed a stick, and tightened the tourniquet. As we helped Alfred to his feet, someone crashed toward us.

"Stand down!" Miss Agnes bellowed, charging into the clearing. "Heavens to Roosevelt, what have you people done? Faye, help Naomi to the car. Carl, get Ralph's body." She squinted at Neb's tourniquet. "Good job, Bristly Dime. Help me get Alfred out of here."

"Stop," Faye barked. "I'm in charge."

Miss Agnes's glare downshifted to neutral. "Fine. What should we do?"

Faye tapped her saddle oxford against the leaves. "Activate Miss Agnes's plan," she commanded, and we sprang into action.

I grabbed Miss Agnes's arm. "How do you know Alfred's name? What's going on?"

"I'll explain later," she said. "Hurry. Before the villagers storm the woods and everything flies apart."

CHAPTER 28

IN THE WIND

An hour later, we sat in Neb's parlor wolfing down cold molasses biscuits as Captain Davis and Faye helped Alfred, in the back bedroom. Captain Davis walked in, his handsome face drawn.

"How's Alfred?" Carl asked, jumping to his feet.

"Still with us," Davis said. "Barely. Miss Irma's sitting with him."

"I did what I could," Faye said, filing in. "Removed as much venom as we could, treated the bite with turpentine . . . I wish I knew more. I wish Mama was here."

Davis glanced at Miss Agnes. "Thanks for the assist, Agnes. Smart, Stick, shouting up to my radio transmitter. Which one of you kids knew how to turn it on?"

"We all know," Rain said. "We've seen you do it a hundred times."

"Speaking of snakes," I said, "the Dime Novel Kids would like to share our evidence against Carl Miller—German spy, double-crosser, and a snake of a different kind. Please arrest him and make sure the FBI receives a full report."

"*What?*" Faye gasped.

Davis perched on Miss Irma's delicate velvet chair, looking

as out of place as an island pony in a hat shop. "I have my own ideas about Carl," he said, "but I'd like to hear yours first."

"I'll get our evidence," Neb said, and took off for HQ.

"Bring my weather journal," I shouted.

"And the portrait Carl drew of us," Rain called, disappearing into the kitchen.

The portrait? Why?

When Neb returned, Rain unrolled the portrait and clothes-pinned it to a ladder-back chair. "Carl drew this," she said. "He signed it, *For my true friends Rain, Stick, and Neb. Love, Carl Miller.* Note how he lit our faces from the side, leaving one side in shadow."

Carl sighed. "Hold it, toots. I can explain."

"Rain has the floor," she replied, and opened Neb's little red book. "Neb found this book on the beach. It's filled with sketches, each one with a neat frame drawn around it. Here's Alfred, with his fox face. And Ralph, with his fat lizard smile. And U-boat Captain Yaeger—all of them half in shadow, half in light."

"They're the same style as Carl's portrait," Faye said, stunned.

"Very good," Rain said. "Carl might as well have signed these sketches too."

I looked at Carl. "We were so focused on Miss Agnes and the Artists, we didn't see you for what you are. We trusted you. A mistake," I said, and Carl looked like I'd stomach-punched him. (See *paralyzed diaphragm*, Volume D.)

To my surprise, Rain sat and gave me a nod. "Stick?" she said.

She's up to something, I thought as I rose. "Interesting, what the artist sees and a scientist asks," I said, smoothing my lab jacket. "I asked myself why Carl drew frames around each sketch in Neb's book—and why he added this spill of shells and seaweed to our portrait."

I plucked a magnifying glass from our crate and scanned the shells. A pattern of tiny letters stared up at me.

Mr. Mac eased in and lowered himself into his chair like it was lined in nettles. *Perfect timing*. I gave him a smile. "Neb is our code expert," I said. "Neb, I'll turn our presentation over to you, if you don't mind."

Neb stepped forward. "Thank you for that introduction," he said, smoothing his hair. He shot his father a quick look, picked up the magnifying glass, and studied the tiny letters. The room went silent except for his breathing. "This is Dirk's code, the same one we recovered at the Oceanside Club," he announced, straightening up. "It's a one-to-one code. Feel free to talk among yourselves while I decipher." He rummaged through our box for the code's key and his pencil, and went to work.

Moments later, he dropped his pencil. "This inscription reads *CM, fisherman and true American*. I assume *CM* stands for Carl Miller."

"It does," Carl said.

Miss Agnes almost smiled. "Very good, Bristly Dime. Nazi code is a challenge."

"It is," Neb admitted, and gazed at Carl, his brown eyes sad. "And since this is a Nazi code, I guess it helps prove Carl is a Nazi."

346

Carl is a Nazi. The words stung like a thousand jellyfish. Rain stared straight ahead, but her chin quivered and her eyes filled with quick tears.

Neb nodded to me, very professional. "I'll pass the presentation back to you, Stick," he said. He sat by his father, his back ramrod straight. Mr. Mac patted his shoulder and Neb smiled.

"Carl Miller a *fisherman?*" Faye said. "I don't think so. Carl doesn't know a sea bass from a blue crab."

"This is spy-craft, not a seafood dinner," I said. I placed the postcard from the Oceanside Club on the table. "This is addressed to Carl's brother. Fritz *Fischer.* Full brothers generally share a last name."

Carl leaned back. "Fischer is my birth name. When my father sent me to Germany, I changed it to my mother's maiden name. Fischer, *Fisher.* It's a pun, calling myself a *fisherman.*"

A silence fell over the room. "It's almost funny," Neb said.

I continued. "You drew most of these sketches on your U-boat. Sailors eating, peering through a periscope, loading torpedoes..."

He rose to stand beside me. "And that's you Dimes, the first day I saw you. And that's Alfred. Alfred Braun—poet, lover of jazz, and my only friend on that stinking tub. I brought this book ashore by accident, and lost it one frantic night. Thanks for finding it, Neb." He turned a page. "That's Captain Yaeger, as you guessed."

"Yaeger," Miss Agnes muttered. "German for *wolf.*"

"He lives up to his name," Carl told her. "He hunts ships like he smells their blood."

Captain Davis frowned—at *me*. "That book's proof. How long have you had it?"

"Proof of what? Nobody knew Carl was a spy."

"I did," Miss Agnes said. "I suspected it, anyway. That Swiss wristwatch is standard issue for German spies. Rookie move, Carl. You should have buried it with your uniform."

Carl studied her. "You used that odd map to lure me in. You knew I'd recognize it."

"Actually, I gave the cards to Stick and Rain to reward them for standing up at that civilian defense meeting. And . . . I wanted to . . . establish a bond with potential allies," she said, shooting me a glance.

"I didn't know she could blush," Neb whispered.

"I admit, I also hoped she'd show you the map. It was excellent bait. If you'd come to spy in my window instead of sending *children*, I'd have arrested you as a Peeping Tom and taken you in for questioning." She looked at me. "I wish you had trusted me."

"How could I?" I asked. "You broke into HQ after the U-boats torpedoed their first ship. We know because you brought in a mouse. A mouse can't climb two hundred fifty-seven metal stairs. It rode in your briefcase."

She chuckled. "Edgar's work again, the little scamp. You're right, I *did* go up, to scan the beach for invaders. HQ has the best view. I assume Otto ransacked it the night before."

"You also burned papers in your backyard," Neb said.

"I didn't want my codes in Nazi hands," she said. "And I couldn't use the fireplace—"

"Because the chimney was full of radio equipment," Rain said.

Faye gasped. "Codes? Radios? What kind of postmistress *are* you?"

Davis grinned. "Please allow me. Everyone, meet Agnes Wainwright, of the FBI."

Fish rot! Miss Agnes is with the FBI?

The parlor went silent. Our chance of ever going FBI heaved its last, hopeless sigh. (See *metaphor*, Volume M.)

"We knew you were FBI," I lied.

"Rubbish." Miss Agnes adjusted her lacy collar. "I may as well read you in. The FBI sent me here to watch for German spies—like Dirk, who I knew from my last assignment, in—"

"Brazil," Rain said. "We deduced that from the map in your cards, the photo in your glove compartment, and the fact that J. Edgar understands Portuguese."

Davis laughed. "You named your cat after the FBI director? That took some brass."

J. Edgar? Of course! After J. Edgar Hoover! How could we have missed that?

"We noticed that," I said. "But felt it too obvious for comment."

"Historically, Brazil's a bit of a training zone for German spies, but I expect they'll come into the war as an ally any day now," Miss Agnes said, resting her hand on the mantel and looking almost good. "I worked as a double agent in Brazil years ago, when Edgar was just a kitten. Dirk—then a German recruit—trained there, and I made it my business to befriend him."

"A double agent pretends to be on one side, but is on the other," Neb whispered to Mr. Mac, who nodded, his face serious.

"You had blond hair and cheekbones back then," Rain said, studying Miss Agnes.

"True on both counts. Never be afraid of change. Well, I've been transferred several times since Brazil, and I lost track of Dirk. Until he showed up here with Julia."

"And how about Julia? How does she fit in?" Neb demanded. He turned to Mr. Mac. "Julia almost fell in love with me but I turned her down," he said, and Mr. Mac's eyes widened.

"Julia remains an unknown," Miss Agnes said. "She's in the wind."

"As in *Dime Novel #72: In the Wind*," Rain murmured.

Why would Miss Agnes lie about Julia even now?

"Brazil," I said, thinking back. "Brazil's in the *southern* hemisphere while we're in the northern hemisphere, which is why Dirk found our night sky so interesting," I added. "We look up on different stars. So. Now Dirk is . . ."

"In custody, thanks to the evidence you Dimes passed to Captain Davis," she said. "Yes, he shared it, along with parts of your story and Carl's," she said before I could protest. "Don't be angry. I outrank him."

"Dirk's in custody thanks to *your* evidence?" Mr. Mac said, staring at Neb.

Neb beamed. Faye's mouth fell open. It felt good, being a known spy-catcher. An honor Miss Agnes and I have in common.

"But *Alfred* came from Germany, which is under *our* stars," Neb said, reaching into his pocket. He held out three coins. "I found this Kraut money in his pocket."

Carl closed his eyes and shook his head. "Poor Alfred. Wrong pocket litter."

Miss Agnes rocked up on her toes. "Pocket litter's the little trash spies carry, to back up their identities," she told Mr. Mac. "Movie tickets, grocery receipts, stamps. And those coins are called *reichspfennigs*, Neb. Not *Kraut money*. Always respect your enemy. Disrespect leads to carelessness, and carelessness leads to catastrophe."

"She likes being the center of attention," I whispered to Rain.

"Like you," Rain murmured as I thumbed through my weather journal.

"Returning to the spy we call Carl," I said, "I'd also like to present this journal entry as proof. *We saw a huge track leading to the sea.*" I looked at Carl. "You *dragged* your raft to the sea, called by lights on the ocean. Long-long-short. Rookie mistake."

"Morse code, *U* for *U-boat*," Neb said.

"Alfred thought it was clever," Carl said, and sighed. "*U* for *Unterseeboot*, in German. We were signaling—him from the U-boat, me from the beach. As for that track . . . Ralph dragged the raft to the sea."

I looked at Davis. "Carl and Ralph came to study the island, the military bases going up nearby, the beach patrols. Today they came to blow up our lighthouse."

"Plus the rinky-dink light tower," Neb said. "And the water tower, where Carl used to hide. I smelled his Old Spice after-shave the day the Artists moved in, only I thought it was Julia's perfume."

"Neb has a nose like a bloodhound," Rain said, and Neb gave a humble sniff.

I scanned my notes. "One question," I said. "Carl and Ralph took the bus sometimes, and sometimes they rowed ashore from a U-boat, just like the spies in New York and Miami. Each time they rowed ashore, the barometric pressure had been high, leading to calm seas. And the wind blew from the east, pushing their raft ashore. But tonight they rowed into the wind, in a dangerously heavy chop." I looked at Carl. "Why?"

"Captain Yaeger," Rain guessed, and Carl nodded.

"Grand Admiral Donitz has ordered us back to Germany. Yaeger announced this suicide mission as soon as we came aboard last night—to leave a calling card for President Roosevelt."

Faye shook her head. "Stop confessing, Carl. Don't you know what happens to spies?"

"We Dime Novel Kids rest our case," I said.

Rain rose. "I helped present our facts," she said. "Now I'd like to present a different view of those facts." She looked around the room. "Carl's a double agent, who risked his life to save us all."

CHAPTER 29

FATE'S MANY FACES

"**A** double agent? Based on what?" I demanded.

Rain studied Carl, her curls gleaming in the lamplight, her brown eyes thoughtful. "Based on what my artist's heart knows. And my strong mind. And the way Mama Jonah teaches me to let little things grow to be big. My heart tells me Carl wouldn't double-cross us," she said. "His heart's good, and mine feels it. And my mind tells me he *didn't* double-cross us."

"And if you let that idea grow, it *only* makes sense that he double-crossed someone else," Faye said. "By the process of elimination, I'd guess Carl double-crossed Yaeger."

"Very good, Faye," Rain said.

"Only, Ralph thought Carl double-crossed *him*," Neb said. "That's what Ralph meant when he called Carl a double-crossing son of a gun, in the woods tonight."

"Exactly. Carl does have curiosity about our island, but he never hurt us. In fact, he helped us. I rest my case," Rain said, and sat down by Carl.

"Thanks, toots," he said, and she leaned against his arm.

We swiveled to Captain Davis, for his decision. "It's always good to entertain different points of view," he said, his handsome face thoughtful. "Thank you, Dimes."

Rain nodded. "Different eyes," she explained.

He looked around the room. "As it happens, I agree with Rain," he said, and Faye gasped.

"Carl *is* a double agent. Ever since he pretended to come talk to me about enlisting, he's given me good information—about U-boats, missions, his hopes of getting home. When I saw him at the party last night, and later saw the lights off-shore, I knew his U-boat had picked him up. I left for Norfolk, never expecting him to return so soon.

"Stick," Davis continued, "good move, leaving the radio open to transmit an SOS. When I realized I couldn't make it by dusk, I stopped in Elizabeth City and radioed Agnes."

"I'm a bit of a musician," she said, surveying her finger-nails. "His call came through just as you three ran by, shouting 'Eleanor!'"

"*A musician?*" Faye said. "You can't even dance. I saw you try at the party."

"*Musician* is spy lingo for *radio operator,*" Rain explained.

"That's why you didn't let Grand *visit* you," I said. "Until finally you hid your spy gear and invited him over so no one would take *our* reports on you seriously."

"Where did you hide the dolls? And the high-caliber lip-sticks?" Neb demanded.

"The linen closet," she replied.

"Carl?" Captain Davis said. "Anything to add?"

"Yes," Carl said. "If I'd known Ralph had gone back for you kids, I'd have stopped him cold. And Davis, I'm sorry to change our meeting time."

Davis pulled a paper from his pocket: "I found your note

when I got home: *Meeting changed. Ralph & me, plus friend Alfred. Sunset TONIGHT. Same spot. CM.*"

"*That's* why you were slinking to my house after you wired the lighthouse," Neb said.

"Davis and I had a plan," Carl said. "Davis would capture us, we'd put on our uniforms, and he'd take us in as POWs—prisoners of war. We'd be safe until war's end. Only, Davis and I planned it for next week, not tonight."

Faye put her face in her hands. "I'm an idiot." I started to agree out of habit, but found too much evidence to the contrary. "Your plan would have worked if we hadn't followed Alfred into the woods," she said. "We saw him . . . skulking. So I closed the store and we followed him. I don't know, he just looked guilty of *something*."

"Guilty of being afraid," Miss Agnes said. "Remember, Dimes: *Never* look scared undercover," she added as Neb's mother walked in.

Miss Irma looked at Carl. "Alfred said to tell his mother he loves her," she said, brushing a tear away. "And to tell you goodbye. He seemed like a sweet boy. I'll pray for his mother."

We sat in shocked silence.

"I'm sorry, Carl," Miss Agnes finally said. "But we must grieve later. Now we must move, and move quickly. Two decisions remain: How to explain the gunfire in Buxton Woods, and what to do with you."

"The gunfire's easy," Faye said. "We'll tell everybody Faye's Brigade held target practice—shooting at snakes. It's ridiculous, but they expect ridiculous from us."

"Then they're nincompoops," Miss Agnes said, and Faye looked at her, shocked. "You were smart today. And brave. I applaud you."

Naomi hopped up. "Ruth and I can open the store and start the rumor mills churning," she said, but Ruth looked at us, ashen-faced, her gray eyes anguished.

"I . . . I don't think so," Ruth whispered. "You go. I need time . . ."

Miss Agnes stared at her, puzzled. Then she took Ruth's hand. "Who shot Ralph?" she asked, her voice soft.

Ruth's thin face crumpled. "It was like a movie and I was a star until I pulled the trigger and he fell. I never thought it would feel this way."

"Ruth, this is a *war*. He was trying to kill us," Faye said. "I shot too."

"He invaded our home, threatened us," Ruth said. "I had every right. Every *responsibility*, maybe. But shooting at cans isn't the same." She put her face in her hands.

Miss Agnes patted Ruth's shoulder awkwardly as Faye sat beside her. "You were great out there, kiddo. We fired at the same time, *in self-defense*. If you hit him, thank you for saving my life, and maybe every life in this room. If I didn't hit him, I'm sorry."

"I can open the store alone," Naomi said. She kissed her sister and started out.

"Wait," Miss Agnes said. "Mr. Mac, these young people risked everything to protect this island today. I hope you're as proud of them as I am."

Miss Agnes is proud? It felt surprisingly good.

"The island is in good hands," Mr. Mac said, and Neb beamed. "Stick? Rain? Your families will be proud."

"I wish Mama was here to see this," I murmured. "Miss Jonah too."

Faye tucked a curl behind her ear. "Don't worry, kiddo. They'll hear all about it—in private, from me."

"Unfortunately, Davis's plan of taking Carl prisoner won't fly," Miss Agnes said as Naomi left. She popped her knuckles—a hidden talent. "I've done some recon."

"Snooping," Rain told Faye. "Like in *Dime Novel #58: Recon, Rethink, Run.*"

"Carl, because your father *volunteered* you into the German service, you have a paper trail—both as Carl Fischer, *and* as Carl Miller," Miss Agnes said. "Just as the American German spies in New York have. Or . . . had."

The color dropped from Carl's face in one sheet. "I understand."

"I don't," Rain said, startled.

"If we turn him in," Davis said, "they'll realize he's a spy."

Carl looked around the room. "This may be my last chance, then, so here goes," he said. "My name is Carl Fischer, I'm from Richmond, and I love you, Hollywood Faye Lawson. That's true. Almost everything else I've told you is a lie." Faye's violet eyes shimmered.

"A few years ago, I swiped a car to show off for a girl, and got caught. It was stupid," Carl said, and we all nodded. "My father made a deal with *Abwehr*—Germany's secret service. He *volunteered* me to fight for the Nazis if they'd keep me out of Richmond's jail."

"That's a terrible deal," Neb said.

"Not in my father's eyes, Neb. He's a patriot—loyal to his homeland, like thousands of German Americans who've headed back to Germany to fight for the land they grew up in. As it turned out, *Abwehr* also recruits spies. I signed up, hoping to get home, and they sent me to spy school."

"Spy school? Get out of here," Neb said. "Do *we* have that? I'm good undercover. There are people at the Oceanside who still think I'm a little old man."

Carl continued. "When I first came aboard the U-910, I brought my file with me: *Carl Miller. Born in Richmond, Virginia, to German immigrants. Speaks German at home; speaks English with a Southern accent. Useful anywhere in the South. Smart, likeable, expendable.*"

"Expendable?" Faye gasped.

"I didn't like that part either," he said. "But a free ticket home? Count me in. I figured I could find a way to Richmond once I got here."

"Only they stuck you with Ralph Perdu," I said. "Who'd kill you if you gave him half a reason. And who'd joined up the same way you did. From a jail cell."

"Yes," he said, sadness shadowing his face. "And they took another precaution."

"Your grandmother," Rain said.

"You're smart, toots," he said. "My grandmother, who I visited for a few days in her beautiful town—Kassel, Germany. My escape would buy her a one-way trip to Auschwitz."

"Where Julia's family went," Rain breathed. "The place that makes Julia cry."

"Auschwitz?" Davis said, looking at Miss Agnes.

"A horrifying and shockingly inhumane camp that will soon be public knowledge in America," she said. "I'll fill you in."

Faye jumped up. "Kassel? Oh Carl, I heard it on the radio last night!"

"I know. Alfred heard it too, and let me know. Our airplanes bombed Kassel flat. Alfred slipped me a note, letting me know my grandmother's probably gone—that Yaeger had lost his control over me. Only, Yaeger saw the note before I did."

"That's why he sent Alfred on such a dangerous mission," Neb guessed. "To get even. To get rid of him."

Carl nodded. "Alfred would have been a dead man even if he made it back to the ship. Neb, that little book you found? My story's written in code, and hidden in the frames. It's for my little brother. In case I never get a chance to tell him, I want him to know who I really am."

"I'll decode it and put it in Miss Ada's library," Neb said. "We'll find him after the war, when life is safe for you again."

Davis paced. "So. We can't turn you in as a POW—you'll be executed. You can't stay here—Yaeger will hunt you down, and if your grandmother survived the bombing, he'll have her killed. You need to disappear, Carl, and I have no way to disappear you."

Think, Genius, I told myself. *Think.*

They say inspiration is a soft thing, like the brush of an angel's wing. Mine hit like King Kong's sledgehammer. "I know how to disappear him."

"Life Rule #33: *The Dimes always have a plan*," Rain said. "Spill the beans, toots."

I jumped to my feet. "Carl, we need your uniforms and dog tags. Yours, Ralph's, and Alfred's. And we need the white ballast stones from beside the church door. All of them." I looked at Captain Davis. "Davis, get the Jeep. Oh. And we also need . . ." I hesitated. Mama says never use a cup of Blunt when a pinch of Subtle will do. "We need a stunt double for Carl. As in *Dime Novel #73: Fate's Many Faces*."

The clock ticked. I tried again: "We need a nameless stranger, from the cargo area."

Faye lit up like South Carolina fireworks. "Stick, you're a genius."

"I know," I said. "Let's go."

That night as the tree frogs sang and the snakes slithered and the stars looked down, we dug three graves on the rise in the heart of Buxton Woods. One for Carl's friend, Alfred Braun. One for Louisiana's lost boy, Ralph Perdu. One for our friend, Carl Miller.

We slipped Alfred in first, his uniform straight and his

identification tag in a little pouch around his neck, the way Germans do. Then Ralph, in the second grave. Then a stranger, dressed in Carl's uniform and tags, with Carl's wallet in his pocket.

Rain stood by Ralph's grave. "I forgive you," she whispered.

"I don't," Miss Agnes said, kicking dirt into the grave. "That's for Edgar."

Carl knelt by Alfred's grave. "I'll make sure your mother gets your message," he said. He bowed his head at Ralph's grave, and then knelt by the stranger's grave. "Thank you, friend," he whispered.

We shoveled the graves full and placed our whitewashed ballast stones over them, to keep the bodies from floating up on the water rising beneath them.

"Pray now, please," Rain said, and took Carl's hand. We bowed our heads. After the tree frogs sang one last hymn, Carl looked down at his shirt, still stained with Ralph's blood.

"Leave that behind," I said, my voice raw.

Faye frowned. "He can't leave here bare-chested."

"That's okay," Carl said, peeling his shirt off. "I have a jacket in my duffel."

"A jacket missing a compass-style button," I guessed. *"But in August?"* I looked at Davis. His shirt would swallow Carl. I looked at Miss Agnes. Too many frills. I smoothed my lab jacket. My heart pounded. "Here," I said. "This is Papa's. His arms kept me safe all my life. I hope they keep you safe too."

I shrugged out of Papa's hug one last time, and handed the shirt to Carl.

"Thanks," Carl said. He put the shirt on and tucked it into his khakis.

I looked at Neb and Rain. We'd stood up for the people we love. We'd lost people, and learned to walk on with their voices in our hearts. We were not little children anymore.

I've grown up and Papa missed it.

Faye had seen it first, but now I felt it. For the first time in my life, my full name—Sarah Stickley Lawson—fit me snug as my skin and deep as my soul.

Captain Davis opened his wallet and took out a twenty—half his month's pay. "This should get you down the road, Carl. Don't come back. We can't save you twice."

"Thanks, but I don't need it." He unzipped his duffel, scooped out a handful of fives, and handed the duffel to Faye. "German spies carry beaucoup cash, as Ralph would say, and I'm happy to spread Hitler's money around. Use it well. All of you."

Captain Davis sighed. "I didn't hear that."

Carl kissed Faye's face, even though by now she blubbered like a pot of rendered fat. As he turned away, the bushes rustled and we jumped. Miss Agnes leaped in front of us, holding her hat pin like a sword. A woman stepped from the forest.

"Relax, rookies," Miss Agnes said, lowering her hat pin. "She's with me."

"Julia!" Rain cried.

"I'd almost given up on you," Miss Agnes said. "Folks, meet my fellow FBI agent Julia Smith."

"*You're* FBI too?" I gasped.

"I am," Julia said. "I wish I could have told you kids sooner, but I couldn't risk giving Agnes away. And I couldn't risk Dirk finding out who I really am."

I stared at her a moment, reshuffling my thoughts. "You're a double agent," I said. "You only pretended to work with Dirk."

Julia nodded and glanced at her watch. "That's right. We suspected Dirk was the advance man for a Nazi spy group. But I needed solid proof. And we wanted the names of as many of his associates as we could get."

"The list we gave Captain Davis from the Oceanside helped with that," Neb said.

"It did," she said. "And Dirk's horrible paintings, which we mailed to New York and Miami, stopped over at FBI stations, where their painted-over code was translated before the paintings were sent on."

"And Dirk's sketchbook?" Rain asked.

"It *did* hold drawings of potential targets, just as you suspected. But to make an airtight case, I also needed the scroll." She smiled. "My job would have been a breeze if you kids were easy to buy off, or scare away."

"But then we wouldn't be us," Neb said, and she laughed.

"Once Mr. Green surfaced, my mission expanded into protecting you three—until Mr. Green was in jail, and then Dirk. Dirk's awful enough, but Green was a violent man."

"That's why you followed us. And why you were so confusing," Rain said. "You were a good guy acting bad."

Like I say, Rain has a way with summary.

"We don't have much time," Miss Agnes said. "I'll take follow-up questions tomorrow. Carl, we'd like to make you an offer: Go to work for *our* side. As a spy. You're good at it, and I've arranged for Julia to introduce you to a friend. We have the bona fides waiting."

"Fake papers," Rain whispered, and Faye's eyes widened.

"You're sending him to the doll healer. Miss Caledonia," Neb guessed.

Miss Agnes winked at him. "Carl? Sixty seconds to make up your mind."

"I'm in," he said. "One hundred percent in."

Rain and Neb rushed him for hugs. Me, I stepped forward, my eyes stinging and my hand out. "I won't forget you, Stick," he said, gently shaking my hand.

Faye stepped up beside me. "Find me when the war's over."

"Count on it."

I held out my fist. So did Rain and Neb. "You too, Carl," I said, and he put his fist against ours, his hazel eyes puzzled. "*Non tatum sursum*," the three of us said.

Miss Agnes smiled. "Latin for *don't mess up*."

Julia stopped just before the undergrowth swallowed them up. "Rain," she said, turning. "I don't know why I'd never seen the part of me that let me think, even for a minute, that you could take my bracelet. But I see it now. And it will never get the best of me again."

"I know," Rain said, her voice soft.

She gave Julia a smile and a quick nod. Rain can be slow

to forgive, but she always gets there—especially if the apology comes from an honest heart. And Julia had finally proven hers.

Carl and Julia slipped into the woods and it was done—all but one last thing.

That night at headquarters, while the island slept and the U-boats listened, Captain Davis fired up the radio and broadcast a message: "Three unidentified German saboteurs were shot dead on Hatteras Island today as they attempted to destroy the lighthouse, the secondary light, and the water tower. We buried them in Buxton Woods. May God have mercy on their souls."

He clicked the radio silent. "That was for Captain Yaeger's ears. Just in case Carl's grandmother is still alive, and needs our help to keep Yaeger's wolves from her door."

ONE LAST NOTE TO THE FUTURE
IF YOU FIND THIS

There's three graves hidden in the heart of Buxton Woods, all three held down with ballast stones painted white. If you've read this far, you know who's resting in those graves and who wanted the bodies to never float up and give their secrets away.

We're proud to have our story, *Island of Spies*, in Ada Lawson's library. We'll add another book beside it—*A Thin Book Written by a Spy*—as soon as Neb finishes decoding it.

You might like to know that two weeks after that fateful night in Buxton Woods, I came home to find a letter propped on the kitchen table, and a note from Miss Agnes, who had proposed to Grand. I've already booked a band for the party: the Dream Makers.

I'll be the only scientist on the island with a secret agent for a grandmother.

Red Dime, Miss Agnes had written. *This came today. No word from the FBI about your junior agent status, but I'm on it. Nice to see Otto painting that new mountain of ballast stones, and carrying firewood and water for Miss Jonah. His father finally sees who he truly is, and that gives me hope for Otto.*

Please tell Titus I'll take the family to Sunday's ball game if the teams scrape together enough players. I can play catcher, if asked. Meanwhile I've gone to Wilmington

with your mother to investigate yet another rumor of cast-
aways. Don't hold your breath.

The envelope she'd left on the table had a New York post-
mark. I slid the letter out.

> Dear Stick,
> I KNEW Jonah looked familiar. While I had
> a few moments in New York, I stopped by the
> city's magnificent public library. I think
> Rain will be interested in this article,
> which I found in their microfilm. It seems
> like something a friend should hand to her.
> Rain's art is as extraordinary as her story,
> which begins in Holland.
> Best wishes to brave children, Julia

I unfolded the article. A newspaper photo smiled at me—
two people in a field of flowers. That's Miss Jonah, full of joy, I
thought. Beside her stood a beautiful, dark-skinned man who
wore Rain's curls and smile. I scanned the article.

ARTIST MARCO VAN DIJK AND WIFE LOST AT SEA

The ship carrying artist Marco Van Dijk and his wife
Flore Van Dijk has been lost in The Graveyard of the
Atlantic, off of North Carolina's coast. There are no known
survivors.

The Van Dijks were sailing to the Netherlands Antilles,

367

in the Caribbean—his birthplace. As a young man, Marco Van Dijk moved to Paris to study art. His work is celebrated across Europe.

The mystery of Rain's ring, solved. *M* for her father, Marco Van Dijk. Finally, she can add his name and face to the puzzle in her heart.

As I refolded the letter, Miss Agnes's Buick roared into the yard and backfired. Schooner barked, car doors slammed. A moment later, a foot fell against the porch.

Ba-BAM.

The door opened and I whirled to face it.

Papa smiled from the doorway. "Hello, Genius. Is it Stick or Sarah these days?"

"It's Sarah Stickley Lawson, through and through. But everybody who loves me calls me Stick," I said, and hurled myself into his arms.

Yours truly,
the Dime Novel Kids:
Nebuchadnezzar Alfonzo MacKenzie
Rain J. M. Lawson Van Dijk
Sarah Stickley Lawson

Hatteras Island, North Carolina, 1942

FROM THE AUTHOR TO YOU

Some books just feel like they want to be written. *Island of Spies* is one of them.

I first caught a glimmer of this story during a family trip to Hatteras Island, where the story is set, when I was about nine years old. In Eastern North Carolina, where I grew up, we go to the beach every chance we get. We always have. As I walked along the shore with my father, I spotted a large, black—*what? A ropy blob of prehistoric goo? A giant egg casing?*

"That's oil," Daddy said. "In World War II, German submarines called U-boats hid right out there, torpedoing our ships," he added, pointing out at the Atlantic Ocean. "The ships still sit on the bottom of the sea, releasing oil for the ocean to churn ashore. That's our secret history." He looked at me. "The spies are secret too."

A secret history? U-boats? *Spies?*

Whether he was fishing or telling a story, my father knew how to set a hook.

Island of Spies grew out of that long-ago stroll along the beach.

This book is historical fiction—a made-up story with history as its framework.

What's true? First, here's what most people know:

For the United States of America, World War II began when Japan bombed the U.S. Navy ships at Pearl Harbor, Hawaii, late in 1941. It was a surprise attack, and almost all of America's ships were either sunk, or badly damaged. As Congress declared war on Japan and their ally Germany, many people panicked, fearing Japanese attacks all along our West Coast.

Now, a secret part of our history—something people are just starting to talk about:

Just a few weeks after Pearl Harbor, German U-boats surfaced off the coast of North Carolina, on the East Coast. And they started hunting the giant ships carrying oil, passengers, and goods up and down the coast, from Canada to South America and vice versa.

The U-boats found the best hunting in the tricky waters off North Carolina, where two mighty currents collide. The area's shifting underwater sandbars and channels are known as the Graveyard of the Atlantic because thousands of ships have gone down there throughout history. Starting in 1942, U-boat captains added to that number, zeroing in on ships carefully crossing those sandbars and sending them to the bottom of the sea.

The people of Hatteras Island heard the first ships explode in January 1942. As ships burned and sank, the frightened islanders waited for help, just like they do in this book. But thanks to Pearl Harbor, U.S. President Franklin Roosevelt had no ships to send. To keep the already-frightened American mainland calm, he censored the news of the terrifying U-boat attacks. In fact, he kept the news so quiet, most Americans never knew of the U-boat attacks that would send more than eighty ships down in North Carolina waters before war's end. In all, almost four hundred ships went down along the East Coast.

The people of North Carolina's Outer Banks—including Hatteras Island—were on their own, just like Stick, Rain, and Neb in *Island of Spies*.

The U-boat attacks are part of our history. What else in this book is true?

The ships' names and the dates they went down are accurate to the best of my ability. I changed the *time* of the very first attack by a few hours, to make the story juicier for you.

Island of Spies uses a lot of spy codes, lingo, and gizmos—all actually used by spies. The fate of the schoolhouse is true and so are the facts in the news stories, to the best of my ability, though Mr. Green (who's fiction) never made the news. Also true: German spies *did* come ashore in the United States.

Another true thing: America dealt with a thousand changes during this war. Young men and women went to war, and other young women like Faye stepped up to handle their jobs, or stepped boldly into new jobs created by the war. Things we take for granted—sugar, shoes, gasoline, and so much more—were rationed to make sure there was enough for the military. That means the government decided how much each person could buy.

Many thousands of people died, mostly overseas, breaking hearts at home.

If you like history (or need information for a book report), pop over to SheilaTurnage.com for more factual tidbits. You'll read about the island's real-life heroic postmistress (who was not at all like the frilly, grumpy postmistress in this book), and the three young brothers who ran their own bus company on the island (you'll catch glimpses of their bus in this story). You can read about German spies here in the U.S., and learn more about the Cape Hatteras Lighthouse and the men who built and ran it.

What's the *fiction* in this historical fiction? The characters and their actions are all fiction.

Readers often ask me: "Where do characters come from?" It's a great question.

There's a bit of my mother, Vivian Taylor Turnage, in Stick. I'd say she inspired this character. My mother loved science and math. When she was a girl in 1942, white girls like Stick and my mom had next to no hope of a science career, and Black girls had even less. Stick is smart and outspoken, like my mother. What led to Stick's invention, the Stick-O-Matic? My mother made one for me when I was ten, to help me impress a group of fourth-graders. (I was the new kid that year and needed all the help I could get.) Using it for a night-light was Stick's idea.

Stick's friend Neb is growing up in the Hatteras Lighthouse compound in this book. His beloved three-seater outhouse, island pony, and home are taken from an interview I did years ago with Mr. Rany Jennette, who grew up in the same light-house compound, in real life. Neb's family is white, like most islanders of that time period.

Stick's friend Rain, a ten-year-old mixed-race girl, lives with her white mom in the island's most interesting house—a huge wine barrel, long as a pickup truck and tall enough to walk around in. A historic photo sparked the idea for Rain's house. Rain's a self-taught artist, and that part of her character was inspired by Ms. Minnie Evans, a Black, self-taught visionary artist who grew up near the port of Wilmington, North Carolina.

As you know, Stick, Rain, and Neb are the Dime Novel Kids. Their enemies, Otto and Tommy Wilkins, were inspired by a couple of boys I've run into here and there. I hope they don't remind you of anyone you know.

If you get a chance to visit North Carolina, I hope you can climb the Hatteras Lighthouse like Stick, Rain, and Neb do—and like I do every chance I get. I hope you see the island ponies, visit Buxton Woods (it *does* have some nice trails), and go fishing where Rain's mother fishes.

As for the three mysterious graves in Buxton Woods, the ones at the heart of this mystery, I've heard whispers about them all my life. I know people who claim they're real, and some who claim they're not. Feel free to draw your own conclusions.

Finally, I hope you've had as much fun reading this novel as I did writing it.

Yours truly,

Sheila Turnage

THANK-YOUS

It takes so many people to create a book!

Most writers work at home, and I am no different. On the homefront: Thanks to Rodney for your love, support, and unnerving ability to think like a spy. Thanks to my extended family for your patience and support: Lauren, Elvis, Olivia, and Harrison; Karen, Alan, Vivian, Julian, and Lillian; Haven, Nick, Taylor, and Jackson; Michael and Susan; Allison and Johnny; and my cousins, aunts, and uncles.

Most authors write with other writers, and I do too. Thanks to the Monday Writers Workshop, author Pat O'Leary, and poet Claire Pittman.

Thank you to Eileen LaGreca for your friendship and the spectacular website.

To agent Margaret Riley King at WME: Thanks for your faith in this book and in me.

Once a book is written, it's ready to greet the world. Thanks to publisher Lauri Hornik for everything over the years, and especially for welcoming me home. To my brilliant editor, Jessica Dandino Garrison, whose dedication to character and uncanny sense of direction made this book deeper and richer than it would otherwise have been, a thousand thanks.

Thank you to sales rep Doni Kay. My characters and I all love you.

There are so many to thank at Dial Books for Young Readers, including copyeditor Regina Castillo, interiors designer Cerise Steel, and editorial assistant Squish Pruitt. Thanks to cover designer Kristin Smith, cover artist Tom Clohosy Cole, and expert reader Sharifa Love-Schnur. Also to Kathy Dawson for acquiring this book.

Last but not least, thank you to the men and women who fought fascism in World War II, and to those who waited at home. I hope we can all learn from reading your pages in history.

Growing up in eastern North Carolina, **SHEILA TURNAGE** fell in love with Hatteras Island's shipwrecks, secret World War II history, and whispered spy stories—which helped inspire her latest book, *Island of Spies*. Sheila is the author of many children's books. Her award-winning Mo & Dale Mysteries kicked off with *Three Times Lucky*, a Newbery Honor Book, a *New York Times* bestseller, an E. B. White Read Aloud Honor Book, and an Edgar Award finalist. Her follow-up, *The Ghosts of Tupelo Landing*, also a *New York Times* bestseller, received five starred reviews. *The Odds of Getting Even* and *The Law of Finders Keepers* rounded out the series with numerous starred reviews, and all four books were Junior Library Guild selections. Sheila is also the author of two nonfiction adult books, a poetry collection, and a picture book, *Trout the Magnificent*, illustrated by Janet Stevens. She lives on a farm in eastern NC with her husband, a very smart dog, a flock of chickens and guineas, one lonely goose, and a couple of sweet-faced goats. She still loves visiting Hatteras Island.

Discover more at SheilaTurnage.com.